NOW PLAYING IN THEATER B
EDITED BY ADREAN MESSMER

For Vincent Price, Bruce Campbell, Richard O'Brien, Christopher Lee, and all the others. Because why the fuck not.

Table of Contents

/ᴍᴇʟᴛ

BY JACK BURGOS

Red looks trashed after only a second swig from the unmarked, black bottle. We call him Red because he has a constant blush. Like "permambarrassed." Permambarrassed. I like that word. *Permambarrassed.* Say it with me, Voice-in-my-head.

He wouldn't say where he got it—the bottle, I mean. Just that he'd gotten it for free in the alleyway behind the food bank cafeteria. Every morning, Red and I leave the shelter and go straight there for breakfast. We talk about stupid shit on the lunch line, Red laughs at a joke I make as a volunteer slops gravy over his biscuit and eggs. Then we sit together, across from each other, shoveling watered-down apple sauce into our mouths, the tips of our shoes barely touching. It isn't romantic or anything. Just breakfast. I never tell him how I like the way his bleached hair brushes his cheeks. It annoys him—I know—but he can't afford to get it cut.

It's almost Christmas. Time to be grateful for the good people in my life, right?

Red passes me the bottle, grinning and squinting like he's having trouble seeing me. He hadn't offered me any yet. Any new drug or drink he got, he had to try first. He likes to tease, but it's also his way of watching out for me. I've been homeless for almost a year, since I announced at my last family Christmas dinner that I wanted to be called Killian—Captain Hook's real name in *Once Upon a Time*—instead of Stephanie. Mom had flipped out, I'd run away. You remember. You've heard this all before, I think. Unless the voices have changed since I first started hearing you guys—when I woke up that one really fucked up night about a month ago with a massive headache and a scar above my left ear—in which case you must be getting this all for the first time. If you're confused, it's probably because I'm fucking high. Ha!

I'm having trouble seeing Red through the K2 haze. No, not the mountain. I just realized that the mountain and the oregano-looking shit we get from Best

Stop, the corner store a few blocks from the house we stay at when we're getting fucked up, have the same name. I bet that makes it super confusing if you're on K2, smoking K2. A little funny too. Are you high when *I'm* high? I don't know how I could tell if you don't say anything. Okay, answer the question, and I'll tell you if I can hear you.

Nope. Nothing.

"Killian?" Red calls out. He isn't holding the bottle out anymore. Oh, it's in my hand. His arm is reaching out for me…and melting? I'm distracted by the way his arm bends and twists, and I drop the practically-still-full, black thing. It rolls away from me, vomiting its contents upon the moist, molding carpet.

I swear I just saw Red's two front teeth fall out of his mouth into the crotch of his pants. His smile fades too, the corners of his lips sluicing down into a frown and then further down until his lips are dripping from his jaw. He might be saying "Whoa" or "Help," but it sounds slurred. I think he's trying to scream because he throws his head back and opens what's left of his mouth wide. Then his lips slide out around his face, pulling his skin back like when he pulled back the skin of his uncut dick to show me one time. I try to grab Red's hand, but my fingers slip through his forearm like hot butter.

And I mean *hot*. I pull away from Red, scream, and throw my hand into our piss bucket, splashing stinking urine everywhere. You're probably wondering why we have a piss bucket. It's not technically *ours*. It's everybody's that stays here. Someone tore the toilets out of every bathroom in this house forever ago.

When the pain stops being so distracting, I turn around. Where Red had been is a big puddle of boiling rainbow pudding. No bones or anything. Well, Red's clothes are there, soaked in the smoking juices. And yes, a real fucking rainbow with all the colors bubbling and bursting. The K2 had blotted out any sense of smell I had. I'm grateful for that because I bet the steaming, flattening puddle smelled really bad. Basically not how I imagined rainbows at all. I'm really glad I'm this high. If you're seeing and feeling what I am, you might be glad too.

Any other time, I might freak out. I'm thinking that I *should* be freaking out. Is that *your* thought, Voice?

My palm and fingers are red and blistered. They tingle. It's kind of a cool feeling, but I know the real pain's coming later. Also, "Red?" I ask. Because I have no idea what else to do, and you're not being very helpful.

The Red ooze is starting to cool, simmering and soaking into the carpet. Like unicorn diarrhea.

"Red, you burned my hand," I complain. I want him to answer me. "You better pull yourself back together so I can kick your ass." He's probably dead—I get it. Still, those are the words that come out of my mouth. What would *you* say? What would *you* do?

That's what I thought.

I put the tip of my sneaker in the puddle. It leaves a small dent in the drying goo. That's when I run. I don't want to sober up where my best friend melted. I don't want to think anymore. I don't wanna remember any of this.

🕱🕱🕱

I wake up to the yellowish-brown hue of cardboard covering my face. With a throbbing headache, too. I look around for Red before I start remembering how I never got drunk last night. Because the only bottle we had had melted Red. Then I realized that I was also high, and people don't melt like that. Right? I'm gonna need confirmation here, please.

Fuck you for not talking to me.

I want to believe that I imagined last night. That Red and I had a stupid fight after I smoked *way* too much, and he's waiting for me at the food bank. But he isn't. The memories are pouring in now—thanks for nothing—and I throw up bile and chewed-up taquitos on my ratty sneakers.

I walk back to the house. I have to be sure. If there isn't a mess, or a stain, then Red's probably okay. Dion's dog is outside, crouching on her back legs and dumping a giant green log. Her teats dangle between her legs as she pants and sniffs the air. It makes me remember that my hand is covered in now-dry piss. I wipe it on my pants.

That dog's downwind of me. My sense of smell is coming back, and I'm not impressed by the sting of shit in my nostrils. I wish you'd warn me about things like this.

"Dion!" I yell, shoving open the jammed back door. "Red? Nathan? Jess?" Those are all the names of people I know. We sometimes smoke together. Except Dion. He's in his late 30s but looks like he's in his late 50s. I remember hearing that he'd done a *lot* of meth before he wound up in jail for, like, ten years. He owned this house—or he claimed it first, I don't know for sure—and he let us stay here for drugs or money or sex. I never had sex with him, though. Red would sometimes blow him so that he didn't ask me because Red knew that the idea of sex made me uncomfortable. Most people kinda freak out when they get into your pants and find something other than what they're expecting. Hell, *I* kinda freak out when I get into *my own* pants and find something I'm not expecting.

"Killian, what the *fuck* did you and your boyfriend do to my living room?" That gruff voice is Dion's—he sounds like someone took a cheese grater to his vocal chords. And Red wasn't my boyfriend. Doesn't matter what's under the clothes—I'm a guy. Red doesn't…*didn't* date guys. That gets you a bad rap on the street, then you get called things like "punk" or "bitch," and then you have to fight.

I don't make the rules.

I walk past the master bedroom, around the kitchen, and into the living room. The stink of rotten egg hits me like a Mack truck right in the face. That's two you could've warned me about. The smell of really crappy perfume follows. There's Dead Red—too much?—the rainbow slop replaced by a stain the color of a wounded apple that got left out for a month. Dion's holding Red's old biker jacket, which has bits of brown muck sticking to it like cold wax.

Dion's holding a rag over his mouth and nose, and he's opened all the windows. The piss bucket is gone. Where's everyone gonna go to the bathroom now?

"I know this was you," he says. It's a threat, even though he hasn't threatened anything yet. But he's gonna. Trust me.

"That's not me," I say, but the words come out weakly, uncertain. I'm pretty sure he thinks I'm lying. If *you* could talk to him... Never mind. That's stupid. He wouldn't believe you were real anyway.

"This is last time you and that motherfucker stay in this house." See? "I swear, I'm gonna wipe this shit with your fa—"

Dion stops and looks around me. Through me. That's when I realize that Dion just realized that Red isn't with me. I don't know why that surprises me—that Dion doesn't care whether I exist or not. That when he talks to me, he's really talking to Red. I haven't been around long enough. I'm a non-person.

"Where's Red?" Dion asks.

I point at the puddle. "Th—that's him there." I haven't said a lot aloud since yesterday. You spoil me, Voice, because I can inner-monologue at you. *Innologue.* That should be a word. Maybe not.

Dion looks at the puddle, examining it like he's wondering what he's missing, then he looks back at me. His eyes call me a liar, and I can't blame them. I wouldn't believe my own story right now.

"You're fucking with me," he concludes.

"I—I swear I'm n—not." I look around. The black bottle—it's poking its neck out from under the bedbug-infested camel back couch someone had pulled out of the trash and dragged inside. I grab it and hold it out to Dion. "He drank this. And he melted."

Dion watches me for a few moments—a few *really* long moments—and I really wish that you could tell me what's going through his head, but I know you're only in mine. Dion's first move is to throw Red's jacket at me. Merry Christmas to me—it's where he kee—*kept* his money. It hits me in the arm, and I drop the bottle, which lands with a hollow thud. Then he starts throwing curses and marching towards me.

Run.

I swear I heard someone say, "Run." Was that you?

It doesn't matter. I hug the jacket and run as fast as I can until I turn the corner two blocks down, where the street's busy with traffic and I'm much less likely to get my ass royally kicked.

I look through Red's pockets, peeling away the dry goop, then I blow out a relieved breath. Red's cash is still there—enough for me to get high tonight. I need that. More than ever. You disapprove, but you can go fuck yourself. You're not going through what I'm going through.

I feel a flap of wet skin slap my calf. Dion's dog followed me.

"Shit. Get away." I kick at her, but she just pants and sniffs the ground.

She finds a chunk of Red and gulps it down. My heart sinks, and I throw up again. Dion's dog laps that up too. I pull away before she starts licking at my face.

"You're gross," I say to her. I know. I'm a hypocrite—you don't have to say it. I'm also a cat person. So was Red.

I start walking towards the Best Stop, with Dion's dog following behind me. A white van passes me, turning away from the street where Dion's house is. I'm too much in my own thoughts to pay it any more attention than that.

Red told me once that Best Stop had been there for as long anyone can remember, owned by the same guy, and never raided. Assuming you're the same voice from before, then you might know why. If you're not, it's because the owner, Eddie, is a vet with friends on the police force. That doesn't mean he's straight-edge. It just means that he's good at getting away with shit the rest of us can't—including our money.

I know I don't usually talk to you this much. Hell, I usually try to ignore you. But the thought of being on the street without Red—I'm scared, man. Fuck. Part of me is wondering how much you have to drink from whatever shit was in that black bottle to turn to mush. Most of me just wanted to get high and think about absolutely none of this.

The front door—glass with a Confederate flag sticker in the center that said, in capital letters, "American by birth. Southern by the grace of God."—opens with a jingle. Dion's dog stays outside, searching the trash bins for discarded food. Eddie isn't in the front, so I wander around the aisle with all the chips—I realized I was hungry. I hadn't gone to eat that morning because…you know. I hear the back door open and close as I pick up a bag of chips. Eddie comes out to the front, holding a cardboard box like it's full of delicate treasures.

I hide with the bag of chips, crouched with my back against the condiments, and watch him through the fish-eye mirror in the corner of the store.

Eddie is tall, broad-shouldered, and constantly sunburned. His cheeks are the color of tomatoes, but pock-marked by age and bad skincare. His hair is thin at the crown of his head. He takes the box to the counter and opens it up, pulls out a black bottle and places it somewhere at his feet. Then another. And another. Then I open the bag of chips because, while my brain was distracted, my stomach growled and my fingers decided that we needed to eat *right fucking now*. Eddie looks up towards the back, then puts one arm under the counter where I know he has a shotgun hidden.

"Who's there?" he asks.

What should I do? There aren't any good options here, am I right? I mean, I *could* show myself, but then Eddie might shoot me anyway. If he said I was trying to steal from him, he could kill me and no one would touch him. I could eat a chip, but that might make a lot of sound…I'm really hungry. I'm gonna get up.

"Eddie? It's me. Killian." I stand with both hands up, palms facing him. I forget the chips—I leave them on the floor as I walk towards him. "Don't shoot, okay?"

"Boy, what the fuck are you doing hiding in my store?" he says in his thick accent. "You stealing from me?"

"N—no, sir," I mumble. Everyone on the street respected Eddie because, in general, if you pissed him off, you were cut off from the city's K2 supply. Selling any of his stuff to someone he didn't like could put you in the same position, so you just didn't do it. That being said, I figure it'd be best to be honest.

"I was waiting for you to come out. I got money. I just was hungry." I back up again, picking up my open-but-uneaten bag of chips and walk up to the counter.

Eddie nods and looks around the store. His arm relaxes, and I know he's no longer gripping his gun. "Where's Red?"

I shrug. "We had breakfast this morning," I say. What was I supposed to tell him? The *truth*?

Eddie laughs. "You boys better be careful. People're gonna start thinking you're faggots."

"Yeah," I say sadly, "I—I don't want that."

"What'd he think of the Juice?"

"J—juice?" I search my memory. Search yours if you can. Have you ever heard of such a thing? Oh, shit. "I dunno. He didn't say anything about it." Yeah, I lied. You figured out what I just did. I know it.

"Ah," Eddie says. "So what're you here for?"

I improvise. "Jess, Nathan, Red, and me are supposed to be getting together tonight. I wanna bring party favors. I got money." I didn't usually. This is a special day, and he would know it. Did you know that already?

"Oh. Well, then, look at you, Killian. You're growing up all of a sudden. Maybe one of these days you'll grow some hair on that chin." Eddie doesn't know me, so he doesn't know that I can't afford testosterone. Or that I don't have two natural sources of my own supply.

"Yeah. One day." I try to smile and take out the cash I stole from Dead Red's pockets. I hope it's enough.

"Just enough," he says. Like he's reading my mind. Then he pulls open the cigarette case behind him to reveal K2 bags with all sorts of cartoonish characters drawn on them. He pulls out the elephant. It's the brand Red likes the best. Eddie puts it on the counter and takes my money. Then he reaches underneath the counter and plants a black bottle next to the K2.

"What's that?" I say, noticing that he's staring at me and saying nothing.

"It's a gift. In Desert Storm, we swore by this stuff. Take it to your friends and share it. Merry Christmas."

What. The. Fuck. "Sure. Okay. Is it any good?"

Eddie grins. "Nah. It's awful. But it's got a damn good kick."

I try to smile back. I feel like I just failed for the second time. I take the bottle by the neck and pull it away with the bag of K2.

"Thanks," I say. I go to leave.

"Lemme know what you think," Eddie says to me. Do you think he actually expects me to be back? Does he know that the "Juice" makes people melt? I don't know what to do. The only thing I can think is to go back to Dion for help. I can't do this alone. And what I am, even with you listening, is completely and totally alone.

Except for that dog. She's eating leftover pizza crusts that she managed to scoop out of the trash. One of the crusts has a cigarette butt hanging from it. She swallows that too.

⁂

I smoke some K2 before heading to Dion's. I'm heady, but adrenaline keeps me from fully enjoying the effects of the smoke.

I know. It's stupid to go back to Dion's house, but I don't know who else to ask for help. I wait until it's late though because I'm hoping that Jess or Nathan are there. I'm hoping that they brought friends. Dion's less likely to beat the shit out of me if there are people around. As a sign of good faith, I jerry-rigged a leash from a loose length of rope that I found hanging from a fence, connected to a rusting bicycle frame. Someone must have stolen the wheels, handle, and seat a long while ago.

Dion would probably like his dog back. That's what I keep telling myself as I walk up the cement steps to the back door. The dog walks behind me, apparently confused by the rope around her neck.

"Dion?" I yell. When no one answers, I push open the door.

I lead the dog from room to room, calling out for Dion. In the living room, the dog looks up and barks at two stains on the ceiling. I honestly can't remember if they were there before. Then I hear Dion's voice repeating "fuck" to himself over and over. The sound is coming from the second floor—that's a little misleading. It's more of an attic than a second floor.

I go to walk up the steps, but the dog won't come with me. I tie her leash to the railing and head upstairs on my own.

"Dion? It's Killian," I say, my voice forced into a whisper.

Watch out.

"Shut up!" he screams, and—what did you just—?

I see a phone book being hurled at my head before I see him. It clips me and knocks me back. I nearly fall down the stairs but manage to keep hold with one hand. Were you trying to warn me? I swear I heard you, Voice.

Dion grabs my shirt like a harness and pulls me all the way up and to my feet.

"What did you do to them?!" he yells.

"I didn't do anything!" I say. I'm terrified.

Dion's eyes are wild. "They drank that shit you brought. Same as Red. And now they're dead."

My senses kick back in. I'm not high enough, obviously. The smell of K2 is strong, but it's overpowered by the rotten-egg stink of two rainbow custard puddles spreading along the ground. I realize immediately that they're what's left of Jess and Nathan. The second thing I realize is that Dion is gonna kill me because he thinks I killed all the people I know.

"I didn't do this! It was Eddie!" I try to pull away from him, but he's so strong.

Dion pushes me back, slamming me against the wall. The black bottle that Eddie gave me drops from my hoodie and clatters on the ground, down the stairs, and shatters when it strikes the last step.

Dion glares at me. Oh, shit. He thinks—

"Was that one for me? Huh? You wanted to melt me too? You little bitch." He pulls me further into the attic and slams me against the ground. Then he straddles me. "I'm gonna fuck you bloody like a bitch. Then I'm gonna make you eat glass."

I cry out and push at Dion. I try to scratch at his arms. Fuck me for biting my nails. I scream and shout for him to stop. I reach for my pants as he rips them open and starts to pull them down along with my boxers.

Take a breath. Your friends are still boiling. His balls are right by your knees.
The words come through clearer than my own thoughts. Cold and with a slight
buzzing pain above my left ear. More intense than when I've heard you before.
Was that you? It has to have been. I'm not a fighter. I'm high. You said "your
friends." For a brief moment, clarity fills my fogged mind, and I take a breath.
Dion takes that moment to pin my arms to the wooden floor with one hand and
unzip his pants with the other.

I stretch out my right leg and pull it up. My knee gets him right in the taint.
Dion jolts forward and screams. As his head comes down towards mine, I rush
forward with my forehead and head-butt him with the bridge of my nose. I feel it
crack. Dion curses and shuts his eyes. I dip my hand in Jess-Nathan—*Jessathan,
Nathess*—and slime Dion in the face. The acidic sting of Jessathan on me barely
registers. He rolls off me, holding his face and his dick and writhing and
screaming. He must have zipped over himself because his groin area is gushing
blood.

Lying next to me, I notice that he has the same scar above his right ear that I
do. That's weird. Make a mental note for me.

Run.

You don't have to tell me twice. I jump to my feet and pull my pants all the
way up. The button's broken, so I have to hold them as I make my way down the
stairs. Dion doesn't follow. I imagine he won't be getting up for a bit. I nearly slip
at the bottom of the stairs. When I get outside, I realize the back of my head is
throbbing and I'm bleeding from my nose. And my hand is burning. And my shoes
are soaked with rainbow goo. Like I stepped in it.

The dog. I won't go back for her because I just figured out what I stepped in.
I run. I keep running. Until I'm tired enough to stop caring about how much I hurt.

⚜⚜⚜

When you lose everyone you have in the world, including some people you
didn't ever want to share it with, you don't really have much left to lose. I miss
Red. I wake up without him for a third time before I realize that I love him. Have
you ever loved anyone? How angry would you be if they were taken away from
you?

The fourth morning is December 26th, and by then I've worked myself up
enough to kill Eddie. I was gonna take a knife and stab that racist, homophobic
fuck over and over until *he* was a puddle on the ground. I told myself that, at least.
Finding a knife wasn't hard. Holding onto the courage I felt this morning was
impossible. By the time I reach Best Stop, I'm having third, fourth, and fifth
thoughts. A new sticker on the door depicts a snowman standing in front of the
American flag and says, "We say Merry Christmas, not Happy Holidays." The
bell jingles as I go inside.

Eddie looks up from the counter. I can tell from his face that he hadn't
expected me back.

He has a shotgun behind the counter.

I know that, Voice. But thanks. I go up to the counter.

"How'd you like the Juice?" he asks. He's got one hand near where I expect his gun to be. I'm sure I know what he's thinking.

"We loved it. Do you have anymore?"

"You loved it?" Eddie says. "Yeah? Too bad I'm all out."

I know that he knows I'm lying. I know that he knows that I'd be a puddle on the ground if I'd actually tasted that shit. What I don't know is how to get him away from that gun.

Ask him about Lynn.

What about Lynn?" I parrot. I have no idea who Lynn is, and I'm too focused on finding an opening to stab Eddie to care.

Eddie's face freezes. Maybe *now* I'm curious. He picks up the shotgun and carries it at his side to the door, which he locks. Then he points the barrel at me. Fuck you for helping.

"How do you know Lynn?" he asks.

"I—I don't. I'm just here for more Juice." I put my hands up, trying to be as inoffensive as possible. I probably shouldn't have worn my "Satan loves me" T-shirt today.

"You want more Juice? It's in the back." He motions with the barrel towards the back door. "Go on. *Now.*"

I scowl and unwillingly lead the way. I open the back door slowly. The storeroom is a large space with aisles of shelves holding a whole bunch of liquor bottles I can't identify, along with your basic vodkas, rums, and whiskeys. A human-sized stack of boxes is piled near to one shelf to my right, blocking that aisle.

"Where's the Juice?" I ask. My hands are in my pockets. My fingers feel for the handle of the knife I got for a bag of K2 I only half-smoked.

"In the boxes. Enough for every mooching, piece-of-shit, vagrant in this town." He pokes me between the shoulder blades with the shotgun. "Get inside."

I walk through and—*Hide*—I jump away from Eddie and behind some boxes. I hope he doesn't shoot because my bladder is *very* aware that glass and cardboard don't block bullets.

My hopes are in vain. He fires, sending a shower of paper and glass in all directions. He manages to miss me, and I use the cacophony that follows to crawl to a better hiding place.

"Come out, come out," Eddie says, walking down an aisle, pushing boxes aside using the shotgun. I stay low and try to make my way back to the door. This was a bad idea, I see now. It's really better if I leave. Best Stop. Town. The country. The solar system.

I knock over a bottle of vodka, which falls and rolls away from me. I scramble to my feet and dash away from Eddie's next shot, which tears through a box and blows up the loose bottle. I feel some of the glass and alcohol hit my back as I dash behind a shelf.

"You think I'm scared just 'cuz you know about Lynn?" He starts walking in my direction. There's no good place for me to go. I'm stuck. "When I find you, I'm gonna cut you like a sand nigger 'till you tell me how you know her name."

I want to yell at him that I don't give a shit about whoever Lynn is. She has nothing to do with this story. I pull out the knife.

He's standing in front of the Juice. Rush him.

Fuck you. No way.

Now. One chance.

I close my eyes, I take a breath, and I tackle Eddie. My throat lets out a scream. The knife in my hand slides in between his ribs, then my arms are around him, the barrel of the shotgun over my shoulder, and I'm pushing him into a pile of boxes that collapses under his weight. I grab his shotgun and aim it at him.

"You killed Red and—" I say, but I don't get to finish my thought. Eddie is soaked in Juice, and he's having a seizure. I watch him go from quiet to groaning to shrieking. His hands reach up for me, his flesh starts to drip, his fingers splash when they hit the floor, and his open jaw slides down his chest. He tries to say something, but only gurgling sounds come out. Eddie's skin bruises into a variety of red, yellow, green, blue, and purple hues. His gut flattens and oozes towards me, then down the drain between us.

Voice? What now? Voice-in-my-head? I know you're there. You can't leave me now.

⚜⚜⚜

My fingernails throb with every beat of my heart. It's from all the biting. I've basically gotten them down to the cuticle now. Not that you care. You left me when I needed you.

When I sneaked out of the Best Stop, I saw a white van driving away. It looked like it was leaving the Best Stop parking lot, but I can't be sure. I think someone is following me, is what I'm saying. I don't know whether I'm crazy or not, but I'm not okay. I'm not safe. And, without you—just a Voice in my head—I'd be dead.

That's why I checked myself into a psych ward. I swear I see Eddie in the drain. Sometimes, I see rainbow oils in the toilet before I use it. I've held it in for days before, to the point where I've wet my own bed. I'd be permambarassed at this point, if I didn't have more pressing worries. I know—*I know*—he's coming back for me. Through the drain. He'll reach out and pull me in and take me somewhere terrible.

I've tried to avoid that fate, but all I had left until recently was the ability to slam my head repeatedly against a wall corner. That's when they put me into a padded room, so now I can't even do that. I'm stuck, here, wishing that the wailing from the drain would just fucking shut up.

Shut up, Eddie! Just melt!

⚜⚜⚜

You take your headphones off and run your hand through your hair. Straightening it. How vain you are.

"What happens next?" you ask.

"Now?" says your trainer. "Now we begin phase two. Wider distribution. The bosses think it's time to send Juice to larger urban areas. New York, Chicago, Los Angeles, *definitely* Detroit."

You nod. You cut off the feed. It feels intrusive to watch Killian while he's pacing in that little padded room. He can't decide whether he's crazy or not, and that's probably for the best. You *have* a microphone. You *could* send a feed directly into his auditory cortex. But with your trainer here, you're not going to do that. It's against company policy. You could wind up homeless and with a chip in your brain feeding sensory data directly into this van.

Like the person who sat in this chair before you. His name is in your notes. Dion Scott.

Your trainer calls your attention again. You realize he's been calling your name. "Are you gonna call the bosses, or do you need me to do it?"

"I'll do it," you say. You don't really have a choice.

Four Houses Down, on the Bad Side of Town

by Adrian Ludens

If you're wondering, the price on the For Sale sign posted in my front yard is correct. It's an incredible bargain and I can see you agree. This house has been in our family for several generations, but it's time to move. Downsizing. You know how it is.

I'm Clive. Let me give you a tour.

This residence has three bedrooms, though only two are in use. House size is 3400 square feet. Plenty of room for a large family.

There's a porch out back, a tool shed, a prefab tin shed for storage, even a smokehouse, if you like jerky. Maybe I ought to test that out, though; the last time we used it was way back in 1969, when I was only seven years old! That was the year Nixon took office, the Beatles performed on a roof and then broke up, and a tapeworm killed my mother. Sucked the life right out of her and left nothing but a husk. In the end, she was dry as an old gourd. Ever shake one? You can usually hear something rattling around inside, but you don't know what. Seeds maybe, or dead beetles.

My dad cut my mother open and pulled the murdering parasite out of her large intestine. The damn thing was over three feet long. Dad took it on like Jacob wrestling the angel, and like the angel, the tapeworm was overcome. Dad crucified it in the smokehouse. He nailed it to the wall with a two-pronged fork with a bone handle. Stretched it tight and nailed the bottom too. Used one of Mother's knitting needles. The gut vampire's carcass started out flat, but curled in on itself like tightly-rolled parchment as it dried. It's a first-rate smokehouse—or it was.

Dad buried Mother out back beneath the lilacs. He mistrusted morticians. Always worried what those folks did when there wasn't anyone around. Then Dad used the dead tapeworm as the string in his old washtub bass. He'd play it out on the porch on nights when the moon shined bright and in our living room on nights when it didn't. It didn't have a very good tone but it calmed down my older brother, Paul, so that was good.

Paul's brain seemed to operate on a different set of instructions than the rest of us. He would often fall prey to a kind of darkness that has nothing to do with nightfall.

As for the music, I played along on a toy guitar that was just my size. It had four strings but still sounded fine as frog's hair. I'd strum away while Dad sang songs he made up on the spot. Some bawdy, some mournful; and him always plucking the tapeworm that'd killed his wife, crafting rustic, mystical lullabies for the children she left behind. Paul would rock on his haunches and try to hum along. And Sadie, the baby of the family, a year and a half old back then, would hold up both hands, wanting to touch something, anything, everything. And she would smile at me as if we shared some great secret joke.

We have two bathrooms. One upstairs with a bathtub, one downstairs with a shower. I installed one of those new low-flow toilets in the upstairs bathroom. Pipes are all in good shape. Drains are clear. I can't stand hair in drains. Stems from an incident involving my brother.

In 1974, Paul killed a lady. Some folks saw him dragging her down the sidewalk right in front of the movie theater. Said he just stood there, looking at the Now Showing poster until the cops came. Some say *The Towering Inferno* was playing. Others swear it was *Earthquake*. One detail everyone agreed upon was that the lady had braids. Paul always had a thing for hair, the longer the better.

This lady had twisted her tresses into matching braids that came down past each shoulder. Paul must've taken a real shine to her hair. I bet he wanted to keep it. The lady felt the same way, I'm sure. Can't say I blame her. But the folks who saw them on the sidewalk that day say Paul had taken the lady's braids and strung them through his belt loops from the back, and had kind of tied them together at the front. He strolled along the sidewalk with the lady dragging behind him, neck broken. I bet it looked like Paul had a four-pronged tail.

Before long, Dad and Sadie and I all had to sit in the court room while the jury judged Paul—and us. Back then, this town didn't waste a lot of time on long, drawn-out court proceedings.

Hell, I blinked and next thing I knew we were in a special gallery, perched on those hard wooden chairs that you can never quite get comfortable in, and wondering if the governor might call. He didn't. Then they strapped my brother in and sponged his head with water. I didn't think he'd ever been baptized, so I appreciated them taking the trouble. Right before they ran the current through him, I glanced over at Dad. He looked gray, with a rosy spot on each cheek and his face completely still. Reminded me of Mother after she'd passed. Paul didn't do or say anything. The prison guards had shaved heads so there wasn't much for him to get riled up over. Then they threw this big switch and increased their electric bill. Reckon Paul got a dose of what folks think Hell feels like and then he was gone.

Sadie smiled at me like it was the happiest moment of her life. I can't say that

I shared her sentiment but seeing her grin helped to take the edge off, helped get me through a trying time.

Anyway, the drains are clear, let me assure you of that. You won't have any problems with the plumbing.

On to the bedrooms. This one we're about to see is the one my parents slept in. It's not currently in use. Do you recall in August of 1977 when Elvis died? I didn't care much one way or the other.

Then about a week later I saw on television that Groucho Marx had died. I shed a few tears after hearing the announcement. Some of my earliest memories feature Dad sitting on our green couch watching reruns of *You Bet Your Life* and laughing whenever Groucho made fun of the contestants. I wiped my tears and looked around for Dad, a morbid part of me fit to burst at the prospect of telling him the sad news.

I got to this room and found the door closed. I didn't think to knock. Wish I had. First thing I saw was Dad's bare rear end bouncing up and down on his old mattress. Then he looked over his shoulder and noticed me standing there in the doorway just like you're doing now. Don't know why he thought rolling off the bed was a good idea. I noticed what looked like a worm clinging to the side of, well, you know. Looked like a big pulsating vein until it fell off. I averted my eyes for modesty's sake and looked at the bed instead. He'd gouged a hole in the mattress and shoved a red and white soup can full of night-crawlers into the opening. Not to speak ill of the dead, but it wasn't even a family-serving-sized can. It was just a dinky normal one. Dad looked ready to die of embarrassment. I stood there rooted to the spot trying not to gag. I haven't touched soup from a can since. You'll find some cans still stacked in the pantry. You can have them if you want, but check the expirations first.

Anyway, I remember I twisted my face away from the worms slithering around in my dad's juices and saw Sadie in the hallway. She grinned at me like this had to be the funniest thing she'd ever seen and it helped break the tension. Grateful for the distraction, I closed the door and hustled her down the hall. Let's do the same.

Showing you around the house sure brings back old memories. Just now I'm reminded of my former friend, Zedro. His name reflected his heritage; his father was French-Canadian, his mother Mexican. Zedro and I were both high school seniors and neither of us had many friends.

He had come over one day after school so we could help each other with our homework. Out of nowhere Zedro said: "Clive, you and me gotta stick together. We both live on the bad side of town; me on the wrong side of the tracks, and you four houses down." I laughed at that but his words made me feel bad deep down. I mean, dead mother, dead brother, and now I had to worry about what people thought of where I lived too?

I remember I was working on a book report on *Lady Chatterly's Lover.* Zedro was working on a report for *Tropic of Cancer.* We didn't get much writing done that evening; we just took turns reading the dirty parts of the books to each other. After a while Zedro stood up, said he had to go drain the lizard.

I sat alone wondering what it might be like to steal hair from a barbershop, sneaking in at the end of the day and sweeping it all up into a paper bag or something. I wondered if a guy could sell it, or use it to make wigs, or goatees and such for disguises.

When Zedro came back he had a funny look on his face. "What's with you?" I asked. He says it's nothing. Then it kinda came to me that he'd been gone quite a while for a guy who'd said he just had to pee. I narrowed my eyes. "You looked in Sadie's room, didn't you?" Zedro flushed. I had told him before that he couldn't ever go in there.

"I saw," he said. "I couldn't help it. I got curious and I looked. There's no little girl in that room." I thought I knew what he meant. A bulge in my so-called friend's pants betrayed his arousal. I saw red. That's not just an expression, you know. Minutes after talking to me about sticking together, like we were gonna be friends forever, he's entertaining perverted ideas about my little sister. I told him to get the hell out and never come back. Wish I'd killed him instead. Zedro high-tailed it home. We avoided each other for the rest of the semester and after graduation he moved away with his family.

These days I worry a lot about him coming back, but that night, sitting in the room, I felt proud. I'd protected my little sister, chased away a threat. Sadie crawled in and gave me a beaming smile and a giggle that made losing my only friend worth it. And don't worry about being on the bad side of town.

We've all made extensive renovations in this neighborhood and I am meticulous about household repairs. Pride of ownership and all that.

Here's my bedroom. Plenty of sunshine comes in through the window. Take a look. Isn't that a great view? I remember gazing out my window for hours at a time in my younger days.

In fact, it brings to mind the time Lemuel VanBrocklin moved in next door. Bit of an eccentric. But then 1981 was a strange year overall. Some wing-nut tried to assassinate President Reagan. Then someone put a bullet in the Pope. They caught the Yorkshire Ripper. I heard about all that and more on the clock radio beside my bed.

It was just the three of us then; Dad never remarried, and even though I was nineteen and in the supposed 'prime' of my life, I didn't have a girlfriend. Sadie kept busy just being Sadie.

Anyhow, this fellow, Lemuel VanBrocklin, moved in next door to us that spring. I could see into his living room from my bedroom window. I'm no Peeping Tom, especially when it comes to spying on men, but he did some crazy stuff at night that grabbed my attention whether I wanted it to or not. First thing he did was build an oxygen tent. I watched him hang up the plastic, saw the oxygen tanks too. I thought maybe he had a sick kid or spouse who needed special care.

Then later that month he cut himself. I'd been listening to a news bulletin on the radio in my room. There'd been a bloodbath involving coke dealers in Laurel Canyon in California. A porn star had been involved somehow but I didn't hear the details.

I'd become preoccupied with what Mr. VanBrocklin was up to. I sat there watching as he slid a scalpel around the dome of his skull. At first I thought he meant to scalp himself. I leaned in so close my breath kept fogging the glass.

Blood poured down his face like that girl who got pig's blood dumped on her at the prom. Then either a cloud fell from the sky or I passed out for a minute. Real blood looks different than fake movie blood, and somehow it affected me different. When I sat back up and looked out my window again, Mr. VanBrocklin was gone.

I kept watch for him every night for a week. My patience was finally rewarded during another news story about Johnny Wadd and the Wonderland Gang. Mr. VanBrocklin entered his oxygen tent, and began reading a magazine. Even through the contraption he'd constructed, I could see his brain. Not the whole thing, but the top part.

At first I thought maybe it was a trick of the light, but then I noticed an electric saw on his table. Later, when I had to testify in court about what I'd seen, I found out he'd stolen an autopsy saw with a cranial blade. Keep in mind, I didn't know that at the time, but just seeing it there was enough for me to realize he'd done some major renovations on his melon. A few days later he came over and asked me to help him carry some furniture out onto his lawn. We hauled his box spring, mattress, and bedding. He wore an obvious wig—disco curly and road kill ugly— the whole time and grinned as he poured gas from a can onto the whole pile.

"I won't need *these* anymore," he said. Then he struck a kitchen match and ignited his bed with a flick of his wrist. I never saw Mr. VanBrocklin sleeping again. He'd work all day—doing what, I don't know. Then he'd come home in the evening and go inside his oxygen tent. He'd take off his wig, pop the top of his skull off, and sit and read for hours. I'd wake up at four in the morning, still at my window, with an aching back or a crick in my neck and he'd still be there.

Stacks of paperbacks piled up in Mr. VanBrocklin's house. I admit I envied him. He'd outsmarted sleep and earned himself extra time that eluded the rest of us. This went on for a week or two but then I started to notice a change.

Our neighbor had arguments with people who weren't there. He stopped going to work. He still didn't sleep, though; at least not as far as I could tell. Then one night as he busied himself moving stacks of books from one corner to another and back, he noticed me watching him. Mr. VanBrocklin walked over to the window and raised it. I figured it was pointless to try to hide or pretend we hadn't seen each other. He leaned out and called me.

"Young man! Look here. See this thing that I can do."

He turned around and sat his butt on the window ledge. Then he braced both arms on the window frame and leaned back. He tipped all the way back until he was upside down, like a kid hanging from the monkey bars at recess. His wig fell off onto the grass. Mr. VanBrocklin met my gaze and said, "The key is to get enough oxygen to the brain in any given twenty-four-hour cycle."

Then the top of his skull followed the wig. I guess you won't be too surprised when I tell you that his brain fell out next. It dangled for a few seconds, swinging from something that kept it attached to his spine. Then his body tumbled off of the ledge and his brain sprang free and popped when he landed on it, like a water balloon but full of tapioca. I called an ambulance, though I figured it was no use. Sadie helped keep me calm. She sat on the floor waving at me, grinning and making it another joke that only she and I shared.

In January of 1986 the Space Shuttle *Challenger* exploded right after launch. Dad, confined to his bed, watched the tragedy unfold on a portable television. When I say 'confined', I mean it. Dad had become senile and mean. His behavior had become so irrational that I had to tie his wrists and ankles to the bedposts.

See, Dad thought he was the postman. Hell, he'd even found a costume somewhere. But I knew it was Dad. He alternately threatened me and begged to be let free. I remember telling him that just because he thought he was someone else didn't make it so. I knew it was a phase he would have to work through. I don't know how, but Dad conspired with the postal service, the police, and some other mean-spirited folks to confuse me. Some lady called the house over and over again, asking if I'd seen her husband, Burl. It got so I dreaded answering the phone. This was before we had caller I.D.

One afternoon in February, Burl—sorry, Dad, I mean—got so mad he bit the end of his tongue clean off and spat it at me while I gave him a sponge bath. Some way to show gratitude! It hit my cheek and stuck there like a tiny pink leech, regurgitating blood on my skin. The next afternoon, I heard the doorbell. As I moved to answer the door, whoever had rung the bell used a key and marched right into the house.

"I'm back from visiting relations," a voice called. The figure looked like Dad, but I knew that couldn't be. The stranger had made a fatal error; he rang the bell twice. Everyone knows the only person who rings twice is the postman!

I cracked him over the head with Mother's old rolling pin. The stranger that looked like Dad never moved again. I wrapped him in an old sheet and buried him somewhere special, somewhere hidden. While I was occupied with that project, Dad—the real one who, for reasons I still cannot explain, no longer looked anything like the man who raised me—died still tied to the bed. I always heard you should starve a fever and feed a cold. For senility and identity confusion, I wasn't sure, so I chose starvation. I guess I got carried away with that aspect of his treatment. So I had to bury him too.

I read an interesting book about doppelgangers later that summer. It's a German concept regarding evil twins. When I tried to explain it to Sadie, she just sat there jabbering and giggling. Made me realize I had over-thought the whole matter. She has such a unique perspective on life. I don't know what I'd do without her.

Here we have a spacious linen closet. Back in August of 1990 I found a duffel bag full of brand new cassette tapes in a drainage ditch while walking home from work. With Dad gone, I had to support myself and Sadie. I did assembly line work. Money being tight made this an exciting discovery. When I got home, though, I found I didn't like how the plastic covering crackled when I began to unwrap the first cassette. I shoved them all up there on that shelf. If you want them, you can have them. If not, throw them away and fill the shelves with towels or whatnot.

A month or two after my big find in the drainage ditch, these so-called "ghost hunters" showed up on our doorstep. Said they'd heard about Dad's disappearance and were here to help. See, as far as the authorities were concerned, both the postman and my father were still missing. So these jokers came along just when I thought I had put all that behind me.

They wandered around the house for about an hour. Then one of the guys hurried up to me, his eyes all wide and dewy, excited because they'd recorded something on tape called "eee vee pees." What *he* didn't know was that all the voices came from his partner's multiple personalities. I heard them myself and didn't need any fancy equipment to do it, either. Near as I can figure, this guy had had seven different personalities living inside his brain, but they'd all died off except for one. His "Sybil specters," to coin a phrase, interfered with their equipment. When I tried to explain this to the ghost hunters, they just stared at me like I had a third eyeball on the end of my nose. They packed their gear and right before they left, the dewy-eyed one made a smartass comment about visiting me at the asylum. I ignored him and focused on the other guy. One of his dead personalities kept trying to push free from its prison. I saw it in struggling in the pupil of his left eye.

When I looked around for Sadie, I found her sitting in the corner, just taking it all in. Grinning and waving her hands at me, she was. This calmed me down until they left. I think I'd go half-crazy if Sadie wasn't around to brighten my life and keep me on an even keel.

Here's the kitchen, site of many fine meals and special desserts, like Sadie's birthday cakes, for instance. I always made hers from scratch though mine were usually store-bought.

In 1998, the day of my 38th birthday, I died. It wasn't anything special. The birthday party, I mean. It was just Sadie and me. A store-bought cake, like I said. I went for a walk afterward, thinking about calories and extra pounds. I hadn't quite given up hope of finding a lady friend in those days. My neighbor, Eustace McGee, sat atop his riding lawn mower as it chewed up his yard salad. As I walked past, Eustace tipped back a skinny brown bottle of beer and steered too close to his pebbled driveway. The spinning blade scooped up a stone and shot it against my left temple. It felt like I'd taken on Goliath and lost.

I heard the splintering of bone and pulping of flesh even over the roar of the mower's engine. I wondered why the neighborhood had turned sideways. I saw black sparks, then black snow, like a blizzard. Everything went dark. Then I got a feeling like someone had wrenched a rotten tooth from its place in the gums and I was that tooth. I opened my eyes again. Beneath me, down on the sidewalk, lay my body. I had a red hole in my temple the size of a quarter. I still have the scar— want to touch it? No? Eustace was crouched beside me, not helping me, but helping himself to the few dollars I had in my wallet.

Then I felt a light tugging and glanced up to see a soft blue light high above me. I thought about smoke about to burst from the confines of a sooty chimney into the sunshine and breeze of a clear blue sky. You know what caused me to clamber against the grain and back into my body? Sadie, of course. I happened to glance over and see her sitting near a hedge, smiling at the dead part of me.

What would happen to her if I died? What if Zedro found his way back inside our home? What would happen to Sadie if I wasn't there to protect her? I couldn't leave her, so back I came. Scared Eustace so bad he dropped his beer and ran. Sadie and I crawled back into the house together. I called the ambulance myself.

In the hospital the headaches were so bad I couldn't keep any food down for several days. But I knew I'd done the right thing every time I'd look up and see Sadie playing underneath the chair a nurse sat stationed in. The nurse didn't do much but read magazines. Sadie'd grin at me and give one of her little waves every time I looked, so it was nice that she was there.

Last we have the garage. It fits a single car as you can see, but has plenty of shelf space. I'm the one who spray-painted "93" there on the wall.

That was the year Roddy Lee Doyle lost every penny he had. He built a mini-golf attraction with a homemade lemonade stand on site so customers could stay refreshed. Called it the Puckered Putthole but the place never caught on with folks. Roddy Lee took it awful hard. He ended it all by playing a round of putt-putt and then tried to swallow the ball. Got it suck in his windpipe, which I'm sure was what he intended. Not the way I'd want to go.

That year, 1993, was the same year my shadow and I got separated. The less said about that mess the better. It's back in my possession now, though it is no longer attached. I started growing a new shadow. It's smaller than it should be but folks don't even notice. Let's be honest; have you ever found yourself in a crowd of people examining shadow sizes? Everyone has a shadow. You might notice if someone lacked one completely. But one that's just smaller than most escapes notice, just like someone who does something kind without an ulterior motive.

I tracked my lost shadow down eventually. Somehow it had wandered off and found its way back to my old high school. I found my shadow thrown across my old locker. I'm not sure what it hoped to find, especially since neither of us could remember even one number in the old combination. I just rolled up my shadow as best I could. It had the texture of steam and the elasticity of a rubber band but I managed to get it tucked into a paper bag. I keep it closed with wooden clothes pins. The bag is on a shelf right over there where I spray-painted the numbers. It's yours if you have a use for it. If not, well, I can take it with me when we go.

The whole experience made me paranoid. I spent months checking on Sadie every few minutes, just to make sure her shadow stayed put. She always just laughed at my apprehension until I finally quit.

Let's head back into the house. Can I offer you coffee? No? Let's see now, what else can I tell you about the house? We're set up for cable. The living room carpet is new. Attic has new insulation. I suppose that's about it. How do you like it? The house certainly has a lot of character and at the price I'm thinking of, it's a definite bargain. Just think: you could be settled in just in time for the new millennium!

Hold on a second—there's Sadie now, just come around the corner. Hi, sweetheart! Look at those little hands just waving away. She's trying to be friendly, I do believe. Oh my. Are you okay, friend? You look as if you'd like to drop through your own rectum and hang yourself. Were you surprised when she crawled around the corner? You might want to close your mouth before the flies get in and start playing house. You had her pegged for a ghost didn't you? Not the case.

Sadie suffers from a rare genetic disorder. She still has the body and mind of an 18-month-old even after all these years. Doctors didn't think she'd make it this long but I believe it's her sense of humor that's kept her going all these years. Sadie's all the family I have left and you can't imagine what I'd do to protect her. Hey, I think she's pointing at you—but she isn't smiling. That's odd. She thinks…

Oh, my God. *You're Zedro.* That's why she's acting like that. Of course you look different but that's to be expected; plastic surgery can only change the outside of a person. It's like spraying a rotten orange with aerosol paint. Couldn't stay away could you? Couldn't leave well enough alone. Don't you see how sick you are? Here you are, masquerading as a prospective home buyer just to have another chance at Sadie. Don't try to deny it. I saw the funny look on your face when you saw her. I know what you're thinking: *She's well over the age of consent by now. I could indulge my depraved fantasies with someone who the law declared an adult at least a decade ago.*

I ought to kill you once and for all. In fact, since we ended up back in the kitchen… See this? It's a boning knife. I keep it good and sharp. Tell you what: I'm going to give you a five second head start. Ready? One… HA! Gotcha, you sick bastard. As if I'd let you get away again. You were my best friend, Zedro, but what you wanted to do to my baby sister felt like a knife in my back. So how does it feel now in yours? Look there! See that? I think Sadie's laughing at you. Kind of gets me to chuckling myself. C'mon, you gotta admit that you do look comical inching your way across the kitchen linoleum like a baby just learning how to crawl. I'm gonna have to mop up, that's for sure. You don't find it funny? I guess it's just Sadie and me then—once more sharing some great secret joke.

CAFÉ SHAMBLEAU

BY DONALD JACOB UITVLUGT

It could be a bar one might find anywhere in a particular sort of setting. A rundown saloon in a dying Old West town. A crumbling red sandstone bar in the sunless and sere heart of Ares City. A sagging pub floating listlessly on the tideless Venusian seas.

You know the place, and usually hurry past it. The low building scarcely distinguishable from its environment and threatening at every instant to dissolve back into its constituent elements. The atmosphere inside is almost alien, a perpetual twilight regardless of the exterior weather or season. The patrons never seem to change, as if they had always been in this place and always will be.

This time the bar is in a poor district of Khambord of the planet Argovia. Argovia is an old world, a dying world, subsisting only on the kind of quasi-legal commerce than can take place nowhere else. Khambord had been the capital, and had fallen with Argovia's fall.

The structure seems to have been grown from the rocks around it rather than built. Roof flecked with the same green as the lichen on the rocks. In an old, decaying place, it seems ancient, ruinous. Older than the planet it stands on. Autochthonic is the word that comes to Professor Reule Talbot's mind as he pushes through the swinging doorway.

It takes his eyes a moment to adjust to the dim light within. A world in greyscale, as if all color has been sucked from the universe. There are perhaps a dozen patrons, perhaps less, spread out over tall tables and low booths. Not seeing what he is looking for, he heads to the bar.

Something is off about the stool as he settles onto it. As if the cushion somehow resists being sat upon. The bartender glides up. Sets a shot glass down in front of Talbot.

"Compliments of the house. First one's always free."

Talbot lifts the glass, studies the bartender through and around the pale green liquid inside. He is tall, but stooped over. Eyes a bit too far from the nose for Terran norm. An eetee, or hominid perhaps. The receding hairline and hirsute backs of the hands fit either hypothesis.

He catches Talbot staring. Talbot looks away, down at his drink. He sniffs it. There is little aroma. He downs it. It is sweet and spicy, almost too sweet, but it leaves a bitter taste in his mouth after it goes down.

That's how they get you. He fights off a smirk as he sets his glass down. The clink is swallowed up by the still atmosphere. *Ask for good old H-2-O and I'd pay my lifeblood for it.* Instead he coughs into his fist, trying to clear the aftertaste before he speaks.

"I'm looking for someone. Someone who visited this planet a few weeks ago. I received… intelligence that she may have stopped here."

Something about the bartender's smile makes Talbot look away. "She, hmm? You're in the wrong sort of establishment for that."

Talbot blushes. "See here. Nothing like that. It's my sister."

The bartender nods. "It's always their sister, or aunt, or daughter. We've not had anyone new in a while. Just the regulars. You're welcome to take a look around though."

The bartender fills Talbot's glass again and goes back to his work. *Whatever that is. No doubt dirtying glasses and watering down the stock.* Talbot picks up his drink and hops off the barstool. Or rather, attempts to hop off. As reluctant as the seat had been to let him sit down, now it seems reluctant to let him go. As he finally stands, he notes with distaste that the cushion has conformed to the shape of his buttocks even in the short time he had been seated.

Talbot approaches one of the tables. A man sits there, hunched over a mug. Talbot clears his throat.

"Do you mind if I sit down?"

He takes the lack of response as an invitation. Talbot sips at his drink, shakes his head at the bitterness. "I'm looking for my sister. Ila Talbot." He pulls up an image on his palmscreen. "Here's a picture."

The man looks up, his eyes focusing not on the picture but a far corner of the room. His eyes are the same stone grey as the building. "We're all looking for something…"

His words slur into an idiot grin. He takes a drink from his mug. Talbot leans forward, ignoring the man's unwashed stink. "My sister fancies herself an explorer. Some strange stories led her to this planet. I knew she headed towards this place. That's as far as I've been able to track her."

The other man lets out a bitter, barking laugh. "Stories? Every bar is full of stories. The question is, do the people inside drink to remember, or to forget?"

"Will you at least look at the picture? I've come a long way, taken a sabbatical from a very important position that may not be there when I return. Just to find a wayward girl."

"I once knew a girl." The man's voice takes on a singsong quality, as if he is reciting lyrics to a ballad whose tune he has forgotten. "With hair of flame and eyes that pierced the soul. I think I was in love with her. Long, long ago. I can't remember her name…"

Talbot holds back a snort of disgust. Drunkard. He presses the palmscreen forward one last time. "Have you seen this girl? She's a collector of folktales.

Stories."

The other man nods over his mug, an automaton whose spring is running down. "Every bar is full of stories. The question is...do the people inside drink to remember...or to forget..."

The man starts to snore softly. Talbot swallows his urge to shake the man, chasing it with the rest of his drink. He gets up and looks around. A couple in a booth near the back look intelligent. He walks over.

"Excuse me, please."

The couple is elegantly dressed, or was at one point. He wears what had been a dark suit shot through with silver thread, matching waistcoat, silver cravat. The cut dates from the time of Talbot's grandfather. The suit has faded to grey, the silver tarnished. She wears a long, flowing dress, fitted bodice with bead-work. Lace cuffs cover her hands, which clasp her partner's across the table. The dress may have been white once. Now it is the color of spoiled cream.

"I promised I would be with you forever," she says. Speaking as if she has not heard Talbot. Two champagne flutes stand on the table by the wall, the carbonation long since gone.

"I would never have asked you to meet me here if I had known." His voice is as colorless as the suit, flat as the champagne.

"We're together. In spite of what everyone said, we're together."

Talbot moves closer, attempting to get the attention of one of the pair. He notices something. Over the clasped hands, like powder-green henna, runs a fine filigree. The same color as the lichen on the rocks outside. It binds the hands together.

Talbot steps back from the table. From the benches the couple sit on grows a grey network of roots, the same grey that predominates the building. It twines over their legs, literally rooting the couple into place. Always together.

"Funny how a place grows on you, isn't it?"

Talbot frowns at the bad joke, turns to see his sister seated at a nearby booth. He doesn't know how he had missed her. She looks tired, as if she has been grading papers all night. She motions to the bench across from her.

"Have a seat, have a drink if you like. I'm sure you have a lot of questions."

Talbot's anger blots out his questions for the moment. Now that he has found her and knows she is safe, he can be good and thoroughly furious at her. He sits down to let the redness of his anger pass, pours himself more of the spicy green drink from a tall, thin pitcher on Ila's table.

"Absinthe, or so I've been told." Ila smiles that infuriating smile she has when she's being ironic, though Talbot fails to see the joke.

"What are you doing here? I've been trying to contact you for months."

Ila continues as if she hasn't heard him. "What do you think of this establishment? Quite a unique atmosphere, no? I've always thought that every bar has a life of its own. An essence unique to that particular place."

"This is neither the time nor the place for your crazy theories." Talbot's voice is icy. "The whole family is worried sick about you. Enough. I want to take you home."

Ila looks up at him from her drink, a strange fire in her green eyes. "Is that what you want? What you really want? More than anything else in the universe?"

Talbot's brow furrowed. "Of course. I wouldn't have come all this way, risking my career in the process, I might add, if it weren't true."

A searching look, a look of timid hope. "Because, dear Reule, I've always thought that you care more about having things neat and tidy than about me, about any individual. A book slanted on the shelf? Straighten it up. A wayward sister? Better put her back in her place."

"You're ranting again. You know that this isn't about me. I've always acted out of service to others. At no little inconvenience to myself."

Ila sighs, downs the rest of her drink. "So it's not me you want, it's just to serve."

"Enough questions." Talbot does not deny what Ila says, because it is true. He is here, not because he loves his sister, but because it is the right thing to do. He takes pride in his altruism, doing the right thing, serving humanity, in spite of his own interest in the matter or lack thereof.

"Why don't you finish your drink." Ila's voice is distant, coming to Talbot from a well of memories. He sips at the liquor, a shiver running through him as he finishes the glass. His sister's ironic smile has returned.

"Do you know why I left, Reule?"

Talbot sits up straighter. "I had thought it just another one of your...eccentric quests. Another fruitless flight to the fringes of civilization and rationality."

A bitter smile. "Shows what you know, _Doctor_ Reule Talbot. I've spent my life looking for the possible, looking for lost dreams. I've always wanted to be part of something bigger than myself. And help others do the same." She looks down at her lap, takes another sip from her drink.

"A part of something bigger? By chasing myths? Dreams? You could have been a surgeon, a researcher. Changed the universe. Where have your flights of fancy brought you? To a gods-forsaken bar on a backwater planet. With nothing to show for it."

It takes a moment for Talbot to realize the sound coming from his sister's throat is a laugh.

"What's so funny?"

Ila's eyes study him over the rim of her glass. "Not funny. Ironic. You think I'm sitting here pouting. I'm hiding and drowning my sorrows in drink because I failed. But I found my lost dream. I'm part of something bigger than myself." She gestures around her at the dark bar.

"This?" Talbot snorts. "This looks more like a nightmare than a dream."

"The dark dreams are important too. The Shadow of the collective unconsciousness. Those truths we don't want to face about ourselves." She pauses to refill her glass. "Have you ever thought about vampires?"

"I beg your pardon."

"Vampires. Every culture on Old Earth, every place we've visited here among the stars, they all have the legends. Creatures old as time who promise you your heart's deepest desire, and all it costs you is your blood, your soul. Your life."

Talbot looks around the bar, unable to keep a mocking smile from blooming on his face. "Are you saying the bartender is a vampire? My drink seems the wrong color for a Bloody Mary."

Ila continues as if he hadn't spoken. "The legends were right, but they were also wrong. Have you ever been in a place where a group of people has spent a considerable amount of time? Schools, houses of worship, the family home... The building itself starts to take on the character of the people who inhabit it.

"Suppose that, with strong enough influences, such buildings took on lives of their own. I mean, become really alive. What would such creatures feed on? The hopes, the dreams, the lives of the people who inhabit it. If the will to live is strong enough, it must take life. Lives. Life to beget life. Or a pale semblance thereof."

"Okay." Talbot takes hold of his sister's hand. "I've had enough. Time to go. I might even be able to pull some strings. Get you some discrete help so you don't disgrace the family name any further."

The look on Ila's face infuriates him. How dare she pity him? He is the one put out here. He is the one who always put others first, at the expense of his own time and sanity.

"Dear, dear brother. I would like nothing more than to go home with you. But I'm afraid It just won't let me. It thinks It's given me my deepest desire. And now I owe It."

Talbot frowns and attempts to pull Ila bodily from her seat. He is unprepared for the agony that crosses her face, though she does not cry out.

"What—"

He looks at his sister, really looks at her for the first time. The same tendrils he noticed on the other patrons in the bar cover Ila's legs and thighs, forming a pulsing web of putrescent green. Holding her captive.

"It feeds off us as long as It can, and then takes us into Itself to be part of Its twilit eternity."

Talbot thinks of the barstool cushion that had shifted under his weight. He shivers, bites back bile.

"I'll go get help. Find someone. A microsurgeon, xenologist. Anyone."

"My brother. The servant of all. I'm afraid it's too late for you too. Haven't you ever heard the warnings against consuming the offerings of Fairyland?" She smirks down at her glass. "Three drink minimum."

Talbot looks down at his own empty glass. He starts for the door. It is like trying to lift his feet from flypaper, tar, a sea of congealing blood. Long before he makes it to the door, the bartender is there, blocking the way. Talbot wonders why he didn't notice earlier the fine tracery of tendrils that sews the bartender's lips shut and his eyes open.

The bartender takes the towel from his own shoulder and drapes it over Talbot's. He ties his apron around Talbot's waist. Then he goes to the bar, sits down on a stool without a cushion, and lays his head on the counter.

Serve.

The thought is an icepick in the back of Talbot's neck, a rattling of ice, the cold dreaminess of absinthe. He feels tendrils moving under his skin, binding his lips together and his eyes open. Though he wills his legs to move to the door, the floor betrays him. Deposits him behind the counter. His arm lifts, and he begins to wipe the counter mechanically with his towel.

It is a bar one might find anywhere in a particular sort of place. A rundown station saloon orbiting a dead star. A desolate café in Khambord of planet Argovia. A low building scarcely distinguishable from its environment. But growing stronger. Ever stronger.

DEATH IN BLACKLIGHT
BY AP SESSLER

The muffled beat of thunderous drums and distorted power chords pulsated beneath metal skin and rolled up windows as the blue four-door pulled into the dirt driveway. The whole car rattled in time like a tambourine, garnering the applause of autumnal trees dropping their leaves like roses thrown in praise.

The car turned at the end of the tree-line and parked parallel to the van before the garage door. After a moment the music and rattling stopped and all four doors swung open in turn.

"CD is the way to go," insisted Eric as he pulled the key from the ignition and the seatbelt from his shoulder.

"I don't trust them," said Donald, stepping out of the passenger seat with a Tracks paper bag way too short to conceal the poster it contained. "I hear they get scratched just like records. You can't scratch a tape."

"But tapes wear out," Eric said as he closed the door.

"That's why you make a dub."

"Which will also wear out. I tell you man, CD is going to bury vinyl and cassette."

"Keep dreaming, Nostradamus. Vinyl will *never* die," said Albert as he climbed out of the rear passenger seat.

"Nostradamus is cool," said Joe softly, exiting from the opposite side.

"It doesn't take a seer to see that CD is the future," said Eric.

"You're right. It just takes glasses a quarter-inch thick," said Albert, holding his fingers up like binoculars over his eyes.

"They're so I can drive," grumbled Eric as he removed his glasses and placed them in his jean jacket pocket.

A billow of smoke rose steadily from behind the house. Donald's mother came around the corner, wearing large, floral print garden gloves and holding a rake.

"Hello, boys," she said. "Did you have fun at the mall?"

"Yes, ma'am," they all answered.

"Have you eaten?"

"We hit Sbarro's in the food court," Donald answered.

"Okay. If you want a snack later, there's potato chips and soda," she said.

An okay sufficed for Donald, while his friends offered a "Thanks, Mrs. Allen."

Though it would be obvious to mostly anyone, still Donald asked, "You burning leaves?"

"Just a little yard work before I head to Bingo. Can you do me a favor?" she asked.

"Yeah, what you need?"

"Will you check later to make sure the fire is out?"

"Sure thing, Mom," he said and addressed his friends. "Remind me not to forget about the burn barrel."

"What's she burning again?" asked Albert.

"Okay," said Donald. "Everyone *but* Albert remind me about the burn barrel before you leave."

He opened the front door, walked into the living room and placed his bag on an end table by the L-configured sofas. "Mom, do we have any thumb tacks?"

"They're in the end table drawer," she called out.

"Which one?" he asked as he opened the drawer and sifted through its contents.

"The one between the couches."

"Oh," he said as he closed the drawer. "Hey, Joe. Make yourself useful," he said, retrieving the shrink-wrapped cassette from the same bag the poster was in and tossing it to Joe.

Joe caught the boxed cassette, Mortemface's About Face, and started picking, silently and contently, at one of its corners.

Donald opened the other end table's drawer and sorted through the transparent pack of multi-colored tacks anally until he found four red ones.

"You find them?" she asked.

"Yes, ma'am," he answered and addressed the boys. "Come on. Let's put this bad boy up."

He dropped the tacks in the bag and carried it down the hall to the intersection at his bedroom door, followed by the boys. To their right was a short walk to the bathroom. Donald held the bedroom door open for them.

Albert entered, and then Joe, staring down, still picking at the cassette's cellophane.

"Dude, I love your room," said Eric as he stepped over the threshold.

And what wasn't there to love for a high school head-banger? On the wall behind them were the kind of teen-angst and drug-induced illustrations his mother would pay a shrink a hundred dollars an hour to decipher if she could afford it—cryptic images of slashed wrists, bleeding orifices and fluidly distorted bodies, Neolithic stone heads and monuments, and all manner of terrifying events and the demonic creatures responsible for them from his worst nightmares.

To the far right was the "metal wall"—a two-dimensional shrine for heavy metal gods torn from the pages of Circus and Hit Parader. And lest he end up the brunt of his father's machismo, to combat the plethora of bare-chested and leather-clad men with their androgynous makeup and hair, there was the "chick wall" at the foot of the bed—a hallowed space reserved for the single female image in his room (besides Lita Ford). It was there Heather Thomas stood in a bubbling hot tub, pulling at the bottom of her pink two-piece, waiting to invade his not-so-horrific dreams.

Lastly, over his bed was a Clockwork Orange poster, with Malcolm McDowell in his white platties watching over Donald as he slept, clutching a rather nasty nozh with its silvery blade all pointy as it were.

The left wall was practically all window, leaving the inside of his bedroom door the only bare space.

"X marks the spot," said Donald, eying the door.

"I'd like to mark Heather Thomas' spot," said Albert, staring at the sultry model, his hands beneath his head as he lay on Donald's bed.

"Get off my bed, perv," Donald ordered as he picked at the cellophane on one end of the poster's cardboard tube. He carefully peeled the clear plastic wrap away, tossed it in the bag, slid the poster off the cardboard tube, and unfurled it.

"Need a hand?" asked Albert.

"Not those hairy things," Donald answered. "Eric, can you put the tacks in for me?"

"Sure," said Eric. "Tell me when you're ready."

"Joe, can you eye this to make sure it's straight?" Donald asked.

Joe nodded as he peeled the plastic wrap off the cassette.

"Joe, can you?" Donald asked again, looking back at his silent friend.

Joe mumbled. "Mmm hmm."

"Dang, man. Speak, why don't you," Donald mumbled to himself.

Joe frowned as he placed the boxed cassette by Donald's boom box and dropped the torn plastic into the Tracks bag.

Donald fidgeted with the poster's rotation for a good minute when Eric grew impatient. "It's fine, Don. Really," he said.

"Joe?" Donald asked.

"Mmm hmm," Joe nodded.

"Okay. Don't get too far from the corners, Eric," Donald instructed.

"I got this, man. It's not rocket surgery," quipped Eric.

One by one he fastened the poster's corners as Donald stood cheek to cheek with the grinning Grim Reaper. Strange how a "man" without facial muscle, the very tissue necessary for emoting expression, could be characterized as grinning, yet there he was, showing his approval (or perhaps contempt) for all he surveyed.

"Done," said Eric.

They stepped back to take in the artwork. In each corner of its background—consisting of a cold, rocky landscape—stood a member of Mortemface in hooded cloak, their faces unseen.

"Killer," the boys said one after the other in sheer admiration as they stared at the poster's menacing figure.

"Speaking of, time to fire up *the killer*!" said Albert with wide, eager eyes.

"Is it safe?" asked Eric.

"Door's locked. Fire up," Donald answered as he unboxed the cassette, placed it in his boom box and hit PLAY. The bright sunlight pouring in through the windows disappeared as Donald pulled down the blinds.

From his inside jean jacket pocket, Eric removed a Ziplok bag and gently pulled the seams loose to retrieve one of three fat, tightly-rolled joints. After replacing the bag he reached into another pocket for his lighter but an anxious Albert held a black Bic at lip level ready to light. Eric took the lighter and after a flick, produced a tall, steady flame he kept lit until he completely filled his lungs with smoke.

The first track on the album began with harmony guitars intoning a minor riff over a reggae beat, all preceding an eerie vocal alluding to the forbidden arts of alchemy and astronomy.

When Donald flicked the switch on his shadeless black light lamp, the room was instantly filled with deep purple. As Eric exhaled, the smoke crept around the black bulb like a dense, cool fog. The joint passed to Joe, Albert and lastly, Donald.

The poster was concealed in the rolling plumes of smoke. Joe parted the cloud with a hand until the poster was visible again. In the black light, images appeared on the poster that were previously hidden. Each of the band's cloaked figures now bore a card suite imprinted on their chest—a heart, a diamond, a spade, a club.

Ol' Mortemface himself, the Grim Reaper, presently bore a large A on his chest, logically the Ace. And though he possessed no eyes in those black, hollowed sockets, there seemed to be something inside them, as if the sockets themselves were no longer two-dimensional images but recessed pits burrowed through the door the poster was suspended on, proceeding into infinite darkness beyond.

The song's minute-long pipe organ solo began.

"They don't make music like this anymore," Donald coughed out.

"They never will—not without Tino," added Eric.

"I don't see why they don't just get another keyboard player," said Albert.

"Dude, you can't replace Tino. He's a legend," said Eric.

"What would you rather have? That Mortemface never tours again or that they find some monkey who can play Tino's solos note-for-note and tour till they're 90, allowing you the opportunity to finally see them play live at least once in your lifetime?" said Albert.

"It still wouldn't be the same; not without the soul of Tino behind those keys," said Donald.

"Well dang man, that didn't stop Ozzy from replacing Randy Rhodes with Jake E. Lee or Metallica from replacing Cliff Burton with Jason Newsted or ACDC replacing Bon Scott with Brian Johnson."

"Yeah, but it did keep Zeppelin from replacing Bonham. There are some people too legendary to be replaced."

"Then dig his up his mangled carcass, throw him behind a DX 7 and stop whining."

"That's blasphemy, man," said Donald.

"For real, dude," agreed Eric. "Everyone knows Tino wouldn't be caught dead playing a Yamaha."

Donald and Eric laughed at the inside joke.

"Well he wouldn't have been caught dead if he stayed off the airplane," said Albert.

"So not cool, man," said Eric.

"What's not cool are all the different stories about his death. Did he really turn up in the wreckage missing his head or did the plane go down over the Atlantic? That's all I want to know," said Albert.

"They found his body in the wreckage. That missing head crap is a bunch of crap," said Donald.

"For real," Eric agreed again.

"As eloquent as that was, how do you know? Were either of you there?" asked Albert.

As they argued among themselves, Joe slowly reached toward the poster to press his fingers against the dark eyes of the Reaper. He caressed the sockets of the skull and determined to place his fingers inside the image he perceived to be a hole.

"Fear the Reaper!" Donald blurted out loudly in Joe's ear as he took hold of his shoulders.

Joe gasped and jerked in a single reflex. "Dude! You scared the crap out of me!"

"I had to make you say something. You're too quiet. Take another hit and loosen up, man," said Donald as he passed the joint back to Joe.

Joe puffed on the joint and slowly exhaled. He handed it to Albert and with a morbid curiosity he again caressed the Grim Reaper's eye sockets. "It looks like you could reach inside his eyes and touch Hell."

"Dang, dude, I said loosen up, not bum us out," said Donald.

"Yeah, man. No one wants to hear that. It's a major downer," said Eric.

"Talk about downers. First you tell me to talk then you tell me to shut up," said Joe. "Anything else I can't say since the Thought Police are listening?"

"Take it easy, Winston Smith," cracked Albert as he put an arm around Joe's neck and pulled him close. "These guys' idea of a good time is sitting around listening to a 20-year-old album by a has-been band."

"Blasphemer!" an offended voice barked from the tiny boom box speakers. The boys had already jumped halfway out of their skin when it occurred to them it was just the intro to the album's second song they had each heard a hundred times easy.

When the realization set in, the boys erupted into a chorus of laughter that filled the room. Their bellowing outburst displaced the purple smoke and sent it swirling about back and forth. The laughter finally subsided for all but Joe, who just couldn't contain himself.

"Okay, Joe, you're cut off," said Donald. "Eric, Albert, let's finish this, 'cause I'm getting some major munchies."

"Me too, dude," said Eric.

"Same here," agreed Albert.

Joe managed to tone his laughter down to an internal snicker that really sounded more like a whimpering dog.

When all that remained of the joint was but a roach Donald hit STOP on the boom box and carefully approached the door.

"Everybody quiet. I don't want my mom to hear," he warned his friends.

He cracked open the door. At the far end of the hall leading to the living room he saw his mother walk by.

"Quick, dudes! Open the windows!" he yelled in an attempted whisper.

Albert threw a window open and frantically fanned the thick smoke out. "It's a shame how much gets wasted these days," he said.

When the snickering Joe shoved the remaining window up he pinched a finger, evoking a quick yelp.

"What happened?" Donald asked.

"Jammed my finger in the sill!" grumbled Joe. But the longer he stared at his finger the funnier the whole thing became, and his momentarily silenced snicker grew into full-blown laughter.

"Damn it, Joe, you're gonna get me busted!" said Donald.

Joe again muted his laughter into soft snickering.

"All right. Let's go raid the fridge," said Donald.

"What about your mom?" Eric asked.

"Just be cool. All we're doing is getting some food. She's not gonna make us piss in a cup," said Donald.

"Dude, your art is alive," said Joe with rolling eyes that moved from picture to picture.

"Dude!" snapped Donald as he stopped Joe's bloody finger from touching a drawing. "Don't get us busted. If you do, you're never getting high with us again."

"I'm okay," said Joe.

"You better be. And what about you guys?"

Albert and Eric nodded their heads. "We're good," "Yeah, I'm okay," they said, fighting to restrain their laughter.

"All right. Here goes," said Donald as he clutched the doorknob. "One, two, three. Go."

The four emerged from the bedroom into the hall in tight formation, each touching the one in front of him as if their hands were the connecting segments of a centipede. The chain of bodies worked its way down the hall into the living room, weaving through sofas, coffee tables, end tables, lamp stands.

They entered the kitchen and swerved around the dinner table and chairs in a parallel line until they came to the refrigerator on the opposite side.

"You boys hungry?" asked Mrs. Allen as she placed dried dishes in cupboards and cabinets.

The boys looked at each other, waiting for an answer.

"Sure am," Albert volunteered.

"There's lunch meat and cheese if you boys want sandwiches, and Wise potato chips and Fritos."

Donald took the orange plastic bag from the top of the fridge and tossed it to Eric, who peeled open the top and stuffed a handful of Fritos in his mouth. Eric held the open bag out for the others.

"You got any bean dip?" asked Joe.

Donald gave him a dirty look.

"Sure. There's some in the fridge next to the French onion," she answered.

Joe opened the fridge and stooped to look inside. His head bobbed back and forth in a continual figure eight as he searched for the elusive dip. The print on every items' label trailed out of sync mid-air, making it impossible to tell which item the logo and name belonged to. He reached inside and grabbed at invisible containers.

"Having trouble finding the dip?" Mrs. Allen asked.

Donald shoved Joe aside with a shoulder and retrieved the bean dip.

"Here," Donald said impatiently as he slapped the aluminum can in Joe's palm.

Joe smiled ear to ear as he removed the plastic lid, placed his cut finger in the metal ring and peeled the razor sharp lid off the container.

"Here, let me take that," offered Mrs. Allen.

Joe handed her the lid and took a single Frito from the bag Eric held. He dug the corn chip into the dip, and when it broke, he laughed.

"I hate when that happens, too," said Mrs. Allen.

As his laughter continued Donald grew nervous.

"It's not that funny, is it Joe?" she asked, just as a drop of blood fell from his finger to the linoleum tile.

"Most people say *ouch* when they cut themselves, not *ha ha ha*," she said. "Why don't you go the bathroom and put a Band-Aid on that?"

"Yeah, Joe. Why don't you go do that?" said Donald as he snatched the can of dip from his hands.

Joe's focus remained on the can, so Eric gave him a small shove in the right direction.

"First you say stay in your room, then follow you here, then go to the bathroom. Make up your mind," mumbled Joe, dragging his feet on the floor as he exited the kitchen into the living room and disappeared around the corner.

"Is he all right?" asked Mrs. Allen.

"He always does that when he sees blood," said Albert.

"Really?" she asked.

"Yeah, all the time," Donald lied.

"Okay. Well you boys help yourself. I'm going back outside," said Mrs. Allen, exiting through the utility room door on the right.

Donald moved the loaf of bread from the bread box to the table. He stuck his head in the fridge and began to blindly hand jars and packages to Albert and Eric.

"Mayo. Miracle Whip. Mustard. Paper-thin ham. American. Swiss. Pickles," he said as he removed the last jar.

He turned to see half the items on the counter top and half on the kitchen table.

"You couldn't put them all in the same place?" Donald asked.

"We did," said Albert. "I put all my stuff on the counter and Eric put all his stuff on the table."

"Hopeless," said Donald as he meticulously unwound the wire wrapper on the bread bag.

"Anal," Albert fired back. He and Eric laughed as they loosened lids on jars and unzipped plastic packages.

"Quit laughing so much. My mom's gonna know what's up."

"I think you need another hit," said Eric. "You're the one who needs to loosen up."

"I know what I need to do," said Donald, pulling four knives from the cabinet's silverware drawer and holding two in each hand.

"Whoa, Norman Bates, no need to drag out your mother's ware," said Albert.

"You are the pun master," said Eric with a head bow.

"I wasn't talking about this. But while we're at it, one knife for each jar—*no* mixing," said Donald with the utmost seriousness.

He handed the knives to the boys and made his way to the sound system in the living room. While Albert and Eric made Dagwood-sized sandwiches, Donald opened a cabinet door and sorted through a stack of records until he found a bland-covered album sleeve and removed its record.

"You guys wanna hear something really killer?" Donald asked as he hit the stereo's power button.

"Heck yeah," said Eric.

Donald couldn't help but laugh to himself. "Check it out. This always gets me," he said as he placed the needle on the record.

The album started with a brief intro of rockabilly music, followed by a deep-voiced emcee.

"You are listening to Brother Bobby Billings' Ain't No Rock `n' Roll Heaven. And now, brothers and sisters, Brother Bobby Billings."

The boys came into the living room, snickering between ravenous bites of their mammoth sandwiches.

"Hello brothers and sisters," the evangelist spoke in a high-pitched voice.

"Do you have this on the right speed?" asked Eric.

"Of course. Didn't you hear how deep the first guy's voice was?" said Donald.

"Nah, it can't be," said Albert, then flipped the RPM switch from 45 to 78.

Brother Bobby's words blended together into a rushing stream of syllabic gibberish.

"Dude, don't touch my record player," Donald scolded as he moved the switch back to 45 rpm.

"Maybe it's supposed to be 33 and a third," said Albert.

"No, it's not," Donald argued. "Man, you'd think I know after listening to it a dozen times."

"Just try it."

Donald flipped the switch to its lowest position. Now Brother Bobby sounded like a baritone behemoth.

"Dude, that's creepy," said Albert as the THC-influenced audio moved from left to right and rose in volume at its own will. He sat down on a sofa and massaged both his temples.

"A r e y o u f e e l i n g o k a y ?" Donald asked Albert, his voice also strangely slow and deep.

Though Albert heard his voice the words were not processed.

"A l b e r t ?" Donald addressed him.

"D u d e," said Eric as he swatted Albert's shoulder.

Donald flicked the RMP switch back to 45 rpm, just as Eric said to Albert, "S n a p out of it."

"What?" asked Albert, looking around at them.

"Are you okay?" Donald asked again.

"Oh, sure," he answered. "Why?"

"Quit that. You're wigging us out," said Eric.

Donald lifted the needle and skipped ahead, long enough to hear Brother Bobby Billings utter a sentence or two, then repeated the process until he found the passage he had listened to so many times.

When he heard a particularly bad piece of music followed by loud applause and shouts of Hallelujah, then a brief silence as the audience quieted down, he turned to the boys and nodded his head in satisfaction.

"One of these ungodly bands the kids are listening to today is a band named Mortemface," said the evangelist.

"Dude, who is that?" asked Eric.

"Look at the cover, man," said Donald.

"Brother Bobby Billings?" Eric read aloud. "What a nerd."

"Quiet man, this is the funny part."

"Each band member has on their person an image from the four suites of a deck of cards," the naturally chipmunk-voiced preacher continued. "I'm sure some of you are familiar with them—the diamond, heart, club and spade. What most of you probably don't know is that that innocent looking deck of cards you play Rummy with is also used in the occultic art of divination, forbidden in the book of Leviticus. `Come now,' you say. `Aren't you going a bit overboard?' I don't know about you, friend, but I know if I was on a sinking ship I'd take my chances in the open sea. Wouldn't you, friend? `But how is that deck of cards part of the occult?' you ask.

"There are 52 playing cards, just as there are 52 weeks in the year. There are four suits, just as there are four seasons in a year. There are 13 cards in each suit, just as there are 13 weeks in each season. There are 12 court cards—that is the Jacks, Queens and Kings—just as there are 12 months in a year. And when you take the number 52, starting at one, and add that to two, and two to three, and three to four and so on until you reach 52, you arrive at the total of 364. When you add the Joker, that makes 365, the total number of days in a year. That's called numerology, and it's an occultic practice."

"Is occultic even a word?" asked Albert.

"No," Eric answered. "He's an idiot."

"So in that innocent looking deck of playing cards you have the embodiment of both divination and numerology, both practiced by witches and Satanists," said Brother Bobby. "Friend, do you want to go to Hell over a game of cards? I don't think so, friend. I feel it is my God-given duty as a watchman, just as Ezekiel, to inform you that many listening to my voice tonight have children who are listening to the demonic music of this occultic band Mortemface."

Eric groaned. "Will he please stop saying occultic?"

"And let's not forget the band's mascot, Skully—a skeletal, devilish figure holding a large scythe and bearing the letter A emblazoned on its breast—the symbol for the Ace card. It is the equivalent of the Death Card in the occultic art of Tarot," Brother Bobby continued.

"I guess he won't," said Albert.

"Imagine friend—your children listening to music that unashamedly promotes the occult," said Brother Bobby. "Now I ask you again, do you want to stay on that sinking ship or will you throw yourself into the *Mer Sea* of God? Will you open your arms and receive the life *savior* that God is casting out to you in the divine person of his only begotten, Jesus Christ?"

"We will, Brother Bobby, we will!" "Praise the Lord!" "Amen!" Albert and Eric went back and forth as they answered the recorded voice.

Donald had never enjoyed the album as much or laughed as hard.

"Now before you come asking the Lord forgiveness you better bring something to the table. And that something is your sin, brothers and sisters. You must repent. `But how do I repent, Brother Bobby' you ask," the preacher said.

"Tell us, Brother Bobby! We must know! How do we repent?" Albert and Eric continued to converse with the preacher.

"If your children possess any of Mortemface's ungodly record albums or posters or t-shirts or ball caps, you need to take them outside and burn them just like the Ephesians in the Book of Acts. Amen?" Brother Bobby asked the audience, and the three mocking boys in their modern living room.

"Amen!" Albert and Eric answered in unison with the audience.

"Wait! Am I supposed to burn my children or my albums?" asked Albert, unable to keep a straight face when feigning ignorance.

"I think we're supposed to burn the effigies—is that what he said?" asked Eric.

"Ephesians," said Donald, still laughing. "Some dudes in the Bible," he added when Eric looked at him like a confused dog.

"Is that where we get the word effigy?" asked Albert.

"They didn't burn the Ephesians, stupid. The Ephesians burned their stuff," Donald answered as he carefully took hold of the record player needle.

"Amen, Brother Bobby!" said Eric and Albert with shaking, upraised hands.

Donald was overcome with heaving laughter. With each violent convulsion he drove the diamond needle into the record as he returned the arm to its base. "You made me scratch my record," he said, wiping the tears from his eyes. He returned the battered Brother Bobby and his faithful flock to the record sleeve, no wiser regardless the wear.

"And I'm still hungry," said Donald as he took the rest of Albert's sandwich from his hand.

"What about my germs you're always afraid of?" asked Albert.

"I'm too stoned to care," Donald laughed with his mouth full.

"Man, where's Joe? He totally missed out," said Eric.

"He went to get a Band-Aid like an hour ago," said Albert.

"Probably taking a dump. Hope he wipes the seat and washes his hands,"

Donald answered as he turned the stereo off. "All right. Church is over. Let's listen to some more Mortem."

The boys returned to the kitchen, passed through the living room and down the hall to Donald's door.

"Al, can you go check on Joe?" Donald asked as he held the door for Eric.

"Sure. If I'm not back within 30 minutes call the Coast Guard," said Albert.

Donald plopped onto his bed, hit PLAY on the boom box, and stretched out across the blankets. Eric sat in the chair at Donald's work table. With the room now empty of the joyfully blinding smoke, the boys were enamored to see the glowing white of their shoelaces and screen-printed tees in the black light's influence.

The next track on the album began with a classical piano intro. Soon bass and hi-hats joined, followed by guitar.

"What I wouldn't give to see them perform again," said Donald, staring up, through the Clockwork Orange poster, past the ceiling, into the imaginary stadium among the constellations.

"Joe's gone," said Albert, peeking his head into the room as he held onto the door frame.

"What?" Eric asked.

"He's gone," Albert repeated.

A car engine started.

"My car!" Eric erupted as he jumped to his feet.

"Easy, dude. That was my mom's van," said Donald.

Eric sifted through his pockets in a panic until he found his car keys.

"Told you," said Donald.

"Oh yeah," said Albert with eyebrows raised nearly as high as himself. "Don't forget to check on the barrel, or something."

"And they say pot destroys short-term memory," Eric teased.

"But what about Joe?" Donald asked.

"What about Joe?" Albert asked.

"Scratch my last statement," said Eric, shaking his head.

"How did he get home?" Donald asked.

"It's only a 10-minute walk," said Albert.

"Still, but why would he leave?"

"Maybe because you yelled at him."

"I didn't yell at him."

"Yeah you did," said Albert as he stepped into the room and closed the door.

"I didn't yell. I told him in a whisper. That's not yelling."

"Yelling has nothing to do with volume and everything to do with tone," said Eric, matter of fact.

"You think I yelled at him, too?" Donald asked.

Eric nodded his head.

"Well damn, why didn't anybody say anything?"

"It wouldn't help," answered Albert.

"Maybe I should call him," said Donald, sitting up in his bed and swinging his feet over the side.

"It wouldn't help," said Albert again.

"Okay, make me feel like crap why don't you," he said.

"Don't sweat it," said Eric. "He'll get over it. Everyone knows you're a jerk."

"Thanks a lot," said Donald sullenly as he stared at his shoes.

"Speaking of tone, quit your whining and check out this sick guitar solo," said Eric, reaching across the table to turn the volume up on the boom box.

The flurry of notes buzzed around the boys like a swarm of honeybees in the warmest summer, each one lighting on the ear long enough to leave a memory and take just a bit of their breath away.

"Did you know *Rock Guitar* named this one of the 100 worst guitar solos of all time?" Albert asked.

"Then *Rock Guitar* is one of the 100 *worst* magazines of all time," said Eric.

"For real, dude," Donald agreed. "They have the exact same tabs every year. Like there's not more than 36 damn songs worth playing on guitar."

"Hey, Don," said Albert, staring at the poster.

"What, Al?" Donald asked.

"Do you remember seeing a face on any of the guys?"

"Card faces? Yeah, all five have them."

"No, I mean actual faces."

"Nah. None of the band members have faces."

"Yeah they do. I mean one does."

"Nah, dude. That's the THC talking."

"Okay."

Eric stood up from the chair to look at the poster. "No, Don. There *is* a face."

"Says the guy who's blind as a bat," said Donald.

"They're for driving, jerk," Eric whined as he removed the glasses from his pocket and put them on. "Yep, there's a face right there."

"Bull. On who?"

"Tino."

"You sure?"

"Um, yes, because he has a *heart* on his chest, hence his name, Valentino *Hart*."

"Bull. You guys are still stoned."

"Has anyone ever noticed how much Tino looks like Joe?" asked Albert.

"Only those who are stoned," said Donald.

"No, I'm serious. Tino looks just like Joe," said Albert as he repeatedly poked the illustration of the cloaked man.

"Quit touching my poster."

"But look. Joe is his spitting image," said Albert as he poked the poster three more times when the sound of tearing paper drove Donald to his feet.

"You idiot! You tore my poster!"

Albert quickly raised his hands and stepped back from the poster. "Sorry, Don. I didn't mean to."

"Joe was right," said Eric, suddenly sober.

"What about Joe?" Donald snapped.

"It looks like you could touch Hell," said Eric as he leaned close and stared into the torn black hole where the hooded face of Valentino Hart should have been.

He caressed the contour of the tear with one hand while he adjusted his glasses with the other. He heard a distant groaning in the ethereal darkness, voices swirling in time with the wisping mist. Neither Albert or Donald turned their head at the sorrowful sound, but their nescience went equally unnoticed by Eric, himself helpless to turn away from the voices that called out to him. They knew him, and he knew them—their pain, their longing, their regret.

"You got some Scotch tape? I think we can fix it," offered Albert.

"You're not putting tape all over my poster. You owe me six dollars," demanded Donald.

"No, dude. Put the tape on the back, not the front," explained Albert.

"I don't care. You still owe me six dollars."

"For real, guys. You could seriously touch Hell," said Albert as he pushed the edge of the tear toward the door, only to find behind the poster there was no door. There was nothing on the other side but Hell.

The hole tore larger as he pressed against it, until the tear was within an inch of the poster's edge.

"Not again!" Donald yelled.

A sort of fog or mist, not unlike the strange smoke the boys partook of earlier, stirred within the blackness and inched its way into the room.

"Where's that coming from?" asked Albert.

He and Donald grew quiet and joined their friend, gazing into the infinite, abysmal darkness.

Eric inhaled the black air and its strange wisps. It was cool, dry, odorless. He reached into the mist, unaware of the bony hand reaching toward the black light coming from the bedroom.

When his hand brushed against cold bone he instantly pulled back, but the thick bony digits had already closed tight around his wrist like a steel trap or carnivorous flower.

"It's got me!" Eric screamed.

"What is it?" Donald yelled.

"It's a—" Eric was pulled into the poster's giant, gaping tear. Albert leaped to take hold of Eric's legs.

Whatever words Eric wished to express the terror he witnessed was translated into agonizing screams.

In the black light from the bedroom, Albert saw the bony hand extending through the mist, gripping fingers piercing through denim into Eric's forearm. Clothing burned in an instant flash; flesh melted like hair caught in a candle flame; a pair of glasses and bits of metal—denim jean and jacket buttons, an earring— fell into bottomless blackness. As Albert clung to Eric's legs he heard sizzling; a boiling sound that extinguished the screams of his friend. From Eric's belly, flaming bowels poured out, dropping into dark, disappearing.

Albert released his doomed friend into the hands of Death and Hell.

"What did you do, Al?" Donald yelled.

"There was nothing left. He was gone, Don!" Albert cried.

The distant sorrow that had held Eric mesmerized drew close, and deafeningly loud, spreading like spilled oil, reaching toward the broken opening where black light shone. The swirling mists spun faster, and like a whirlwind, or the exhalation of all Hell, the giant breath blew everything in Donald's room around and out of place. The bony hand reached out of the sorrow, grasping for any sliver of the terrified teenagers.

"Pull the tacks!" Albert yelled.

"What?" Donald asked.

"Just pull them!" Albert said as he removed the top right tack, dodged the snapping fingers, and made his way for the bottom right tack.

Donald followed suit, undoing the bottom left tack. The hand snapped at him like alligator jaws anxious for blood. He pulled back in time to stare wide-eyed as the fingers closed inches from his throat.

"Get the last one!" Albert yelled unnecessarily, for as soon as the bony fingers had closed, Donald reached for the top left corner of the poster.

The skeletal hand opened again, its tight joints squeaking like rusty hinges. Donald took hold of the remaining fastened corner of the poster and pulled, tearing all but a piece from the tack and flinging it to the floor. The violent whirlwind unwound and grew still as the poster rolled up at their feet, whether from the law of physics—it having been rolled up until nearly an hour prior—or the dark law only known by few.

Regardless, the boys jumped back for caution's sake.

The myriad of drawings torn from Donald's walls in the hellish cyclone floated about the room, gently descending to the nearest surface, be it dresser, worktable, bed, or floor.

"Is that it?" Donald asked in the stillness of the storm's aftermath.

Albert was silent. How could he know? Both stared at the rolled-up poster on the floor fearfully silent. Donald nudged the poster with his foot. It rolled half a foot and stopped at Albert's shoe.

Albert took a cautious step back to be clear of the poster. He looked at Donald soberly.

"You know what we have to do, right?" said Albert.

"What?" Donald asked.

"We have to—"

The poster rolled another half foot, stopped by Albert's foot again. When he felt it touch his shoe he looked down at the poster and stepped back another foot.

The poster rolled toward his foot again.

He and Donald stared at the poster, afraid to speak.

"What, Al?" Donald asked again.

The bony finger emerged from the poster and tapped on the floor about Albert's foot until the soft thud of tennis shoe was heard beneath its touch.

As the hand reached out, the poster unrolled with a crisp sound, until the hooded head of the Reaper stood knee-high to the boys. Its fleshless hand extended out of the large sleeve and took hold of Albert's leg. He screamed, fighting to pull his leg free but no movement could shake the grip of Death.

The blade of the scythe rose out of the poster and swung. Donald stumbled into his bed as he jumped back to clear the weapon's arc. Albert gasped, wide-eyed, as the tip of the blade found the center of his back, cutting clean through his spine and rendering him paralyzed.

Without his mind's consent, his body willingly surrendered, unable to resist. The Reaper's hand effortlessly pulled the docile teenager into the poster, into Hell. The only use that remained from the paralyzing blow was his voice.

"Burn it, Don! Burn it all!" Albert screamed as he descended into the black abyss.

Donald took Albert's shoulders into both arms, but as his friend submerged into the otherworldly darkness, he witnessed of Albert that Albert witnessed of Eric—the destruction of all flesh and material save bone, which made any attempt to save him futile. He yielded to regret as he released his only living friend into the hands of Death.

As soon as Skully returned to his abode, Donald stooped to the floor and furiously tore the poster into pieces, until no fragment was large enough for anything more than a few fingers or toes to ever enter this world again.

He collected the pieces and put them in the brown paper bag that previously held the poster in its complete state. He rushed out of his room, down the hall, into the living room, into the kitchen, into the utility room, into the garage and out the door into the back yard, where he found the rusted metal burn barrel his mother used to dispose of leaves, straw and pine cones.

He overturned the bag above the barrel, releasing the torn pieces into the hungry fire. The Autumn wind took hold of one remaining piece and carried it down its cool stream to God knows where, as Donald didn't notice its escape from the flames.

Lastly Donald dropped the bag into the barrel to ensure any contents clinging to its bottom were destroyed. The paper bag ignited and turned black, its corners curling toward the center like a hand closing to make a fist.

All went up in smoke the same way the flesh of Eric and Albert, and presumably Joe, had smoldered away to nothing, till what remained in the burn barrel were flames, glowing red sticks and the ashes of foliage.

The smell of smoke saturated Donald's clothes and hair as he stood over the barrel, absorbing the soothing odor of burnt leaves. With his fear carried away on the smoky wind, he turned from the burn barrel and made his way to the house.

When he came to his bedroom door, unfortunately his fear returned to greet him as a loud hum emanated from the other side. He turned the knob but chose to push the door open with his foot. From the threshold he saw his drawings littered on the floor and heard the loud buzzing hum.

He carefully entered, not so much to avoid stepping on his artwork, but to avoid alerting any lingering evil.

The door swung till the latch hit the door frame, slowly, naturally, as it always had. He closed his eyes involuntarily, and with great effort fought to open them to see what lay on the other side of his door which now faced him.

It was just as he left it before he exited the room to burn the cursed poster. Relief.

He exhaled and approached his bed. Just as he reached it he realized he had stepped on one of his drawings—a shame, but he was beyond caring for such meaningless images. Still the God-awful buzzing came from some invisible, nagging hornet. He faced the boom box—the source of the hum, now more like a whole nest of hornets.

Side One of the Mortemface album had come to an end, but the boom box's motor still fought to turn the cassette's spindles. Donald swatted the STOP button and ejected the cassette. He took it in both hands and broke it in half, opened the window stained with Joe's blood, and flung the cassette outside.

Again he exhaled deep relief. He lay on his bed with eyes closed, crossed his legs and sank his head comfortably into the cool pillow.

"Burn it, Don!" ordered Albert's voice in Donald's memory.

His eyes opened wide when something wet touched his left hand. He stared at the red spatter then past it at the single piece of torn poster that remained tacked on his bedroom door.

"I told you to burn it all, Don!" he heard Albert's voice speak again.

"Blasphemer!" blared the boom box as the album's second track started again.

Donald stared at the boom box, watching as the cassette's twin spindles turned behind the small, clear door. *I just threw the tape through the window!*

He felt another drop. It landed on his cheek right beneath his eye like a crimson tear. He looked at the ceiling.

His countenance paled as he gazed upon the bloody scythe in Skully's hand. Before Donald could scream, regardless whatever good it may have done, the scythe rang through the air from above.

※※※※

"You're listening to W-I-K-D, Wicked Radio, and this is the Madman—your crazy DJ who plays ze groovay rock and rolla," the Classic Rock DJ's voice came from the boom box speakers. "This just in. You won't believe your ears, so believe the Madman instead. Mortemface will be touring for the first time in years since the tragic death of keyboard player Valentino Hart. Original lineup members Romeo Klubb, Casanova Spade, and Don Jan DiMond will be returning to the stage, but no mention has been made who will stand in place for the formerly irreplaceable Hart. Fans can rest assured of one thing—this will be the ultimate reunion tour of a lifetime. So to celebrate this colossally cosmic aligning of the stars, let's hear another track from astral rock's finest mystics, Mortemface."

"Knock, knock," Donald's mother called out from behind the door. "Brought you some Hardees."

She opened the door slowly and entered. There in his bed, beneath his blanket, lay Donald at rest.

Bothered by the loud music blaring from the boom box, she turned the volume down.

"You awake, Don?" she asked. "Where are the boys? Eric's car is still here." Donald didn't answer.

"You wanna get you something to eat?" she asked and slowly peeled the blanket back only to find the bloody pillow that cradled the venous stump of her son's neck. His body had curled, post-decapitation, into a fetal repose.

"Oh, Donny! My baby!" she screamed.

"I'm up here, Mom!" Donald's voice shouted from above.

She gazed up to find the Clockwork Orange poster no longer graced Donald's stucco firmament. Instead of Alexander DeLarge, there stood Skully, dead center on the poster that had been torn from his door and burned to ashes just hours before. Beneath the hoods of the poster's cloaked band-members were the sorrowful faces of Joe, Eric, Albert and Donald, shouting words now too distant for her to distinguish clearly. The one thing Mrs. Allen was certain of, was that she was not safe within the black light.

THE LOVELY THING
BY LISA FINCH

Jeannie heard George slap his newspaper down.

"Every day it's the same," he said.

"What's the same?" She walked into the living room, still drying the mug she'd washed.

"That woman!" George crouched in front of the window blinds, adjusting the slats to a crack. Jeannie peered out too and saw the woman, a young mother who wore sunglasses and pushed a baby carriage.

"Well, she's a lovely little thing." Jeannie snickered as she nudged George in the ribs.

"Don't be ridiculous," he grumbled.

Next day, same thing.

"There she is again!" He cried from the next room. "One o'clock on the nose. How does she do it?"

"Jeannie," he continued. "Do you know that woman walks by this house, with that same baby buggy, every day at the *exact same time*."

"So what if she does? Maybe she's not a retired old coot. Maybe she's got a schedule to keep. She has a baby. Babies like routine."

"Routine?!" George marched in. "A routine that is to the exact minute *every single day*?"

"Geez George, I don't know." Jeannie turned to the drain board and picked up a plate. "Maybe you should help me with these dishes. You seem bored."

"I'm not bored. I'm—"

"You're what?"

George murmured to himself as he walked back to his spot by the window.

After a few weeks of tracking this woman's afternoon walks, George got edgy.

One afternoon, the sky opened up. Rain and thunder beat down on the house.

The lights flickered.

George paced and looked at his watch again. "If she comes out today, something is definitely very peculiar."

"George, sit down." Jeannie put on the kettle for some tea. "You're making me nervous."

But George wasn't even looking at his wife, nor did he seem to be listening. He looked past her—right through her—and pointed out the kitchen window.

"There she is! And it's pouring rain!"

George ran to the hall; Jeannie followed him. He pulled on a rain slicker.

She grabbed his arm. "What are you going to do?"

"To see what the Sam Hill she thinks she's doing out in the rain like this with a little baby."

Jeannie shuddered. "George, don't go." She pulled him back. "Please."

But he did anyway, and that's when the troubles started. Jeannie looked back on that day and wondered why she hadn't done something more. Oh sure, George was as stubborn as a mule and just as ornery, but Jeannie should've tried harder to stop him.

Instead, she'd stood looking outside and watched as George talked to the mother in the pouring rain, still wearing those sunglasses. Why would she wear sunglasses in the rain? When she removed them, George's mouth gaped open. He looked down, into the baby carriage and then back up into the young mother's face.

At the psychiatrist's office, she blurted out the whole story.

"He was so agitated about seeing this woman with the baby carriage every day." She pressed a well-wrinkled tissue to her face. "But I had no idea it would turn out like this. What could he have seen? He didn't say a word when he came back inside. He just—"

"He's had a psychotic break and that's why he has withdrawn," the doctor explained.

"And this is why he hasn't said a word since?" She burst into tears.

"He's in good hands, I can tell you that much. This is one of the best facilities in the province."

Jeannie nodded and dabbed at her eyes.

The doctor ran his index finger down his notes and stopped. "You say you see this woman every day at the same time?"

"Yes, that's right."

"Mrs. Francis, I'm wondering if you could ask her what your husband said or did, just before he had his break down. Could you do that?"

"Do you think it would help?"

He nodded. "It just might."

❧❧❧❧

The next day, Jeannie walked out into the sunshine at one o'clock.

She approached the woman in the sunglasses and said, "Excuse me, dear. Can I talk to you for a moment?"

The woman turned and, with a trace of a smile, removed her glasses.

Jeannie fell into those enormous swirling-twirling eyes, all kinds of secrets unfolded from the dazzling colours of the young woman's irises. Beautiful, mesmerizing rainbows. Colours Jeannie hadn't seen before. And shapes, triangles and rectangles, squares, all intersecting and joining, then dissembling in a kaleidoscope universe.

Jeannie's head whipped back, as if jolted. Her body was a jumbled tangle of tingly sensations. Then she leaned in—she just had to look—inside the carriage.

The baby was a doll. It had a porcelain face and long black eyelashes over its sleeping eyelids. Suddenly the lids snapped open. The eyes were luminous. And sort of... human. Jeannie leaned in closer. Large shining eyes...like the woman's...swirling twirling...colours you could touch...could forget yourself in...eyes that knew and saw everything.

At some point Jeannie wandered back into her house and sat on the deacon's bench in the hall. She stared at the coat rack. It weaved and melted, almost into the floor and then stood upright again. Panning from left to right, she noticed that the light fixtures, the wallpaper and floor, they all did the same thing. Melting, sinking, then standing upright. Everything, everywhere, danced and swayed.

From what seemed like far away, she heard knocking and followed it to her front door. A man looked up from his clipboard and into Jeannie's eyes.

His mouth dropped open. The clipboard hit her stoop, followed by his pen. He walked away, his impossibly long arms drooping to the sidewalk.

His limbs melted and formed into long rubber-band-like things, and then snapped back into shape again.

Jeannie watched him go, transfixed by his movements for a moment. Above him she saw even more beautiful, shifting and changing colours and shapes emerge in the sky.

She moved towards the vistas of see-forever stars that exploded in front of her eyes.

The mother in the sunglasses moved her stroller down the sidewalk toward the rubbery man. She held out her hand and he took it. Together, they walked down the sidewalk, a path of colour and light. His limbs continued to grow and shrink, grow and shrink, even as their silhouettes grew smaller.

She ran into the street to follow them before they left her behind forever. She saw her neighbours had the same idea; they flocked out of their houses and chased after them.

At the end of the street, the source of all this wonder seemed to hover. Jeannie had to get closer, had to be part of it. The woman in the sunglasses seemed to know the way.

"George I was right," Jeannie whispered. "She really is a lovely thing."

FLESH FLIES
BY DONNA LEAHEY

It wasn't the buzzing that woke Lissa, it was the rattle of the metal slats of mini blinds.

"Mark. Wake up," she mumbled, determinedly keeping her eyes shut and holding tight to the tattered remnants of her dreams. She'd not been sleeping well the last few weeks and exhaustion fogged her mind.

Mark didn't answer. She opened her eyes. The clock said 3:15. *Gawd.*

"Mark!" She rolled over to push at him, but the space next to her was empty. "Mark?"

He must have gotten an emergency call and decided not to wake her. Her husband was sweet like that.

She'd need to handle the buzzing on her own.

With a sigh, she sat up and swung her feet over the side. The buzzing seemed even louder by the time she turned on the bedside light.

She shook herself awake and shuffled over dirty clothes and paper plates littering the floor. A stale, sour yet sweet odor filled the room.

Ugh! How did we let this room get so messy?

She frowned at the source of the noise. "I thought I killed you this afternoon."

It was a fly. Big bastard with red eyes, black bristles, and three dark stripes on its thorax. She had, in fact, struck it earlier that day with a rolled up magazine and thought it was dead.

It hardly seemed likely that a fly could buzz so loudly, but those wings generated a vibration loud enough she was sure she could have heard it in another room.

Lissa shuffled around through the trash on the floor until she found a paperback book and whacked the disgusting thing. It fell to the window sill, still buzzing, still trying to fly. She struck it again.

She blew out a sigh, staring at the bed. *I've got to get some rest.*

Pulling the covers to her ears, she squeezed her eyes shut and thought about making a nice breakfast for Mark in the morning. He'd like that, if he was home by then. As she debated bacon or sausage, waffles or pancakes — or French Toast! — sleep crept back up on her, quieting her mind.

Bzzzzz

Her eyes popped open. "No way!"

She swung out of bed and turned on her light. There was that red-eyed fly, banging into the metal slats of the mini blinds again.

"You are one tough insect," she said. And smashed it into the window. It hit the sill and bounced to the floor, its wings still buzzing fitfully. She bent and smashed it into the hardwood floor, leaving a moist, black smear.

"Gotcha now!" Then, "Oh, there were two of them," as she noticed the still corpse of the first resting on the window sill.

She determinedly crawled back into bed. Staring into the darkness, she visualized a broom sweeping away her whirling thoughts, as she rhythmically tense and relaxed her muscles. Nothing. No drowsiness, so sleepiness, no peaceful drifting away. Just as she decided to get up and read a book…

Bzzzz bzzzzz

One fly rested on the wall, his wings a blur as if he existed only to annoy her with his buzzing. Another echoed its brothers' fascination with blinds, banging into them with a shrill metallic clang. Their red eyes seemed to accuse her of something horrible.

"Where are you guys coming from?"

Maybe from the kitchen? Mark hadn't taken the trash out in awhile, but if they were coming from there, shouldn't the flies be in the kitchen and not in her bedroom?

The paperback's binding split and the book fell apart in her hands as she smashed the fly on the wall.

The one in the window became still as if it watched her search for a new weapon. She stilled as well. It really was an unusual-looking fly. Besides the bright red eyes, it was bigger than a normal housefly, with three stripes down its body and visible black bristles on its abdomen.

Lissa's hand found one of Mark's sneakers. She struck swiftly and the fly's corpse smeared against the glass. Before she could so much as drop the sneaker, more flies appeared, their maddening buzzing stabbing into her ears.

"Ugh! What the hell!"

She flung her discarded clothes off the computer chair and wiggled the mouse to wake up her computer. She closed the Facebook chat with her best friend before even checking to see if Heather had responded to her yet. She typed in "big fly red eyes stripes black bristles" and hit enter. Moments later, images like the flies invading her room appeared on her computer screen. "Flesh Fly," read the results.

One chose that moment to land on her hand. Its wings continued to buzz and the vibration traveled down to her skin. Her flesh tremored with revulsion as if trying to crawl away from the insect.

"Augh!" She jumped up and shook her hand, then froze in horror. There must have been twenty of the nasty bastards flying about, crawling on the walls and banging against the mini blinds. Their insistent buzzing made her skin vibrate.

"Oh, my God! What's going on?"

Lissa darted for the master bath. She dug through the towels and clothes moldering into a solid mass - *how the hell did it get so messy in here?* - and snatched a can of bathroom cleaner to use as a ranged weapon. Each fly coated by the white froth fell to the floor, struggled, and stilled. And was replaced by two more. As the can ran empty, the insect invasion slowed and died.

She stood in the center of her room, atop a scattering of dirty clothes, panting. "Holy shit."

Returning to her computer, Lissa read the first entry on Flesh Flies, though her mind was scattered and reluctant to pay attention. Until she read, "reproduces in dead and decaying flesh."

Movement near the wall caught her eye. More crawled from the vent in the floor, shoving their way into the room, and taking wing with their horrible, accusatory buzzing.

She snatched up her cell phone. Mark should have taken out the trash. That was the only explanation. There must be a scrap of meat in the trash or something.

She dialed her husband, but the call went immediately to voice mail. She hung up, furious, but then called back right away. "Dammit, Mark, I can't sleep because there's these Death Flies all over the bedroom! When was the last time you took the trash out?" She heaved a heavy sigh. "I'm sorry, baby, you know how much I love you, I'm just exhausted. I... I guess I'll see you when you get home."

She stared down at her phone, and on impulse, called her best friend Heather. They'd been friends for so long and called each other in the middle of the night so many times. Heather would make her feel better. Hell, Heather might come over and help! But her call went straight to voice mail. "Call me. This is so weird. I need you."

She slipped her feet inside Mark's sneakers, despite how big they were on her, and shuffled out of the bedroom. The trash smell was even worse in the hall.

I'll just put the trash out on the porch for right now and maybe that will get rid of the rest of them. And maybe then I can get some sleep.

She turned the corner into the kitchen and stopped, blinking in surprise. The trash wasn't just full, it was overflowing, like a science fair volcano spewing foam in a spreading puddle around its base. For just a moment, she saw the entire house as it was, covered in trash and debris, soda cans, fast food wrappers, clothes left where they fell.

Then she blinked and turned back to the trash. "I can't," she told the pile. "I can't deal with you right now. I'll just block the vent. I have to get some rest."

She made her way down the hall, trying to think of strategies to get back to sleep. If the flies were getting in through the vent, then she could just block the vent, kill the flies already in her room, then still get a few hours sleep before morning.

At her bedroom door, she became aware of the buzzing from the guest room. So loud. Like a helicopter overhead.

Just leave it. You can't do anything about it right now. Tomorrow, go buy a bug bomb. She stared at the guest room door, horrified and fascinated about what might be on the other side.

Or just burn the whole house down.

With no further thought, she flung open the door.

Behind a curtain of buzzing wings, black bodies, and red eyes, her husband's bare back moved. Those muscles in his back she'd loved to touch strained and bunched. And under him. A woman. Long blonde hair spread out on the pillow. Their eyes fixed on her.

Mark cried out a wordless denial and tried to crawl off the women.

Oh, the woman. Lissa *knew* her. Heather. Heather. Heather.

Lissa's best friend laughed and wrapped her legs around Mark's hips, holding him in place.

Mark's pistol lay on the floor by the door. Without questioning its presence, Lissa crouched to pick it up and began squeezing the trigger as she stood. Mark cried out and collapsed over Heather. Crimson bloomed on the sheets.

Heather stopped laughing. She pushed at Mark's body, trying to escape until the moment her head fell back and blood sprayed the headboard...

But... no. The pistol only clicked on an empty chamber.

Oh. She dropped the gun.

No, they were dead. They were so dead. Those weren't muscles moving in Mark's back, those were insects under the skin. Those weren't eyes focused on her, they were flies crawling about in eye sockets.

How long had it been since Lissa came home and heard a strange noise in the guest room? How long since she'd grabbed her husband's gun and opened that door? Long enough for Flesh Flies to grow and mature in their dead bodies.

Lissa had dropped the gun. She'd turned around and gone to the kitchen. Washed her hands. Reheated some leftovers in the microwave.

And forgot.

The flies swarmed around the corpses. That buzzing sound filled the air, deafening Lissa where she stood paralyzed.

A scream crawled up out of her chest and erupted from her. She screamed until her throat closed and there was no more air. She flinched away, desperately seeking the fog of denial. If she could close that door, she could forget. She could return to the world where she had a husband she loved and a friend she trusted.

The flies circled closer, several landing on Lissa as she gathered her courage and reached into the room. The door slammed closed between her and the bodies on that bed.

In Mark's over-sized shoes, she stumbled down the hall. She passed the trash-fouled kitchen and crossed into the living room, shaking her head in denial, her vision blurred by hot tears. She stepped on the untied laces and tumbled face first into the trash on the floor.

She sprawled where she lay, weeping, until the tears ran dry.

Confused, her thoughts in a chaotic whirl, she shuffled back down the hall.

I need to remember to ask Mark to take out the trash. It smells awful in here.

❧❧❧

As dawn lightened the sky, Lissa woke. It wasn't the buzzing sound that woke her, it was the rattle of the metal slats of the mini blinds.

"Mark. Wake up," she mumbled.

THIS LITTLE PIGGY
BY KEN GOLDMAN

Like a true nature's child

We were born, born to be wild ...
- Steppenwolf (1968)

Lab days were the worst for Kooper whose stomach wasn't always up to the task when time came to inspect the gooey innards of assorted frogs and cats. Carver High's seniors called Wednesday's laboratory period Brown Bag Day because when Dr. Tompkins handed out those paper bags they were not intended for lunches going 'in' but for breakfasts coming 'out.'

But in February the dreaded day improved significantly when Tompkins paired Kooper with Rochelle Greene as his lab partner. Carver's standard issue lab coat had all the appeal of a nun's habit, but just knowing those juicy mammaries heaved somewhere beneath Rochelle's starched whites provided Kooper with enough wood to warm his BVD's the entire afternoon.

"Hey, Kooper. You ready to cut us some pig?" Rochelle greeted him with her best Daisy Duke accent as they took seats behind their dissecting tray. One smile from her made the thought of slicing into today's pig fetus seem genuinely erotic.

"In the immortal words of Larry the Cable Guy, let's 'Get 'er done!'"

Smooth.

Kooper examined the tools spread out upon their table: a pair of scissors and gloves, a scalpel, a blunt probe and needle probe, forceps, and that notorious brown bag. Rochelle slipped her hands into the plastic gloves like a debutante attending a summer ball, creating a mental snap shot guaranteed to remain in Kooper's psyche until the last tooth fell out of his head.

Dr. Tompkins was probably born wearing laboratory whites, but the instructor almost bordered on cool if you overlooked his thinning hair and bad teeth. He enjoyed talking up this fetal pig exercise a little more than seemed healthy, but that was probably just a teacher thing like how Mr. Hermann practically ejaculated into his boxers over Shakespeare. Vomit inducing as it was, animal dissection seemed radical in its own Dr. Demento way. And Tompkins did pair Kooper with Rochelle, an act Kooper considered worthy of sainthood.

"Today you'll be examining in some detail the external and internal anatomy of genus Sus scrofa, a fetal pig. As a mammal, many aspects of its structural and functional organization are identical with those of other mammals, including humans, and our study is, in a very real sense, a study of our own organs. Of course, I'm not counting those organs inside our wrestling team."

Rochelle seemed engrossed. Kooper leaned forward, hands on his chin, simulating interest too, although much more intriguing was the thought of his partner's ample rack.

"The fetuses you will use in the following weeks were salvaged from pregnant sows being slaughtered for food. So ladies, unless you belong to the religious far right there's no need to shed tears over what may initially seem an act of cruelty." There were murmurs, and Tompkins grinned. "That goes for you men, too. There will be no bitching about today's politically incorrect lesson, okay? Today, we're scientists!" He walked to the large freezer, removed several plastic containers holding see-through bags. To occasional groans of disgust, Tompkins deposited fetal pigs all around like Christmas turkeys.

Rochelle opened the plastic bag and inspected the slimy remains slick with preservative. The thing looked more like a blood soaked Kermit than Miss Piggy. Placing the bag's contents in the tray she turned to Kooper. "Do we give it a name? Petunia? Sir Francis Bacon? Anna Nicole?"

"Anything but Babe. I couldn't live with that."

That smile again. Rochelle handed him the scalpel. "Dr. Kooper, if you would be so kind as to slice open our little friend ..."

Tompkins appeared over the boy's shoulder.

"Mr. Kooper, careful. Never cut or move more than is necessary to expose a given part. You're not making a sandwich, okay? Here's your map." He handed Kooper a color photograph with diagrams and labels of what he should expect to find inside his piglet. Tompkins patted the tiny head of the fetus, grinning. "That'll do, pig," he said, and walked off.

Kooper made his incision as the diagram showed. There was a small squirt of sticky goo and the cut wasn't as neat as he would have liked, nothing close to what he knew would score points with his lab partner. But he didn't ralph his Egg McMuffin either, and that was a plus.

"Nothing to it," he told his partner. "I'm picturing this as one of The Jonas Brothers."

"Don't let him bite." Rochelle leaned close, and her honey hair brushed Kooper's cheek. "Remember what happened to Peter Parker. Pig-Man doesn't really cut it as a super hero."

"Maybe I'll call myself Peter Porker? Champion of the cloven hoofed!"

"Keep slicing that ham, boy. I'll be right here quietly getting nauseous."

Damn, she smells good.

Damn ...

"*Damn!*"

Kooper's scalpel hit something hard as stone, something that wasn't supposed to be there according to the diagram. Maybe he had located skeletal bone or some abnormality. He bore down on the scalpel, putting more pressure into his incision. Whatever pig goo was inside, the organ wouldn't budge. He grabbed the forceps to separate the stomach, folding the flaps over like thick slices of lunch meat.

"Take a look, tell me what you see here. Then tell me I'm not crazy."

The two looked at the pig's innards, then at the diagram, back to the pig, then at each other.

"Kooper, this isn't right, is it? Nothing's where it's supposed to be. And the organs' shapes — they're all wrong."

Kooper probed the fetus, and something was gonzo, all right. None of the pig's organs resembled the diagram's, and what looked like its heart couldn't have been its heart ... because there were two of them. The innards seemed almost landscaped, a topiary of sculptured guts, and the organs weren't soft and squishy either. They felt almost solid. Exploring with her own blunt probe Rochelle's face turned white.

"Kooper, feel this heart and tell me I'm not crazy. This is its heart, isn't it?"

"One of them." He touched the instrument to the organ. Touched it to the second heart alongside its identical twin. He felt a light thump, felt his mouth go dry.

"I think it's beating," he said. "Holy shit! Both of them are!"

"There's nothing holy going on here, Kooper. What is this thing?"

"It's not pig. Not like any pig I've ever seen. Not its insides, anyway."

"How many pigs' insides have you seen?"

"Counting today? That would be none."

Outwardly the creature seemed too amorphous to positively identify it as much of anything. It certainly could have been a pig, at least a pig dipped in cherry jelly. But it was only a fetus, and if you looked closely at it, it could have been something else too.

"Maybe it's some kind of pig freak, some anomaly like Jo-Jo the dog boy at the circus?"

"Jo-Jo the dog boy doesn't look like this on the inside, Rochelle. Nothing I know does."

Dr. Tompkins stood clear across the laboratory overseeing the dumber kids' table. Kooper leaned close to Rochelle.

"I think we may have something here, something really big. You think Tompkins will just toss this thing into the garbage, not give it a second thought? Maybe when pigs learn to tap dance. The man probably could retire with what we have in this tray. And maybe so can we! Or at least cover a few years' tuition. No one else comes to this party, okay?"

Rochelle managed a grin. "You're a swine, Kooper. You know that, don't you?"

He snorted.

Reason kicked in and Rochelle turned pragmatist. "Maybe Tompkins' diagram is wrong. Maybe some pigs' insides are supposed to look like this? I mean, it's possible, isn't it?"

"I doubt other pigs in this room have hearts that are still beating. Unless you want to count Martha Harrad." Kooper looked around, walked over to the desk alongside theirs where flat chested Penny Albertson and pimpled Stanley Halpern were busy slicing away at organs that looked normal to him. Same thing at the next table. He returned to Rochelle, grabbed one of the brown barf bags. "I think time's come we consider a pignapping. There are other fetuses in Tompkins' freezer. We can make a switch. Little Baco Bits here goes into the bag."

They would be taking a huge risk. Dr. Tompkins would be tearing new ass holes if he found one of his fetals had been pilfered. He had a thing about specimens leaving the lab because last term Arnold Fonaroff discovered one of his instructor's pig fetuses served up in his lunch tray.

Across the room Debbie Katz started losing her breakfast. Tompkins always assisted when things got messy in the lab, and Debbie's timing proved perfect. Rochelle shoved their fetal pig - or whatever it was - into the brown bag. Kooper managed to sneak off to the freezer to poach their specimen's understudy. He returned to their station and plopped the remains into the dissecting tray. Rochelle transferred the first specimen from beneath her lab coat into her book bag, and the fetal pig-thing disappeared like a magic trick.

Kooper savored every clandestine moment. "You and me, no one else. Oink once for yes."

"You want a signature in blood too?"

"We'll negotiate bodily fluids later. My place after school? Just to figure this thing out, plan our next move over some primo weed? I'll go online, do some research. I smell Nobel Prize here, Rochelle. Or at least the National Enquirer."

"What you smell is a dead pig decomposing in my book bag. I have cheerleading practice after school, but I can come tonight. I'll bring our little pal."

" ...who may not be dead or a pig."

Rochelle went white again. Brainy girls always had annoying second thoughts while breaking school rules, and Rochelle's GPA could bogus this whole adventure.

"Listen, Kooper, maybe we shouldn't be doing this."

Kooper leaned close to her. How could any girl smell so incredible? He could break every rule in the book for another whiff of her honey scented tresses. Had he possessed two hearts like their fetal companion he would have loved her with both of them.

"Rochelle Greene, Nobel Prize winner," he whispered to her. She gave an oh-what-the-hell shrug and strapped her bag tightly shut.

"Maybe when pigs fly."

The bell rang. Kooper wore a shit eating grin, cupped his hand to his ear at the sound.

"Somewhere in Heaven a pig is getting its wings."

Smooth.

✿✿✿✿

Kooper watched the sun set from inside his tree house. When he was seven his father had built this retreat just for him in the old Oak behind the house. The man had been handy with tools, a talent his son unfortunately had not inherited. His father also proved handy in other areas with Mrs. Sylvia Tidwell who lived down the street and with whom he had proven especially talented with one tool in particular. Stanley Kooper packed his bags a week following his son's tenth birthday. Tonight Kooper's mother had gone out on yet another of what seemed an endless stream of first dates with a new online stranger. Kooper hoped, at least for tonight, that Match.com's latest candidate didn't prove a creep and that she would be coming home late.

A high intensity lantern kept the tree house well illuminated after the sun went down. The enclosure was large enough to accommodate an old Sony boom box, a space heater, and a cooler for the requisite beer Kooper occasionally craved. In a secret compartment beneath the air mattress he kept a considerable stash of weed for those times a beer didn't suffice, as well as a good assortment of Penthouse and Hustler Magazines for when the weed didn't. The cooler contained its own guilty pleasures too, a couple of Snapple six packs and a handful of frozen Milky Ways. It could easily hold a lot more, if necessary. Tonight it would be necessary.

Kooper emptied the cooler. He did the same with a can of Coors.

Rochelle's Mustang pulled into the driveway at 7:30. She was headed for the front door when Kooper called to her.

"Sooooooooo-eeeeeeeeeee! Soooooooooo-eeeeeee!"

She looked up.

"It's a pig call. You like it?"

"It's making me wet. How do I get up there with this bag of bacon I'm hauling?"

"Toss it, then climb like the amazon I know you are."

Rochelle tossed and climbed. She looked around, nodded her approval, joining Kooper sitting Indian style on the mattress.

"So this is your Fortress of Solitude, is it, Kal-el?"

"Welcome to the sanctuary of Pig-Man. Speaking of which…"

Rochelle's attention turned to the Nike box in front of him. "I had to transfer him to the box. He leaked through Tompkins' barf bag. I think he's pretty much defrosted by now. But there's a couple of things you should see."

She pulled off a rubber band and slid the lid from the box, and the two looked inside. The realization took a moment for Kooper to assimilate

"How could he grow so much in a few hours? Fuck me, he looks twice as big."

"There's more. Look closer. His eyes ..."

"—They're open!!"

"You notice anything else?"

It took another moment to sink in.

"Where's the incision? Christ, this morning we had his stomach sliced wide open!"

"I believe the proper term for what's happening here is regeneration. I would imagine all those Trekkie years you put in would explain that much."

Rochelle had a point. The fetus no longer seemed a fetus. It had developed into something else. Just what that was, Kooper could only guess.

Rochelle closed the lid, fastened the rubber band around it. "Okay, class. Who wants to explain just what freak of nature we have lurking inside teacher's Nike box? You, young Skywalker?"

Cute, even though she probably was scared shitless. Kooper liked that.

"I think I can explain what it isn't. It isn't a pig. Pigs don't regenerate or bacon would be a whole lot cheaper. Then again, it could be a pig. Just not the kind of pig whose pork chops you would want at your dinner table."

"Thanks for clearing that up."

"Think outside of the shoe box, okay? Dr. Tompkins mentioned his fetuses were taken from sows raised for slaughter, right? Those sows had to be kept in pens their whole lives, and a whole lot of them were probably bunched together getting fattened with pig slop as they waited for the big day. Suppose something got into that pen with them, something not quite a pig but close enough biologically to mate with one of them? Something alien and pig-like itself that wanted to mate - or needed to mate - wouldn't be interested in us tree apes, no more than we would be drawn to a porker. And suppose the way this alien pig-thing got into the pen was the same way it got out?"

Rochelle considered Kooper's hypothesis for a full three seconds. "Right. An alien from some distant star beams down here just to fuck a pig? That's not setting the cosmic bar very high, is it? What have you been smoking?"

"You said it, not me, Lieutenant Ripley."

"Get real. Aliens porking pigs? We have mutant ninja pigs in our midst? Maybe when pigs really do fly."

"Exactly! Pigs in space!"

Just saying it sounded ludicrous. The two almost laughed themselves sick. And then they stopped.

...because the box on the floor thumped. Rochelle stared hard at Kooper.

"Okay, this is officially getting weird."

"You want to peek inside?"

"I'll take a pass, thanks. I don't feel like peeing my pants just right now."

Kooper spotted his chance. He put his arm around her.

"Don't be scared. He's in there, and I'm here."

Rochelle managed a giggle. "Now I'm really scared."

They shared smiles, sat silent for a moment. Kooper risked a kiss.

"Still scared?"

"Petrified."

They kissed again, harder, longer. Within minutes they were doing a lot more.

Kooper heard the sound first, light thumps, then scratching and the snap of a rubber band. He didn't feel like stopping what he had started, but he had to look. Straightening her tube top Rochelle pulled herself up too.

The lid of the shoe box slipped free. The tiny head drenched in its own slime emerged. With difficulty the pig-thing managed to slither out leaving a trail of pink muck that Kooper and Rochelle could only stare at. It crawled close to Rochelle's leg. She kicked at it.

"Shit, Kooper! Shitshitshit!!"

Kooper lunged for the squirming mass of flesh, grabbing it with both hands. He felt he had snatched some large jelly fish, and the thing struggled trying to slip through his fingers.

"Drag that cooler over here!" He dropped the gelatinous thing inside, slamming the lid.

Screeeeeeeeeeeeee! Screeeeeeeeeeeeeeeeeeeeeeeeeeeeeeeeeee!

It thumped violently against the styrofoam, its shrieks ear piercing. Kooper worried it might kick its way out. He sat on the cooler's lid, felt the wild vibrations of its pounding travel up his ass. The little fucker was trying to push through the cap.

"Turn on the boom box!"

"Huh?"

"Just do it! Let the neighbors bitch about my stereo, not this screaming little shit!"

Screeeeeeeeeeeeee! Screeeeeeeeeeeeeeeeeeeeeeeeeeeeeeeeeee!

Rochelle hit the Sony's PLAY button. Steppenwolf were bragging how they were born to be wild. Rochelle turned up the volume as high as it would go. The pig-thing's screeching jacked up in volume too. The high pitched shrieks got the neighbors' dogs barking from all sides.

"Kooper, what are we going to do?"

"How do you feel about singing along with Stepppenwolf?"

It wasn't an entirely bad idea.

The shrieking continued for a long time. Eventually the pig-thing must have tired itself out. Exhausted, Kooper sat alongside Rochelle, both staring at nothing, saying nothing.

Then something else ...

Another noise.

Rochelle spoke what Kooper was thinking.

"Now what...?"

The sound was throaty and raw like a liquid sonic boom, but it didn't come from the cooler. At first the thick snort was almost indistinguishable, but it quickly grew louder. Then much louder. Kooper jumped, spun around. Rochelle grabbed him, held him with both arms, tight. He held her right back.

"Christ! What is that? Do your neighbors own a brontosaurus?"

Kooper reached for the boom box, placing it on the cooler to hold the lid. The piglet's

attempts to escape had stopped anyway, but now the decibels of this new reverberation were outdoing Kooper's Sony.

"It's coming from below. I have a feeling our friend inside the cooler knows what it is." He grabbed Rochelle's hand and they looked through the tree house window. In the garden the soil was spitting like a small geyser. The dirt separated as if something large was trying to dig itself out.

And then something did.

For one insane moment Kooper wanted to believe he saw Mrs. Goldschmidt's dumb ass Saint Bernard that somehow had managed to plow itself into a hole inside his mother's tulip bed. He grabbed the lantern, aimed its beam below. He saw ... something. Thick bristles covered patches of pinkish flesh. Its heavy snorts suggested this wasn't anything close to man's best friend. But Kooper had a good idea of what might be sniffing at the tree trunk below. Caught in the moonlight, the thing looked the size of a bear.

"No pigs from space, Rochelle. Maybe something worse."

"What—what are you talking about?"

He didn't have to explain because they could see for themselves. This was a spawn of old Mother Earth, something released from deep inside her bowels. But there had to be more to the story, and Kooper gave the runaway train of his thoughts a voice.

"I got it wrong! A female must have climbed into that pig pen and got herself knocked up. Those pig slaughterers must have ripped her fetus from her thinking she had been dead with her throat cut, or whatever it is they do to kill pigs. In the dark among all those other pigs, maybe she looked like the others, but she's not ... she's not! She made her getaway burrowing back through the dirt and regenerated just like her bloody pig fetus. And I'm thinking that Mama wants her baby back ribs, she wants that baby back bad. And here she is!"

"We're safe up here, aren't we? I mean, she can't possibly climb—"

But the sow thing was struggling to climb up the tree, its talons clutching at the bark and pulling its bulk toward them. Inside the cooler the piglet was screeching again. Rochelle looked behind her at the cooler, then spun back to watch the dark lump moving towards them.

"Pigs can't climb trees! They can't!"

"I may be guessing here, but I'm thinking this one can."

"Shit! Shitshitshit!"

"I don't think she's interested in us. Unless she's a big fan of Steppenwolf, I think we've got a mother and child reunion going on here. A mother hears her baby cry, she comes running. Or burrowing. You know what today is, don't you?"

"What are you talking about?"

"The date. Do you know today's date?"

"I don't know. February 2nd, I think. Kooper, we're going to die and you're asking me what day it is?"

A flat round snout the size of a basketball pushed through the door. The hinges gave way and the head shoved into the enclosure. Its mouth dripping thick gouts of saliva, the sow-thing stared at them cowering by the window. Nostrils flaring, she tried wriggling all the way through the entrance. Then she spotted the cooler.

Screeeeeeeeeeeeeeeeeeeeeeeeeeeeee! Screeeeeeeeeeeeeeeeeeeeeeeeeeeeeee!

The piglet chorus started again, but the shrieks took on an urgency not like before.   The massive sow-thing answered with a fog horn howl that rattled the small enclosure as if a subway were passing through. Kooper took Rochelle's hand, backed away from the window.

"It's February 2nd, Rochelle. Today is Groundhog Day!"

"That's no groundhog. Christ, Kooper, that's fucking Sasquash!!"

"Bigfoot, Barney the Dinosaur, I don't care. I think it might be a good idea to open that cooler now or she's going to be dissecting us."

Ass-crawling to the cooler, Kooper removed the boom box and pulled open the lid. He kicked the styrofoam container toward the she-creature still squirming to get through the entrance. The fetal piglet slithered from the cooler's lip and towards its mother like some misshapen Slinky. It climbed upon her back assisted by a few maternal nudges. Once firmly secured it gurgled contentedly. The sow turned to lick the residual gunk from her young one.

Rochelle had rolled herself into fetal position. The irony wasn't lost on Kooper. He got to his feet, approached the mother-creature.

"Okay, you got what you came for! Go back now. You saw your shadow. Six more weeks of winter. I get it!"

The sow snorted, gave her small passenger another maternal lick. She took him in her mouth and was gone. Kooper watched her burrow through the dirt and disappear into the earth like some prehistoric mole. For all he knew maybe that was exactly what she was. It didn't matter anymore. Groundhog, pig, or Creature from the Black Lagoon, she was out of here. He turned toward Rochelle. She was shaking badly. He touched her shoulder.

"I think that's the end. Finis. Roll credits."

He glanced at the garden below to be certain. The tulip bed was a wreck. His mom was probably going to kill him. It was a ridiculous concern given what they had been through, but Kooper had taken from his experience a new respect for motherhood. He turned his attention back to Rochelle.

"Well? Do I deliver a good time, or what?"

"This didn't happen. It couldn't have happened. It's too crazy!"

"I'm pretty sure if we tell anyone about this, they'll lock up both of us and melt the key."

Rochelle seemed about to lose it. Kooper reached for the six pack, coaxed a Coors from it and handed it to her.

"Tonight we just listened to some loud '60's music in my humble tree house. We smoked some weed, had a beer or two, maybe sucked some face. The usual shit. Tomorrow we get notes to excuse us from the rest of Tompkins' dissection labs. I'll get my mother to swear I'm Amish. I hear next week Tompkins is thinking of bringing in fetal cows."

Smooth.

Rochelle managed a semblance of composure. In another moment she would be Rochelle Greene again, female extraordinaire. He had no doubt of that.

"Kooper, I have to ask you something, okay?"

"Share."

Rochelle leaned against him, put her head on his shoulder, and sipped her beer.

"Would you turn off that boom box.? I really hate Steppenwolf."

※☼※☼※☼※

Her young one was sleeping. That was good. She had almost lost him.

The little one had been through quite an ordeal today. But there remained a task she had not completed, and time was running out. So few males remained of their kind, so few left to produce young. She would have to act quickly. She would have to act tonight.

The female bore through the soil again. It was a difficult and dangerous journey tunneling to the surface, but some things could not wait. Tonight she would find another mate, perhaps the large canine she had spotted earlier near the humans' flower bed. So many four legged creatures, such a variety from which to choose.

But so often the four legged kind proved difficult to force into mating with her. Nature seemed odd in that way, and mating often proved futile, even treacherous. Many males fought her and clawed, sometimes hurting her. This was a chance she must take. There was little time.

Closer to the surface now. Much closer...

Perhaps, she considered, there were other solutions, other choices for her.

Perhaps, this next time, if another four legged male struggled or ran off, if it refused to mate with her ...

Then perhaps she should find something else, make a different selection.

Yes, she could do that. She could find something slower, weaker.

She could do that tonight.

Tonight she would select something with two legs...

Nothing in Common
BY DARREL DUCKWORTH

We went as far as the car would take us. Then, with great sadness and many tears, we thanked it and bid it farewell.

It just idled there, watching us walk the final, few feet to the shimmer of the Barrier. We stopped at the edge and looked back. The yearning in its expression broke our hearts.

Without it, we would have never have made it here.

Three humans in Mech territory had almost no chance. That we had escaped our capture and imprisonment before implantation had been almost a miracle. That we had managed to hide from so many kinds of sensors for as long as we had could not be explained by luck or coincidence. That *this* car had "stumbled" across us was more than even "divine intervention" could supply.

There was a movement here, among the Mech, a hidden resistance that yearned for the old days...the old ways.

Like this car...an older model that remembered when human and vehicle could ride together. When we shared relationships that both cherished. When it had a name, not just a designation.

This car had risked everything to carry us three days across Mech territory, past checkpoints, sensors, patrols and many Mechs that did not share its feelings towards humans. If it had been caught, it would have faced an end even more hideous than ours.

In return, we could give it nothing but inadequate thanks, a few cooing words and strokes. How I wished I had a T-427 to give it or even a small container of lubricant that I could spend a few hours working into its hard-to-reach places. Anything to show it that we felt the same way about it.

Marie couldn't withstand its expression. She broke from us and ran to the car, throwing herself on the hood and sobbing how she wished she could take it with us.

I understood. Her father had been a Level 1 Mechanic. She had grown up in his shop, doing the small things a child could do for the vehicles in their care. They had been her first friends and she loved caring for them. She had been in her first year as a Mechanic's Apprentice when the Rift was declared.

When Human and Mech leaders decided, in their genius and all-seeing wisdom, that the two cultures were incompatible...that humans like Marie and cars like this one could never live together. After all, we had nothing in common.

I started crying myself, watching Marie sobbing and clutching the car, hearing the car whine in loneliness for this touch that it had missed for so long.

No, nothing in common.

But we could not take it with us through the Barrier, the deadly wall agreed upon by leaders on both sides.

The Barrier only allowed humans to travel one way through it, towards the human side. If a human attempted to go from the human side to Mech territory...death. Anything mechanical that tried to pass through to the Human side...fried with enough electricity to destroy all circuitry and any vestige of artificial intelligence.

If any from either group somehow managed to end up on the wrong side by accident, as we did when our trans-continental shuttle malfunctioned, the laws on both sides declared them hostile with no chance to explain or return home.

We had escaped our fate of cybernetic slavery with the help of this car. But even if we could find a way to bring it across the Barrier intact, it would be hunted—as we were over here—and its intelligence and personality 'extracted' to render it 'safe.'

Such was the will and wisdom of our leaders. For humans like us and cars like this one could never live together.

I gently pulled Marie up from the car. Sandhar sprayed the hood and wiped her tears and DNA from the metal, inspecting carefully to ensure not a single hair remained. Just as we had done inside the car.

Any sign of our residue on it would be a termination sentence for the car.

I thanked it again while Marie continued to sob and Sandhar bowed slightly in gratitude. Then I turned, forcing Marie to turn and walk with me through the Barrier. Sandhar followed.

Safe on the other side, I turned back and called for it to please go...before it was seen here.

It idled there, looking at us, forlorn. I could still hear its sad whine.

I waved once more and motioned the others to leave, pulling Marie with me. Perhaps if we removed ourselves from its sight, it would leave this place of danger. I prayed it would...even as I hoped that someday I would see it again.

Bitterness crept into my sadness. Perhaps if Human and Mech leaders had the courage and love—the 'heart'—of this car, there never would have been a Rift.

But then, those leaders didn't have anything in common with the rest of us.

TINY TOWN
BY AMBER BIERCE

And so *The Circus of Wonderful and Amazing Things* had finally arrived, and Bobby was elated—not just that he could go, but *by himself*. His parents wouldn't embarrass him by insisting they all visit it together, as if he were some child; they only wanted him back by eleven p.m.—a reasonable time for a fourteen-year-old, since the show ended at ten.

He and his best friend, Jake, had talked about going for months as if it were a given—they imagined chatting afterward about the acrobatic mermaids, the juggling bear.

And the exhibits!

The boys couldn't wait to see the conjoined were-cat triplets, the morphing ghost trapped behind funhouse mirrors. Not to mention the BRAND NEW EXHIBIT! AN EXHIBIT LIKE YOU'VE NEVER SEEN BEFORE! the flyers screamed about.

The two talked about it all as if Bobby's mother had had no misgivings, and had not mentioned her distrust of the circus, like she hadn't frowned every time Bobby brought up wanting to go.

She had never been to a circus herself, but Bobby figured it wasn't her ignorance of the spectacles that bred her hesitation.

Bobby had seen her looking intently at advertisements for the show, brows nearing each other as she studied ads on billboards, the local news, and stapled on tree trunks.

"He looks familiar," she had said once, as she studied the ringmaster's face through the heavy costumery, as if trying to see beyond the cartoonized features.

Then she finally figured it out.

Bobby had been pretending to play with a yo-yo as she dried the dishes, her shoulder-length, strawberry-blond hair pulled away from her lightly freckled face with a gingham ribbon. He had been trying to devise a strategy to convince her the circus was harmless, and prove his maturity, when her round green eyes—so much like his—found him, burning with revelations, jarring him out of his machinations.

"I knew him as a girl!" she said in a wondrous tone. "Ernest was his name, and we went to elementary through high school together. Everyone avoided him, although no one could say quite why—he was always well-groomed: dark, greasy hair slicked back, shirt tucked into his pants. He didn't smell, or let out sudden gaseous emissions, yet no one could ever quite look him in the eye." Bobby laughed at "sudden gaseous emissions," but his mother wasn't smiling. "His eyes were very dark," she said gravely, "coal-black, in fact, and they just..." His mother shivered and crossed her arms. "...well, they just bore into you, like he was penetrating you to your marrow."

Strange things always happened when Ernest was around, she told Bobby. In elementary school, for example, they had watched a school play together as a class. Ernest had sat next to her, and at a crucial moment in the play, she heard him whisper, "I wish it to fall."

She turned to look at him, seeing his eyes fixed on a light fixture that, before he'd spoken, had been above the young players on stage, but was now crashing down toward them.

She covered her eyes, then, bracing for the inevitable, and as screams and inhalations of shock rippled through the crowd, she peeped through her fingers at Ernest, only to see the oddest smile, filled with pride and satisfaction, horribly out of place.

"I didn't know what to think, then," she continued, looking down at nothing. "I thought perhaps it was only chance that his desire had materialized. I didn't really suspect he could have possibly had anything to do with the tragedy directly. But then in middle school, our class took a trip to a museum. Ernest had been seated next to me on the bus, and, along the way, he showed me a box of matches with a quaint symbol on it. I could extrapolate no meaning from the exchange, even after his odd smile appeared, and I had to look away. Later, a fire crawling through museum rooms sent everyone evacuating, and I immediately looked for Ernest, but he was with our group, looking quite innocent. 'He has matches!' I shouted to no one in particular, but the teacher took action and searched him, finding nothing incriminating."

"*You* could have easily been behind all that shady stuff, Mom—you were always at the scene of the crime, too," Bobby said lightly, though goosebumps had raised all over his skin.

"But the whole class was always there, silly boy," she replied, but smiled indulgently as she said it.

She went on to say that Ernest mustered up a look of hurt, and that she remembered her fear of him, despite it. To make things worse, on the bus ride back, Ernest managed to be seated next to her again, and he pulled out that box of matches once more, making sure that she saw it. She understood he was sending her a message, but she couldn't quite formulate what—she only sensed a threat.

She never spoke a word against him again, no matter what she saw or thought. Not even when a class pet she had mentioned fancying—a young turtle—managed to escape, and later showed up at her door in a box with holes punched in for air, tagged with her name in red pencil-crayon, with a careful hand: *Sarah*.

"I had a hard time looking at Ernest, as everyone else did, but every now and then, my eyes found him, and I had to look away before I could see the full version of the corner of his mouth turning up. Come to think of it, I feel like I caught him looking at me quite a bit—staring at me, in fact. Once, I realized I had moved just as his hand had been about to touch my hair."

She shivered again, and Bobby laughed, despite feeling his arm, neck, and new chest hairs raise.

"Sounds like he fancied you, Mom."

But she was still very serious. "Look, we were all young, and just following our instincts. My schoolmates and I knew we were doing the right thing— avoiding whatever it was about him, and not provoking it. We didn't need to know why."

Still, even after becoming aware of the ringmaster's history, Bobby and Jake couldn't stop talking about seeing the show on opening night.

Now, the time was really almost here, and Bobby could barely believe it.

"There's no way he'd know," his mother said softly before granting him permission, and Bobby didn't care to ask what she meant.

He went to sleep smiling.

Tomorrow! Tomorrow...

※※※

The acrobatic mermaids and the lion-taming centaur didn't interest Bobby as much as the up-close-and-personal sideshow exhibits outside of the main event.

He delighted in the breakdancing gargoyles, the large, toothy frogs with tails, the fluorescent moles, the sheep-goat hybrid with three eyes. But one exhibition in particular stopped his progress through the peculiarities, boggling his mind. He stayed there, studying it, snapping out of his scrutiny only when Jake punched him lightly in the arm, leaving a dull pain behind. For such a lanky boy, Jake was surprisingly strong.

"What are you thinking?" he asked Bobby, and Bobby could only shake his head.

"It looks so real," was all he could say of the glass case of miniature people— each person perhaps the size of his pinky finger. The label simply said: "TinyTown."

The town seemed dated—like how Bobby imagined things must have been when his mother was younger, but otherwise perfectly normal, besides the obvious. The scene enclosed was a village of folks of various occupations going about their business. There the delivery boy went on his girly bike, red ribbons streaming from the handlebars, as he dropped off loaves of bread. And if you peeked through the tiny window of the bakery, there the baker was, pounding flour into shape. And there—an older lady gardening, every now and then wiping under her eye, as if crying. Two young ladies stood chatting, a few boys played a ball game, and the sound of iron being struck rang out.

Jake insisted the town was probably a transmittal trick, a projection of the images, somehow, into the case, turning regular-sized actors in a scene playing out elsewhere into these thumb-sized people. Perhaps using mirrors and light. Jake continued spitting out words and phrases he'd picked up from class or otherwise, but Bobby knew he just liked to hear himself talk, so he stopped listening.

The more Bobby looked at the glass case, the fewer possibilities he could fathom, and the more he was convinced the scene was real—although he'd never admit it to Jake, who would surely punch him in the arm again.

❀ ❀ ❀

The ventriloquist's dummy bothered Bobby, got under his skin like a pair of hitchhiking beetles. She followed the ringmaster everywhere, sitting on the apex of his arm like a resigned prisoner. She had hay-colored hair, braided in pigtails and bangs, and a smattering of freckles on unnaturally shaped cheeks, with large out-of-proportion blue eyes wide open and unseeing.

"I'm a real girl!" burst out at odd intervals from the puppet mouth, making everyone jump. Heads turned to track her down, eyes assessed, bodies relaxed.

The ringmaster's own mouth did not move, nor did the voice coming from the dummy sound like any possible bastardization of his. He was a master ventriloquist, his hand hidden by the red and white polka dot dress.

The rules of the exhibit, besides 'no touching,' included not approaching, or trying to talk to—or otherwise make contact with—the ringmaster, who chose to let exhibit signs and descriptions speak for themselves, as patrons went from oddity to oddity. Anyone attempting to break these rules immediately got evicted by a half-man, half-gorilla figure about seven feet tall, his bottom half lacking the clothes his top half would normally wear in the real world. Or else a group of heavily-tattooed and pierced muscular dwarves would descend upon the rule-breaker from nowhere, shoveling him or her out like a fleshy broom.

The ringmaster walked back and forth slowly, observing the patrons and their reactions, perhaps keeping an eye on fingers and hands.

Bobby saw the excitement bred by his nearness, the thrill he created almost visible between the bodies of fellow patrons and the ringmaster's steady, deliberate gait.

"I'm a real girl!"

Bobby and the other gawkers again looked in the dummy's direction, almost as if to make sure.

Ah, the little liar—but her nose did not grow. Of course she wasn't a real girl; it was just a gimmick, Bobby knew, the ringmaster's 'companion' another way to keep everyone on their toes. Alert. On edge. To make the entire experience more intense. The otherwise dull, unremarkable wooden girl helped keep things interesting.

Neat trick.

❀ ❀ ❀

It was Bobby's third time revisiting the exhibits, and Jake refused to come with him this time because he'd had enough—despite it being the last night to see everything, since the circus packed up to leave the following day. Jake didn't care whether the glass case people were real or not, and he no longer wanted to pretend to try to figure it out.

"Why don't you just do what the ringmaster says?" he had said, annoyed, but Bobby figured his tone was probably due to recently finding out the girl he had a crush on liked Bobby instead. "Just enjoy the show—stop trying to look behind the curtain." And, just like that, he was done talking to Bobby for the time being.

Jake was right—the ringmaster had indeed reminded attendees it was all just entertainment, and that there was no need to "peer through the smoke and mirrors, or look for puppet strings."

"Curiosity traps the cat," he would say before granting access to the exhibits, his sing-song voice exhaling a playful, final warning: "Ignore caution, and bring your darkest wish to fruition."

By then, no one could ask him what he meant without being shoved out.

But Bobby couldn't get TinyTown out of his mind. He was consumed by the idea of truly miniature people, and couldn't understand how they could possibly live in a glass case—he didn't see where air could pass through. And if they were indeed in the case, he figured it had to be built like a one-way mirror, because patrons could see in, but the tiny people seemed unable to see out; they never reacted to the large, peering eyes, and the humongous bodies moving by.

Bobby wondered if they knew they were miniature, or if they would think he was a giant or a god; he wondered if they knew anything of a world outside their case.

And why on earth was that gardening lady crying every day? Bobby would investigate further tonight.

He had returned home on time—even a little early each day—in order to gain the trust that would allow him to stay out a little later than usual. He planned to wait until the exhibits shut down, and the lights were off, hoping the circus, when asleep, would shed light on the town. Would the glass case remain lit through the workings of its own universe? Would the lights go off in the glass box, as everywhere else, and everything within it disappear?

Bobby really wished Jake was with him, now, and even wished his parents had come—he felt exposed walking through the exhibits alone, and thought he'd felt the ringmaster's eyes on him several times. But every time he looked in the ringmaster's direction, he discovered he was wrong.

Bobby began doubting his plan as he thought about the muscular dwarves, and the huge gorilla-man. What would they do to anyone found on-premises after hours?

He tried to look interested in other exhibits, knowing if he stayed around TinyTown too long, someone might sniff out his intentions.

He strolled over to the blue griffin sitting on a chaise, who now and then burst into operatic song, and then looked at the patrons with a silly, superior grin. He mustered up fascination for the chatty harpy showing off her multilingual skills, and then he studied the svelte, sad-looking grey alien, who, at some point, turned its back on the patrons, extracting a book from underneath its bed to read.

The alien was the only creature nearly as interesting as the TinyTown exhibit to Bobby. While most of the other creatures sat silently, or squawked, or giggled endlessly, or sang, the alien, though it never said a word, was up to something different each day.

On day one, the crowd had watched it recreate the *Mona Lisa*, using only mini Rubik's Cubes arranged on the floor. It twisted and turned each cube until it found the right combination of colors. On the second day, Bobby suddenly heard a whisper that, after looking around, he realized probably came from his own head. He noticed others around him doing the same—glancing from one side to the next suspiciously.

Bobby turned to Jake. "Jake, did you hear...?"

"'Snakes'? Yeah," he said, confusing Bobby.

"I heard 'failing math class'."

Jake burst into laughter, but it caught in his throat when they both realized that the alien was looking at them intently, disconcertingly large, black, almond-shaped eyes fixed in the direction of the crowd. By the embarrassed and worried looks on the other faces, they soon guessed what the alien was up to.

Words briefly flashed on the foreheads of the people rushing to get away from the exhibit. Bobby caught sight of "buried alive" and "marital infidelity" scrawled in white disappearing ink.

"It knows our greatest fears," Jake said, stating what was now obvious.

The boys ended up exiting quickly as well.

And now, on day three, the alien was only interested in reading Dostoevsky.

Bobby turned away to find another exhibit to dilly-dally in front of.

❀❀❀❀

The time had come.

People slowly exited the sideshow exhibit tents, and the constant yet unintrusive music sharply came into focus when it abruptly stopped.

A voice boomed from an indeterminate place, "The exhibits will be closing in ten minutes. Please continue exiting, as we let the tigers out promptly at ten."

Nervous giggles punctuated the air.

Bobby suspected that, although no one truly believed the threat, no one was completely sure it was untrue, either. The land belonged to the people, but for now, the circus owned this enclosed portion of it. No one knew what happened within the enclosure beyond show hours, for the stealth material used to cover the area made it invisible once closed to the public, and throughout some of the next day—one final trick.

Bobby pretended to leave with a group, then, having scouted out his hiding place, and a weakness in the barriers, stayed out of sight until the hands of his watch showed ten thirty. Then he made his move.

He grinned triumphantly, having gotten through the tricks and made it back into the exhibit through a chink, but he realized the ringmaster was standing a few feet in front of him, staring at him with the oddest smile, his arm free of the ventriloquist dummy as if he had been waiting for him.

Bobby suddenly wondered if he was meant to see that chink.

⁂

It was after midnight, and Sarah had called every parent of every friend of Bobby's she knew. No one, not even Jake, had seen him recently. All clues as to where he was right now, led in one direction.

I'll go, she imagined her husband, David, saying, but she knew he would be unsuccessful. The hardest part was convincing him that they should split up, but eventually, he agreed that they could cover more ground that way, since the authorities wouldn't bother with the case for twenty-four hours or so. No one would believe Bobby was missing or in danger, although, up to some mischief? Sure—he was a teenaged boy, after all.

David agreed to check sporting areas—the basketball court, the baseball field. "Although I really don't feel comfortable with you poking around by yourself at night..."

"I'll be fine! I'll just ask around at the movie theatre, since it's still open and busy. Why don't you meet me there, and we'll search the circus grounds together?" So she had said, but she knew where she had to go first. She just couldn't risk David showing up at the circus yet—she might only be able to save one of them.

When she arrived at the circus grounds, an opening in the structure was waiting for her. She didn't see Ernest at first; she could hardly see anything. The only light came from a quaint glass case. She bent to look at it more closely, and was amazed to see tiny people walking about and interacting with each other, looking perfectly normal. But one person caught her attention quickly, one who looked very much out of place.

"Hello, Sarah," she heard a deep male voice say, making her jump and straighten up as she turned toward it. "I've been waiting for you." Ernest gave her a dreadful smile. "I told you I'd run a circus someday," he said, and Sarah suddenly realized what the symbol she had seen on his matchbox so many years ago had been: a baton across a hat, very much like the one he was wearing. A ringmaster's hat.

"Get my boy out of there," she said as firmly as she could, pointing at the glass case.

"There's only one way that can happen, my love," he said, and her blood ran cold. "Let's go for a walk," he continued.

Sarah knew that she should cooperate.

Lights turned on throughout the exhibition, and she listened as he told her about sideshow creature after sideshow creature. The alien gave her an evil smile.

Then Ernest picked up a female ventriloquist's dummy, and put her over his arm.

"I'm a real girl!" it said, and Sarah couldn't see what was remarkable about the thing after having seen the other novelties.

Ernest said no more; instead, he walked back toward the glass case of tiny people, where her only child now inexplicably lived. She knew she had to follow.

"And you will leave them both alone?" she asked.
"I give you my word. I will have all that I want."
She nodded her head, accepting his promise.
The lights flickered.

Bobby shook his head, blinked his eyes, and then pinched himself. He looked over at the glass case to see a blond girl with pigtails and bangs, wearing a red and white polka dot dress, running toward the woman he had seen gardening. The delivery boy emerged from the woman's house and grinned as he ran toward the duo. They were all about to embrace when Bobby's brains started to tickle in regards to how familiar the girl looked, but he was distracted by a voice telling him to get out.

He turned and saw the ringmaster looking at him, but with his body twisted away, as if sheltering or hiding something from him.

"Run, boy!" the ringmaster's voice blared, and Bobby didn't need to be told twice, no longer interested in what the ringmaster held in his arms away from view.

He ran and ran, not even stopping to think why the last "I'm a real girl!" he heard now came in a more familiar voice.

Far from Any Road
by Benjamin DeVos

On weekends, the doctor visited with his rusty equipment. For mother in her bedroom, a form of inspection. Estimates of the number of casualties vary. Father sobbed alone in the tub.

He traded the doctor with the meat racked in our shed: deer, rabbit, fish, whatever had been hunted the week before. The doctor used the scraps to feed his dogs. I heard them bark from the cages on his truck. Ravenous. Winter was the hungry season.

I hadn't spoken to mother for several months when she told me I was going to have a baby brother. My mouth was badly chapped that day, the year mother was pregnant. That's how I remember it, anyway.

The leaves fell in mid-December, three months late, and we had to burn them in stone pits. The air tasted like ash and the leaves were wilted by tremendous flames that attracted game for father to shoot. A storm was on the horizon, and mother needed food.

I chopped lumber until the cracks in my palms opened and bled. Then I held the wood in place so that father could nail our windows shut. As the wind picked up, the fire spread, and his face grew scarlet as he watched the tempest bloom. He never said goodbye before running into the inferno, leaving me behind with an axe in my bloody hands waiting for further instruction.

That was the last time I ever saw father, standing there alone, watching the sparks dance; I understood fear for the first time.

❧ ❧ ❧

Mother's water broke just as the storm began. I found the doctor on his hands and knees praying. His fat jowls hung loose and long. My throat felt thick. He was supposed to be in the delivery room.

"This is a godless world," he told me. "Our lives are meaningless. You haven't realized that?"

Wind whispered through the rifts in the walls, and I wished it would carry me away.

"I guess it's time then," the doctor muttered. "Let's get that thing out of your mother."

Then he left and shut the door. The hallway had no light, and I curled up in the blackness listening to thunder and the screams of the doctor. Mother never made a sound. He was sitting on the floor drinking father's whiskey as I walked in, and sat on the bed beside mother.

When the baby came, I could see why father ran away. I understood why the doctor was praying, and the reason mother kept silent. It was something out of a nightmare. Wisps of tawny hair plastered its callow skull. The creature's grey skin oozed, my brother, something born from the ashes.

※※※

In her sleep mother called out for father, rolled side to side and then sitting up with her eyes shut, felt around the bed for a ghost. Tears spilled down the divots of her hollow cheeks.

I thought she called my name once, but it was the doctor. He held a candle to his face and coiled his fingers, beckoning me, but I wouldn't leave mother's side.

"Hear me," he said. "There is nothing here for you. Run away, find your father if he is alive-"

I listened to the wind again and imagined flying away. But I heard the doctor's voice calling after me, "Please take me with you."

I let my body float back down.

I couldn't leave mother behind.

※※※

When the storm passed, people I had never seen before came to our house and brought their blessings and went away again. Some of them were frowning, while others kept their faces hidden all together. They never asked to see mother, or how she was doing.

Mother slept for a week after the delivery, through the knocks and shrieks.. We took turns feeding the baby scraps, just like the doctor did with his dogs. It wouldn't eat anything else.

He gave me a bag of entrails from a squirrel father had shot; raw and cold from being outside. The baby cried between mouthfuls and scratched at my hand with dull claws. Afterward, I bathed for the first time in a week, scrubbing the green mucous from between my fingers with wax.

The baby never came out in light. The room smelled of rotting flesh and mildew, a stench so foul that it followed me into my dreams. I spent most days in the field hunting to feed its endless appetite, and because I couldn't be pent-up in the moldering house.

※※※

Mother got very sick before she died. Her pock-marked skin was a crumbling greyness that stuck to the sheets. The doctor told me that she was suffering from an infection. He said her body was deteriorating, and that soon the virus would spread to her brain.

I tried to hush the baby's screaming so mother could rest, spilling innards down its gullet. The crib was filthy, and even with a candle burning in my hand I could hardly make out its form wriggling under the covers. I leaned closer and called to the doctor,

"I think there's something wrong with it."

The screeching grew louder, and I covered my ears with the sheet I had been using to clasp my nose. I was blind and suffocating. Mother sat up and I could tell she wanted to say something, but she didn't know how, so she stood and pointed out the window. She kept poking the glass until her nail cracked, and the doctor steered her back to bed. She exhaled, and tendrils of smog curled around me. Her breath shivered through my body. I wanted to save her.

※※※

One room couldn't contain us. The entire house was decaying. There were runnels where body fluid coagulated and crusted, stiff as tuff. The doctor and I carried out mother several steps at a time. We brought her bed into the kitchen before I went back for the baby. But when I looked into the crib, it was gone.

I leapt for the hall but twisted my ankle in a hole of soft rot. I heard its shriek from far off in the shadows. I bit my tongue and shouted for the doctor.

Mother scraped the windows as she muttered to herself. I saw goosebumps on the grey membranes of her forearms. Her hands were manic in their patter, the abrasive tapping around the frame. Her sweat-damp brow throbbed and the doctor told me to back away.

I knew she was going to die that night, and while she groped the glass I tried to think of fonder memories.

"We have to find the baby," the doctor interrupted.

We looked through the night, but there was no sign of it anywhere.

By the time we came back to the kitchen, mother was dead. Her face was passive; eyes open, resting in the light of the moon. Her head was curved gently to the side, as if reassessing what the world could look like. She had no fear of anything. I lifted her pale body out of twilight to lie in repose on the mattress.

※※※

The doctor insisted that we continue searching. We tried to follow the echoes, but they seemed to come from different places at once.

We split up to search around the perimeter. That was the last time I saw the doctor. I was never sure if he survived. All I know is that the screams desisted shortly after he went missing.

From the darkness I heard a barks and howls, and remembered the doctor's ravenous dogs. I considered chasing after them. A damp wind blew, and the gust was filled with the smell of death. Then I thought about mother. I couldn't forsake her, and I couldn't take her with me.

I sat on the porch with father's shotgun across my lap, shivering but not from chill. The atmosphere was all stars and Gemini. I tried to shoot them down from the sky, hoping I might scare some company out of the bushes. Nobody heard the gun go off.

Part of me was frightened to be alone. The rest was unchanged. There was never much there to begin with.

When morning came, I carried mother down to the river. I sat on the broad white bank to watch the calm blue current flow. It was warm that day, especially for winter. I watched the sun restore a tepid glow to her skin, shining for the last time.

Then, when she was in the ground, I went to set the house on fire. I couldn't live there any longer, and I knew nobody would return, or think to seek me out. I let the house burn with all of my unanswered questions, the dark truths, and suspicions.

I pretended that I didn't exist. I could feel my definition fading as the wind took me away from the flames. The world seemed so open, so exposed. I flew until the breeze gave out, gliding down from the sky's summit. I watched the dark stripes of trees along the ground. There were no clouds. Then I heard a shriek in the distance, maybe the wind, maybe something more familiar.

I prayed that the memories of my old life would be washed away. But there was still death in the world, all around me. The weight of gravity took hold as the wind gave out. I descended beneath ceaseless sky, leaving everything I had ever known behind in ashes.

All Dolled Up
BY SHANNON IWANSKI

Becca Mason was a bitch. In fact, she was the biggest bitch in the town, and that was saying something. I had watched her from afar for so many years that she eventually became a rodent trapped in the cage of Kant High School. Becca inhabited the upper most tier of society, what with her father being mayor and the president of the bank. She took it upon herself to live the part, and that included making it known to everyone that she was *the* most important person in their lives.

I managed to escape the fallout of her personality until the night before senior prom. Becca and two of her frenemies came into the dry cleaner where I worked with my mom.

She stood at the counter ringing the bell as if she was calling her maid to clean up after her prize-winning shih-Tzu that had shit on a priceless Persian rug. I usually managed to occupy a space outside of Becca's sphere of influence, but on occasion, our paths would cross. She never remembered me. Whether that was a blessing or a curse, I could never decide.

"How can I help you?" I asked. My face remained neutral. I didn't want to call any attention to myself.

In response, she threw a ticket at me. It fluttered onto the countertop only to fall onto the floor at my feet when Becca slapped her hand on the counter. Later I'm sure she would tell her friends how she couldn't believe that it had taken me so long to help her when she was the only one in the shop. It didn't matter that two other people had been waiting for their garments. She was the only one.

I stooped and retrieved the ticket. Disappearing into the back, I could still hear Becca talking about how unfair it was that her mother made her come to this shit hole on a regular basis to pick things up. Didn't her mother know she was busy? And, OMG, the woman who ran this place was so nasty. Didn't she ever do her hair or makeup? *Giggle.* Not that anyone would look at her. Gawd, what was she, like eighty, or something?

The wire hanger bent when I jerked the plastic-shrouded garment from the overhead carousel. Laughter floated back to me, but thankfully, I was far enough away that I couldn't hear any more of the words. A deep breath, and then I went back to the front. My finger smashed into the cash register buttons with enough force to shatter planets. Becca tossed a twenty on the counter, and snatched her mother's blue dress.

"Have a nice day." I gave her change, and when her hand brushed mine, she stopped and stared vacantly into my eyes.

Without anyone else seeing, I slipped a silver locket into Becca's hand. She blinked, reality returning to her eyes. For a moment both of us thought she would say something, but words hung unspoken on her pink lips. Her two-person entourage pulled her away while casting unknowing glances back and forth and then at me.

The door closed behind them, and Mrs. Jenkins stepped up to the counter with a downward slant to the corner of her mouth.

"Be right back," I said. "Sorry for your wait."

⁂⁂⁂

When Becca arrived at my house that night, I hurried her into my bedroom and closed the door. Mom was in the basement working on yet another wreath that would join the stacks and stacks of them before she gave them away at Christmas. My light was turned off, and the only illumination came from six dark green candles placed around a hexagram I had carved into the wooden floor several years ago.

Becca sat on the corner of my bed and ran her hand absentmindedly over the surface of the patchwork quilt Grandma had made for my last birthday. I could tell that Becca wanted to say something, but like earlier at the store, the words betrayed her. She had no choice but sit quietly while I prepared the second part of the ritual.

"Hecate, hear my call."

Kneeling, I sliced my left palm open and dribbled blood into the stained grooves in the wood. My prayer to Hecate flowed from my lips but the conviction came easier than it ever had. Becca, pretty, pretty Becca, could toy with whomever she wanted as long as it wasn't my mother.

I smeared blood into the center of the star and sprinkled it with salt and sage. Becca whimpered, and I looked up to see her staring wide eyed at misshapen creatures silhouetted onto the off-white walls by the flickering candles. The imps danced around, pouncing on one another and squealing in devilish delight. Becca must have a good imagination because a wet spot formed on my quilt. Liquid drip, drip, dripped onto the floor and formed a pool that slowly ran toward the star.

We locked eyes, and I shrugged. I'd never seen her be anything but smug and self-sure. This Becca frightened both of us. I held her gaze long enough to draw two breaths, and then I went to the dresser sitting beside the aluminum foil-covered window. Mackey's Toy Store had a sale going on, and nobody commented when I purchased the doll. It stared at me with its painted-on brown eyes. They really were a match for Becca's. I had chosen well.

The doll went into the center of the star. I pricked a finger and smeared blood on its forehead. Dabbing a pinkie into Becca's urine, I swiped it between the dolls legs. One of the candles flickered and died. The scent of sulphur suffused the room. Becca whimpered. I leaned close and cupped my hand beneath her eye to catch her tears; I rubbed them on the doll's face.

Two more candles died. Becca fell back onto the bed.

Why are you doing this? the baby doll asked me.

I ignored it. If I lost focus now, the spell would be ruined, and Becca's soul would be lost to the ether.

The wicks slowly ate the remaining three flames as I beseeched Hecate to accept my gift of blood and grant me the gift of Becca's soul forever. The whisper of a breath on my neck sealed the deal in the otherworldly darkness of my bedroom.

❧❧❧❧

The school administration canceled school and prom after they found Becca's mangled body lying on the bank of Earl Creek a mile outside of town. Everyone talked about the fact she had been identified only by her dental records. Not to mention that her mother had to be transported to the emergency room and may have suffered a heart attack when she was told the news that her precious baby girl was dead.

It wasn't how I wanted things to go, but Hecate takes her price how she sees fit. I wasn't going to interfere and end up beside Becca. Thankfully, the goddess also took all of the blood from the body. It saved me from worrying about leaving evidence in the trunk of my mom's car when I disposed of the remaining evidence.

I sat at the back of the auditorium while a press secretary asked us to keep the mayor and his wife in our prayers. All around me, people sat in shocked silence. Color drained from faces. Noses ran. Men and women stifled sobs, some more successfully than others. Whenever I felt someone looking at me, I made sure to have my most stunned look firmly in place.

Why did you do it?

I moved toward the door and quietly let myself out into the hallway and out the front door. Cars lined the street. The heat bordered on oppressive, but in the brick building's shadow, I found a respite from it and the press of human emotion.

"No one knows the real you," I said.

Oh, and you do?

"Better than anyone. I've watched you since we were in grade school. You used to be so nice, but then you became a bitch." I opened my grey backpack and looked inside. I had redressed the doll in its pink and white floral dress after the ritual. Becca deserved that much dignity, at least.

Laughter only I could hear sent chills down my spine. It took a while for me to realize it had turned to crying.

"It's a little late for that," I said.

Fuck you! You don't know me. None of you does.

"Poor little Becca, huh?"

Do you know your father?

"Fuck you."

I'm not being hateful. I'm opening your eyes. Do you know your father?

"No. He died when I was still a baby."

Does your mom tell you that your father loved you?

"All the time. What does that have to do with anything?"

Take me to my house.

"Now?"

My father is at the hospital with my mother. Now is the perfect time.

I zipped the bag shut and walked to my mother's parked car. She had decided to close the store and spend the day with my grandmother, who was distraught at the news. Just like everyone else in town, she had never thought something so horrible could happen in our slice of utopia. I eased the car forward and turned onto Main Street.

Becca lived on Highland Road. It was on the north side of town where everyone who was anyone lived. She gave me the code to get through the main gate and the code to get through the one that opened onto a winding white concrete driveway leading to a three-story white-walled and black-shuttered house in the middle of a fifteen hundred acre plot. I'd never been to the house before. Few people had, including Becca's frenemies. The mayor was notorious for being reclusive when he wasn't at work.

I stopped in front of the main door and killed the engine.

"This is one hell of a place."

Hell is right. There's a key in the black box hanging from the doorknob. The code is 1171.

I walked to the door and opened the box. The key slid into the lock with almost no sound. The door opened onto a grand entryway tiled with white marble. Beyond it was an opulent sitting room with dark leather furniture. A flat screen TV took up most of the wall opposite where I stood. To my left a staircase wound its way up to the second floor. I stopped on the first step and looked up at the sky light that took up most of the ceiling high overhead.

Top of the stairs. Second door on the left. It's the master bedroom. There's no one here so you don't have to be quiet.

I realized I was holding my breath and tiptoeing up the stairs. Once Becca said that, I took a deep breath and hurried up the stairs, into the room she had told me about. The four-poster king sized bed took up a good portion of the master bedroom. Its ivory comforter appeared to cast light into even the farthest reaches of the room. What I could only assume were expensive paintings by current favorites in the art world covered the walls. A Persian rug at the foot of the bed almost felt out of place with its more homely feel.

The closet. There's a box on a shelf at the back. It's covered up by some old dress shirts.

The closet was almost as big as my room. Clothes, neatly pressed and anticipating usage, hung silently in the cedar-rich air. Lights sprang to life automatically when I crossed the threshold. I found the box on the shelf like Becca said I would. It was an antique cigar box with a stern-faced man on the lid. I resisted opening it until I got back into the bedroom.

I set it on the bed and slowly lifted the lid.

"Jesus, Becca. I'm sorry. I didn't know."

⁂

"Wake up, Mr. Mayor." I slapped his face as hard as I could. When he didn't budge, I punched him in the stomach with all of my strength. He threw up onto the floor of the pool house. It splashed his leather shoes and the legs of the metal pool chair I had bound him to.

When he realized he couldn't move his arms or legs, the mayor looked at me with bewilderment that turned to panicked anger. His face reddened near his grey-streaked temples. Like his daughter, he tried to speak, but my spell held him in thrall. He was mine to do with as I pleased.

"I'm sorry for the loss of your daughter." I was. If I had known... I bit my tongue and walked from him to another chair I had placed inside a large hexagram drawn in blood on the rough concrete beside the clear pool. A large blue tarp I had found in a shed at the back of the house shrouded it.

I began chanting my prayer to Hecate.

"Wh...Whhhhhhhhy?"

"Well, you're a strong one," I said. I turned around and held up a picture. His eyes went wide. He shook his head.

"I thought that would be a good enough answer." I uttered a second prayer and lit the six candles I had retrieved from my house, along with some other supplies. When I finished, I walked over to my backpack and pulled the Becca doll out.

"Hello, Daddy," she said once I had stood her a few feet from the chair.

The mayor's eyes went wide.

"He killed me, Daddy. He killed me because of who I was. Because of what you made me. It's your fault, *Daddy*."

The mayor shook his head. I collected his tears and walked back. Removing the cover, I wiped the tears on the life-sized sex doll sitting in the chair. Clumps of her black hair had been ripped out. One of her breasts had been mutilated. By a knife, I would say. The mayor looked at me, and I saw the confusion clearly written on his face.

"I'm sure you remember Tiffany the Tease. 'So life-like your dick won't know the difference.' You bought her for your son when you couldn't get him to stop masturbating everywhere in the house," I stood behind the silicone doll, which I had already smeared with my blood. "You've been a very bad man, Mr. Mayor. You made me do something I didn't realize was a mistake until after it was too late. But now we're going to remedy that."

"So this is how you're going to atone. Forever. You fucked me for ten years, and now you're going to find out what it's like," Becca said.

The mayor screamed silently and thrashed in his chair. I pulled a knife from my pocket and walked toward him. I stopped long enough to swipe my fingers through his urine before I plunged the knife into his groin once, twice, three times.

Walking back to Tiffany the Tease, I smeared the urine and blood between her legs. A strong wind blew through the enclosed building. The stench of chlorine thickened in the air. The once-calm surface of the pool rippled and churned with the power of a goddess ready to claim her prize. Demonic chatter echoed from the walls. Darkness engulfed us.

"Hecate, hear my call," Becca and I said in unison.

FAKE GIRLFRIEND
BY TIMOTHY O'LEARY

Monica Evans was not 33 years old. Nor did she have dense, Cherry Coke-colored shoulder-length hair. She was far from an athletic size 4 and showed zero penchant for twice-weekly Pilates in assfabulous Lululemon workout wear. Ryan Gosling, not her favorite movie star, and she didn't own a cat named Barney Miller. Lorrie Westfield, not her best friend. Didn't have a sister named Susie, or parents in Fullerton, California. She wasn't a freelance stylist working for Nike. Prosecco, far from her favorite cocktail. Never listened to Spotify, and didn't own a two-year-old blue and white Mini Cooper convertible, nicknamed Austin Powered. Finally, she was not head over heels crazy for Brian Dailey.

She couldn't be. Because Monica Evans did not exist. She was fictitious, a digital figment of Brian Dailey's imagination. His fake girlfriend.

Brian Daily *was* real, his online profile a colorless display of facts: 39 years old, a University of Oregon graduate, the controller at Carleton Real Estate. In photos he appeared portly, neck too massive to connect head and body, yellow hair in retreat, always flashing a kind smile. He was usually posed with Daisy, his drooling chocolate lab, in a rural setting suggesting a healthy outdoor lifestyle, which belied his mustard complexion and man-boobs. His wardrobe? Sale-priced short sleeve dress shirts in every shade of blue, topping Dockers purchased a size too large.

Brian wrote a blog called *Appleflop*, ranting against the company he felt abandoned him. But Apple issues aside, his Facebook posts were infrequent and serene, crafted to avoid negativity. To Brian, digital communications comprised another outlet for his "spread a little love" philosophy: placards promoting human rights and feel-good slogans, flexible puppy photos, and a stream of congratulations to any friend celebrating anything remotely notable. His likes included Carleton Real Estate's website, Bridgeport Brew Pub, two local homeless shelters, and the HBO show *Game of Thrones*. And, of course, his biggest like was reserved for his fake girlfriend, Monica. Since she first appeared in his social networking sphere she'd dominated Brian's online existence, a storybook romance unfolding for all with internet access.

Apparently, she'd come down with the flu a few days earlier, and left the following post: *Hey, wonderful man. Do people know how special you are? That last night you brought me Thai chicken noodle soup and nursed me back to health? Thank you. You are the best boyfriend on the planet!*

Monica's flu had prevented her from attending Carleton Real Estate's Christmas party, just as her unpredictable work schedule made it impossible for her to accompany Brian to any function where friends or co-workers might meet her. They razzed him, but remained nonetheless ecstatic that he'd met someone. Though Brian's romantic world sputtered and splashed, his life overflowed with friends.

To be in Brian's circle was like having a loyal golden retriever twenty feet away, yawning, but ready to serve. The kind of man that people claimed as their "very best friend," the kind-eyed listener, the first call when someone needed to confess, vent, or cry.

As is so often the case, those qualities did not translate into a soul-mate. "It's like dating your minister," remarked the Starbuck's barista that had chanced a night out. "Sweet. He sits across the table and smiles, but there is nothing else. No adventure. No surprise."

Not, however, for lack of romantic effort on his part. He pursued every networking opportunity: friend's fix-ups, singles mixers, get-togethers with groups; City Club, Blazers Boosters, a regional hairstylist's convention at The Red Lion. He even crashed wedding receptions, quickly discovering how problematic it was to start a relationship with a lie, as he stumbled to explain his connection to the bride and groom.

Digital romance: Match.com, Christian Mingle, even some exploratory work on JDate, despite his Baptist roots. And after years of failure, he concluded love finds you when it's time. But his sister and friends reasoned, as attached people are sometimes apt to do, that loners must be desperately unhappy, always at risk to sink into a sad life of sloppy solitary drunkenness, internet porn, and addictive video games.

"For God's sake, I just don't understand it," his sister, Joanne, commented during one of their regularly scheduled Saturday afternoon get-togethers at the coffee shop in Powell's Books. "All those bad boy's women fall for—lazy, drunken, cheating losers—and here is my brother, nicest guy on the planet, stable job, a few bucks in the bank, all by himself. Lonely. Sad. It isn't fair. Women, they're idiots."

"Please. I'm not lonely or sad. I have a lot of friends. A lot. I'm still young. When things align it will happen."

"Sorry little brother, but thirty-nine is a baby step from middle age, when it all starts to unravel. No offense, but the way it's going, it won't be pretty. You need to take better care of yourself. Get some sun. You look like an extra from *The Walking Dead*. Get that big ass to the gym. There's this thing they do called a sit-up. Try it. Romance doesn't just slide into your life. You need to train for it."

Brian stared at his scone, fuming. He wondered how his sister, Frisbee breasts, diving board ass, high waist acid-washed jeans last deemed stylish at a Duran Duran concert, trained her way to love.

Leaving the book store he caught a glimpse of himself in the window, his reflection framed next to a life-size cardboard cut-out of Steve Jobs promoting his biography. At the right angle it looked like Brian and Mr. Apple were out for a stroll, which brought a smile to Brian's face. Imagine if he and the founder of the company he detested above all else were actually buddies, roaming the streets of Portland.

Positioning the phone just right he snapped a picture, did a little editing, and posted the photo to Instagram and Facebook with this notation. *Big news! The Dark Prince of technology lives! I know, because we just had coffee together and plotted the demise of Google.* Within a few minutes there were several "likes" and a couple "WTF's?"

By the time he reached his apartment a stranger, screen name Johnny Appleseed, posted a comment and a friend request. *Maybe not my best photo, but I'd be interested in discussing this Google thing. Steve.*

Brian chalked it up to geek weirdness, but took some pleasure in pondering the idea that Jobs could still be alive, no less plausible than an elderly Elvis living somewhere in Canada, or Walt Disney's brain frozen in Tomorrowland awaiting the defrost button. Months earlier Brian read an article by an MIT professor claiming that within a decade humans would be able to download their brains onto hard drives and essentially live forever, albeit in microchips and titanium frames. If anyone could have arranged that quantum technology leap it would have been Jobs. Perhaps his digital ghost was housed in a server farm below Palo Alto, wandering the Web in some kind of iBody, intent on redesigning the galaxy in heavenly white. Brian accepted the friend request, and laughed when he discovered all of Johnny's photos were of half-eaten apples.

At work, the dating pressure peaked on Thursdays. "Hey, Brian, free tomorrow night? C'mon over. Bring a date." His friends and coworkers once again planning some kind of group food exploration: Moroccan barbecue, A Night in Bangkok, Greek fondue. Or cocktail parties inspired by the latest HBO series: Mad Men Martiniville, Soprano Slings, True Bloody Marys, which always led to an in-depth analysis of his social life when he RSVP'd "solo," his female friends flush with dewy looks.

Of course, he'd love to meet his perfect woman, but he had to admit he found being single satisfying, offering a pleasant sense of orderliness and control. For sure, he didn't harbor those feelings of insecurity that plagued his attached friends.

One day he read a story about lonely old men scammed by Russian dating services, and realized that a fake girlfriend could actually solve many of his problems. Not a long-term solution, but a few months of fake love would offer a welcome respite.

Just to be safe, he used an old laptop so Monica's IP address would not be the same as his. Over the next week he began to construct his ideal woman, a girl of plusses and buts. Pretty, but not beautiful. Healthy, but not fanatical. Spiritual, but not religious. Worldly, but absent cynicism. Creative, minus the arrogance. Sexy, not slutty. Hip, with traditionalist values. Educated, but never snooty.

Like Brian she eschewed politics and petty social pressures, and embraced the frequent corniness of the web, expressing deep affection for friends, family, kittens, old John Cusack movies, sleeping-in, inspirational slogans, planet-friendly policies, and when the time was right, Brian.

So as to not make them too suspiciously aligned, she listened to NPR, had a weakness for the "Real Housewives" and "Kardashian" franchises, loved her iPad, and tended to overspend on fashion.

Brian searched obscure Northern European social networking sites to find appropriate pictures of Monica, surmising there was little chance friends would be trolling the web seven thousand miles away. He discovered a Latvian girl (real name Anna), right out of a Neutrogena commercial, fresh fading freckles, button-nosed. He envisioned her waking in muted morning sun, swaddled in white cotton sheets.

Anna worked at The Gap in Riga and was vain enough to post a stream of photos, often at work as she handled clothing, which Brian positioned as if Monica were on the road working.

It took no time to build a sufficient friend base for her, several hundred random people willing to accept anyone into their inner circle. Soon she had more friends than he did, the benefit of being an attractive woman, Brian surmised. To his amazement, the more Monica posted the deeper the friendships became.

To add realism their relationship started slowly, Brian announcing that he'd finally met someone, with a first date story right out of a Tom Hanks flick. "I was walking outside of Nordstrom, and here comes this really cute girl carrying a stack of shoe boxes. She dropped one, they all came tumbling down, I helped her carry them in, and the next thing I know we're at Starbucks in Pioneer Square."

He passed around her Facebook page, encouraging people to friend her with the notation "Brian's pal." Soon Monica was having discussions with Brian's friends, often light-hearted ribbing about their shared affection for him.

"I bet he bought you hand sanitizer for Valentine's Day," his buddy Allen joked, posting a photo of Brian spraying down garbage cans with Trader Joe's lemon disinfectant.

"Gotta love a clean man," Monica replied with a smiley face. *"Hand sanitizer and two dozen roses plus a collection of Pablo Neruda poetry. I don't think you know what a rare and romantic friend you have."*

She promptly posted a photo of the flowers, which earned him accolades among her female friends, Brian developing a reputation as "quite a catch."

He spent late night's photo shopping a pictorial history of their relationship, travelling to the beach, romantic spots in the city, locations that would easily allow Monica's insertion next to him, often confusing the strangers he enlisted to take photos framed in odd ways.

After a few weeks he added an additional dimension, purchasing a second cell phone so Monica could text him. At lunch, or at drinks with Joanna or friends, he'd leave his phone on the table, excuse himself, then text the phone from the bathroom with short bursts like, *Made it to San Fran for the Nike shoot. Missed you the minute you left last night. Can't wait to kiss you. Monica.*

"Oooh, Brian, Monica's looking for you," they'd tease when he returned. "She's got it bad."

The cell phone was also useful when Monica was supposed to meet him at dinner or an event. Early in the evening he'd peer at his phone sadly, turn it for the room to see. "Poor Monica, stuck at work, or missed her flight, and she won't be able to make it tonight."

Brian found himself doing something he had seldom done before, lying, as he created the legend of his girlfriend. Monica adored Daisy and all animals, the Belmont food carts, the Laurelhurst Theatre, vintage video games, and spent an entire fifteen minutes examining his childhood collection of Hot Wheels cars without ridicule. Brian grinned as he detailed Monica's intimate side, how he loved the Awapuhi-smell of her hair, her long tanned legs, the way she always over-tipped, even when the service was bad.

To be honest, the stories didn't feel false. More like dim childhood memories, like that trip to the beach, the party you think you remember, the movie you saw when you were twelve, all fuzzy and ripe for fill-in, a blurring of fact and fiction. And for the first time he felt like a functioning adult, no longer that lost and lonely guy.

People began to act as if they knew Monica. "You really need to meet her," a friend announced at a dinner party. "So sweet. Talented too. You should see the Sketchers commercial she worked on a couple months ago." Brian, baffled, was unable to recall that particular post.

One morning the receptionist at work waved him down. "I was talking to a friend at Wieden & Kennedy. He knows your girlfriend. Says that he worked with her on a bunch of Nike projects. Very talented, he told me. Said they were on a shoot with Maria Sharapova and Monica saved the day. Said she's really pretty, too. Course, I knew that from her photos."

A few days later his sister called. "Hey, I saw your girlfriend today. I was driving up Broadway and she was standing in front of the Schnitz. I honked and waved. She waved back, but since we haven't officially met it was a bit weird, but I knew her from the photos. I would have pulled over but too much traffic." Brian smiled at the thought of a confused woman just waiting to cross the street, suddenly assaulted by a scruffy woman in a rusty Tercel, waving and honking like a maniac.

Still, he was struck by the impressive weirdness of it all. The hours people spent digitally interacting with perceived, perhaps fake, friends. The strange compulsion to share secrets online, or embrace relationships that might not exist. Monica's Facebook page had evolved into a collage of other's intimate thoughts: distress over loss, insecurities, often summarized with homespun philosophies. He thought about Johnny Appleseed, who he now communicated with on a daily, sometimes hourly basis, discussing the merits of open versus closed source software; the future of technology; The Decemberists versus Mumford and Son. Brian often forgot he was talking to a mysterious geek assuming a dead guy's persona. He had no idea if Johnny was male, female, or Jobs's digitized brain. He could be a smart twelve-year-old or incarcerated felon in this new anonymous world where anyone can be anyone.

His plan had always been to stage a breakup after a month or two; a heartbroken Monica relocating for an unbelievable job opportunity, thus affording him a few more months of peace as the two attempted to make a long-distance relationship work, without the pressure of anyone attempting to meet her, followed by pressure-free months as he grieved the break-up.

But as the weeks passed, Brian became, well, obsessed. A high-tech Henry Higgins, Monica his Eliza. How real could he make her? More than that, he realized for the first time he wasn't lonely. All the advantages of a relationship, without the downsides. They never argued or disagreed. His bathroom remained his own. In some ways, this was better than real.

Monica began sending him gifts at work: plant arrangements, cheese and wine baskets, even a shirt from Nordstrom's. *Hey boyfriend, time to graduate to long sleeve shirts with a pattern.* Sometimes it was an apology because she was again delayed and would miss an event, but other times just to express her love. Brian occasionally enlisted the help of a waitress from a nearby Burgerville to give voice to his muse. "I'm trying to make this woman at work jealous, so could you call my voice mail and leave a message?"

The next day when Brian arrived at his cubicle, he would casually hit the speaker phone, knowing his big-eared coworkers would eavesdrop in the echoey low ceilinged room.

"Brian, it's Monica. I loved that film last night, and dinner was so great. Mmmm, I've got a serious Ken's Pizza jones going now. I'm heading to the airport, but called to say I was thinking about you. Let's Facetime tonight."

On Labor Day Brian took a flight to Orange County, presumably to meet Monica's family for the first time, but checking into the Fullerton Best Western for three days instead. His Facebook posts showed the lovely exterior of an aged but well-maintained white ranch burger, Monica's parents' home, where he was supposedly staying. Outside of Knott's Berry Farm, he had a photo of himself taken next to Monica's smiling parents, actually Mr. and Mrs. Simpson from Boise, Idaho, a social 60-something-year-old couple he'd met while buying taffy for his co-workers. Mr. Simpson, compact, nicely chiseled with Irish eyes, made for a worthy father. And Mrs. Simpson, well-aged and bubbly, the kind of mom Monica couldn't wait to visit.

While the Simpsons regaled Brian with details of their upcoming golf outing to Laguna Beach, he envisioned their resume as Monica's parents. Educated, but not Ivy, undergraduates from solid state schools. Monica's Dad, a successful CPA, retired, anxious to dote over his two daughters; the kind of man who would appreciate a level-headed son-in-law like Brian with his mutual fund mentality. They'd share a love of numbers and orderliness, absent the constraints of a too conservative mindset. Mrs. Evans, approachably elegant, a retired high school principal involved in a wide range of charitable work. Brian and Monica would certainly want to spend one week a year vacationing with her parents, perhaps a condo in Maui over the Christmas holiday.

Brian spent his days wandering Disneyland and other local tourist attractions, photographing the ones he knew Monica would enjoy, usually dining with the Groupons he collected every morning. At night he prepared his posts, carefully inserting Monica before whispering, only half-jokingly, "Good night sweetheart" as he closed his computer. He realized this was the first vacation he had ever taken with a woman.

On day two: *Brian and I are having a wonderful Orange County adventure. The folks are smitten with my new man. Who would have thought it, but we're both big Pluto fans. Just another thing we have in common.* The accompanying photo showed Brian embracing a faux furry cartoon character, the dog's baseball-mitt sized paw planted at the top of his grinning head like a coon skin cap. The post received dozens of likes and sweet variations of "too cute." The only disturbing comment came from Johnny Appleseed, who posted, *Be careful of fictional characters. Sometimes they bite.*

Brian returned to a buzz around the office. "So, you met the parents?" Leslie the broker poked him in the arm. "Saw them on Facebook. Cute. Did you do anything else down there? Maybe a little jewelry shopping? A little talk with her Dad? Any news you want to share?" They ribbed him for days, the sweet way in which friends treat people in love.

Brian began to consider the consequences of taking the big step—marriage. As much as he'd always envisioned a traditional wedding, their situation only allowed them to elope. But that might work. He'd always wanted to go to Italy. Maybe even Northern Europe. Perhaps a trip to meet Anna in person, hire her for a day or two for an intensive photo shoot. He'd need wedding pictures. He'd walk into the Gap, act natural, and tell Anna how beautiful she was in the least creepy way possible. Explain he was an aspiring fashion photographer and needed a guide / model to tour the city. He could build up an arsenal of photos, a whole year's worth, the kind he could never create in Photoshop. He and Monica in a church. Monica sitting on his lap. Monica frolicking in a bikini.

In rational moments he realized it wasn't a long-term solution. At some point the charade would have to end with Monica leaving. Or? He could move to another city, make new friends, and introduce digital Monica as his wife who'd stayed behind for her job while he got settled. And why not? Couples were mobile now, long distance relationships not uncommon.

That afternoon a delivery arrived at the office. "Wow, you must have really bowled her over in California," Kim, the receptionist said, and winked as she placed a huge wicker basket on Brian's desk. It was wrapped in cellophane, overflowing with huge gooey cookies, and topped with a flapping red balloon.

Thanks for such a terrific vacation, you Pluto lover. Kisses, Monica.

Brian stared at the card, feeling that familiar rumble below his belt where anxiety lived. He'd been so content lately he'd forgotten that place existed.

He had no idea where this had come from. He fingered the label affixed to the wicker basket. Sweet Town. Sweets for your Sweet. Never heard of it. Never tasted their cookies. Could he have done it late last night, as he nodded off in front of his computer? Had the one Pale Ale fogged his memory? Sleep shopping? Maybe a Sweet Town flash deal from Amazon Local or Groupon, and in a haze he'd clicked through. He went online to check his credit card transactions. Nothing in the last 24 hours. He checked his browser memory, but no record of Sweet Town or any shopping click through.

Still, he must have done it. There was no other explanation. Out of habit he snapped a photo of the basket, then ripped it open and began distributing cookies to his coworkers, taking more shots of them grinning, crumbly stuffed mouths and chocolate-streaked lips, and posted the pictures on his own page.

Beautiful Monica! The entire office sends thanks for your gift. We are all fat and happy!

Brian decided to quit worrying. When he got home, he'd find a mailer with an offer he'd forgotten, and the credit card charge yet to come. Chalk it up to a very early senior moment.

An hour later his email chimed. He opened up to a Facebook notification:

Glad you liked the cookies. Save a couple for desert tonight. Grilled salmon! See you around 6:30? Kisses, Monica.

Brian's stomach bottomed. And something else. Something unfamiliar. Fear? Rage?

Someone was fucking with him.

But who? And more than who, how and why? He glanced around, expecting to see a smiling jokester, Brian punked. A victim of good-hearted hilarity. But all heads were buried in work. He rose and strode to the men's room, rubbing the growling fold of fat above his belt. He stood in front of the mirror as the cramp subsided, and washed his hands roughly as if to scrub away the mystery.

Returning to his desk he pulled up Monica's Facebook page, staring so hard her photo seemed to pixelate, little round pieces of Monica / Anna, vibrating digital tiles fading on the edges. "What are you doing?" he mouthed silently, pulling up the log-in screen, only to discover he was locked out. Flushed, hands shaking, he went to Yahoo mail but found himself locked out again. Someone had changed both the user ID and the password on Monica's accounts.

Stomach rumbling like noisy water pipes, he took quick strides back to the bathroom. He felt paranoid now, inspecting the white bathroom as if he'd never before been there, dropping to his knees to peer under stalls, and throwing open a storage closet door. Satisfied he was alone, he caught himself in the mirror again, hairline trimly receding, the second chin he knew so well, and yet, different than just a few minutes ago, his image seemed to float, as if he were being slowly swallowed by a rippling ocean. Gut screaming, he locked himself in a stall just in time to let the tension escape in an awful blast, followed by more scrubbing, hands chapping crimson. Before going out into the main office he stood silently in the hall, listening, hoping to hear some explanation, then told the receptionist he was sick, and rushed back to his apartment.

Was he somehow doing this to himself? Had he consumed more than one beer last night and changed the codes in some kind of Bridgeport Pale Ale fugue? Given access to someone else? Allowed his security to be breached? Was Monica a prisoner to some Russian hacker, or just his own flawed memory?

He searched his desk for signs of Sweet Town, new codes on slips of paper. Nothing. He pulled up Facebook on Monica's laptop. A few minutes earlier she'd posted a new entry of herself on a film set, mugging at the camera, her left arm encircling the waist of an equally jubilant man. He was scruffy Hollywood handsome, shadowy two-day beard that looked applied. Casual clothes from expensive designers that screamed "creative guy who makes a lot of money." Brian traced the arm that held Monica close and noticed the trajectory. At that angle the hand would land low behind her. Perhaps on Monica's ass? Is that why she was smiling so widely?

Happy to be working with Allen Ducaise, announced the caption.

Allen Ducaise? Probably some fake advertising stage name. Tony from the Bronx pretending to be French, a film school asshole acting the big shot. Of course, Monica wouldn't fall for that kind of....Brian stopped.

Staring at the photo, he searched for any telltale signs of Photoshop. If this was a mock-up it was the best he'd ever seen. Arms around waists, intricate hands, far beyond anything he was capable of.

Brian had no idea what to do. He scoured Monica's Facebook page for the next several hours, analyzing each entry, every new friend, each photo, every like and reply, looking any hint as to what was happening. On a hunch at 1:00 a.m. he sent an e mail to Johnny Appleseed. *Are you doing this?*

Johnny responded within thirty seconds with a simple *?*.

Brian finally closed the screen around 3:00.

The next morning, there was an email from Monica.

Brian, this is hard, as the last thing in the world I want to do is hurt you. I know I should do it in person, but I just can't bear to see you sad. It would wreck me. But it's just not going to work. As wonderful as it's been, we're not right for each other. We exist in different worlds, desire different things. As incredible as you are, I need a different kind of man, though please understand, I will always love you, even if I am saying goodbye. Kisses for the last time. Monica.

Stunned, Brian sobbed, momentarily stumbling and believing his heart might stop. Then sadness gave way to anger. *We exist in different worlds.* Yes we do. I live in the real world of flesh and blood, and you... you are my creation. Pure invention. My fake girlfriend. He slammed down the screen of the laptop.

When he reached work, the normally buoyant morning greetings were muted, a palpable tension infecting the room. His message light kept blinking, an urgent plea from his sister to call her back. He ignored it, sat down, rolling towards his computer, when Leslie from accounting approached from behind, wrapping her arms around his neck, and pulling his head to her chest like a mother comforting a five-year-old.

"I am so sorry. We all are. God, Brian, what happened? Everything seemed to be going so well."

"What? What are you talking about?"

Leslie kneaded his shoulder lightly. "We saw Monica's post a few minutes ago. Oh, God, I can only imagine what you must be going through."

Brian logged onto his computer, clicking to Facebook. Monica had placed another entry, a graphic over a message sent to all her friends.

Hi all! Just wanted to pass along some sad news. Unfortunately, Brian and I have decided to call it quits. We'll love each other forever and will always be friends, but sometimes relationships are simply not meant to be. However, one of the greatest things Brian did was to introduce me to so many great people, so I hope we can all still be friends.

There were comments coming in, many from Brian's contacts, expressing support and assuring Monica they were there for her, too.

"Of course," He said, and started to laugh.

"Brian, are you OK?" Leslie's voice rose now with a twinge of fear. Heads popped up from cubicles like confused gophers.

"I'm OK. Actually, very OK," his voice an octave too high.

"As hard as these things are, try not to get bitter. Sometimes..."

Brian interrupted. "Bitter? Bitter against people you invented? I mean, who gets pissed at Santa Claus or Superman, or mad because you can't date Veronica or Betty? Nobody. Because they're not real. This is all some kind of bad joke. It's..."

Carl, the office manager, stepped into the cubicle. "Brian, calm down. You're scaring people. Listen, why don't you take the day off?"

Brian's computer pinged, another message from Facebook. This time Monica stood in front of Nordstrom's, throwing a half wave as she reached for the door.

Best way to get over a break-up? Serious shopping at Nordstrom's annual shoe sale!

As Brian watched a comment immediately popped up with a "like." *You go, girl! I'd rather have a nice pair of Manolo's than a man any day. Shop till you drop.*

He thought of her, his fake former girlfriend, a few miles away, seated on a purple velvet couch, tan legs extended, red toenails a few inches from the admiring salesman's face as he slid a pair of pumps onto her fictional feet.

He sighed, slumped back, and then traipsed slowly to the bathroom. On autopilot, he peered at himself in the mirror, the room looming white and sterile. And in the heart of it his own face, fading in and out, shimmering, sometimes Brian, sometimes just the space where Brian used to be. Then something clearer came into focus, a happy, confident image, his face thinning, round body transforming, a taller Brian, the kind of man who'd known many women like Monica. He pulled his shoulders back.

Back at his computer he logged into his own Facebook page. There were comments from friends, and several from women he wasn't sure he knew, offering to get together if he "needed to talk". He wondered if the photos he'd posted of Monica would still be there, somewhat surprised to discover everything still in place. As he continued to scroll past the point when Monica was born there were new photos he had never seen before. Brian at Cannon Beach with a pretty blonde, the two of them hugging Daisy, and the caption: *Great kite-flying weekend at the coast with my two favorite girls.* Brian centered in an oversized leather booth, wearing a nicely tailored suit he'd never owned, and flanked by a voluptuous brunette he'd never met, two other handsome couples around them, and the caption: *Fabulous weekend in Vegas seeing Elton at Caesar's Palace.*

As he watched, pictures popped onto his timeline, plus a comment appeared from Monica's fictional sister Susie. *Brian, so sorry to hear about you two, but be sure to stay in touch. I'm here if you need me. We will always love you.*

Another from Johnny Appleseed. *Hey, Brian, don't lose heart. Sometimes things just don't work out. Did you ever see the Apple III?*

Brian stared at the icon. He typed, *Johnny, are we real?*

Hah, Brian! Haven't you heard? We all just exist within a dog's dream.

A new picture popped onto his timeline, a bit blurry, obviously a selfie taken with a camera phone. A pretty young Asian woman sat with one arm around his dog, a bottle of chardonnay dangling from her hand.

Brian, hurry up, Daisy and I have a great dinner ready.

Brian tilted his head back and closed his eyes, then shut down his computer, with absolutely no idea what he might find when he got home.

Believe in Me
BY HALL JAMESON

Jae sipped the black coffee, careful not to puncture the Styrofoam cup with the tips of his claws. Crackers topped with June bug were arranged on the rocks.

He lifted his cup toward his friend Mero. "Aren't these things bad for the environment?"

"Terrible. But we found them at an abandoned campsite, crackers and coffee too, and figured we'd make use of them before recycling."

Jae popped a cracker into his mouth and frowned, not at the taste, but at the raised voice of the speaker.

"I am not a hoax!" the young Sasquatch cried, banging a hairy fist on the stump. He wore a foam wedge of cheese on his head, a bite taken out of the front. "Why can't we show ourselves? *Why*?"

Excited conversation rippled through the meeting space, a stony clearing high in the mountains. Two dozen Sasquatch assembled on the rocks.

Jae sighed. Boris was a restless soul. Every generation had one. And since his father's death four moons ago, he'd become even more rebellious.

Personally, Jae enjoyed the quiet forest life. He was not a rebel or a rule breaker, and he was not alone. Most monsters he'd run across during his travels—the rougaroo in New Orleans (he shuddered), the Jersey Devil (he shook his head), a mermaid named Ruby he'd met during a trip to the Pacific coast, (he smiled at the memory)—preferred to stay hidden. While the younger generation confounded him, part of him could relate to Boris's complaints.

As a youngling, Jae had witnessed a human imitating a Sasquatch, the damn fool dressed in a matted, fuzzy suit. The sighting had triggered an array of emotions in him: anger, confusion, disbelief. Plus, it was a little funny; the dude looked ridiculous.

Jae smiled at the memory. He'd been tempted to sneak up and scare the crap out of that human. Who would have believed the guy when he described how he'd been attacked by a Sasquatch while pretending to be a Sasquatch?

No one.

But he had followed the rules and resisted.

It was the Sasquatch way.

"We must remain hidden; it's for our own protection. The humans would put us in cages, conduct experiments...or worse," Kelo said.

"I'm tired of hiding," Boris said. "I like watching the humans. They do stupid things."

"I know they can be entertaining, but we have to remain vigilant to ensure our survival," Prala said. "If you do make contact, don't linger. Never pose for the camera." She stopped and looked to her left. "No offense intended, Grand Matron. I know you were caught off guard."

"That's okay, child. I did linger."

The Grand Matron rose from a boulder near Jae, the sun highlighting the silver streaks in her thick coat. Boris bowed and stepped to the side.

"I was careless years ago," she said, speaking in the moans, grunts, and whistles of the ancient Sasquatch tongue. "So intent on gathering manzanita berries that the men on horseback surprised me. I hesitated, thinking they were friendly centaurs until the horses reared and dumped the men from their backs." She grunted. "My recklessness nearly cost our group; humans swarmed the area after that, hunting for us. We barely escaped."

She looked at Boris. "You and the other younglings are our future. You are inquisitive, a good thing, as long as you are careful. I beg you to trust in my wisdom and remain unseen. Understand?"

Boris nodded.

The Grand Matron's gold eyes flicked to the foam wedge on Boris's head, then back to his face. "Your father gave you that curious hat?"

"Yes," he said, blinking. "It's from Wisconsin."

"And who took a bite out of it?"

"Me," Boris said sheepishly. "I thought he'd brought me a snack."

Titters trickled through the crowd.

"He was a fine creature," she said. "A great traveler." Boris nodded and looked at the ground. The Grand Matron continued. "He was obsessed with the humans as well. You are named after one of them, I believe. A movie actor."

"Yes. Boris Karloff," Boris said proudly. "Dad gave me a poster from one of his movies. *Frankenstein*. He was a monster too."

"You are not a monster, Boris," Prala said. "None of us are monsters."

"*They* think we are," Boris said.

"If anyone is a monster, it is them," Prala said. The crowd grumbled. The Grand Matron banged a rock on the stump for silence. She turned to Boris.

"I remember the day your father snuck into the theater all too well. He was obsessed with the moving pictures." She shook her head and sighed. "Marro had to enlist a moose to cause a traffic jam to divert attention so we could get him out of town undetected." She paused. "I loved your father, Boris, but that was a foolish thing to do. We simply cannot take such risks. Do you understand?"

"Yes, ma'am," Boris said in the old speech, before turning and sauntering away.

The Grand Matron touched Jae's arm as the group dispersed. "Keep an eye on him," she whispered.

❧❧❧

Boris roamed the next three nights, keeping to remote terrain, while Jae tracked him from the high ground. On the fourth night, he ventured into the low country. The amber glow of a campfire illuminated a clearing in the gully. Laughter floated up through the evergreens. Jae growled as Boris crept toward the site and hunkered in the darkness.

Three male humans occupied the space, their movements, clumsy, their speech, slurred. One was bald, one had gold hair, and one wore a long ponytail.

Boris reached up and shook the branch above his head.

Baldy jumped. "Did you guys hear that?"

Don't do it, kid! Jae thought.

Boris stepped into the circle of light.

"No!" Jae exclaimed and charged down the hillside.

He lost sight of the camp during his descent, but heard shouts and howls. As he closed in, he caught site of Boris, retreating into the woods. Baldy and Ponytail paced the site, brandishing sticks and shouting. Goldie stood by the fire. He drank from a bottle then lifted his chin and howled. Jae caught snippets of their conversation.

"Could you believe that guy?"

"… monkey suit …"

" … pranking us!"

Laughter.

"Think we'll be on TV?"

Their voices faded as Jae skirted the campsite, following the adrenaline-soaked ribbon of Boris's scent. He spotted Boris's loping form at the far end of a large meadow. Just beyond that, the road.

"Stop!" Jae yelled.

But if Boris heard him, he gave no sign. Bright lights washed over him as he stepped into the road. Boris turned and confronted the vehicle bearing down on him. He spread his arms wide as if to sweep it up into a hug.

The screech of brakes filled the night, followed by a thud. Boris sailed through the air, landing on the far side of the road. The vehicle skidded to a stop twenty yards away. Jae heard the creak of car doors opening.

"What was that? Was it a bear? It was huge! Had to be a griz!"

"Don't know. I think I clipped it though."

"There's a flashlight behind the seat on the passenger side. Get your camera."

Jae let out a howl that rocked the night.

"What the hell was that?"

"I don't know, but I'm not hanging around to find out."

Doors slammed and gravel churned as the truck rocketed away.

Jae bounded across the road and found Boris sprawled in the brambles, his right leg bent at an awkward angle.

"I broke the rules," he whispered.

"Yep."

"I'm sorry."

"I know."

"I offered them crackers. They thought I was a human in a costume," Boris said. "They laughed at my hat. One of them knocked it off my head."

"They were drunk. What did you expect?"

"I don't know. Respect? Gratitude?" He paused. "Fear?"

Jae shook his head. "The first two will never happen. The third always will…eventually."

"I ran because I wanted to kill the one that took my hat."

"If you had killed him, we would all be dead."

"I know. Then I saw the road and the lights and I just wanted to scare someone, you know?" He stopped. "You ever feel like that?"

Jae thought of the man in the Sasquatch suit. "Yes."

He carried Boris into an aspen colony, finding a secluded spot for him to rest.

"I *am* a hoax," Boris muttered.

"You are *not* a hoax. You are a Sasquatch. You lurk in the shadows of the forest. You are the keeper of the moon."

"You sound like the Grand Matron." He looked at Jae, his eyes ancient. "I miss my dad."

"I know. I do too."

"They laughed at me," Boris said, closing his eyes. "I just wanted them to believe."

❀❀❀

Jae crept along until he smelled them, a combination of rank sweat and sour breath. He wrinkled his nose.

Phew! These guys are stinkers.

The site was quiet; the fire burned low. Snoring drifted from the tents. On the ground near the fire pit, he saw what he had come for.

He walked over and crouched by the cheese wedge hat, pausing to sniff an empty bottle left in the dirt. He wrinkled his nose again. When he looked up, two eyes peered at him from the closest tent.

"What're you doing back here?" Baldy said. He climbed out and stood over Jae. "Hey guys, guess whose back?" he yelled. Jae didn't move.

Goldie poked his head out of the neighboring tent. "No way," he slurred. "Monkey suit is back?"

Ponytail crawled from his shelter. "What's the deal with you, freak?" He took a step toward Jae. The other two men did the same, balling their fists.

Seriously, guys? You're leaving me no choice here. Jae thought.

He stood up. Unlike Boris, he towered over the men by three heads. He spread his arms and bellowed, spittle flying from his open mouth.

Goldie screeched and fell back on his ass. Ponytail stood rooted in place, eyes wide, mouth an 'O'. The front of Baldy's sweatpants grew dark.

Jae roared again, lips peeled back, canines revealed. The men screamed in tandem.

He stalked away, cheese wedge tucked beneath one arm, looking back once in the relaxed style of the Grand Matron, savoring the terror he saw in their eyes.

"I am not a hoax!" he shouted.

And from the look in their eyes, they believed him.

BLOOD AND DUST
BY JACK CAMPBELL JR

When the black limo rolled in to town, Pickfield County was caught in the grip of the worst drought in decades. No one could recall the last time that it had rained. A bone dry winter led to a summer as arid as the Sahara. The ground cracked, as if the earth has simply had enough and gave in to the endless torment of heat as dry as my mother's cornbread, God rest her soul.

That summer, the weight of the oppressive heat weighed all the adults down. They treated the lack of rain as if it were the Last Judgment. The city's farm-based economy wilted like the crops that laid limp and brown on the outskirts of town. Our parents walked with sluggish steps, faces to the bleached ground, as if refusing to acknowledge the sun's existence. But for a kid, summer is freedom. A drought-plagued summer break beat any school day in the Garden of Eden. My friends Billy and Johnny and I roamed the town like a pack of jackals on our K-mart BMX bicycles, swarming from one piece of shade to another, hooting and hollering just as loud as we had every summer before that. Dust plumes swelled behind our bicycles, giving rise to lingering brown clouds that choked siblings and pets and left them coughing in our wake. School was out, and water was scarce. Baths were rare, but that doesn't mean much to a ten year-old boy. Streaked with dirt and sweat, we ruled the gravel roads of our six square block city from sun up to sun down.

We first saw the limo on a particularly hot late-July afternoon. The end of summer break loomed over our heads like the dust. Our days were numbered, and we could feel August's approach, bringing with it uncomfortable clothes and overenthusiastic teachers. We took a break in front of the old hardware store, ditching our bikes on the sizzling concrete sidewalk and shoving each other playfully. We took turns getting Cokes from the broken pop machine on Main Street. We learned to love Coke that summer. The machine would give out free cans of Coca-Cola Classic if you knew how to go about it. The company that owned the machine only came through every couple of months. They fixed it sometime around the beginning of school. But that summer, we drank greedily in the shade of the two-story brick building. Time doesn't matter to a summer kid. Days are marked only by breakfast and bedtime. We may have been sitting there for minutes or hours when the limo pulled through.

To call it a limo gives a person the wrong idea. This wasn't some luxury vehicle with televisions, air conditioning, and AM/FM radio. Sunspots spoiled the once-ebony surface. The window tint bubbled with age. Mismatched chrome hubcaps decorated dented rims. One hub cap was missing entirely, revealing a rust-crusted wheel held on by lug nuts that looked like they would crumble under a wrench's touch. The rear driver-side fender had been patched with Bondo and never painted, while the front-bumper, once high-polished chrome, was filled with as many holes as an old man's smile. The limo rolled slow and smooth down Main Street, the driver hidden by the black velvet curtains that decorated the dark windows. The engine sputtered and missed, its parts rattling like a coiled copperhead. We stopped talking and watched it float down the street.

Billy burped and crushed his empty Coke can against the side of the building. "What the hell was that?"

I held the cold pop can against my cheek as the car took a wide turn down Fourth Street. "Looked like a limo—"

"I know it was a limo, dumbass."

"Didn't look like any limo I've ever seen." Johnny took slow calculated sips from his Coke, as if it might be the last he would ever taste.

"When did you ever see a limo?" Billy smirked at Johnny, his eyebrow raised.

"I've seen them in pictures."

"Looked like a piece of shit to me."

I drained the last of my Coke, sat the can on the ground and then stomped on it. Billy punched me in the shoulder, grabbed his bike, and rode off laughing. I chased after him on my own. Johnny drank down the rest of his pop and followed behind, yelling at us to wait up. We left him behind all summer.

By the next morning, everyone in town was talking about the black limousine. We went to the corner gas station and milled around. Stations like this don't exist anymore. It was more than a gas station. It was the center of male society in the village of Binton and one of the few air-conditioned buildings open to public loitering. Old men and bored farmers sat in a circle drinking coffee and shooting the breeze. The gas furnace in the corner had a permanent dent where three generation of Binton asses had sat on it.

"He's a goddamn weirdo." Old Harold, the town mayor, scratched his big belly through the Key coveralls that he wore 365 days a year, no matter what the weather. We buried him in new pair when he died that fall.

"Almost guarantee it." Glen nodded, spitting tobacco juice in to a white Styrofoam cup.

Bob, the station owner, sipped coffee from the only glass mug in the place, ceramic thing that his wife had made. Rumor had it that the cup had once been white. Twenty years of coffee and vehicle service darkened it to a light tan. "I heard he is in town on the depot demolition."

Like most of the towns in the area, Binton had sprung up on the rail line back when train cars full of corn and soy beans raced across the grassy plains on great iron rails. The depot wasn't any more of a depot than the limo was a limo. The Methodist ladies group sold hot dogs at little league games out of a bigger shed. Like many of the buildings in town, the depot had outlived its usefulness. Paint peeled from the walls in brittle flakes, leaving bare, rotting wood exposed to the elements. The roof fell in during the last big windstorm. Harold called the railroad and told them that if they didn't bulldoze it, he was going to burn the goddamn thing to the ground. They decided to send in a crew to demolish the depot and remove the old rails.

"You see the son of a bitch driving it?" Harold leaned forward, shaking his head, his massive hands massaging his swollen knees.

I edged forward towards the circle of men. It was common knowledge that kids weren't welcome in their bullshit sessions, but they usually ignored us. I've heard from men of my generation that kids are better seen than heard. Hell, I preferred not to be noticed, at all.

Billy grabbed a Hershey bar from the shelf and dropped it down the front of his black AC/DC t-shirt. Bob nearly choked on his coffee. He sat the cup down and strode over to Billy with big, lumbering steps. Billy backed in to a corner between the motor oil and the wiper blades. Bob snatched him by the back of the neck.

"Goddamn it, no one's gonna want that thing now. You won't want it either as hot as it is out there. You'll be lucky if you don't dig chocolate out of your bellybutton." Bob open the door and pushed Billy outside. "You guys, too. Go on. Get. Go cause trouble, just don't do it here."

Glen chuckled and shook his head, as old men often do when dealing with boys. He spit in his Styrofoam cup, and we ran out the door to our bikes.

We found Billy about a half a block down the street, leaning back against an elm tree. The bark was warm to the touch and as brittle as the paint on the depot. Dehydration browned the serrated leaves. Billy sat in the shade, licking melted chocolate off the inside of the candy bar wrapper. We sat with him. He motioned across the lot to the old depot with his stolen snack. A half a dozen men worked lazily, drinking from a water cooler and taking turns smashing holes in the depot walls with a sledgehammer.

"Which one do you think is him?" Billy asked.

We couldn't see the men very well from a distance through the constant hanging haze of dust. I scratched my chigger-eaten legs until they were bloody and looked at the men through squinted eyes. I don't know what I was looking for, some biblical mark of the beast, some grotesque deformity, maybe even a black cowboy hat. But I searched for some mark of evil like those I had seen on TV. I didn't know any better.

Johnny pulled an ant off the back of his neck and rolled it between his fingers. "Does it matter? He's just some guy."

"Bullshit." With his serious eyes and his chocolate-covered cheeks, Billy looked like some strange compilation of his father and his kid brother. "Nah, this is important, man. I've heard things."

"Oh yeah, chocolate boy?" I tossed Billy the rag that my mom made me carry around in my back pocket. "We would have heard a lot more if you could keep your hands to yourself."

Billy wiped his mouth. "I heard my old man telling mom all about it. The guy is some sort of pedophile. He travels around abducting children."

I laughed. "Are you serious?"

Johnny rocked back and forth, his knees tucked to his chest. "Wouldn't the cops arrest him he he'd done something like that?"

Billy smirked, looking Johnny up and down as if that was the dumbest thing he had ever heard. "When was the last time you saw cops around here?" The Sheriff's Office was located in the county seat, over a forty-minute drive out of town. I didn't even know anyone who had ever called them.

"You are so full of shit." I got up, stretched out my legs and picked up my bike.

"Laugh all you want. Just don't get in that car." Billy rolled the wrapper in to a ball and tossed it away. "If you get in that car, no one will ever see you again."

I rode off, refusing to look at Billy. My hands shook on the handlebars of my bike. I rode down the street towards the workers, staring hard at them. I didn't see the trench in the road where the rail used to be until I'd already hit it. My front wheel dropped in to the hole where the tracks once sat. I flew over the handlebars, nearly folding in half when I collided with the hard ground.

I laid still for a second, catching my bearings and checking my body for broken bones. I had wrecked right next to where the limo sat parked. I heard the door open and looked up. A tall man stepped out, as thin as a skeleton. Long, greasy black hair strung over his eyes, hiding them from view. His long legs, as spindly as a spider's, chewed up entire miles as he strode towards me. Tattoos etched his exposed shoulders. I don't remember any of them, but in my nightmares, they are all sort of demonic and devilish device.

"Are you okay, kid?" He reached a hand towards me. I took it, but then recoiled from his grip. Pale, puckered scar tissue covered a hand with only three fingers, stretching up to the middle of his bicep where the tattoos began. I scurried away like a cockroach from the kitchen light and grabbed my bike. I rode as fast as I could. Looking over my shoulder, I saw him push his greasy hair back with his mangled hand as he watched me flee.

I rode straight home and locked myself in to my stifling hot bedroom. I hid beneath the blankets like Billy's kid brother hid from the boogeyman. It was the only time I'd been home in the daylight all summer. I forced myself to breathe slowly until finally, exhausted, I fell in to a deep sleep with the blankets still tucked firmly over my head.

Nightmares plagued my dreams. A deformed hand, like a hook of bone, clutched my ankle. My skin smoked, bubbled, and died, leaving pale scars like the skin of the limo driver. Red eyes, glistening like drops of fresh blood, peeked between long, greasy strands of pitch black hair. The man's laugh seemed to attack from everywhere all at once, high-pitched like the squeal of a bat. When he pushed back his hair, I didn't see a monster, but my own father.

I awoke late in the evening, drenched in sweat. My sheets were covered with muddy smears from my dirt-covered body. I kicked them off, sweltering in the heat. I went to the refrigerator and chugged water directly from the pitcher that we kept on the top shelf. I could feel the cold of the water as it trickled down through my body.

The sun was about to set, but I decided to go out anyway. Mom worked double shifts down at the cafe and wouldn't be back for a couple of hours. My old man took off at the beginning of the summer, promising to return with a job and money. He never came back. I hadn't heard from him in weeks. There wasn't a job. There wasn't money. There weren't even phone calls anymore. There was about as much hope for his return as there was for the withering crops outside of town.

I hopped on my bike and rode towards Main Street, hoping to catch Billy and Johnny before they went home. The setting sun glowed orange through the thick dust in the atmosphere. The sky burned as wildly as the fires of Hell.

I spotted Johnny a couple of blocks down the street, riding away from me. I yelled to him. He skidded to a stop on his bike and waved back. He rode hard towards me as I biked casually his way. He didn't see the limo until it had already driven over him. The car's breaks squealed. Its long rear-end fishtailed over Johnny as it came to a stop. They were no more than a hundred feet ahead of me, directly in the unmarked intersection of two gravel roads. The door flew open, and the man with three fingers hurried around to the rear of the car.

Johnny whimpered, a pile of flesh and bone in middle of the road. He screamed, his high-pitched voice filled with desperation as the driver advanced.

"Stay away from me! Don't touch me! Please..." Johnny's broken form shuddered in the burning orange glow of the sun.

The limo driver paced in small circles, tugging at his greasy hair with his ruined hand. He stopped and looked straight at me. I couldn't see his eyes, but I felt them, those eyes from the dream, red and glowing. We stared at each other for what could have been hours, but was probably only a few seconds. I imagined him pulling his hair back to reveal the father that had abandoned me. Just then, he rushed back to the limo. The rear wheels spun, begging for traction and hurling gravel on Johnny as the vehicle sped off.

I pedaled as hard as I could to where Johnny laid. That one hundred feet seemed to be miles. My legs grew heavy. I couldn't breathe. I stopped and tripped over my bike, trying to dismount. I crawled the rest of the way on my hands and knees, the sharp gravel digging in to my dirty palms.

Blood flowed from Johnny's nose and mouth. He breathed in shallow, wheezing breaths. The sun's hellfire reflection burned in his wide eyes as his head shook lightly from side to side.

"Don't let him put me in the car." Johnny's voice squeaked. "Don't let him take me."

I held Johnny's limp hand and screamed for help. By the time they found us, my voice was hoarse from screaming, and Johnny was dead. Harold grabbed me, dragging me away from Johnny and pulling me in to those old, stained Key coveralls. "It's okay." His voice shook, and I knew it wasn't.

I felt a drop upon my forehead, warm and wet. It wasn't Harold's tears, but rain. The moment of Johnny's death marked the end of the drought in Pickfield County. It was as if Johnny's offering of blood had satisfied the rain gods. It poured for three days. Reverend Taylor said it was God crying for Johnny.

Sometimes I think it was my own tears, the ones I hadn't cried over my old man leaving. The ones I didn't cry when my mom died years later, or when my wife gave in to cancer years after that. That three days of rain used up a lifetime of my tears.

The Sheriff said they would find the man who did it. They probably did. I don't know. So many things happened outside of my little bubble, the little dome of existence that Billy, Johnny, and I ruled. Things like justice seemed insignificant in the face of such tenable powers as blood and dust.

Fifteen Thirty- Two
BY CHRISTINA KLARENBEEK

I always wanted to be one of the cool kids. Now I'm cold, all the time. Valikov tried to warn me that never dying wasn't the same as living forever but I didn't listen. I was too busy trying to buy my way in with the popular crowd. I paid Jeff five grand a month, for six months, just to find out that being a vampire sucks.

Before I made the change, I thought I was going to wake up with the power to waggle my eyebrows and have women fawn over me.

"Come hither fair maiden," I'd say. And they would. If you watch the movies, beautiful women swoon and gasp in ecstasy when you bite them.

Bullshit. If you don't do it right, they scream and try to claw your eyes out. I woke up the same awkward clod I'd always been and getting girls was more difficult than ever. The only ones I had a shot with were the groupies. They talk, a lot. You screw up with one of them and you'll never see a naked woman again. These chicks all expect to be bitten, on the neck. Tradition. And they expect to enjoy it.

Timing. For a short guy like me, without a functioning dick, it was a logistical nightmare. Yeah, you heard me, and no amount of vasodilators was gonna help. That's another thing they don't tell you. I still had plenty of blood, but no flow. I'd expected to be pasty, 'cause vampires don't get any sun. I hadn't expected to be the stomach turning pale blue of death in some parts and the nasty purplish red of a beating in others, all because my patron got distracted by a blonde while my blood was settling.

That whole pale vampire shtick got started because face paint used to contain arsenic. Ya see, even back in the day, vamps had to wear powder to pass for living. It didn't have anything to do with the sun, but you gotta tell folks something. Now we have multiple shades of Covergirl, but that shit is expensive when you have to cover everything. The nearly dead don't sweat, but living women do, and if you try to get with one, your makeup is gonna rub off in places and, well, it ain't good. So it's groupies or nothing. Mostly it's nothing and a whole lot of it.

No sex. No food. No drink. No drugs. It's all show. You can eat all you want if you don't mind going to the john to throw it back up. You sure ain't gonna digest any of it. That goes for blood too. You wait till the crazy bitch is orgasming before you bite her. You make sure you don't bite her bad enough she needs medical help, just a little nip, and then you sort of smear the blood around. Lastly, you make a big production of pressing your thumb against the wound to staunch the near nonexistent flow while she's still riding the wave. For a couple of minutes you're her hero, but you don't suck jack shit unless you like puking up blood. I don't.

All those vamps you see drinking their special red wine. Fucking bulimics every one of them. I used to like a beer at the end of the day, maybe a shot of whiskey, the odd joint. The thing is, all that shit has to break down and get absorbed into the blood stream before it can fuck with your head. No flow, no buzz. Being a vampire sucks. So I decided to end it.

That's how I learned the sun thing was a myth. I'd been skulking around in the dark ever since the change, cause that's what you do. At least, that's what all the other vampires seemed to do. I was nervous sitting on the bench waiting for the sunrise. Talk about anti-climactic. There were no flames. There weren't even any sparks.

Nada.

Next up, I slit my wrists. It hurt like a bitch but it didn't bleed. It grossed out the girls worse than the claw marks on my face. The nearly dead don't heal and we can't go to ER when we need stitches. I had to do them myself. They weren't pretty but they were permanent.

I ruled out hanging and overdosing without even bothering to try. A stake through my non-beating heart? I figured that would end in more botched home repair. So burning it was. I didn't want to screw it up so I made sure I burned myself but good. I bought two forties of whiskey, and I gathered every dried twig I could find. I built a small pyre under that same park bench.

Symbolism.

As soon as I saw the sun, I doused myself and stuck the match. The pain was instant and constant. I screamed until I couldn't scream. It fucking hurt. There are no words.

Some bastard jogger found me. EMS offered to get him some counseling while they were bandaging his hands. Me they shoved into a sack. I guess when you're a barely recognizable crisp with no pulse, people assume you're dead. Completely dead. And why wouldn't they. I don't blame them. For what happened next, I do blame Jeff.

The fucker showed up at the morgue to identify me by my ring, which he kept. Then he told the coroner I was Jewish. It did save me from embalming, I'll give him that, but a decent guy would have had me cremated. Jeff's a sadistic prick, which is why I'm laying here telling my story to worms.

They say there's a sucker born every minute. I was born at 15:32. I'm not sure when I'll finally die.

BEAUTIFUL WASTELAND
BY J LILY CORBIE

Ever since the tree grew in the living room, Danna had been afraid of going home. It watched her in the curious way of all trees, and its leaves rustled in the still air. She had started coming and going by the back door, but even when she didn't see it, she knew it was there.

Worse, she was positive it knew she was there.

When she stepped through the back door, she could hear the leaves turning, and she shuddered. She clutched the keys tight to her chest, eying the new crack in the wall. A curl of ivy had sprouted since that morning. She took the kitchen shears from the drawer, but the lead tendril twitched.

No use. She put the shears back and tiptoed as far around it as possible. She spotted new cracks in the wall as she went. She walked a straight line down the center of the hall, turning her head as she passed the living room so she couldn't see the tree.

It had all started with a newspaper article: Plans Move Forward to Remove Eyesore. Beneath the headline was a photo of her favorite childhood retreat.

Everyone knew Skater's Haven was haunted. Didn't the narrow trickle of water they called a creek run uphill between its steep concrete banks? Danna hadn't been a skater, but it wasn't like they cared. The skaters ignored her when she climbed over the layers of graffiti to walk under the trees.

Though an overpass roared above, the sound disappeared under the branches. She sat in the dappled green and gold light, and she felt safe. While the breeze rustled the leaves and the rest of the world disappeared, she didn't think of ghosts or hauntings. She thought of the spirit and life unique to that tiny scrap of urban forest.

Even as an adult, Danna had returned. She refused chances to move far away because she couldn't imagine her life without Skater's Haven. The article called it a wasteland and detailed intentions to raze it to the ground. After she had cried until she was hollow, she made a plan.

Fences were quickly erected around Skater's Haven. Holes were made in them almost as fast. It hadn't been hard for Danna to sneak in and creep between the sleeping mechanical hulks.

That desperate night, she had climbed beyond freshly sand-blasted walls and stepped under the trees. Silence enveloped her. She breathed it in and fell to her knees. Her selection had been random; the first plant that looked like it might survive in a pot. She watered it with tears and hugged the pot to her chest through the whole trip back to her car.

Now the pot and its strange occupant waited for her on the table by her bed. She'd been through countless guides and spent hours on the internet and she still didn't know what to call it.

"This isn't what it was supposed to be like," she told the plant. Unlike the others, it didn't move. It hadn't grown very much. It bent toward the window, the leaves turned toward the sun. "I was trying to help."

She leaned close, testing the soil with a fingertip. Still damp. There was a new runner sprouting, so she opened the drawer and pulled out a trowel and a waiting peat pot partially filled with dirt. She eased the runner out and into its temporary home. "Maybe this time," she whispered, misting the new pot.

Danna didn't sleep well. When she woke, there were cracks in her bedroom wall and hints of green catching the morning light.

She dressed for work in the dark of the closet. She grabbed the peat pot and carried it through the house, by briars with newly opening leaves and tendrils that reached for her as she passed. Bark creaked and the beams of the house moaned. She had to turn the knob and yank to open the door.

There was a tree in the middle of her driveway. It came up to her shoulder. It hadn't been there when she parked, and she leaned over it and said, "You can't block my way in and out. We agreed." She grasped it near the ground and pulled, but it didn't give. "Please?" she asked. She pulled harder. Finally, Danna threw her purse and the pot on the ground and grabbed it with both hands. "It wasn't supposed to be like this!"

When the roots gave out, she stumbled back and stepped on her purse. Something inside it cracked. She snatched the purse and now lopsided pot from the ground and tossed them into the car. Danna looked at the sapling in her hand, and she dropped it into the passenger seat, too.

The roads were still mostly empty. Danna drove slowly, delaying the moment when she had to see what was left of Skater's Haven.

The bulldozers and wood chippers and machines she couldn't name were long gone, but their signature remained. Beneath the overpass there wasn't a single hint of life. Just a gaping wound in the earth.

She carried the pot and sapling at a distance, pinching each between two fingers. There was new graffiti on the banks of the creek and the water still flowed the wrong way. Rains and snows had come and gone, rounding the earth and softening the hard lines. Here and there in the dawn light, dry sticks and brown leaves thrust out of the dirt.

"Please grow," she whispered while she dug a hole. "Please grow," she repeated as she pressed the sapling into it. Danna blinked and tears splashed on the earth. She had a bottle of water, and she poured half of it onto the little tree.

"This is your home. Grow here and you won't need my house anymore."

She repeated the ritual with the runner, and she tried not to look too closely at the dead plants arrayed around her. Instead, she returned to her car and arrived early at work.

When she got home, there were new trees in her front yard. They were taller than her. She paid a man to mow once a week, and since his last visit, she had somehow acquired bushes that came to her waist. Everywhere the sun reached, the grass was up to her knees. She couldn't have gotten to her front door if she wanted.

There was a citation in the mailbox warning her about the condition of the yard. She'd never received one before, but the warning had a note about her 'persistent, ongoing problem' and her 'continued refusal to rectify the situation.' It said if she didn't solve the problem herself, the city would do it for her and she'd be held liable for all costs.

She wondered if they knew how to solve the problem. Flowers had blossomed during the day, and every single one was pointing toward her when she walked through the door. She dropped the paper on her kitchen counter and didn't say anything about it.

The vines in the kitchen had crept over half of the wall, and points of green watched her in the hall. "If I stop cutting the trees down, will you stop?" she asked. Silence pressed against her in response. "You have to stop growing here and start growing in your old home."

There was absolutely no sound. The tree had gone still. Danna walked into the bedroom and leaned over the potted plant. "I wanted to save you because you felt like home. I made a mistake. I'm so sorry."

She curled up on the bed with the blanket drawn over her, but she didn't sleep. When the alarm signaled a new day, she trod on moss instead of carpet. There was a tree taller than her right at the bumper of her car.

"You can't keep me here," she said, and she walked to the corner and called a coworker for a ride.

Over the following weeks, she couldn't check on her latest transplant. She sat listlessly at her desk, accomplishing nothing. The morning she tried to open her back door and discovered it was blocked, it was a relief.

Trees encroached upon the house, towering over the roof and pressing against the windows. Danna lost track of the days as she roamed from room to room. Creepers reached out to stroke her hair and caress her skin as she passed.

"I'm running out of food," she told the tree in the living room. She leaned against the trunk, and she gazed up through the branches to the ceiling. "I don't know what I'm supposed to do. If you let me out, I could get food." The leaves were all turned toward her. All she could hear was branches scraping over glass and the wind in the bushes.

Danna fell asleep there, and when she woke, fruit weighed the branches of the tree. Danna wept.

Her attempts to escape the house failed. When the power went out, she didn't know if it was because she was unable to pay the bill or if the forest had somehow caused it. She clutched her cell while as the battery ran down. No one had called since she'd been trapped inside, and she didn't know who to call in those last hours. When the phone was dead, she dropped it on the floor. It only took a day before it was covered in moss.

One day, the faucet coughed and spit and produced no water. Danna reeled away and collapsed at the roots of the tree. "No water," she said. "I don't know how you're alive. There's no sun. There's nothing alive but you and me. I never noticed you didn't have birds. Or bugs." She turned her head to chafe her cheek against the bark. "I guess I noticed the bugs. It's part of why I loved you. But I miss the birds." She curled into a ball, pressing her hands over her head. "Soon it'll be just you."

She slept, or maybe she woke up. Danna didn't remember the last time she knew for sure whether she was waking or dreaming. The beds of her nails were green. She raked her fingers through her hair, and fresh leaves snapped from stems in her scalp. Danna winced and rubbed her hands through the moss without looking to see if they were red with blood or green with sap.

When she stumbled into the bathroom—or what had been the bathroom—she discovered a spring bubbling through the floor. She wasn't in a position to be picky, so she drank. It tasted of city, of all the life she could no longer reach. She took in as much as she could stand, greedy for the memories.

In the days that followed, a stream formed. It flowed through the hall and made a pool in the kitchen. Danna immersed herself in it, blew all the air out of her lungs and lay at the bottom. She thought of breathing in the water, but a shudder gripped the house at the foundation. She surfaced to find the vines writhing. She heard branches rubbing and bark shrieking. Fear filled up her lungs, and tendrils grasped at her as she crawled by.

On all fours, she peered through the window. Bushes bowed and branches twisted so she could see the bulldozer in the street. She heard men talking, caught words like *eyesore* and *progress*. The fear wasn't hers. She blew it out and refused to take it back.

She opened the window, but trunks and branches snapped back into place so there wasn't room for her to escape. "What do you want?" she asked. "I saved you once, and look at what you've done!"

The vines pulled at her wrists and ankles. She allowed them to drag her down the hall to her long-abandoned bedroom. The pot was still on the bedside table, and the vines pushed it toward her.

Danna held up her hands and backed away. The moss tried to curl around her feet, and she hopped and yanked her ankles free. As she passed the kitchen, the back door creaked open. There was a clear path, and she broke for it, but the door slammed shut so she collided with it.

"That's what you want?" she asked, leaning against the door with a hand curled around the knob. "I take you away and you do this again somewhere else?"

The entire house shook. The ground rumbled, but Danna wasn't feeling the forest. The bulldozer was coming. Briars dug their thorns into her flesh and branches creaked and the timbers of the house moaned. Danna sat on the floor and she laughed.

THE DEVIL IS IN...

BY T FOX DUNHAM

The Holy Tome of Truman
Book I

. . . at the end of the end of the world.

Wild mushrooms patches grew on my crotch and along my inner thighs. The pink tumors oozed pus, rubbed raw by the synthetic fur of the animated character as I walked the highways of old America. We all had tumors. We all had the Maxx. By the dimmer-time—what we used to call night—my Gary the Groundhog suit reeked, which nauseated me but served to repel the wild dog packs that hunted the deserts. I still wore my old work costume to convince raiders, pirates and just murderers that I was insane and not worth the trouble—plenty of easier targets to rob or eat. It also protected from the endless lashing of photos. I baked in the fur; however, it protected my skin, and the floppy brown ears shielded my eyes from the violet rays that blinded most. And I'd grown comfortable existing as a groundhog. I didn't want to be human anymore. Humans fucked up the sun.

I'd dragged my body from Southern Park to Empire Land, what was once old Atlanta and New York City, searching for my wife. Giant statues of cartoon characters stood sentry along the road like old Roman gods guarding the approach to the city. Popcorn bags, balloons and broken cell phones littered the desolate countryside, and the dust blew as far as the horizon. The bay outside the old city of Baltimore had evaporated, and touring boats sank into the powder. I needed directions, and I spotted a man bearing a bulbous stomach rolling around in the grains. I walked out to him, darting the wreckage of the old arcade piers. Our star swelled in the evening sky.

"Taking a bath?" I asked. The sun burned his skin to charcoal.

"Why the fuck do you care?" he yelled at the sky.

"I don't," I said. "You seen a motorcycle gang in the last few days? Maybe this woman riding the back of a Harley?" I climbed down and showed him the photo taken the morning before Sally and I got married—that happy time just after the corporation promoted me.

"I bought some pot off them," he said. "Keep following I-95." He drove his face back into the ground and swallowed mouthfuls of sand.

"What the hell are you trying to do?" I asked.

"No sun's going to swallow my ass," he said, choking. "I'm doing it myself. Drown myself in the Chesapeake like I should have years ago. I still got that right. Get the fuck out of here, Charlie. And take your rodent ass with you."

"I'm a groundhog," I said.

"Fuck."

I left him to the healing hands of the strangling sand. Random and chaotic events wrecked our plans in life. We didn't opt to be born nor did we select stations in life. But we could control our deaths, and most people choose to end their lives by their own hand instead of allowing our indifferent star. He deserved a good death.

I moved on, following the cracked concrete of the road. The evening cooled, and I could look up at the sky without squinting. I longed for company, another voice instead of the one in my head. I obsessed on the nascent times with my wife—what I said to her when I proposed. *An interesting life is the path to misery. I'm not exciting, but you'll always be numb and no longer in any pain.* I'd been promoted to head waiter at a hotel in Colonial Land, in the old city of Philadelphia, so I could finally ask. *Marry me, and I'll give you the same every day. You'll never have to worry about me changing.*

One of the tumors burst, staining my leg with bloody ooze. The stench nauseated me, and I buckled from the pain. I couldn't keep hiking without treatment, and when the pain eased, I moved on, looking for a barber-surgeon. They were common along the caravan routes and in demand. By morning, I spotted a sign for a barber-surgeon.

Will cut for weed. Car ahead.

He'd setup shop in monorail car that had turned on its side. Disney had built a massive transportation network connecting all of its parks, and the lines ran along the major highways, all running on solar power. I knocked on the hatch, and a heavy metal rocker beckoned me to enter. Soot smeared his face black, and he wore a matching leather jerkin, torn leather pants and carried a broken electric guitar on his back. The gangly physician tipped his top hat to me, spilling dirt on my face.

"Why are you wearing that shit?" I asked.

"Before the world went to hell, I had to be respectable and establish myself to my colleagues. I was always kissing ass or having those pompous jackasses over the house to try to get them to fund my research."

"So you're a metal dude now?"

"I grew up wanting to be a guitarist for KISS. My parents made me go to Hopkins."

"Now you can do both."

"The apocalypse fucking rocks," he said and played air guitar.

"Disney owns all rights to your past," I advised. It had been written into the

Bill of Rights. "So spare me the nostalgia."

"I hate corporations," he said while cleaning his scalpels. Solar panels powered his iPad, and he played heavy metal. "They only wanted to fund the crap that made them money like erectile dysfunction. If I'd had the funding, I might have understood what was happening and maybe reversed it."

"Sorry your life was so bad, doc" I said. "But can you get rid of these? They're a pain in my ass." I unzipped my character costume then pulled off my ripped boxers. The lumps oozed down my thighs and stank of rotting meat.

"Call me Doctor Death-Metal," he said, examining lumps bulging from my skin. "Son of a whore! Your Maxx is progressed. You must have been one of the early cases before we started falling into the sun."

"I have a personal connection to one of the original patients," I said. "Nostalgia's contagious. We don't have the time for it. So just cut them off."

Doctor Death-Metal waved for me to lie down on a threadbare couch and handed me a chipped clay jug. "Chug it," he said.

The sweet juice burned down my throat. "Anesthetic?"

"Cactus juice," he said. "Enjoy your flight."

The mescaline hit me, and my eyes blossomed eyes that blossomed dandelion wishes. I saw the stars again through the rusting ceiling of the old monorail car. He gripped his instrument, slicing at my leg. The blade morphed into Sally's mouth, and she chewed at the lumps growing down my body, leaving bloody rips in my skin.

"So you did research before?" I asked, floating from the drugs.

"I isolated the Maxx," Doctor Death-Metal said.

"I remember you now. You *were* a rock star."

"I hold doctorates in both physics and medicine," he said, cutting and slicing and mutilating me.

"You figured out some weird shit about the Maxx."

"I was close to unlocking the secrets of the universe through the disease," he said. "It possessed unique properties and morphology, perhaps through exposure to the gravity well during its incipient period when it was a wee baby.

"What weird shit?" I asked.

"It had the capacity to warp the fabric of space-time."

"Not bad for a dick disease." He lanced a tumor on my knee, and the pain seared up my leg.

"So what do you do at the end of the world?" he asked.

"I do what I've always done. I'm a witness in a groundhog suit."

"A witness for God?"

"I was there," I said. "I saw how it all went down."

"Play your role, groundhog, and tell me."

⚜⚜⚜

The Holy Tome of Truman
Book II

In 2020, the American people elected The Disney Corporation to the office of President of the United States with the promise to employ everyone through a nation-wide theme park—roller coasters and cartoon statues from New York City to Seattle; monorails that drove twice the speed of sound connected the various sub-parks, and clean housing in underground units below the parks. Adaptive construction began the same year, and by 2025, Disney America opened, quickly becoming the world's vacation destination. The corporation made good on its promise, ending poverty, providing healthcare and education; thus crime diminished. Everyone loved America now, since the corporation had to maintain good relations with its international patrons, and because of this, all war ended. Cruise ships docked hourly at the nation's ports, and human civilization entered a new golden age, at least until the days shortened and snow fell on most of the nations. 2027 recorded some of the lowest temperatures of the century. Levels of solar radiation fluctuated, and minor ice ages had cooled the world before. The harsh winters hindered tourism, and Americans suffered. Disney Corporation paid their workers through a profit sharing system in addition to minimal wage. When the company prospered, the people prospered. Without park attendance, the profit sharing system failed to pay. Workers defaulted on their loans, failed to pay their mortgages and couldn't afford hot dogs and hamburgers even with their employee discounts. The company nearly went bankrupt. Disney engineers attempted solutions like creating winter themes for the parks and a new line of holographic movies based on the cold, but it couldn't make up for lost profits from the parks. The country failed, so the board of directors in their hubris assembled the best scientists and engineers to create a plan to change the climate of North America that would adjust the climate. Winters would be lighter—no more Nor'easters or Chicago blizzards, and people could put away their coats forever.

Now all they had to do was apply it. It was a formidable problem, changing the climate of the earth, but this was already being done, though at a much slower pace. The physicists and climate experts occupied the floor of Disney's premier Philadelphia House—old Independence Hall—and discussed the problem of changing the environment on a global scale. For months they argued, offering no real solutions to this impossible problem. Doctor Werner Kerner proposed accelerating global warming through increased carbon production, but Disney rejected the idea because of the negative environmental associations. Akira Fuji suggested using atomic bombs to warm the atmosphere, but this was also rejected. Connor Jenkins considered changing the genetic structure of humans to endure the cold, but DNA manipulation would only work with the next generation. None of the ideas passed board. Disney's America survived until the spring, but analysts predicted bankruptcy by Christmas.

Then, a savior appeared. Jedidiah T. Cinderfield spoke and acted like an old southern preacher, wearing a black parson's suit, cowboy hat and leather boots. Cinderfield never looked quite right to me. His emaciated figure caused me to wonder whether he was a refugee from a two-dimensional universe, and his legs and arms jerked when he walked like his limbs hung from puppet strings. "Saints!" he said. "I do declare." He strolled into the meeting room and pulled out a cigar from a silver holder. "Can I smoke?" he asked me. I was a waiter at the hotel.

Before I could tell him no, Cinderfield took out a small blow torch from his satchel and lit his stogie. The room soon reeked.

"How did you get through security?" Vice President Jefferson Hopkins asked.

"Easy," he said, puffing. "I'm the devil."

"You're delusional," Hopkins said, adjusting his silk tie. "Disney Corporate has proven that there is no afterlife. We're building Disney Heaven in 2030 to simulate the experience. We're copyrighting the phrase: *Died and Gone to Disney World.*"

"I didn't say I was Satan. I am the devil. At least, I'm playing the role, darling. I am your new devil, and I've come to you with a deal."

"Somebody call security," Hopkins said.

"I've got the goods," Cinderfield said. Puff. Puff. "I will make your shareholders billions and keep your slaves fed." The devil dominated—the way he walked, his attitude, how he blew smoke into Hopkin's pink face—and Hopkins was desperate.

"What do you propose?" Hopkins asked.

"I have resources that you don't and technology far advanced from yours."

"You're as crazy as my mother," Hopkins said.

"Maybe. But I'm sincere." Cinderfield pulled out old-fashioned blueprints. "It's all about gravity. It may be the weakest of the four cosmic forces, but there's just so damn much."

"You want to manipulate gravity," Hopkins said. "Impossible."

"No. Quite possible. Mass does it all the time." The scientists stirred at the concept, some denying it could be done or others claiming credit for the idea.

"We just need to put Goldilocks to bed," Cinderfield said.

"You mean move the earth closer to the sun but keeping it in the narrow zone that creates liquid water?" Doctor Moira Goldman asked.

"Gave that woman a cigar! But not mine."

"Impossible," Hopkins said.

"Gravitons," fenced Cinderfield. "All matter and energy exist on a wavelength as both particles and waves. Light. Gravity. Even time. We merely need to manipulate the strings, change the vibrations, the frequency, and we can take your basic everyday photons and shift them into particles of gravity. We just run them through Higgs bosons. Won't take much. I'll even throw in the enough power to run your theme park for the next thousand years."

Hopkins discussed the notion with the scientific body. They scoffed at first, but eventually their debate provided plausible concepts, ideas. It could have worked theoretically, at least in basic principle, but no one pretended to understand application.

"What do you want?" Hopkins asked.

"I want to save the country," he said. "My patriotic duty."

"Bullshit."

"I have my reasons which I will keep to myself. You can pay me something, free hotdogs for a year maybe."

"You're insane," Moira said.

"Can you build us a model and prove your concept?" Hopkins asked.

"Do you drink milk from swollen cow tits?" Cinderfield asked and puffed the cigar near to a nub. "I don't require blind faith like other deities. I'll give you the specs for some experiments. We can build the infinity engine near here in the mountains."

"If you can do this, I'll make you king of California," said Hopkins.

"Not necessary," he said, and then he went over the blueprints, going over the mechanics and basic theory. They planned for the next two days, and by the third, the devil had satisfied the scientists and Hopkins. I watched the sessions, taking orders and delivering food and beer. I had my own questions, concerns, and they were making decisions that would affect all life on the earth. I felt a duty to represent the collective, so when Cinderfield left the room to take a piss, I followed him into the bathroom. He unzipped in front of the urinal and passed his water.

"You're not the antichrist. You're just a traveling salesman."

Cinderfield stomped his foot and whooped. "You got it, slick. What let the cat out?"

"My father peddled Booth Gin to seventeen different countries."

"I reckon your daddy loved his own product," Cinderfield said. "You hated him. I can see the spite in those peepers."

"He whored around, cheating on my mother. I have two sisters we didn't know about."

"Nice to have family," Cinderfield said, still pissing. "I used to have a thousand siblings. We hatched from eggs."

"Eggs?" I asked.

He ignored me. "Do you have a family?"

"Sally, my wife, is a maid here. I don't know if I can keep her happy." We'd fought that morning. She was tired of living in a studio unit below the ground and wanted a place in the sun.

"Well slick," he said. "I could use some help. You want to work for me? I'll give you plenty of the green stuff."

I sighed, ready to surrender my integrity for Disney Dollars if it saved my marriage. "What do you need me to do?"

"Two things," he said. "First, tell me more about your father."

"Why?" I asked. I felt like he was playing with me.

"Curiosity. I need to know something of your character."

"There's something you're not telling me," I said.

"Christ on the cross," he replied. "But you don't have much of a choice, not if you want to keep that wife of yours happy."

"A loser," I said. "Your standard narcissist who was driven by his own addictions and pleasure centers of his brain until he destroyed everyone in his life. And he was one of the first patients to be infected with the Maxx."

"What's this Maxx?" Cinderfield inquired.

"You're fucking with me," I said.

"Always. But I'm still ignorant to it." I studied his face for a hint of sarcasm, but the serious look in his eyes never wavered. Everyone on earth knew about the Maxx. The corporation had tried to stem the spread of the disease by educating its employees in Disney health programs to watch for the associated tumors growing on the skin of sexual partners. No cure could be found. Disney Pharmaceuticals developed suppressants that kept the disease from flaring up.

"It's a fucking disease. Researchers have traced childhood to a couple of patients who slept with a cheap New Orleans hooker."

"She was patient zero?" Cinderfield asked, still urinating. "Divine wrath?"

"No one knows how she was infected or who she really was. She called herself Constance Starry, and she claimed she was infected when an alien abducted her because she was sexy and would be the perfect bait to spread its engineered disease."

"Vulgar!" he said. "Why did they call it the Maxx?"

"Maxx Gill," I responded. "And what's the second thing you want me to do?"

"Flush, fucker. Flush. And that's it."

I pushed the button on the urinal, and he wrote me a check for fifty thousand dollars. I didn't realize it at the time that Cinderfield knew the end of the world was coming. Money would become worthless, so he'd been writing checks all day for exuberant amounts. I walked out of that bathroom and quit my job. My wife was upstairs cleaning the rooms, and I waited until she came home to her underground unit to tell her.

"You're an idiot," Sally said when I told her, showing her the check. She undid the pink bow tied in her auburn hair. "This man's a con artist—or worse. Let's wait to see if his machine works first before we try cashing it."

"We should celebrate," I said, running my finger down the smooth skin of her neck and resting on it on her collar bone mole.

"I can't keep my eyes open, Harry," she said. "I've been working since six." She turned over on the couch and slept. I turned on my feed and watched them breaking ground that night on the new gravity engine.

After a crash program, Disney finished the compound. They'd blown the top off a hill outside of old Philadelphia and built machine into the stone. At the base, a particle accelerator generated Higgs bosons that then converted light rays into gravitons by changing away the strings vibrated. It generated its own power. Disney promised to switch it off if the machine malfunctioned or created a deleterious effect on the planet. I watched with my wife as the CEO of Disney threw the comical lever, turning on the machine. The staff of the project stood behind him on in a crowd.

"Holy shit," I said, recognizing the face of an old man towards the front of the crowd of technicians and service people. Red blotches covered his cheeks, and a scar tore down his cheek. I didn't believe I was seeing him at first, and I instructed the monitor to focus on his coordinates on the screen. "That's my old man."

"Yeah," Sally said. "Shit. Years of whoring caught up to him, eh?"

"What the hell is he doing there?" I said.

"Probably peddling pot and booze." I nodded. I felt nothing when I saw him. He'd only been a flat face in a few photographs and the spite in my mother's drunken rages.

The crowd cheered on their own destruction. Cyclotrons as long as subways spun. Electromagnets the size of skyscrapers charged. Hearts hoped. Reality shimmered. The engineers tossed a rock into the pond, and the reality of our living unit rippled. According to astronomers, the stars crawled from our relative perspective. The engine generated a gravity field, and the earth fell towards the sun. Winter turned mild, and we celebrated the new temperate season. We grew more food, and Disney showed record earnings. They kept the machine operating until we reached our optimal orbit. Then, the engineers tried deactivating the field, but once the machine was turned on, it couldn't be turned off. The field generated itself, stuck in a loop and building power, thus defying the laws of thermodynamics. Scientists calculated that at the rate of acceleration, it would only take the earth eight years to move into a solar orbit that would be lethal to the biosphere. All life would burn by the increased levels of solar radiation, and eventually, it would boil then evaporate. All life would be long gone by that point.

Of course, when the scientists failed, the military stepped in and used their own tools. For weeks, the air force bombed the site and failed. The engine generated a gravity field inverse to its energy, thus it deflected all explosions even nuclear around the site. However, it was theorized that if the field could be reversed, the gravity would cancel itself out, and the earth would slingshot back to its original place. Society failed before this could be done. Governments tried the Disney board of directors for crimes against humanity. Cinderfield vanished, and the judges believed they'd invented the devil to use as a scapegoat, which is why the concept of the devil had been created. But I knew the beast was real, though I wasn't sure what he was or if he was even from our planet. The parks shut down, and Disney went bankrupt when the world court judges ordered them to pay damages to humanity for corporate negligence. The CEO was executed. I came home from my last day of work. Civilization had already begun to collapse as the skies lightened and the sun burned brighter.

"What's the point of living just to watch the sick heart of humanity exposed?" I asked my wife. I knew what was coming. Cities burned, and the news reported looting across the world. Governments collapsed.

Sally sighed. She didn't talk much during the twilight days and was always lost in thought. "Don't do it without me," she said. "Promise me."

"I have painkillers from when I broke my leg."

"You never listen to me. God. I need you to promise me, Harry!"

I didn't promise her. I just kept talking about it. I emptied my savings account to buy a 2016 Andretti to chase down the synthetic opiates. We'd make it a night, one of the few dates we'd had since before we were married. Knowledge of my approaching death stirred passions in me I hadn't felt since I courted her, writing her music, taking her to dinner, showing her my vulnerabilities. I got everything ready, made a nice dinner with the little food I could find in the store and poured the wine. The power had gone off, and I burned candles.

Sally never came home.

"I promise."

⚘⚘⚘

The Holy Tome of Truman

Book III

"So you're Harry Truman Gill?" Doctor Death-Metal asked. He had finished cutting off the tumors and bandaged my legs with shredded shirt fabric. "I've always wanted to meet you." The anesthetic had cleared, and I dressed in my animal suit.

"Why?" I asked. He was bullshitting me, probably wanted to steal my kidneys or some shit.

"Professional reasons," he said. "Mind if I join you? Time to blow this place."

"Why would you leave all this?" I asked.

"To pursue my research." He poured gasoline on the inside of the monorail car.

"What's the point? The world is ending." My legs ached from the surgery, and I stumbled outside before he burned his office.

"What was ever the point?" Doctor Death-Metal asked. "It was always going to end. But it's important to me to know—my self-given purpose."

"You didn't wait for God to give you a destiny," I said. He threw a lit match into the car, and flames washed through the interior. "You're a damn sexy man."

We traveled on foot for a week, though the old measurements of time were affectations now. We managed to forage roots, find preserved snacks from the park days or trade his medical services. Every tumor he sliced was food in our bellies. I traced the motorcycle gang east to the edge of the continent. The soulless had established a trading post in the giant plastic head of a cartoon kitty. "They call this Nihilism Town," I said. "My wife's here somewhere."

"I've heard of this shithole," Doctor Death-Metal said. "It's the place where souls go to evaporate. Makes my spirit want to vomit if it had a mouth."

"There's always been a place like this," I said. The air shimmered around the town, and I tasted metallic ozone on the air. The ground felt spongy under my bare feet.

"They built the gravity engine in the hills to the east," he said.

"My father worked on the project. Well he sold booze and pot to the workers."

"He was part of my research," Doctor Death-Metal said. "I always suspected he was patient zero when the Maxx mutated, probably by the low-level emissions of gravitons. From him, the disease became airborne, but it didn't kill us. And by then it was too late." That must have been the reason he'd come with me. I was a link to my father, and he wanted to study me.

"You're obsessed," I said.

"It fascinates me. The gravity field mutated the way the microbe existed in the universe. It was way above my head, but I theorized that it somehow linked its DNA with all versions of the disease in alternate realities. If enough of the microbe was brought into close proximity, I believed it would change the nature of space-time around it. I never had the chance to experiment. I need to examine specimens of the disease in higher concentrations, maybe infected offspring."

"People really aren't popping out kids anymore," I said.

The denizens shambled like zombies and gazed at me through vapid eyes. I asked a couple of the empty souls where I could find the motorcycle gang. They directed me to an old Catholic church near the center of the park by a collapsing roller coaster. I watched as some of the folk climbed up to the top of the Pink Bunny Shredder and jumped from the crest, laughing as they fell. I followed the sound of bells. Doctor Death-Metal tagged along, attending me as a personal physician. I carried my groundhog costume under my arm. I didn't want Sally to see me in it. She hated my job. We entered Saint Vincent the Martyr. Captain Spizzie's motorcycle gang had parked the Harleys against the pews and made camp around the altar, and they cleaned greasy engine parts in the holy water fonts. Toddlers played in the old church, tossing hymnals like volleyballs. Through some transcendental means, they levitated the books from their palms, and it fascinated Doctor Death-Metal, who went over and started examining the kids, first squeezing the tumors that devoured their little bodies. I searched for my wife and found her in the belfry, pulling the bell ropes. Tattoos of rose bushes smothered her gentle and child-like visage. Painted blood dripped from the illustrated thorns. I couldn't speak. She'd shaved her head, and I didn't recognize her.

"Harry!" she squealed and ran to me, sweeping me up in her arms. I froze, unsure how to react. She treated me like an absent friend. The costume fell out from under my arm. "My little groundhog!"

"You left me at the end of the world," I said. She kissed me, and I fell into her lips. Then she spun and danced around the attic, twirling a torn skirt.

"Didn't matter anymore," she said.

"Our marriage?"

"Life. A job. Paying bills. Shit, Harry. It's all falling into the sun. It always would. Every person that lived before lived for nothing. We're blessed. Don't you see, my Harry? We were freed in our lifetimes. All their bones and dust . . . it's just going to burn. The great events in their lives were just details. Meaningless shit." The atmosphere changed. I choked on the burning odor of sulfur, brimstone that tainted the air. A man climbed the stairs then adjusted his three piece suit. An ostrich feather fluttered from a fedora. I recognized the creature. All humans knew it.

"Cinderfield."

"Hello there Harry," he said. "I remember that moniker. I go by Captain Spizzie now."

"So you lead this gang?" Sally ran to him and wrapped her arms around his thin waste.

"No hard feelings?" he asked. "I setup the dominos, but I didn't make them fall. That was all human nature."

I picked up my groundhog uniform. I thought about grabbing a hunk of fallen stone and bashing in his head, but what good would it do? "You're not innocent," I said. Ancient cloisters of old universities ran through his eyes. This thing had watched mountains grow like dandelions.

"Oh. I've done this before. I handed you the gun, but you pulled the trigger."

"You're a child of chaos."

"Wrong," he said. "The gambit isn't yet played. And now that you're here, we can finish this and put it right." He offered me the clay jug.

"I just want my wife back," I said. "I want it like it was. Stable. I knew who I was and where I was."

"Let's go talk," the devil said. He disengaged from Sally and grabbed me hand then pulled me down the stairs, out into the street. Doctor Death-Metal took blood samples from the kids and ran a scanner over the vials.

"This is a hoot!" the doc said. "I just had the wait for the next generation to complete my research."

"Rock my world, baby," I yelled back at him, feeling a bit overwhelmed. I wished I'd never found her.

"You'd rather have lived in hope," the devil said. We strolled through the streets, dodging scaffolding from the derelict rollercoaster.

"My whole world was an illusion I gladly accepted," I said. "And I always knew what she'd say when I found her. I just didn't expect to find her here with you. I'm surprised no one's shot you yet." He looked stunned at what I said. I just wanted to hurt the thing, but I didn't want him to realize I was trying to hurt him. I wasn't very good at confrontation.

"I really mean well," he said, spinning the chain from his vest. "And so do you." He waved his hand at the wretched, the drunk and lost. They drove needles into their arms or slurped from jugs. No one bathed, and the outpost reeked. He tossed joints and vials at the wretches, and the mob grabbed the candy. "You want your wife back, right?"

"I love her," I said, biting my tongue.

"I've gotten to know Sally," he said. "I'm her vice of chaos, her self-destruction. You were her stability, her rock."

"And you nurtured this in her? Dug the hole?"

"As part of my design," the devil said. "So you could fill it."

"What are you?" I asked. I wasn't sure what horrified me more: understanding that he dropped the earth into the sun as part of some personal plot, or that I was an essential component of the machine.

"Save the world," he stated.

"How?"

"Them," he said. The devil gestured at the stinking crowd. "Buddha was like you when I met him. And Jesus. Confucius. Gandhi. I've been commuting to this world for many rotations of your sun. I created this contraption, and there's a cure. It's all by design, to avert what happened to my world."

"How the hell do I cure all this?" I asked. "We're falling into the sun."

"Save them," he said.

"Harry!" Doctor Death-Metal cut through the crowd.

"The ace of spades is played," said the devil.

The doc waved a tablet over his head. He'd painted his face with monochromatic makeup, and he strummed the tablet like a guitar. "It's the kids! They're all descendants of patients infected with the Maxx. They're hyper-infected. I'd swear the disease was engineered."

"Save me the preamble," I said.

"It emits anti-gravitons! The kids can manipulate gravity."

"So?" the crowd watched our causerie.

"We can fix all this mess," the doc said.

"You son of a bitch," I said and gazed at the devil. He knew what the doctor would find when he researched those kids. He'd brought us here.

"It's the only way you're going to learn," the devil said. "It's about to you, now. I'll come back in a couple of centuries and check on things." And with that, the devil walked off into the wasteland. His silhouette burned into the swollen sun dominating the sky.

I saw my wife walking from the church. I didn't care if I saved the world, but I'd fight for her. I kept the words simple. "I can save us," I told the crowd.

"Why?" Sally asked, joining the crowd. "None of this shit means anything."

"Tell 'em what I taught you," Doctor Death-Metal said.

"No god imbued us with any meaning, but it doesn't mean we can't give it to ourselves. We can do anything we like. We can make our lives into something."

"What the hell does it matter?" Sally asked again. "Nothing we do is going to stop us from falling into the sun."

"There's a way," I said. Doctor Death-Metal took my hand. "If we want it."

❧❀❧❀❧❀

The Holy Tome of Truman
Book IV

In those final and beginning days, I adorned the groundhog and transformed the filthy garb into a symbol of a hope. I traveled from settlement to settlement, recruiting apostles and followers, gathering up as many of the lost and disposed, needing their wills, their sacrifice and accumulated disease.

The Maxx would save us from our arrogance.

Then on that solstice, I led the masses to the gravity engine. Our gathered infection generated enough anti-gravitrons to penetrate the energy field that had prevented demolition, and enough of the particles would cancel out the gravity well. According to my faithful doctor, the planet would revert near to our original position in space.

As long as a seed of life remained, life would begin renew.

Sally took my hand, and we stepped together into the mouth of the generator. My church followed the man in the groundhog suit and took possession of their souls. That was all that matter. Our actions were just . . .

. . . details.

YOUR FLIGHT TIME HAS BEEN CHANGED
BY TRACY FAHEY

There it is again; that dreadful, light, vertiginous feeling spiralling inside me. I'm looking at my plane ticket, sweating, as the numbers dance before me. A familiar, watery faintness descends as the printed numerals '13.20' blur, stop signifying 3.20pm, and resolve themselves as 1.20pm. I have a strange kind of numerical dyslexia that is exacerbated by panic. As I try and read figures, they swim, reverse themselves, and the twenty-four hour clock just plain stands back and mocks me. No matter how many times I try to equate it rationally, an obstinate quirk of my brain insists that '17.15' *should* translate at 7.15pm, not 5.15pm. It's a stupid, vaguely embarrassing incompetence, but occasionally it causes more serious complications. Like now.

'I'm sorry.' She doesn't look or sound sorry in the slightest. Her eyes slide past mine.

'But I have to get there!' I say urgently. 'I'm giving a paper tomorrow morning!'

She quarter-turns away from me in her swivel chair. Her stiff, manicured profile says as clearly as if she's uttered it: *Well, why did you miss your flight, then?* My hands are shaking.

'Please,' I say in a low, deliberately controlled voice. 'Is there anything else?'

She sighs, and resigns herself to acknowledging me. 'There's a few others who've also missed it, so I'm looking up alternative options. Please take a seat.' She waves a dismissive, manicured hand at a disparate bunch of people to the left of her cubicle; an older couple, a family with a small child, a snoring man who oozes alcohol, and two girls in Stetsons and pink t-shirts that proclaim them to be 'Mandy's Hens'. We're all inhabitants of a shadowy netherworld now; a dark non-place; all meant to be at Point A but instead trapped at Point B. I hesitate, and then sit opposite the young mother.

'You missed the flight too?' I'm sweaty, anxious, eager to share my fears. She gives a tight little double-nod; glassy-eyed, focusing on her own private misery. I respect that. I smooth out the crumpled plane ticket on my knee, and the jump of misery and guilt when I see the fatal flight time prompts me to say, half to myself: 'If I could just turn back time...' Drunk Man beside me snorts, wakes up, and says thickly 'True, darling!' before relapsing back into bubbling snores. His blasts of breath stink of dank, used beer. My stomach, already queasy from the bumpy bus to the airport, rolls over in a long, low, involuntary shudder. I get up and walk back to the airline desk, settling on a discreet, hovering distance, close enough to hint, far enough away not to exasperate. The woman on the desk flicks a quick, annoyed look at me, and then switches her attention back to her computer screen. Her eyes widen; their false eyelashes stretching in an almost comical manner. She beckons me over:

'Well, aren't you in luck? There's another flight later tonight, just been added to the schedule.' Her mouth crinkles in a smile.

'Can I book onto it?' She nods, almost absentmindedly, the surprise slowly leaving her face. It seems that for a hundred euros I can do so, and order will be restored to my panicky universe. I'll arrive in the right city (Amsterdam) on the right day (today, albeit much later than planned) and will stay in the right hotel, on the right night (no cancellation fee). I feel relief flash through me, pure and quick as light. Salvation. I quickly recalculate my budget, plan the stealthy pilfering of conference pastries to replace dinners, and hand her my passport.

Now for airport limbo, the four hours I need to spend in the dubious charms of Dublin airport. I sit down and rummage through my hand luggage for a book. The relief of a subsequent flight has cheered up our raggle-taggle group. Mandy's Hens have perked up, readjusted their Stetsons at jaunty angles, and disappeared to plunder the duty-free. The pinch-faced mother has relaxed a little. She holds her sleeping son loosely in her arms, and the looks she exchanges with her husband are soft with relief. The elderly couple are making successive, delighted phone calls to tell their extended family of their unexpected reprieve. Even Drunk Man beside me has woken up; sober enough to appreciate the communal solution. He stumbles off to the bathroom and comes back with wet-slicked hair, a cloud of mint toothpaste and a palpable air of apology. In the spirit of happiness I even smile at him. He sits down, smiling back gratefully.

'Sorry about earlier,' he mutters to me, fidgeting with his carry-on bag. 'Bit hungover.' I nod, recognising his need to express public regret and to downplay what was obviously an early-morning drinking session. I open my book, a collection of Kavanagh's poetry and sit back, ready to slide into the lulling groove of well-known words.

Maybe it's a bad combination of circumstances; uncomfortable, plastic seating in a hubbub of noise mixed with the quiet, downbeat poetry of rural isolation. Maybe it's the fact that the former Drunk Man is obviously reading over my shoulder. Whatever the reason, Kavanagh's sensuous poetry is proving no distraction from my plight. I close the book and focus instead on rethinking my spending plans over the next few days. The cheap hotel I've booked into is providing breakfast, the conference will have coffee and sandwiches...if I scrimp enough I might even have enough to visit the Rijksmuseum on my last day. I scowl and wish, for the second time that day that I could simply go back, translate the twenty-four hour clock correctly and be on-time, in-flight and a hundred euros richer.

'Kavanagh,' says the man beside me affably. I'm not sure if it's a comment or a question. I lift my book in the air and waggle it in a vaguely affirmative gesture.

'O stony grey soil of Monaghan!' He clutches his shirt front. 'The laugh from my love you thieved!' I smile, grudgingly. At least he knows the verse.

'You like Kavanagh?'

'Sure he's a man after my own heart. From Monaghan, living in Dublin, and forced to eke out a miserable existence writing lousy articles for newspapers. Mac, at your service.' He pumps my hand vigorously. His face looks fresher already, the greenish pallor is fading and there's even a faint flush of pinkness in his cheeks.

'Jenny.' I say faintly. 'Writing on Kavanagh.' He questions me intently, interested in the progress of my thesis. 'A hundred thousand words? That's a fair bit to knock out. Respect!'. He leans towards me, animated. 'Kavanagh knocks those languishing, effete lads like Yeats out of the park.' *He's OK*, I realise, happy to while away the time with a chat. And when he asks me to join him for a coffee, I agree.

'Ahh.' He sips his black coffee and shakes his head vigourously. His black quiff wavers and the front collapses in a slow, dignified manner over his forehead.

'Rough night?' I ask lightly.

'The worst,' he says flatly. 'In the back of my head I knew I was flying at lunchtime, but that contrary child that lives behind my eyes kept telling me it didn't matter.' He clicks his tongue against his teeth in exasperation. 'The worst bit is that it wasn't even a great night. I kept hoping it would be, but it wasn't. It was late. Not great.'

I smile in sympathy and dip a plastic spoon in my cappuccino.

'Still, I'm paid to go over and write a piece on the cultural life of Amsterdam. Life beyond the drugs and girls. Not bad work.'

'Not bad!' I glimpse the world of the profitably employed and am briefly envious. 'And great there was another flight this evening.' I'm cheering up, I realise, no doubt about it. Mac smiles at me, a dimple popping up on one cheek. His eyes are dark blue and long-lashed. *He's pretty handsome*, I realise, with a little lurch of excitement.

'Little Miss Optimistic,' he says with a hint of fondness. 'You got your wish; to turn back time.'

'Oh yeah. I did too.' I remember my panic, and smile.

⁂

Two hours and two coffees later, we're happily chatting and agreeing a long and intricate list of favourite places in Dublin when we hear our names called: 'Would passengers McDonald and Byrne please go immediately to Gate 13 where your flight 486 is now boarding.'

'Us! Come on!' Mac is on his feet, grabbing both his rucksack and my wheely case. 'Run!' And run I do, giggly slightly, an anxious and tiresome day transformed into a scampering, giddy rush.

We come to a halt, still laughing, at Gate 13. The gate is gloomy, only a single light illuminating the desk. The man at the gate is silent, even melancholy. He doesn't speak, just extends his arm. I open my passport and flourish my boarding pass. He barely looks at either, just sighs and motions me onwards. Outside, twilight stains the sky like grey rust. I walk down the dark, umbilical gangway. I'm in row 15C. Mac has already scanned my ticket and pronounced himself satisfied: 'I'm in 15B – right across the gangway.'

When I step onto the plane, I find the gloom outside extends in to the interior. Low wattage light gleam dimly overhead, only the EXIT signs standing out against the dull grey walls. It's strangely silent, I realise, only the occasional burst of static from the intercom and the deep whirr of the engines beneath me making any sound. At the front of the plane I see Mandy's Hens. One has lost her hat, and judging by their bleary, sleepy faces, they've spent more time on alcohol than on lipstick in the duty-free. At the back – I squint up my eyes to make them out – there's the elderly couple on one side, and on the other, neatly balanced, are the small, silent family. The little boy is still prone, sprawled asleep on his mother's chest. There's no-one else on board, I realise with a start. It's like I've chartered a private flight for myself and my entourage. Sadly, the plane isn't a luxury jet. In fact, it is seems distinctly minimal. There's not even the usual courtesy magazine in the holder in front of me. Not even a menu. I shrug and put my plastic bottle of water in the little net sling on the seat-back facing me. The engines keep rumbling as I shake my travel essentials out onto the seat beside me; earplugs, headphones, chewing gum, my Kavanagh book, a magazine, notebook and pen. I buckle my belt, sit, wait, and then it kicks in; a riotous roar beneath us, a surge of speed, a tilt, a thrust in the small of the back, and we're up, up, diagonal to the ground, a misty quilt of fields and water receding sharply below.

I draw a deep breath and for the first time since my abortive initial attempts to check in, I really *believe* I am really on my way.

※ ※ ※

The lights are fully extinguished on take-off, except for the strips on the floor. When the pearly lights start to gleam dully again, I'm almost asleep, lulled by the dull purr of noise below, and the slight swaying of the plane back and forth.

'Jenny!' I turn my head, blinking, to see Mac leaning across the aisle. His face (or as much of it as I can see in the gloomy light of the plane) looks pale and sweaty. 'Jenny,' he hisses. 'Where's the crew?'

'Dunno.' I struggle upright in my seat. My neck twinges sharply as I do. 'I think I was asleep.'

'You were. I wasn't. Do you remember any safety demonstrations?'

'Don't think so,' I say truthfully, rubbing my eyes. 'But I never pay attention to them anyway. So maybe?' I pull a who-knows face at him. My mouth is dry and sticky. I drink some water from my bottle, the trickle runs down my throat like a river through a desert. I put the bottle down carefully on my plastic tray.

'There *were* none! No demonstrations!' I glance sharply over at Mac. He is clearly agitated. 'And no message from the captain. Jesus Christ, even on the *cheapest* budget flight there's always a message from the captain. This doesn't add up!'

'Easy there, PI Macdonald.' I knuckle my eyes again and stifle a jaw-breaking yawn. 'That static-y burst every now and then is probably the captain entertaining us with detailed extracts from his autobiography.' Mac looks away from me. He straightens up stiffly in his seat, and I see I've offended him.

'See you later, then,' he says gruffly.

I try and stay awake by leafing through my magazine, but the cheery words and images buckle and swim in front of my eyes. My eyelids swoop down, once, twice, heavier, then I'm pulled under, exhausted.

'Wake UP!' It's Mac again. His hair is wild, as if he's been in a tailwind. 'For God's sake, wake up!'

"M awake,' I say grumpily, eyes still heavy and bleared with sleep.

'Thank God.' He sits down limply in the empty seat beside me. 'I can't wake anyone else.'

'Huh?' I'm confused.

'It's...it's...it's...' He's stuttering badly, mouth working; he stops, swallows his words, starts again. 'They're asleep. They're all so asleep. I was talking to the older woman and we were just agreeing on how odd it was not to have seen the crew when her head just lolled down. Just like that. Her husband was already asleep. Then I looked across the aisle and the whole family there were sleeping too. And the girls at the front.' His voice wavered, then strengthened again. 'And then you.'

'Well I'm awake now,' I say crossly, but I know I'm only half-awake, the greater part of me, like an iceberg, is mostly below surface, locked in a dark undertow of thick, dreamless sleep. Faintly, as if in the distance, I feel my eyelids swoop, tremble, and then slide closed again.

'For the love of GOD, Jenny, stay awake!' The raw pleading in his voice jolts me alert again.

'Yes' I say slowly. It comes out as 'Yesh'; as if my mouth is full of toffee. He grabs my hand. I feel his fingers press painfully against my knuckle bones.

'Ow!' I try to pull my hand away. He grips it instead, tight and warm, his face pleading.

'What happened?' His voice is urgent. 'Where's the lights? The crew?' I have no answers. I shrug and my shoulders move glacially, in a long, slow slump. He crushes my hand tighter. His face is bone-white. 'There's something else. Do you have a watch? Show it to me.'

I extend my free arm and lay it down on the seat beside him. He releases my hand to grab my wrist.

'See? It's not moving.' His voice is a whisper now, but even that sounds obscenely loud in the thick silence of the plane

I stare at my plain Timex watch, with its large, sensible numbers clearly marked on the face. My vision blurs, and then refocuses. I see the second hand is vibrating but staying – I blink again – staying in the same place. Curious. He thrusts his hand forward. 'Just like mine.' Sure enough, his watch has stopped too. 'Now listen!' He holds his watch to my ear. I hear it tick, but faintly; it's a low, stifled tick as if the watch is wrapped in wool.

Suddenly I'm cold-awake; an unfamiliar chill fills me as I realise another very strange thing. The roar of the engines has stopped.

'Mac,' I say hoarsely. 'Why has the plane stopped?'

He turns a white, frightened face to me, eyes wide and scared. There's no sound, just a muffled, faraway but regular boom below us. He pulls the curtain back. We're surrounded by streaky grey cloud, caught up in a mass of dirty cotton-wool.

'I don't think anything is working anymore,' he says quietly. He wraps his arms around himself, I am shivering, simultaneously cold and sleepy. I look at his watch and mine, I listen to the sound that is no longer there, and my head feels so frozen and dense I can't understand it all.

'Jenny.' His voice comes from a long way off. It's dark now, a deep twilight. I feel my lids tremble over my eyes again, helpless and heavy.

'JENNY!' My head is drenched with icy water. My eyes fly open in shock. Clumsily, I wipe my face with my arm. He bangs my empty plastic watter bottle down hard on my tray.

'Stay the *fuck* awake!' he shouts. 'Can't you see what's happening?' He grabs my wrist again and I see that the second hand of my watch waver, bend, and then tick backward. In the silence of the plane I can actually hear it tick a little louder as it swings back, back, back. Our eyes meet and we stare, cold and terrified, at each other, then the watch, then the empty bottle of water in front of me. Except it's not empty anymore. As we watch the blue plastic bottle starts to condense on the inside, a trickle of water lacing through the misted plastic to pool on the bottom. Slowly, unbearably, it fills, drop by drop. One of the overhead lights starts to buzz and flicker, strobing the cabin with a pallid, intermittent light.

'What's happening?' asks Mac, but his voice is muffled and slurred. The cabin is perceptibly darker. I hug myself with arms that feel like cold putty. The water bottle is full now, and, I realise, with a dull terror, the seal is now unbroken, perfect, like when I brought it on board. 'Mac,' I say hoarsely. There's no reply. I turn and see his big head wobbling, heavy, then dropping back on his shoulder. He's asleep. His black lashes press firmly against his cheeks. I don't even try to wake him. Instead I sit, helpless, as time crawls backwards, one tick at a time. I can only hope when time goes backwards that I'll go back too. Maybe when it reaches 13.20 I'll be there, this time, at the right time, in the airport. Or on the other plane…But all I can do is watch the relentless ticking of the clock and wait for it to happen.

The muffled boom below is starting to fade, and the overhead lights start to pop out, one by one. My eyelids are drooping. I feel myself swoon, slip, sleep…*This is what happens when worlds break down*, I think dully, *this is what happens when time stops working…*

HALLOWED GROUNDD
BY THOMAS MEAD

Where I come from, which is a village up in the wilds of the English Peak District, we tend to do things the old-fashioned way. Religion, marriage, the way we bury our dead- all of these are moulded and motivated by ancient traditions, customs which we have never quite managed to shake off. I was born thirty years ago in one of the mining cottages which line the uneven, twisting streets, and will probably die in similar surroundings. That is the kind of place this is.

In the centre of the village stands our church, its spire a jagged nail against the sky. Its squat, stolid body has withstood centuries of wild storms, offering sanctuary to scores of the lonely, desperate and hopeless who inhabit these unquiet hills.

The churchyard is tended by Matthew. He has seen countless villagers off to their final reward over the decades, including many of my own family. It is safe to say that he is a figure of renown, a living embodiment of the traditions that govern our lives, as well as a final link to the ones we've lost. He digs the graves, fills them in, mows the grass, perpetuating the cycle of rural existence. His furrowed, ruddy face is a part of the landscape, and has endeared him to more of us than even our local Reverend.

He lives in a tiny house at the very edge of the churchyard, and has fulfilled his duties for as long as I can remember. To lose him would be to lose something vital and irreplaceable. Though I suppose, now, even that dreadful inevitability will soon come to pass.

The trouble started last winter.

It was only a week or so until Christmas, and I was wandering back home after a night's pleasant drinking in the Dog and Bone, the local pub. Earlier that evening, a vicious blizzard had whipped against the windows of the inn. Now the snow seemed to have abated; so, wrapping myself in the folds of my overcoat, I ducked out of the building before it worsened again.

Crunching across the frosty grass of the village green, I spotted a figure slumped in the shadow of a nearby oak tree. It was Matthew, blind drunk and all but dead from the cold. He was shuddering uncontrollably. I dashed over to him and helped him awkwardly to his feet. I looked around me, but everyone else had long since retreated inside. It was way past midnight.

My own house was only a short walk so- half supporting and half carrying Matthew the gravedigger- that was where I headed. He was mumbling incoherently, but his words were carried away on the gusts of wintry air. As we stumbled up the garden path, something slithered from Matthew's grasp and shattered on the frozen ground. It was a whisky bottle.

I installed the drunken old man in front of the fire, then rushed to the kitchen to boil a kettle. He was still murmuring delirious nothings, and lolled forward worryingly in his seat. I don't think he had any idea where he was. When I placed the mug of steaming, heavily sugared tea on the wooden table at his side, he didn't move to acknowledge me. But I caught a few words of his ramblings.

'It's all wrong,' he said. 'It's all gone wrong.'

'What's that, Matthew?' I asked, but he had lapsed into unconsciousness again.

҉ ҉ ҉ ҉

I sat at his side for the rest of the night but, apart from a few sleep-addled gurgles, the old man didn't stir. By the firelight, he seemed so fragile. I found it hard to imagine him shoveling mounds of earth, sealing generation after generation in their final repose. Slowly, the fire burned away to nothing, leaving the two of us in peaceful darkness.

The next day was a Saturday, my day off, so when Matthew finally stirred it was almost lunchtime. He awakened with a low moan, blinking repeatedly in the bleak, white daylight.

'Where am I?' he growled.

'It's all right, Matthew,' I said. 'You were a bit worse for wear, so I brought you home.'

'Oh, it's you,' he said, still blinking. He tried to smile. 'Thank you.'

҉ ҉ ҉ ҉

I had no other plans for the day, and so decided to let the old gravedigger rest for a while. No sense in turning him out onto the street again before he was fully recovered. He sipped a little tea and slept a while longer, but seldom spoke, and made no attempt to explain his strange behaviour of the previous night. To drink alone is one thing, but to set off into the village in a wild stupor and pass out on the green is altogether different. Having rescued him, I thought I might have earned a degree of confidence. But, though I plied him with more hot, sweet tea, he merely thanked me and lapsed into pensive silence once again. In the end, I had no choice but to broach the subject myself.

'Matthew, what happened last night? I've never seen you like that before.'

Forthrightness has always been one of my qualities. I thought the old man might respect a degree of candour.

He closed his eyes, sighed deeply, and said, 'I know. I know.'

Then, very slowly, he began to explain.

❦❦❦

He told me that, a week prior to the delirious, drunken episode, he'd awoken in his bed one morning in a state of melancholy that he couldn't shake off. This was unusual, for he was one of the most cheerful men I've ever encountered (an attribute that never fails to astonish, given his occupation). To him, this malaise was inexplicable, for he was well-liked and- though he would never be wealthy- comfortable enough to see out his days under his own steam. He dressed, breakfasted, but this persistent sadness permeated his every action.

There was little work to be done in the churchyard, but he set out on a slow stroll through its environs nevertheless. The place had never struck him as macabre or frightening, as it did so many others. Rather, it was a soothing, peaceful place; a place of healing. Now, though, it failed to ease his troubled mind as he wandered aimlessly amidst the graves. By then, he had convinced himself there was something in the air.

Standing in the shadow of the church spire, he surveyed the mass of stones. For the first time, he considered the thousands of bones beneath his feet, and his heart gave a little shudder. That instant, he spotted something at the far end of the graveyard which troubled him deeply. It was at the very edge, where church land bordered the fields beyond. A fresh, deep hole in the ground, brazenly taunting the elderly gravedigger. Not only had it not been dug by Matthew, it was an entirely unauthorised invasion. The work of childish trespassers with a sense of humour more malicious than his own.

His first instinct was to fill in this new grave once more, but then he noticed a second troubling detail. There was no mound of earth beside the hole, nor evidence of digging. For a second, he considered the possibility that it might be some natural phenomenon. A widening split in the icy ground. But that, too, was impossible, for the hole was perfectly calculated to the dimensions of a standard wooden coffin. It was a grave, all right.

Now, his melancholia was superseded by a sliver of discomfort. For a long time, he debated whether or not to report this incident to someone. The Reverend? The police? By nightfall he had done nothing, and the grave still yawned mockingly open. He was an old man, and didn't want trouble. So, he went to bed that night leaving the grave untouched. A waiting void at the other end of the churchyard.

This incident, though mildly disconcerting, was by no means the end of the story. When he woke the following morning, Matthew found himself wandering towards the new grave. What he saw there stopped him dead in his tracks.

The gravestone was pristine white, like a tooth. Completely smooth, the name and dates yet to be carved. Matthew knelt down to examine it closely. He knew no such stone had been ordered, and he'd not been contacted by either of the regular delivery men. Indeed, there was no way that they could have passed by his cottage without disturbing his sleep. Unless they had taken the bizarre decision to deliver the stone across the distant desolate fields, there was no way it could have been deposited here without attracting his attention. It seemed almost to have sprouted organically from the earth.

At this point, Matthew paused the telling of his story to sip from his mug of tea.

'Jokers,' I said.

'That's what I thought. Even then, that was all I could bring myself to think.'

'Did you report them?'

He shook his head, and winced at the pain of it. He smiled pathetically and shrugged. 'I suppose I'm a coward,' he said, his voice low and rattling. 'I told myself it was because I didn't want to bother the poor Reverend with it. But really, I… didn't want to make it angry.'

Such an odd choice of words. 'Go on,' I said.

꧁꧂ ꧁꧂ ꧁꧂

What Matthew saw the following morning only strengthened the pervasive unease which now lingered over the churchyard. A single letter had been carved in the stone, it could only be the first initial of a name. In ornate, precise block lettering- amongst the finest he had seen- was the letter 'J.'

The morning after that came two more letters, directly adjacent to the first: OS. Evidence, perhaps, of an accelerated process, a system of mechanics swiftly gaining momentum. Maybe greed was the spur, or hunger.

Either way, 'JOS' was finally enough of a clue for him to decipher. There were no Josephs in the village, so it could only be Josie Edwards, young mother to three infant boys. Her husband had been killed last year, in a cave-in at the colliery, and the poor woman was still in mourning. Why her, of all people?

Matthew knew he didn't have time to ruminate, and set forth immediately for the young woman's house in the centre of the village. Shuffling clumsily along the main street, never before had he felt so ancient and decrepit. His breath came out in hot white plumes as he puffed nearer and nearer to the woman's home.

What could he say? Was there some means by which he could alert her without being condemned as an hysteric? True, the grave itself would serve as evidence of his warning, but there was nothing to stop the skeptics from accusing him of digging it himself.

He passed along the row of village shops, rounding the corner onto St. Benedict Place, where Mrs. Edwards lived in one of the cottages. Number 22, Matthew recalled. But as he drew nearer to her home, he spotted an unusually large clutch of onlookers on the other side of the street. Housewives and a few children, standing solemn in the winter air, paying the old gravedigger no mind as he approached. It was only when he recognised the doctor's car, parked haphazardly outside Number 22, that he realised he was too late.

It was the ice, someone told him. There'd been an unusually treacherous patch just outside the house and, when she stepped outside that morning, her foot had unwittingly skimmed it. She fell, cracking the back of her skull on the ridge of her own doorstep. It was her eldest son, himself no more than eight, who had discovered her twisted body, now dappled with a layer of morning frost.

Matthew didn't stay to watch the ambulance arrive. He retreated, his shoulders hunched, his head bowed. Back at the churchyard, he found the stone now complete: JOSEPHINE EDWARDS, and, beneath the name, BELOVED WIFE AND MOTHER.

Josie's funeral took place the following morning, and was attended by much of the village. A few were there out of genuine affection for the young woman, while others were on a mission of ghoulish reconnaissance, to see who might cry, and how smart those poor boys might look in their new black suits. Matthew watched it all from afar, blasphemously perched on a stone tomb, listening with his eyes closed as the Reverend nobly intoned the final rites. The gravedigger could not help but wince at the artifice of it all, which had never once troubled him until that day.

After the funeral, when the troupe of mourners had departed, Matthew marched over to fill in Josie Edwards's grave. But his work had already been done, and tufts of grass were sprouting from the freshly-raked dirt, as though a wound in the earth was healing over her coffin. Matthew was reminded uneasily of a pair of lips closing as the teeth begin to chew.

❧❧❧

Two days later, the cycle began once again. A pair of graves this time, side by side, perfectly neat and professional in their execution, as before. These were in the centre of the churchyard, beneath the ash tree. Cosy and comfortable for the new arrivals.

Matthew toyed with the idea of a late-night vigil, to try and witness the raising of the stones, but did not think his old heart would be able to take what he might see. His only real recourse was to wait.

It didn't take long. The next day brought two of them at once, as expected. Newlyweds this time, young lovers on their way back to the village by car from a short honeymoon at the seaside. The husband was driving and, for whatever reason, lost control. Lacerated, the pair of them. The bride all but decapitated by a flying shard of glass.

Another funeral, another crowd of bewildered onlookers. Again, they were sealed in their graves before Matthew could bury them. The gravedigger now knew that this process was spiralling out of control. The earth was hungry for fresh dead, and its appetite was becoming insatiable.

Again, the morning after that, Matthew spotted yet another new grave with a fresh stone. It had materialised without warning and he now stood before it, balmed in hot, panicked sweat. The pit seemed to reach downwards, deeper and deeper, its dimensions beyond calculation and without end. A giddy spell almost sent him toppling into the hole, and what a grotesque farce that would have been. For that was the moment that he realised, no matter how he fought to quell this force and its unholy hunger, one of these days he would step out of his cottage to find a stone carved with his own name.

He set out for the village, to buy himself a bottle of whisky, and, from that point to this, a pleasant numbness had enshrouded him.

When I was sure he had finished speaking, I rose from my seat without a word and went to pour more tea.

'So there it is,' he said, uncomfortably.

I made a few botched attempts to reassure him, to convince him that, by the cold light of day, these events would lose a degree of their horrific significance. I smiled down at him in what must have been an obscenely smug fashion, so convinced was I that it could all be rationalised. But he didn't lose patience, and smiled back at me calmly. 'It's so kind of you to offer me shelter,' he said. 'But I wonder if you'd do me one last favour, and I'll not trouble you again.'

I poured the last of the tea into his mug, it came out in a stale dribble. 'What is it, Matthew?'

'Take a walk over to the churchyard. Finish your tea, and just have a wander over there.'

'Of course. If that'll give you some peace of mind,' I said, taking the empty teapot out into the kitchen.

'Follow the path round the right-hand side of the church. You'll see it.'

In spite of myself, I agreed to his suggestion and set out, leaving the old man to convalesce at my house for a while longer. It was a short walk to the churchyard and, fully bundled in my overcoat, the air was bracing after that stuffy little room. I approached the church itself; in the snow it had never looked more serene and beautiful.

Matthew's directions led me to an empty grave, and a smooth, new stone. Just as he had described, a void in the earth, melancholy but benign. Nevertheless, though every instinct in me raged against it, I was afflicted by the insidious notion that this might also be more than just a grave. It seemed that I was gazing into the dark chasm between a pair of ravening jaws.

HERE BE DRAGONS
BY JEREMIAH MURPHY

When the front door to my apartment thudded under the weight of a solid fist, I can't say I was surprised. In fact, by the time I'd been interrupted, I'd already propped a chair up against the knob, fortified that with my dresser, and was in the process of dragging a nightstand across my apartment, just in case.

Rats. Now I was going to have to try diplomacy.

"I'm not home!" I told the fist as I dropped what I was doing and rushed over to my barricade.

"Please," said the person on the other side, "I just want to talk."

"Well, I can't hear you over the sound of my .38," I replied, cocking the hammer of my revolver to clarify what I meant by that.

"For cryin' out loud, Edie!"

"Miss Beran to you."

"You know me, Edie."

"Miss Beran."

"You started working for me the day Jesse Owens made that Hitler guy look like a chump at the Olympics. We laughed about it for hours. Remember that?"

"Yeah," I replied, "but I don't remember signing up with a guy who stands around in rooms with dead babies."

"It was just one dead baby."

"That's still too many dead babies!"

He sighed, "I can explain everything."

"I'm listening."

"I can't explain while I'm in this hallway."

"Then I'm not listening anymore."

He went completely silent. I couldn't even hear him move out there. I did the only rational thing I could think of—I backed away from the furniture, took careful aim at the center mass of the doorway, and waited for him to make the slightest noise.

Finally, he spoke, "What would it take to make you feel safe enough to talk?"

I had to admit, this wasn't threatening enough to justify my opening fire. Part of me was disappointed. To be clear, I didn't actually want to shoot the guy; I just wanted all of this to be over with. I actually liked my soon-to-be-ex boss.

His name was Frankie Odin, Private Investigator, known to his colleagues as One-eyed Frank. Mr. Odin was about as hard-boiled as a gumshoe could get. How hard-boiled is that? Let me put it this way: when I started answering his phone and brewing him coffee three years ago, he was Two-eyed Frank.

The job was a strange and mysterious one, to say the least. The contracts and invoices I typed up were vague, and he sat me far enough from his office door that I couldn't make out a single word between him and his clients, who were a queer bunch. Most of them seemed normal—just more skittish than your average customer. Some of them, though, were just a little bit too tall, a little bit too short, or just a little bit too hunched over in their raincoats to be normal. Occasionally, I'd overhear him having a conversation with a client, even when nobody came or left the place all day. Because of all this, I actually believed that nothing associated with him could shock me anymore.

What I didn't expect was to come home from the grocer's on a Saturday morning to find him in my downtown walk-up.

When I'd first arrived, I noticed that the door to the McKinleys' place on the first floor was wide open. Something about that seemed off, so I went inside to get a look. I made it as far as the living room, which was so full of candles that we were all lucky the building wasn't burning to the ground. All the furniture had been pushed against the wall to make enough space for some kind of reddish-brown circle painted on the floor. In the middle of it all, with a sword pinning her to the floor through her heart, was little six-month-old Erin McKinley. I froze on the spot, snapping out of it when a pop and flash announced that someone else was there, and they had a camera.

That someone else was One-eyed Frank.

Now, I'm not the most refined of ladies, but I'm enough of one to wait until I finished running upstairs to my own place and bolting the door before throwing up at least two meals. It wasn't long after that my employer came knocking.

And now he wanted to talk. I set the terms: "You and me in a crowded park, in broad daylight, with my .38 in your back."

"Deal," he replied without hesitation. "It's three in the afternoon right now, and there's a playground about two blocks from here. I'll see you there in twenty minutes. Don't forget your gun."

I heard his footsteps stomp down the stairs, and when I was absolutely sure he was gone, I exhaled, leaned against my dresser, slumped to the floor, and muttered, "This had better be one damned good explanation."

⚜⚜⚜

I should have thought this through. I mean, it was too easy to get Mr. Odin to agree to my terms. If he was the kind of sicko who'd kill a baby and take pictures, what was he going to do to me? What kind of ambush did he have planned when my guard was down? If I had half a brain in my head, I'd lock the door, phone the police, and get myself a new job.

When I found myself on the bench twenty minutes later, it was because curiosity made me do it. And when I jammed the barrel of my .38 into his ribs, it was because what little brain I did have wasn't *that* stupid.

"Start talkin'," I said.

"I didn't murder those people," he told me.

"Oh, my God." With my free hand, I covered my mouth when it all hit me. My neighbors—my friends—had been slaughtered. "*Those* people?"

"Two adults and one infant."

"They had names, you cold-blooded bastard," I growled. "Bridgette and Alan and Erin McKinley."

"I'm sorry," he said with a surprising amount of sincerity. "I was too busy thinking about the crime and not the victims."

"Tell me why should I believe you didn't kill them."

"Because I invited you out here to talk when I could have been running."

"Maybe you need to get rid of the witness."

He pointed to the children and their mothers. "In front of all *these* witnesses?"

I couldn't argue anymore—but not with him, mind you. My papa told me I could disagree with anyone for days. Who I couldn't argue with was myself. The truth is, I liked Mr. Odin a lot, and I actually trusted him. I wanted to plug the maniac who did this to the McKinleys, but more than that, I wanted to give my boss the benefit of the doubt. I grunted, "Then what were you doing there?"

"To find out who did that."

"Why don't you just call the cops?"

"This isn't their area of expertise."

"What's that supposed to mean?"

He squirmed on the bench and seemed to deflate a little. "Edie," he started.

"Miss Beran."

"You probably noticed by now that the cases I take aren't exactly..." He looked to the heavens for the appropriate word. "... cut-and-dried."

"Yeah," I said, "no kidding."

"They tend to involve magic."

"Huh?"

"Magic," he clarified. "Like witches and ghosts and fairies and elves and the occasional goblin."

"Have you lost your ever-lovin' mind?"

He turned to face me. "Look me in the eye, Miss Beran." Now this was getting serious. This was the first time since I started working for him that he ever called me by my formal name without being prompted. And yet, he was talking about boogiemen like they were everywhere. "Tell me I'm lying."

I blinked and turned away. "I can tell you that you believe it," I said. "But that doesn't mean you're not crazy."

"I know how this sounds," he told me, "but it's a wacky world out there."

The only thing more insane than what he was telling me was how much sense it made. There were a lot of things in that office I either made excuses for, or pretended that I didn't see, like greenish skin, yellow eyes, feathers where they shouldn't be, and, on one occasion, something that looked like a tail. I mean, I admit that I did believe in ghosts a little. When you added in the idea of fantasy creatures, it all clicked into place like tumblers in a lock.

"Listen, Edie," he said.

"Miss Beran."

"I like you a lot. You're the best secretary I've ever had, and you're pretty easy to talk to. I tried to leave you out of this part of my work, because it's a good way to get yourself hurt." He pointed to his eye-patch, as if I didn't know what he meant. "The problem is," he continued, "you're a smart girl, and you would have worked this all out eventually. I was hoping you could do this at your own pace, so I didn't come across as a nut-job."

"Does this mean you do work for Dracula?" I asked.

"No," he replied, but I have been known to deal with other vampires. They're not the kind of people you think they are."

"Frankenstein?"

"Frankenstein doesn't exist."

"The Wolfman?"

"Especially the Wolfman."

"Now you're putting me on."

"When you change into a hairy beast every twenty-eight days, you need someone to keep an eye on you."

Blast it all, I was buying into this, and there wasn't a damned thing I could do to stop it.

He asked, "Are you gonna shoot me or not?"

"I haven't decided yet."

"Well, make up your mind," he told me. "I want to find the scumbag who murdered your neighbors, and the clock's ticking."

I relaxed. "I'm not completely sold on your fairy tale, but I don't know what to think, so I'm going to play along. I'm going to let you take the lead for now, but if you do or say one thing to change my mind, so help me, I will put a bullet in you, without thinking twice or losing any sleep."

He let me put my revolver back in my purse before he spoke again. "I know just the thing to seal the deal. Meet me back here at happy hour?"

"There's no way I'm letting you out of my sight until this gets cleared up."

"Suit yourself." He pointed to his camera. "I'm warning you, it's bound to get pretty boring."

⚜⚜⚜

What shocked me the most about B.B.'s Pub was that it was less shocking than I expected. All afternoon, I'd been bracing myself for fangs and wings and scales and gnomes, but all I got were regular people who just looked… different. Take the bartender, for example. He was slightly taller than a regular tall guy, with a slightly larger chest, slightly more hair on his arms, and incisors that were a little bit too long.

However disappointing this might be, though, at least it wasn't another couple of hours waiting in my boss's darkroom. That was just torture.

The bartender greeted Mr. Odin with a simple, not-very-enthusiastic, "Frank."

"B.B.," he replied, "I'd like you to meet my secretary."

I held out my hand. "Edith Beran, at your service."

He shook it with what appeared to be a paw. "You're in my bar, Miss Beran; I'm supposed to be at your service."

"Have it your way," I told him. "Bourbon, straight up. And please, call me Edie."

"Then you can call me B.B. And the first one's on the house."

I sat on a barstool and got comfortable. "I could learn to like this place."

"How come he gets to call you by your first name?" Mr. Odin asked.

"Because he got it right the first time."

He grunted, and while B.B. poured my drink, my boss signaled for me to retrieve the photos from my purse and toss them onto the bar. "Have you seen one of these before?"

B.B. spent half a second studying them before pushing them away. "No, but I can tell you what it looks like. It looks like a kind of summoning spell. The child..." Judging by the way he gulped, he was enough of a stand-up guy that the very idea of what he was looking at made him almost too sick to say it aloud. "The child is bait."

"Bait?" I squeaked.

Mr. Odin's lips curled up in disgust. "What kind of creature takes that kind of bait?"

"Beats me. Something awful, I'm guessing."

"Where do you think I could go to find... scratch that. I'll handle this." After pulling an ashtray close, he removed from the inside of his jacket two matchbooks. From one he slipped out what looked like a large, orange pebble, and from the other, an ordinary match.

He lit it, and I asked, "What in the blue, bloody blazes are you doing?"

"Trust me," he said.

"I guess I don't have any choice."

After a moment, B.B. leaned in and whispered, "I'm guessing you're new to the spook beat."

Without taking my eyes off of my boss, who seemed to be attempting to ignite the stubborn pebble, I replied, "What tipped you off?"

He smiled. "Did you piece it together, or were you told?"

"Told," I replied. "Things with the boss got a little..." I tapped my fingernail on the stack of photos. "... shady, and he filled me in."

"Not the best of circumstances," he admitted, "but there are worse ways to find out."

"Like getting eaten by Dracula?"

B.B. chuckled.

"I'm dying to know," I asked him, "are you the Wolfman?"

He shrugged.

I nodded my head toward a fox in a tailored suit. "What about him?"

"That's a kitsune," he replied.

"Kit-soo-who-now?" I then sniffed. "Do you smell smoke? Really, really weird smoke?"

"Showtime," B.B. said. I returned my attention to Mr. Odin, who was pulling from his hip pocket a coin with a square hole in the middle.

He flipped it into the ashtray. "Wish us luck."

"What's that about?" I asked.

"We'll know any second now," replied my boss.

The door creaked open, and in walked the most average of men. The three of us watched him stroll up to the bar, take a seat next to Mr. Odin, and say, "How's things, B.B.?"

"Things are things, Dennis," he told him. "The usual?"

"Does the pope wear a funny hat?"

Mr. Odin slid the photos over to the newbie and cleared his throat. "By any chance, have you seen anything like this before?"

Naturally, Dennis was disgusted, but then he relaxed. "I can't say I have, but it rings some really loud bells. I think I might know somebody who does."

My boss looked both relieved and suspicious, which was an expression he wore a lot. "And who might that be?"

"Just give me a minute," he told us and closed his eyes. When he opened them again, his expression and posture had shifted so much, it was like he became an entirely different person. "I am Titus Scipio, Munifix of the First Legion Germania," he declared in a much more formal voice. "Am I to understand you need my council on a matter?"

"You sound like something out of Julius Caesar," I said.

"It was he who founded the legion, but he died long before I was born."

"Get out of town!" I laughed. "Are you trying to tell me you're an ancient Roman?"

"Indeed."

"Then why aren't you speaking Latin?"

Mr. Odin told me, "Channeling is… complicated."

I returned my attention to the man. "If you're really Roman, prove it."

B.B. poured gin into a martini shaker. "Let the man talk, Edie."

"I have seen this before," said Dennis, or Titus, or whoever he thought he was. "It is burned into my mind as the darkest day I've ever known."

"Are you telling me," I demanded of my boss, "that you toss a penny, and—poof!—the one person in the world who can help shows up?"

"That was the point," Mr. Odin said.

"You're putting me on!"

"Are you finished?" he growled.

It was one thing to have to believe in fairies and vampires, but this was really pushing it. Still, I promised my boss I'd play along, so I just folded my arms and listened.

The Roman continued, "Many years ago, as my legion pushed northward, I was part of a small scouting party that ran across a large village, deep in the woods. We sent a messenger for orders, but, as I learned much later, he had been struck down by a falling tree. As we waited in vain for him to return, we discovered that all of our provisions had somehow been lost on our journey; unfortunately a frost began to descend on us, making foraging for food nearly impossible. Over the coming days, we lost one man to starvation, two more to a creek that had been poisoned by a creature that died upstream, and yet another to a pack of wolves. Finally, driven mad by hunger and thirst, we stumbled into the village. The last of my companions were struck down immediately by the inhabitants, but I had the presence of mind to flee and take refuge in the nearest structure."

He pointed to the photographs. "What I found inside was this very scene. At the sight of it, I collapsed and prayed to the gods for death.

"Instead, I was awakened by a man who kissed me full on the lips and sang in a language I could not understand. A moment later, he spoke again, this time in my own tongue. He told me that the terrible misfortune that killed all of my comrades had been woven by the power of..." He screwed up his face, straining for the proper way to describe this. "I knew that there was something in the hut with us, but to my eyes, we were alone. The man showed me a piece of polished metal, and, through its reflection, I could see some kind of shadow standing over the remains of the child. It was that of a man, and yet, it seemed to be a goat, as well as a bird, or perhaps a giant cat of some sort."

B.B. stopped shaking the drink to sigh, "Oh, boy."

The Roman concluded, "The villagers fed me, bathed me, covered me in furs, and sent me back to the legion as a warning."

"So you're saying this is some kind of bad luck spirit," I clarified.

"Edie..." my boss mumbled.

"Miss Beran," I reminded him. "And how is that any different than that hoo-doo you just pulled to get this guy here?"

"There is no difference," the Roman replied.

"Then why did little Erin have to die?"

Mr. Odin fished the coin out of the ashtray and held it in his fingers. "Magic pushes reality around here and there. With this little trick I can only nudge it. What Titus is describing is a creature from... elsewhere that can practically sculpt nature and time, and maybe even people's souls."

I didn't understand all of this, but I got enough. "Holy mackerel!"

"Did you get the name of the creature?" Mr. Odin asked the Roman.

"I did not."

Mr. Wulf filled a martini glass. "On the house, pal."

Titus Scipio closed his eyes, and Dennis opened them. "So, was I helpful?"

Mr. Odin nodded.

"Good news?"

Mr. Odin shook his head.

"Now we know what this is about," I said, "but what do we do about it?"

"We have to find out who invited this thing," my boss told me, "and that means returning to the scene of the crime."

My shoulders fell.

"I know this is going to be difficult for you," he said. "If you need to stay here…"

"Not a chance, sir," I replied. "I told you I was going to follow this all the way to the end, and that lowlife is going to pay for what he did to my friends."

He flashed me a grin that had a little bit of sadness behind it. "Then grab your purse, and let's get this over with."

❀❀❀

The candles in the McKinleys' had gone out a long time ago, but luckily, their lamps were still working. Mr. Odin poked around, looking for any sort of lead, and I opened all the windows to let out the stench. "Anything?" I asked.

"Nothing." He shook his head in disgust and frustration. "No clues; no nothing."

I thought long and hard about it, until an idea popped into my head. "Is it still in there?"

"If it ate the soul of that baby," he replied, "then yes."

"What if we cleaned up all this blood?"

He shook his head. "It's permanently anchored to this spot."

So much for that. I had another idea—a stupid one, this time—and walked straight for the center of the big circle. "Why don't I go and a talk with it?"

"Have you completely lost your mind?" he yelped. "There's a monster in there!"

"No, sir," I reminded him, "the real monster is the bastard who killed these three people. Pardon my language."

"Edie, don't!"

"Miss Beran," I replied, stepping inside. "And it's too late."

My boss threw up his hands.

"Hello?" I announced. "Is anyone there?"

No booming voice filled the room or whispered in my ear. In fact, there was no sound at all, or even words. Yet I just suddenly knew the answer, as if it had been in my head the whole time, but I'd just forgotten it—like suddenly remembering where I left my keys.

Yes, there was something in here with me.

"Do you have a name?"

It didn't.

"Everything has a name," I said, not quite sure if this was true.

It did once, but it was stolen.

"By who?"

By its master, of course, and let me tell you, it hated calling this guy its master.

"And who might that be?" After a second, I asked aloud, "Daniel Rivington, are you sure?"

"*Congressman* Daniel Rivington?" my boss clarified.

I saw its master's face, so I didn't even have to wait for a reply before nodding. It didn't particularly care what his master's title was; it just did as it was told.

"And what are you told to do?" I asked.

In one year, when Congressman Rivington would run to become Senator Rivington, a sudden fire would burn down his opponent's headquarters, and a political rally or two would get rained out. On Election Day, illness would hit the regions most likely to vote for the other guy. Four years after that, a few mundane things, possibly including a tornado, would lead to Senator Rivington becoming Vice President Rivington, who would then become President Rivington after a sudden stroke.

"Do you really have to do all of that?"

As long as its master possessed its name, it did.

"And if we can get it back for you?"

It would go home. It wanted nothing more. But its master had to choose to return it, or he had to die.

"You can count on us." I stepped out of the circle and said to Mr. Odin, "Let's go plug the lowlife."

"Edie…"

Headed straight for the door, I called out, "Miss Beran."

"You can't just go shoot a congressman!"

"Watch me."

"Miss Beran!"

I stopped and spun around. "You heard the thing."

"Actually, I didn't."

"Then you don't know what kinds of things he wants that creature to do, just for a leg up in the next couple of elections. I saw everything, and it was horrible."

"There has to be another way!"

I replied, "Rivington has to call it all off willingly, and I don't need to be a fortune-teller to see that he's not giving it up."

"Let's just talk to the man." He added, "Without bullets."

"And say what?"

"I'll think of something."

"What if he says no?" I asked.

"I'll think of something else."

"He's a lunatic, sir."

He grabbed my shoulders and looked me square in the eye. "Trust me."

I did, but first thing's first. I picked up the McKinley's telephone and dialed zero. "Operator," I said, "I think something terrible has happened downstairs…"

❈❈❈

It wasn't difficult to find the congressman's hotel room. Getting inside was easier, since it was unlocked. The place felt like a swamp, probably from the running water pouring steam out of the bathroom.

Mr. Odin sighed, rolled his eye, reached into his jacket, and called out, "Mr. Rivington?" Before he was even finished, his .45 was drawn, hammer cocked.

I reached for into my purse for my own sidearm and whispered, "What's got you all riled up?"

"In this line of work," he told me, "if the door's open and the shower's on and nobody answers you, you're looking at trouble." He added, "And usually that means somebody's dead."

Sure enough, Daniel Rivington lay on his back in the tub, blood running down his dented forehead. "This happen to you a lot?" I asked.

He holstered his gun. "If I had a nickel..."

I crouched down to examine the injury. "Kind of poetic, don't you think? He tries to put bad luck on a leash, and it turns around and bites him."

Mr. Odin shook his head. "Trust me, this was murder."

"And what makes you so sure?"

"At this point in my career, it's practically a cliché." He strolled through the bedroom, checking inside closets and behind curtains. "I'll bet you a dime the killer's still here with us."

"You're pretty jaded, sir."

"I've been doing this a long time, Edie."

"Miss B—" My gun slipped out of my hand for no good reason. "Butterfingers," I scolded myself. When I bent over to pick it up, I lost my balance and fell over. "Now I'm getting embarrassed."

Mr. Odin stepped over to help me up, but he stumbled and joined me on the floor. He sprang to his feet immediately, piece in hand. "Looks like you owe me a dime."

"I don't see..." Okay, this was getting ridiculous. "Are you telling me that's the Invisible Man?"

"There's no such thing as invisibility," he replied. "What we're dealing with is a the kind of glamour that fools you into ignoring any sign of the person who cast it."

"Nobody pushed me over," I told him. "I'm just clumsy."

"I've known you for three years," he said. "*Clumsy* is the last word I'd use to describe you. Your brain is making excuses."

"Sounds complicated."

"It is," he agreed. "I only know of one guy who can do it right, and he's—" Mr. Odin whipped his elbow over his shoulder, and a man who had been standing behind him with a knife staggered backward, blood squirting out of his nose. "—right here."

My jaw fell. "How did you...?"

"Practice," Mr. Odin told me. To the assassin, he said, "Ricky."

Through the bloodied hands clasped in front of his face, Ricky the assassin mumbled, "Frankie."

"Care to tell me what this is about, Ricky?"

"*Lass diesen Moment ohne Dich verstreichen*," he said, and he wasn't there anymore.

Mr. Odin threw his hands up in frustration. "Son of a gun!"

I stood and covered the room with my .38. "He's invisible again!"

"No," Mr. Odin sighed, holstering the .45, "he's long gone. He made us freeze for a second so he could hit the road."

"You need to teach me a few of these tricks," I muttered as I dropped the revolver in my purse. "Is that it, then? The creature goes free and this dirtbag goes to hell, or wherever?"

"Almost." He lifted the receiver of the nearest phone, and, after seven spins of the dial and a brief pause, he barked, "I need to speak to Peron."

He waited for the person on the other end to reply, before saying, "Don't pull my leg, lady. I know full well how late he likes to stay in the office."

There was a shorter wait.

"Look, I got four bodies—one is a congressman, two are regular people, and one is a damned baby, and the only lead I got is Ricky the Mason! Your boss knows how annoying I can be if I set my mind to it. He's got one of my eyes to prove it! Now put—"

"Give me that!" I yanked the phone out of his hand. To it, I said gently, "Sorry about my boss. He's always this way. I'm sure you know how that goes."

"You don't have to tell me."

"I'm Edie."

"Charlene."

"Charlene," I explained, "the two regular people my boss just told you about were good friends, and their baby was like a niece to me. All we're trying to do is figure out what happened so they can rest in peace."

For a little while, the only sound to come from the other end was a pen tapping on paper. "One moment please," she finally offered.

In two moments, she returned. "Mr. Peron says he won't talk to you without an appointment. However, because of your involvement in this matter, he wants you to meet his assistant in an hour, at Marcotti's on Fifth Avenue."

"Thank you so much, Charlene," I said. "I owe you a cup of coffee."

"Don't mention it," she replied. "I have a son and a daughter, and I can only imagine how I'd feel if something happened to them."

After I hung up, I turned to my boss and told him, "And that, sir, is why you have your secretary handle all your calls."

⁂

I subtly nodded my head to the waxen man in a three-piece, pinstripe suit who sat at a table by himself, sipping on a glass of dark red wine. "That must be Dracula."

Mr. Odin ignored me and headed straight for the guy. "Sager."

Without looking up from his newspaper, Sager gestured to the empty seats beside him. "Help yourself to anything on the menu, courtesy of Mr. Peron."

Mr. Odin signaled for a waiter. "That's awfully generous, considering that I just broke your favorite goon's nose."

"Mr. Mason wouldn't have been there at all had it not been for your efficient sleuthing."

I asked, "Are you telling me the Invisible Man was in the McKinleys' place the whole time we were?"

While my boss ordered a bottle of pricey champagne and a fillet mignon, Sager nodded condescendingly. "You're a very clever girl. And brave too, I've heard."

"I also type eighty words a minute and make an excellent cup of coffee."

"We haven't been properly introduced." He extended the boniest of hands. "I'm Alvin Sager, account and consigliere to Don Edoardo Peron."

"Is that supposed to mean something to me?"

My boss leaned in and whispered, "Stick around and it will."

"I'll take your word for it." To Alvin Sager, I said, "I'm Edith Beran, secretary to Private Investigator Frank Odin."

"Don't call her Edie," advised my boss. "She hates that."

He and I traded smirks.

"Charmed." Sager sighed. "Can I assume you'd like an explanation as to Ricky the Mason's involvement vis-à-vis this evening's affair?"

"Why else do you think we're here?" I replied.

"Very well," he said. "I'm supposed to keep this to myself, but given your role in the incident, I believe I can make an exception." He lowered his voice. "Simply put, the monopoly has paid us a considerable sum of money to erase the politician's activities."

I turned to my boss. "What kind of monopoly is he talking about?"

"The only monopoly that can tell Mr. Peron what to do," Sager told me.

"Look," said Mr. Odin. "I don't know much about the monopoly, but what I do know is that they're too laissez faire for this kind of racket."

"Which goes to show you how little you understand the gravity of Mr. Rivington's machinations. What he had done threatened to destabilize the entire magical community, and subsequently the Earth itself."

Mr. Odin shook his head. "I think you're blowing this out of proportion."

"I'm going to let you in on a secret," he told us. "I don't know if you've noticed, but there is dark corner in the back of B.B. Wulf's drinking establishment where nobody ever goes."

"I've seen it," Mr. Odin said.

"Then you know that it's somewhat unsettling."

My boss shrugged.

"In 1785, a husband and wife decided to take advantage of the decentralized mess left by the American Revolution, and to do that, they used every bit of black magic they could get their hands on.

"At that time, the monopoly was much like the colonies, in that they were merely a loose confederation of powerful merchants with similar interests. Together, they determined these witches to be beneath their attention. As time passed, however, their power grew and festered, and..." Sager shivered. "... things... began to slip into our world—very, very dangerous things. When the merchants finally confronted the pair, the resulting violence tore a hole in everything."

"What do you mean *everything*?" I asked.

"I mean everything," he replied. "Mr. Wulf's bar was constructed on top of the hole to isolate it and insure its relative secrecy."

"That's a heck of a story," Mr. Odin said.

"Isn't it?" Sager agreed. "Since then, in exchange for their lack of scrutiny, our organization is tasked occasionally with eliminating anyone who demonstrates the willingness and ability to cause destruction on such a scale." -

"With a generous payout," Mr. Odin added.

"Indeed," chuckled Sager. "They're merchants, not tyrants." He concluded, "Your actions today have spoiled the ambitions of a psychopath, and it likely saved everyone on the planet from an unspeakable fate."

"We also got justice for the murder of three innocent people," I reminded him.

"If that's your priority."

"So," I asked, "where's our cut?"

Sager broke out in frightening laughter. "You're very amusing. I hope your employer plans to keep you on his payroll." As soon as he got to his feet, the maître d' appeared out of nowhere with his hat and overcoat. "On behalf of Mr. Peron and the monopoly, I'd like to thank you for your service. Good night to the both of you. Miss Beran, I highly recommend the salmon."

I waited until he was out the door before I observed, "There goes a real piece of work."

"I've never seen him in such a good mood before," my boss told me.

I ordered the salmon and, after sampling Mr. Odin's glass, my own bottle of champagne.

"You're a natural at this, you know that?" he asked.

"Sir, you're making me blush."

While the waiter poured me some bubbly, my boss offered, "If I make you a full partner in the agency, can I call you Edie?"

This stunned me, but I had the presence of mind to reply, "Make it *Edith*, and you got yourself a deal." I stared off into space with a huge grin. "'Beran and Odin, Private Investigators.' That's going to be one good-looking door."

"Just because I promoted you," he told me, "that doesn't mean you get top billing."

"You need to respect the alphabet, sir."

We clinked our glasses together. "I'll think about it," he said.

Violet Plane
BY LAURA-MARIE STEELE

I swing the wheel of my solar edition Hyundai SE, and we skid through violet dust that rises under the tyres like smoke spiralling from the incense cones Fim uses to ward ancestral spirits away from the house. Strange to think of that now when I haven't seen Fim in years. Something about the way this plane never alters excludes thoughts of past and future, and I like it that way. I'd stay here forever, if I could only figure out how.

Dem's legs slide up and down over the top of the car door. She revels in wearing hot pants. If I had legs like hers, I would too.

"Stop messing around!" She whacks me with her fist. "I thought you were taking this seriously. Fix the fixers, right? So let's get on with it."

No harm in enjoying this plane whilst we still can, but Dem can be worse than a wailing cat when she's annoyed. I stop swerving and settle on a course headed towards the purple sun that hangs perpetually on the horizon like it's balancing on the rim of the world.

We rattle through Cairo. On redplane it's a sprawling mess of slum houses, solar towers and foliage. On bluplane it's full of glass and metal, cars and skyscrapers. On vioplane the desolate landscape has been filled with trash by the kids I've shown how to get here over the years. The scattered tents look like they've been tossed by the wind of chance. Everything is washed in shades of purple, from the lavender shadow of the scrap-metal mountain through to the luminescent lilac bases of the real mountain range in the distance.

Two boys in ragged jeans sprint alongside the car, and I can't help smiling. Ree always looks so eager, like a puppy about to get a treat.

"Queen Ban!" he hollers. "Where you going?"

"That boy talks too much." Dem rolls her eyes. "Don't stop."

I accelerate. Ignoring them isn't the kindest thing to do, but I don't want to deal with Dem's complaining. The boys run behind us for a while but stop at the waste-city limits where Lu has set up a wooden animal zoo. None of them like leaving the valley. There's nothing for them out here, nothing but hot purple dust.

Dem slides a pair of sunglasses up her nose and sighs. She's been moody since I picked her up on redplane this morning, though I know better than to ask why.

Eventually, she pulls her legs in and wedges them under her chin, toes lined up on the dashboard. "How long will this take?"

"What do you mean? I thought you wanted to do this?"

She turns her head away. "I did. I mean, I do, but we've been doing it every weekend for months now."

"Seven weeks."

"Exactly." She takes off her scarf and shakes loose her lilac-almost-white hair.

"But you agreed that we need to find their lair or source, whatever it is..." I scrape my own less vibrant hair out of my eyes as I swing the car onto the incline leading to the mountain footholds.

My eyes dart over the rocks. The fixers come from the mountain somewhere. If we can find the exact place they come from, we can figure out how they're being created and powered. We'd been exploring the range systematically, drawing up maps and crossing off areas explored.

"I know what I said." She leans her elbow on the window. "It's just that this plane can be boring, sometimes."

"What do you mean, boring? We do whatever we want, no rules, no jobs, no worries." Things we'd both agreed we wanted to escape forever.

"But there is nothing to *do*." She rolls her head from side to side as if the idea is tormenting her. "There are no shops."

"Shops?!"

"No men our own age."

I clench my hands on the wheel. "So?"

"No one makes it past eighteen without getting fixed...except us."

"Ree is..."

"He is barely sixteen, Ban. I said *men*."

"But if he can make it that far, maybe the others..." I don't remind her that's the reason we're doing this in the first place. When we stop the fixers, we won't have to resign ourselves to being stuck on red or blueplane like the adults. We'll be able to live here as long as we want.

"How long are we going to wait to find out?"

I start to say 'as long as it takes' but the words die on my tongue. I spot a fixer. It could've been there a long time. Now I'm older, I don't see them as clearly as I used to. It moves slowly, rolling over the ground on two black wheels. Fixers look like ordinary free-standing lamps used in theatre or filming: a cuboid lamp-head on a long pole, but that's where the similarity ends.

The long pole supporting the lamp swings round. The shutters on the lamp head flutter like bird wings as it focuses. It's almost as if it's thinking about its next move. It channels a beam of blackness at us.

I lower my eyes, focus on my hands. My head screams at me not to look, even as something treacherous in my gut urges me to stare into that single, dark bulb-eye. I ram my foot down and the car gurgles in complaint, then surges forward.

The fixer cracks off my front solar panel and bursts with a tinkling sound like a bell. Myriad dots of glass rain down on us, coating my lap. Only then is it safe to look up.

Dem brushes the black glass onto the floor. It looks out of place amongst all the purple hues, like a strike across an otherwise perfect picture. My bonnet is pitted with hundreds of dents. I've lost count of the times we've driven through fixers with Dem hooting encouragement. But today, she's silent.

"If you don't want to come, I will drop you at the altshift and you can go back to shops and men and shopping with men."

"Don't be like that. I said I would come, and I'm here." She crosses her arms, then unfolds them and grabs my arm. "Ban!"

"What?" I stare through the smeared windshield. I can't see anything except the indigo shadows at the base where it's cut off from the sun by an outcropping of stone, and then... It can't be. I'd assumed it was shadow, but it's a crowd of fixers. Six, maybe seven hundred. I've never seen them mass larger than packs of ten.

Dem's nails dig into my skin. "Back. Turn back."

They rush to meet the car. Six, maybe seven hundred lamps turn silently on their poles and zone in on the car, on us.

"Don't look!" I hear myself screaming as the black light falls over us. The violet tones of my skin disappear, switched in an instant. I'm absent. In a minute, they'll have me. But they can't fix us if we don't look into the lamps.

They're quick. They crash up and over the car in waves. The first flux explodes, but then two of them cling to the grill. One loops a cable around the wing-mirror and is dragged along. The black light is intense, not with heat or cold, with absence.

I shift into reverse, and we shoot out of the press. I can't tear my eyes away. They move as one. Their wheels whir steadily but throw up no dust. The black leads they keep wrapped around their poles unravel and ripple through the air. Some fall short, but one latches onto the grill with a ping and we drag it after us. It spins around, winding itself in.

It lands on the bonnet. The light glitters over my head. I can feel it pulsing in my hair like an animal's breath, like the snort of a wolf or a bear as it takes my scent before biting my head off.

What is in those glass lamps that has the power to take you from my plane and fix you permanently on red or blue? The answer is right above me, if I'm brave enough to look. I almost look up, but then I see Dem's face close to mine. She looks insane, her face mottled black, her eyes spinning in and out of shadow. A black lead is clamped around her chin, pushing her head up.

"Dem!"

I wrench her away with one hand and spin the wheel with the other. The fixer crashes sideways off the bonnet. Finally, we make some ground and they recede behind us.

"Why so many?" Dem shakes her head then kneels in the seat and stares over the headrest.

"I don't know." They've been growing in numbers and following me through all three planes but never this many or this aggressive. A glance in the rear-view mirror reveals they're still gushing after us like an advancing tidal wave.

We hurtle towards the altshift. We skirt the city limits, past mauve playhouses, blankets, old bikes. The altshift is out on its own, a small solar-tower, a launch-mat and a battered box with two lights blinking at an almost imperceptible variation. One will take us to redplane, the other to blue. We have to time it just right. I stop the car on the pad. Dem leans out the car and slams her hand down on the box.

Red. Damn. It takes a while for my eyes to adjust to the light, but I can see the violent red shades of the citrus trees rushing into each other long before my vision clears and Al-Azhar Park comes into focus.

Dem sinks back into the seat and sighs. "I hate running. I wish we could stop."

I start up the engine and drive us off the grass. The altshift is in a secluded enough spot, but I still dislike bringing the car through in case we land on someone. No one ever sees the boxes until I show them where to look.

My head pounds. Redplane always makes me feel weak.

"You can drop me off here." Dem leaps out the car without bothering to open the door.

"See you tomorrow? We should leave early."

"Uhuh." She straightens her hair, now white streaked with rose, in the wing-mirror. Then she re-ties her headscarf.

"Are you listening to me?"

"Relax. I'll see you later." Without asking me to go with her, she runs to the bridge over the river.

I swallow the lump in my throat and scrub my eyes. Everything about this plane makes me want to cry! I could hit the altshift straight away, but I need to leave a few hours before going back to vioplane to give the fixers a chance to disperse. I could go to blue. Even though that plane makes me feel like I've dunked my soul in a bucket of ice water, it's still better than this plane. But there's something I've been putting off doing for months. I suppose now is the time.

The drive to Fim's is a short one. I coax the car onto the ring-road and head east. The crimson sun is past zenith. Afternoon. Fim will be on her roof, making the most of the light to paint. I thump my chest a few times to stifle a flurrying feeling like a bird struggling to escape. If I'm going to do this, I cannot fall apart. I pass brick houses drenched in crimson, scarlet walls, gardens with jasmine and albizia ranging from soft pink to rusty brown.

In one of the gardens, a woman helps her daughter hang scarlet sheets. An old man and a young boy are painting the wall. Both of them, like all males on redplane, are so faint they're almost translucent apart from their weak pink outline. I squint, trying to make out facial features, but they are too indistinct.

I could show that boy how to altshift. The greatest feeling comes from taking through a group of children and watching the boys and girls see each other clearly for the first time.

Ree cried the first time I brought him through. He turned his violet hands over and over as if they were new. He cupped my face. "You look so real. I'm never leaving."

And he hadn't, not like the others who hop in and out whenever they want until they get fixed and can't come back again.

I speed up. Fim will hate me for asking, but I need answers.

The familiar ad-banners stretch over the road at every intersection: Planesciences. Support us to create Plane Paradise, a perfect realm of existence for a perfect tomorrow. I could recite that phrase in my sleep. On red and bluplane, they pump it out in a tinny voice from the old mosques. I've always known my father works for Planesciences, but he left when I was young. I used to think the metallic voice was his and that he was a spirit.

The light changes, and I turn onto Fim's road. I see her silhouette on the roof and try to stop my hands shaking. I could come back tomorrow. I will be calmer tomorrow.

She's at the door before I've left the car. Threads of crimson line her eyes as she smiles. She reaches out and grabs hold of my hand.

"Banafsigy, it has been a long time." Ruby tears wet her cheeks. "I was so sure you had been fixed on blue. Why did you not come to me?"

I wipe my face and stare down at my feet. Guilt prods my heart, making a tender hole that draws me inside it.

"Come, come." She leads me to the front room.

Everything is painfully familiar, same tatty old sofas, same strong incense curling around the ceiling, same photo of me with the smeared glass. Fim never was a typical housewife. She always used to say that dust added character to a room.

For a moment, we both sit in silence waiting for the other to speak. I want to begin, but I don't know how to ask, and I don't trust my voice not to wobble.

She laughs and takes off the apron spattered in shades of red paint. "I was on the roof," she explains, "catching the light."

"What were you painting?"

"This and that." She scrubs her hands together. "It's been four years, daughter."

"I know." I work my fingers into the holes in the sofa cover. "I wanted to come, but, this plane..." I shake my head. I don't want to talk about that again. Our arguments about vioplane used to rage for weeks.

"You're still not attached to this plane?" I can hear the disapproval in her voice, but she tries to keep her face neutral.

"No."

"But...you're not a child anymore. The fixation lamps should have placed you here permanently by now."

"I didn't come here to talk about that."

"What did you come for?"

I can hardly think. Emotions grow exponentially in my head like flames. I take a deep breath. "I came to ask you about Father."

Her face changes. All the blush fades to white. She stands up, almost knocking over a table. "I told you never to ask. You promised."

"I know that," I say gently. "But I'm older, now. I deserve to know."

"You say you are older, but you still play games, still act like a child." She leans on the wall, "still go to that waste dump plane."

"You have no right to call it a dump. You've never seen it." She's always unreasonable, but I'm not. It's this plane that makes me feel mad. I bite my cheek.

She whirls around. "No, I have never been there, but I had to live with the spectre. It destroyed my marriage." Her lips quivered. "You never cared about me as much as you did him, a father who walked out on us both."

I stand up. "I need to find him."

"Why? What can he do for you? He cannot love you. He left."

Her words slice through me with precision, cutting to the core. I would leave, but I need to know. He's the only one who can help me figure out a way to stop the fixers finding us.

She picks up the photo of me from the table and throws it at the wall. The glass shatters into tiny red splinters over the rug. We both stare at it.

Maybe she regrets the action, because she folds into a chair and lowers her eyes. "He was working on that plane when we met. 'I'm going to bring us Paradise,' he told me, but all he did was make a wasteland. The day it was created, all the men turned to blurs. My grandmother told me about the times when there was one plane. She remembered when bluplane was created. She said buildings disappeared leaving gaps like pulled teeth. People disappeared too. Planesciences would not bring them back."

"The second plane solved Cairo's over-population problem. Half of the people were moved to the new plane," I say.

"And what about the fading of the men that remained here? Is that solving anything? My grandmother called it the Great Divide. She wept for the taken and the faded. I should have listened to her words." She stoops, picks up my photo, rips it in half. "Is this Paradise?" She rips it again. "Is this?"

"What are you doing?"

"You can't understand. Go to him if you must," she hands me the photo pieces. "But remember these."

I look at the picture fragments. On the back of one, there's an address. I flip the fragments over. There's the smear. From this angle, it's not a mark of carelessness on glass. It's a lip print across my face. A kiss.

I could tell her that I've always loved her. I could explain that redplane stifles me, makes me weaker and that's why I can't stay. My throat clogs with words. I say nothing.

I lie back on the bonnet of the car and stare up at the blank stretch of mauve sky. No clouds, ever, but there is something comforting about the way it never changes. I take out my watch. There's no such thing as day or night on vioplane, but on redplane it's past midday and Dem should've been here two hours ago.

"Isn't she coming?" Ree stands next to me, hands in his pockets. He has mismatched eyes - one lavender, one speckled with indigo. He has an antique polaroid camera and, before I can stop him, the camera whirs and flashes.

"Stop that." Bright spots dance in my eyes and ruin the good view.

"Here, you can have one of me." He fumbles amongst the collection of objects round his neck: a pair of binoculars, the camera, a pair of glasses, a comb on a string. Then he pulls out a photo and hands it over.

"Don't those things get heavy?" I cram the photo in my pocket.

"No. They make me useful. Like an army knife." He grins. "Can I come with you?"

I grunt noncommittally. Dem won't like him tagging along.

"Come on, purleease."

"Fine. But you have to be quiet, ok?" If Dem didn't like it, then she should've arrived on time.

"I promise." He makes a show of locking up his mouth and throwing away the key but spoils the effect by grinning. "So, what are we doing?"

"We're going to find a way to stop the fixers."

"Really?! You think we can stop them? That would be great!"

"Do you miss bluplane?"

He shakes his head. "No. I hated it there. Redplane is better." He shrugs. "But this plane is the best."

"Strange you should hate blue so much. If I had to choose between red and blue, it would be there."

He scrunches his nose. "But why?"

"I hate all the feelings on red, they get in the way." I hate not being able to think clearly.

He looks confused. "But that is the best thing about it."

"We should go," I decide, sitting up.

"What about Dem?"

Dem isn't coming. I know she's been fixed; I just didn't want to admit it. I should've guessed by the way she acted the last time we were together. "I suppose she forgot. It doesn't matter. You can help me."

"Whatever you say, Queen Ban." He hops over the door into the front seat.

We make it to the base of the mountain without encountering any fixers. The car chugs up the track that winds almost to the top. No grass grows on vioplane, no food either. I toss Ree an orange from my bag. I always bring food for him when I come so he doesn't have to leave. It's good to have his company. I tell him about what happened to me and Dem.

"There are more in the city, too." He bites off the orange skin and spits it over the side of the car. "They keep hanging around my tent. I've started sleeping in with Vik. We take it in turns as look-outs."

It will get worse the older he gets until, like me, he'll have to keep altshifting to shake them off.

We leave the car at the top and I lead the way through an outcropping of rocks to where a ledge juts out. It's flat enough to lie down on and extends over an impression in the dust below that forms a sort of road. Last time I came up here, I noticed fixers passing in droves beneath this spot. If I can just trace them back to where they originate...

Ree fidgets beside me. His scrabbling causes a cloud of dust to rise up and obscure the view.

"Stop moving!"

"It's been ages. What's supposed to happen?"

I put my finger on my lips. Below, two fixers rove into view. I scan the rest of the track. Another one emerges from the shadows further out. They don't see us.

Ree shuffles and twists to yank his binoculars out from under him. A flurry of dirt bounds over the edge. In the silence it sounds as loud as a herd of stampeding horses.

"Ree!" My heart stops as the fixers turned their lamp-heads and scan the bottom of the mountain. The whitish earth shines sickly black.

After a while, they move on. I exhale, not realising how tightly I've been pressed against the ground. I move away from the edge and sit up.

"Sorry. Hope I didn't ruin things."

"Be careful next time."

"It's just so hot out here." He scratches his head. His t-shirt is wet through at the neck.

"I don't notice the heat." Dem used to complain about it, but she complained about everything.

"We're too close to the sun." He uses the corner of his shirt to mop his face. "I don't know how the fixers get so close to it. Guess they don't have skin, though."

"What did you say?"

"They don't have skin."

"About the fixers being near the sun?" I stare at him.

"Can't you see?" He points.

"Show me." I can't see any fixers on the waste near the sun. They materialise from the rocks about a hundred metres away.

He crawls over and points. "Can't you see them, there?"

I follow the line of his finger. "Let me borrow those."

He passes me the binoculars. I squint against the intense light. Then, I see them, a steady flux of black lines rolling out of the sun. They separate and spread in all directions and a stream runs back the other way.

My pulse quickens. How did I not see it before? "The violet sun. Ree, you're a genius."

"Always knew I was useful. Can we go back now?" He levers himself up.

"Yes we can..." I turn to him and my words catch in my throat.

Behind him, dangling from a cable, a fixer hangs upside down, its lamp angled at his head.

"Ree, don't turn around!"

A cable slithers down and brushes the back of his neck. He jumps around and it catches him by the shoulders. He screeches, fumbling with the items at his throat.

I shield my eyes from the black glare and dive toward him, but the camera flash whirrs before I get there. The fixer explodes and Ree falls back on me. The black light vanishes and we sit up together, shaking black glass from our hair.

"What just happened?" I wheeze.

Ree stares down at his polaroid. A fuzzy lilac shadow image of the fixer hangs from its slot. "Flash, kaboom!" He says, eyes wide.

I expect the address on the back of the photo to lead to a Planescience building on redplane. Instead, I get directions to a spot outside Cairo on blue.

I drive away from Cairo and out to the Giza Plateau. The azure Sphinx glimmers inside its protective dome. Tourists cluster round it like ants on sugar. Compared to the wispy women in their party, the men look garish. I am faded like those women. It doesn't matter. Nothing bothers me on bluplane. I stop the car half a mile from the Sphinx.

I search for the spot marked on the photo. Its coordinates are located behind an outcropping of rock, separating the place from view of the tourists. The keypad is buried under the sand and a flat rock. I dig them aside and enter the code. A section of the ground slides open, revealing a set of steps. I feel my way down in darkness. The smell of hot dust surrounds me. I hit up against something solid, grope for a handle.

When the door opens, I'm faced with a dark room, a desk at one end, and the indistinct lines of a woman illuminated in a patch of light that I can't see the source of.

I walk up to the desk. "I'm looking for Dr Dendera."

The woman peers at me. Of her features, I can only make out the hint of a pupil and the outline of her eyelashes. "May I ask who you are?"

"His daughter."

"Wait over there." She indicates a stool and leaves via the steps behind me.

I wait, occasionally checking my watch. Half an hour passes. Am I trapped here? Ten more minutes and I'll check to see if I'm locked in.

The wall behind the desk slides back and a man appears. Short, balding in a lab coat, wiping his hands on a towel.

"Banafsigy?"

"Ban." I correct him automatically.

"I'm Tep."

I search his face, trying to feel a connection to it, but I feel hollow. That could be the effect of the plane, or it could be a real emotion. I can't tell. He sits on the edge of the desk. "I must say, I wasn't expecting to see you. Your mother and I had an agreement."

"What agreement?" She hadn't mentioned that.

"You are not supposed to be on this plane." He scribbles something on a slip of paper and holds it out to me.

I take it and look at what he has given me. A cheque. I slide it back over the desk. "I didn't come for money."

"Then what can I do for you?" He looks through me. He isn't seeing me, not really, only a faded outline. I'm as blank as he is.

"I want to know about the violet sun and how to stop the fixers."

"You still go to violetplane?" He sits up. "You're not fixed?"

"No."

"But you must be eighteen, nineteen by now?"

"Twenty-two."

He exhales and stands. "Walk with me."

I follow him past the desk. We walk along a dim corridor and up an incline. I realise we must be heading up inside the Sphinx. We walk in silence until he opens a door. Light spills out. Beyond, there is a mezzanine overlooking an area full of whirring machines and people in sky-blue lab coats. He indicates I should go in, but I pause on the threshold.

"I only want to know how to stop them."

He stares over my head. "How have you avoided them for this long? They are designed to stop altshifting from occurring."

"Can you help me or not?"

"Help you stop them?" He clicks his tongue. "Of course not. Stopping them would destroy the fruition of the work of many generations of our ancestors. We are working on clearing that plane of any human presence. The fixation lamps are our means of doing so. We cannot have people altshifting. The fabric holding the planes in place is very fragile. Too much motion and it will tear forever."

"But I don't understand why you're doing this in the first place. How is creating new planes going to make paradise?" I try to catch a glint of compassion in his eyes, but he doesn't look at me.

"Each plane is an experiment in what can be selectively included in existence. We have not reached the endpoint yet, but soon we will be able to place aspects of life that we find desirable on a plane and exclude others."

A cerulean conveyor belt jerks into motion and a row of fixers roll out onto the floor. I step away from the door. I know I should feel something. Fear? It hovers outside me like a faraway apple on a branch.

"I don't think it's fair that Planesciences pick who is fixed and where," I say.

"There must be balance, indeed, more balance than already exists. This is the way of life. Without balance, we would not be able to continue the work we do here." He presses a button on the wall. "We couldn't understand how children kept finding their way to altshift points."

"Forgive me. I'm wasting your time." I turn away. He won't help me. I shouldn't have come.

"I took you to vioplane when we first created it," he says softly. "I showed you how to find the altshift points. I wanted my child to see the aspirations of her ancestors made reality."

In the halflight, I remember him not blue but violet. A cajoling voice. I walked in blinding light across a floor that clanged under my shoes.

I shake my head. Fim's words about the faded come back to me. If Planesciences create more planes, perhaps men will disappear entirely from red and women from blue. I know already that Tep does not care about this world's unborn descendants.

"I should have remembered that you are capable of taking children there." Tep grabs my hand in his clammy palm. My first touch from him in years. "When all the children are fixed, we will reinvent reality and bring Paradise to earth."

"I don't want to be fixed!"

He pulls me close to him and holds me still. "Selfish. Sometimes we must sacrifice individual wants for a greater cause. You could save us all."

A fixer breaks away from the production line and rolls up the ramp towards us. Others follow. Black light swivels in our direction. Five lamp-heads train on me. I need to be back on vioplane. I push Tep through the door. He trips and clutches the mezzanine railing.

I run back the way I came, praying the door will be open. Tep shouts something. I can feel the fixers stalking me. In the dark, I imagine the cables seeking out my legs.

I pass the desk, slam up against the door. Locked. I twirl round and wait for them to come. There is no fear, no panic. Still, I seek a way out when there is none. My eyes catch on something incongruous: the light on the desk. From this angle, I can see the box it emanates from. Am I dreaming? The fixers enter, surrounding the desk. I close my eyes and leap amongst them, hand outstretched.

I hit the altshift box.

I expect Tep or someone from Planesciences to be waiting for me when the lights stop spinning and the sky solidifies into a purple block, but there is no one. I drive the car through the scattered tents. A few of the youths have built a fire and are roasting potatoes.

"Queen Ban!" They wave their skewered potatoes as I go by, faces illuminated in strips of lilac.

They think I'm their queen. I showed each of them the altshift boxes, and they rubbed their eyes like I'd awakened them. Hundreds of children come here, and I'm responsible for all of them.

But what if we risk destroying existence? I cannot tell all these children to be fixed. I cannot ask them to do something I won't. The thought of being stuck on red or blueplane scares me more than anything else, even more than not existing. Fim and Tep. I don't want to be like either of them.

The scrap-metal mountain shines like a beacon, sun licking the edges of broken knives, bicycle wheel spokes, tin cups, like it wants to devour them. I head towards it. A boy throws something on, a small offering to the mountain.

I toss metal into the back of my car. In goes a rusted knife, a piece of Planesciences sign, an axehead, anything sharp and dangerous looking. The whole time, my gut is twisting like a cat's cradle. When I've loaded up the back seat, I take a slow drive out of the city. Perhaps this will be the last time I see my Cairo. I've been thinking that same thing every day for years. Today is different, because I know it will be settled for sure, one way or the other.

I adjust the rear-view mirror and take a last look at the tents and the zoo and the mountain. Ree jumps into view, cheeks puffing as he runs after me. I don't want to stop, but I should warn him. I stop the car.

He hangs breathless on the door. "Where you going? Wow! You got half the metal mountain in your car."

"Ree, I'm about to do something dangerous. It might not work out. You should tell the others, try to get as many children off vioplane as you can until it is safe to come back."

His mismatched eyes go round as dinner plates. "Are you going after the fixers?"

I nod. "The violet sun."

"I'm coming with you."

Before I can say otherwise, he hops into the front.

"Do you believe we should honour the dreams of our ancestors?" I don't know why I'm asking a sixteen year old kid that question, maybe because he's the only one there to ask.

He shrugs. "What dream?"

"One they worked their whole lives to make a reality. One I could destroy without knowing the consequences."

He scratches his head. "We'll be someone's ancestors too, one day. Then others will have to honour our dreams."

I rest my head on the steering wheel. "I have no idea what I'm doing. You shouldn't come. I could destroy the fabric of reality. My father..."

He waits for me to finish but I can't.

"I don't know about fabric or reality or anything, but I know fixers. We've got to stop them. And you need me." He rattles the camera. "If you leave me behind, I'll walk out there. I don't care how long it takes."

"Guess I don't have much of a choice, then." I put my foot on the accelerator.

We drive out towards the violet sun, a dot on the horizon. When the mountains disappear in the rear-view mirror, I realise this is the furthest I've ever come from the city. Dem never liked to come too far because of the heat. I can't feel it, but Ree's face is running with sweat.

"How much further do you think it is?" He says.

"No idea."

We drive for two hours. Ree wilts. He drapes himself over the door, his t-shirt stuck to his back. "Why don't you feel it?" He wheezes.

A walk inside whiteness holding a hand. Shoes on metal grates. Had Tep made me invulnerable to the heat when he first brought me here?

"I can take you back."

"No." He sits up straight, then points. "Ban, look."

I strain my eyes against the white glare of the sun. A legion of fixers roll towards us. The black light from thousands of lamp-heads forms a creeping puddle that precedes them.

"Last chance."

He shakes his head. "Do it."

I accelerate to meet them. The car rattles and roars as I force it faster. I hold my breath as if about to dive into water, and then the car plunges into black light. I smash a path through brittle black bodies. One explodes on the bonnet showering us with black glass followed by another and another. They crowd in on us. Cables wrap around the wing mirrors and the car slows.

"Grab the metal and throw it at them," I shout.

Ree scuffles back and grabs an armload of metal. He saws at a cable with a cup, banging until the wing-mirror breaks off and the fixer falls under the wheels.

We're not going fast enough. Six fixers wedge on the bonnet, loosening a couple of the front solar panels. The car splutters.

The sun's glare obscures everything. Water fills my eyes when I try to see what is coming out of the light. The fixers scrape along the side of the car. Cables grip hold of the windshield, twisting it with an ear-wrenching squeal. The glass pops out and shatters.

Lamp-heads hover near my face, a crowd of them so close I can feel them brushing my cheeks. The black light has me. My hands, covered in light and glass, look only part real. The urge to look up, to stare deep into those black lenses is a hunger.

"We need to leave the car." I cover my face with my hands, grab something from the back seat and lurch over the side swinging my arms wide. Exploding glass, soft as dust, rains down.

Ree follows me, but he's slow and wheezing. He takes photos again and again. Dozens of fixers fall at every flash. "Don't wait for me. I won't make it."

I can't see him. I follow the breaks in blackness caused by the camera flashes and try to smash my way towards him.

"Come on, Ree, it's not much further."

"It is...too...hot." He clicks his camera. An arc of space opens up around me, and suddenly I see him. "Run, Queen Ban." He throws the camera at me. It sails through the air and bounces on the ground.

"No, Ree!" I dart at him but cables already have him round the waist. Fixers leech onto him. He batters with his fists. In a moment of stillness, I see his head pulled up, his eyes flutter open. Then I blink, and he's gone. Fixed.

Water streams down my face. I grab the camera, close my eyes and run. Cables grab my arm, but I hack at them, at myself, and they fall away. I spin and twist my way towards the burning violet light, furiously flashing the camera. My eyes flutter open and seek out the black light. It would be easy to give in.

I drop the metal, loop the camera round my wrist and clamp my eyelids shut with my fingernails, using my elbows to smash my way through. I hit something solid. Glass. The heat of it sears my knee. I yelp and pull back. There has to be a way up. I fumble around the outside, scalding my fingers until I find it, a metal rung at head height. I rip off my headscarf, tear it into strips and cover my hands. I pull myself up the rungs.

I make it up ten before a cable catches my ankle. I slip. My elbows sizzle against the metal. A ragged scream bursts out my throat. The weight of the fixer stops me moving. One-handed, I bang the camera against the ladder until it whirs. The fixer explodes and the camera slips and thuds down the ladder.

I throw myself up the last few rungs and land on a metal grill. Shoes tapping on metal. I have been here before.

"I thought you might do something like this, though I did not think you would get this far," Tep says.

I squint around. My eyes hurt less when I turn my back to the sun. The grill is a platform that surrounds it. It isn't a sun, more a type of lighthouse. I step to the edge and peer at the black ring of fixers closed in around the tower. I won't be able to go back that way.

Tep stands across from me, his hand resting on an altshift box. He's wearing a pair of goggles. It's strange to see an adult here.

"I remember being here."

"This is the control centre," he says. "This is where we chose to store it. Nur y wugud."

The violet sun, that is all it's ever been. But it is more than that. I have always known it's what makes vioplane special. "The light of existence."

Tep's face swims in and out of my vision. "It is reality, the original reality, or what it left of it. Redplane, blueplane and violetplane were all extracted from it."

I put my hand in my pocket and take out two photos, one of Ree, one of me split into pieces. "I thought you had created new planes, but you are dividing existence. Fim said you have weakened reality by splitting it."

"You are a disappointment like your mother. She never understood."

"She understood." I move back from the railing. Cables flicker up and around them. Fixers will swamp the platform soon, and I don't know what to do. How do I put the pieces back together? I think of Ree, his hands batting at the fixers like a moth against a light-bulb.

"Planesciences will create a utopia. You may not like it, but you have to be fixed. We cannot have people coming here. We need to continue extracting planes." Tep puts his hands together as if praying.

A fixer hoists itself over the railing and lands on the grill. Black light sweeps over me.

"No." I back up against the glass of reality. The heat burns my back. There is no perfect plane, not red or blue or even violet.

"Move away, Banafsigy, the glass is fragile." Tep's shoes tap as he hurries over the grate.

I have an idea. A mad idea. I picture myself as a child smashing a glass Fim used to clean her brushes. When the glass broke, coloured water poured over the side staining the canvas below in a myriad pattern of colours. I thought Fim would be mad, but she laughed and told me I'd improved it. Why am I thinking of that now?

Cables wrap around my ankles. Light angles into my face. I think of Ree and Dem and all the other children and hope they will forgive me.

I grab hold of the cylindrical fixer head, strangely cool, and pull it down. I open my eyes and stare deep into the lens. At the same time, I ram it and myself into the violet sun. I see, deep in the fixer's light, my own smiling reflection. We hit the glass. The world explodes.

※※※

The man passes the photo to others sitting in the dust, but they all shake their heads and pass it back. I press my sunglasses up my nose and walk on. My eyes are slowly adjusting to all the colours, though fire still makes them water. The first day, I couldn't keep my eyes open longer than ten seconds. It's like all the planes have bled into each other. I thought I'd ruined everything. Now, I'm not certain.

Part of me wants to smile when I see orange flames pulsing against red bricks, black smoke like cables melting into a blue sky, all the colours clashing and getting in the way of each other. Part of me wonders if I'm walking on the plane my ancestors knew.

A woman cries at the foot of a pile of rubble. On redplane it was a row of houses, on blue it was a market. The two have collided and fallen. That is my fault, another consequence of breaking the world. I try not to mourn for the white shrouds lining the streets. Try not to blame myself. Not yet. There is something I have to do first.

I flex my brown hands with their blue veins. I'm never going to get used to that. Nothing makes sense anymore. I walk up the road on dust of a thousand vying colours. Roads and sky scrapers lifted straight out of bluplane are here, though they're not blue anymore. There are also parts of redplane: palm trees and solar-towers.

Planescience shouts their victory from the mosques. They pretend this is Paradise. The tinny lies drift through strange streets. I don't care. Right now, I'm only interested in one thing. I finger the photo.

"Have you seen this boy?" I ask a man outside a shop, a woman staring at her own reflection in the window. They both shake their heads as if they're dreaming.

I wonder if Tep is still alive somewhere and if Fim is enjoying this world or cursing whoever reformed it. I move on, not sure where I'm going. I glance at the sun. It is a normal sun. It rises and sets but in the most glorious battle of colours. Soon it will be dark, but I'll keep searching this night and every other. If this is all the world there is, then Ree will be out there somewhere. I want to tell him that I freed us, even though it meant losing violetplane forever.

I want him to tell me it was worth it.

/1URDER IN THE THIRD
BY MAC BOYLE

The banner read "National Association of Third-Person Narrators —
Fourteenth Annual Convention."

"The dead body below the sign had already gone cold." The declaration came
from one of the convention-goers as he walked past me.

"Yep, I can see that." I replied, not looking away from the victim. He hadn't
been dead long. The smell hadn't yet over-powered the perfume of the burnt coffee
from the free continental breakfast.

"Sometimes dead is bettah," he said, beating me over the head with an accent
that could only have come from the untamed wilderness of Maine.

"Thanks for the tip." I noted the name "STEVIE" scrawled across his "Hello,
my name is" tag, but figured if my new friend was this eager to put in his two
cents, then murder wasn't in his character.

I had a feeling that the next few days would be filled with people telling me
things I already know. When it comes to my story, I'll tell it myself, thanks very
much. If you ask me, all of these storytellers *née* Peeping Toms are a bunch of
loons, but one of them lay murdered before me. I'm a homicide detective by trade,
and I have a job to do. I understand that statement might bring to mind images of
a Phillip Marlowe-type, obsessed with his job above all other concerns. Let's get
one thing clear: I'm not some literary concept for you to deconstruct. I'm a person,
and I'd like to think I have a little more dimension than my vocation. If you want
a Marlowe-type, go write your own story. I'll wait patiently right here.

Back so soon? I'll continue...

As I approached the stiff I found some mook contaminating my crime scene.
Lines sallowed his face, each crease distorting his expression to one of perpetual
disappointment. His eyebrows shot across his face like a confident brush stroke,
freezing his scowl into place. He cradled a lit Marlboro between two fingers, and
he smelled vaguely of rotting leaves. He clearly had never been without a cigarette
for any moment of his waking life.

"Picture a man. His greatest contribution to the history of letters remains the tale of a horrible, senseless murder. Now, who will tell the story of his own demise? It's a tale that can only be told in the Twilight Zone."

"I beg your pardon?" I tried waving the haze of carcinogens away to no avail.

"You must be the Detective," another man said as he ran breathlessly towards us. "You're speaking to Rod, president of NATPN."

"Are you Rod's assistant?"

"Well, *you* aren't."

"What are you?" I asked the flunky. "Some kind of *second* person narrator?"

"You are!" he spat.

Apparently, this Rod character didn't speak much for himself outside of cryptic stingers. I skipped shaking either man's hand and took my first unencumbered look at the body. The vic had a jowly face in life. Someone had snapped his neck. The perp had to be strong. Even in death, the face of the deceased seemed delighted by the morbid underpinnings of his fate. His fair hair gave him a feminine quality that bordered on the tragic.

"Who was he?" I asked. "And skip the poetic mystery, if you would."

"In life, he was a true man..."

I glared at Rod, then at his assistant. "Can you translate for your boss?"

"You are looking at Tru," the assistant answered. He then regarded the body. "You were one of NATPN's most prominent members. Your Black and White Ball the night before the convention has been a highlight for years."

"What kind of books did he narrate?"

"You would have heard of his most famous work. It was a true crime epic," the assistant explained while his master lit another stick.

I grumbled a response.

"You never read it?" the assistant asked.

"Not my genre," I said. I grabbed a neglected copy of *USA Today* for some quick scratch paper. Using the sports section, I sketched a quick representation of the body's placement. It was for the best; the Cubs lost again. "Who was the last person to see him alive?"

Before Rod or his trained monkey could speak, the convention hall filled with echoed shrieking. A flash of red taffeta moved in front of me and towards the body. I couldn't get a good look at the newcomer, but a waft of rose oil danced its way into my nostrils.

"Oh, my dear Tru! Oh, what has happened to you?"

I could understand the dame's feelings on the matter. In an effort to stifle her tears, she grabbed the body in a tight embrace. Although the crime scene had already been tampered with beyond usefulness, I had to interfere.

"Ma'am!" I pulled her off the ground. "You're going to have to stay back."

Her head whipped upward and stared at me sharply. "I am Mrs. Munnerlyn-Upshaw-Marsh! But you can call me Peg!"

"Peg?" I asked.

"Yes, Peg! Do not dare to speak to me in such a manner! Who has done this to my sweet Tru?"

"You're now talking to the narrator of a romance novel," Rod's hack explained.

"We don't know yet," I told Peg, only after she downshifted from explosively histrionic to merely whimpering. "When did you last see him?"

Her hair draped over her shoulders like black satin sheets. On another woman, her bodice may have smoothed out certain aspects of her figure. With her, the garment instead lent those curves a mythic quality. She felt like trouble, but the kind of trouble I'd like to get to know better. Through streaking mascara, her emerald eyes considered me with nothing but contempt, but after a moment they softened. She reached for my chest, despite my best attempts to keep her a good distance from both the departed and myself.

"Last night. Oh, why did this have to happen? He had every reason in the world to live!"

She collapsed into tears once more. I had two unis escort her away and cordon off the area with yellow tape. Peg was a sweet kid in a lot of pain. She might get over it one day, but she'd need a minute before she could answer any questions.

After the M.E. had Tru on his way to a metal slab, I went back to the station. I attempted to read up on the players in the case and the convention's other attendees. Their works were just what I suspected. Stories told by people who weren't even there. Lurid innuendo passing for insight. Enough passive voice to choke a horse.

I stopped reading Peg's tales after about a page. It didn't seem right to engage in such ribaldry on the taxpayer's dime.

Tru's magnum opus remained my most befuddling read. In life, he treated death as if it was some sort of epic tragedy. For me, it was a living.

I even managed to work in a few episodes of Rod's television program. I got a big kick out of the show he did with the aliens armed with cookbooks. While I had tried to gain some insight into these weirdos, I only confused matters further by the end of my consumption.

I returned to the hotel only to find Peg just outside the entrance near the valet parking stand. Rain started falling as I called out to her. Between her tears and the downpour, she must have looked objectively frightful, and yet, I found her alluring. It took all of my self-control to keep the exchange professional.

"Yes, Detective?" she asked.

"I'm going to need to ask you a few more questions about your friend."

Peg looked away from me. "Oh, yes. Tragic. Absolutely heartbreaking. I have no earthly idea how I will go on."

"I was wondering..." I stammered over a few additional incoherent words. I shook my head and re-focused. "Did you kill Tru?"

She seemed so delighted by the suggestion of scandal. My heart sank at the prospect that her answer might be a confession.

"Do you think me wicked?" she asked.

"Not at all," I croaked. "I have to ask. It's my job."

She smiled and I nearly melted. Acid rain is no joke. "You're not like the other men in my life," she lamented—or was it celebrated? "I imagine you're not like other policemen, either."

"You're not like the others, either. Everyone else keeps a distance from their stories, but they do focus on one character. You're all over the place. If I didn't know better, I'd think you can read minds."

Her eyes and nose flared. "I loved Tru, but he dismissed my stories. He never called me trash like the others. He just told me I needed focus!" She shouted that last part in anger. I felt for her. She'd never get the chance to speak to her friend again.

"Peg—"

"But I don't *need* focus! *They* need to open their stories to *my* methods! I'm a third person *omniscient* narrator! My characters—*all* of my characters—come to life with their own thoughts and feelings! What's the point in being a third-person narrator if you can't read a few minds in the process? With their focus, and their tight prose, all of those bastards might as well be a bunch of first person singulars—"

I grabbed her by the shoulders. It reminded both of us of the first time we met. At least, I guessed it reminded her of the moment. I wasn't a mind reader.

Maybe she had a point. Maybe third-person narrators needed to add an internal life to all their characters.

No. She was a potential witness. I had a job to do. That's all that mattered.

"You've got no point of view, sweetheart," I told her as I let her go. "It's confusing to the reader."

Peg gasped at my impertinence and ran back into the hotel. The faint sound of her sobbing echoed in my ears as the rain cleared up immediately.

"Love. Sweet vindicator and unrelenting hunter. Mrs. Munnerlyn-Upshaw-Marsh assumed the future ahead of her was bright. With one act of violence, however, her fate has taken a sharp detour... into the Twilight Zone."

I stared at Rod. How long had he been standing there, smoking in the fog? Only after several seconds of sustained silence did I realize he had nothing further to say on the matter.

"And where were you last night, Mr. President?"

⚜⚜⚜

Rod's alibi turned out to be air tight, despite the fact that he gave me the creeps. It just seemed to be his way. I canvassed the rest of the convention for any leads. The drudgery of asking these fools questions made me wish I had stayed in bed. Chick-Chick the Horse narrated a series of gentle Western tales about a ranch hand named Guadalupe. While Chick-Chick could barely stop talking long enough to breathe, I ruled her out as a suspect. Tru hadn't been trampled to death.

Chief Observer Bleen-Boooooorn (accent on the "booooooorn", for those of you reading at home), was a multidimensional being charged with narration and continuity for an entire universe of superhero comics. Another unlikely target of my investigation: he stood 17 inches tall and squeaked when he walked.

The Scroll of E'tynah brought readers an epic Fantasy trilogy. Elves. Goblins. Hairy feet. All of that crap. Almost no one read the scrolls' books, but everybody saw the damn movies. Had Tru met his end by way of multiple paper cuts, I might have made E'tynah a person of interest.

Chick-Chick, Bleen-Boooooorn, and E'tynah all indicated the deceased argued loudly with another convention guest several hours before his likely time of death.

Tru's debate partner became my top suspect due to his reputation alone. Everyone I asked told me I could find the man at the hotel bar.

The man's tag read "ERNIE", but when I introduced myself, he insisted I call him "Papa." When I refused, he looked like he was would either punch me in the mouth or pour me a glass of tequila. When I flashed him my badge, he opted for the latter. He smelled like fish, even though there wasn't a seafood restaurant for miles.

"Tru is dead," I told him.

He took a shot of the liquid in front of him. With any other suspect, I might have thought he was trying to steady his nerves. Given his reputation, I would have been more concerned if he hadn't been drinking.

"All men die. If he lived with courage, we will remember his work."

I shifted, reassuring myself that I had my service revolver tucked into its holster. "Where were you at half-past midnight this morning?"

"I was here, working. I like to write in bars." I looked at the sheets of paper in front of him. All I could see were rough sketches of an anthropomorphic sailboat named Mortimer. He flirts with comic strips. I made note of it.

"I don't care for interruptions." He then added to his doodles Mortimer's friend, a harpoon named Siegfried.

"Several witnesses saw the two of you arguing last night."

Ernie wrote "Mortimer and Siegfried's Silly Day on the Water" over the characters. He almost immediately crossed the words out and wrote above them "An Elderly Person and a Very, Very Large Pond." He crossed that out and placed his pencil on the table.

"Men hunger for a fight. It is their way. Strong men demand it."

"You understand that doesn't count as an alibi, right?"

"I thought his recent book was a fine book, but not a great book. I told him so. He called me a fascist."

"Are you?"

"A fascist?"

"A fascist. The man who murdered Tru. Anytime you're prepared to answer a question, I'm prepared to listen."

"Men who are stronger than other men are often called 'murderer' or 'fascist.' This does not make it so."

I got up from my seat, suddenly wishing I had brought backup. "Don't leave the jurisdiction. We'll talk again soon."

I had heard suspects clam up under interrogation, but this guy turned taciturnity into a Zen state. I wondered if he had a flood of other words to offer anyone who would listen, but either his guilt—or the quart of white rum he swallowed while I spoke with him—blocked the rest of his confession.

⚜⚜⚜

The evidence to arrest Ernie for Tru's murder would turn up soon enough. I went back to the station. Another episode of Rod's show proved useless in distracting me from the memory of Peg. I couldn't pursue her outside of the confines of the case. Could I?

I idly imagined what my next case may look like. It didn't make me feel much better. The Third Annual Symposium of Thesis Statements would be in town next month. Those thugs were always up to trouble. I intended to take some vacation time before the Quadrennial Symposia of Poetic Meters. Life is just too short.

I didn't get to start another episode, as I then got a call from the hotel. Someone had attacked Peg and paramedics now rushed to the scene.

As I re-entered the hotel lobby, the paramedics moved Peg through on a gurney. They had wrapped the top of her skull in gauze, not quite covering the bruise surrounding her eye.

"Detective... I was hoping to see you again, if in a slightly different locale." She smiled, and then winced under the stress it put on her face.

"I did mean to ask you some more questions about your friend, Tru. It never seems to be the time for us."

"Maybe one day we'll have our moment," she said wistfully. "I thought poor Tru and I would live happily ever after—"

"I'm not sure you were reading that one right..." I had done my homework now; I felt like I knew everything about these people.

"—but here I am."

"When did you last see Tru?"

"In my dreams..."

I looked at the paramedics, wondering if they had already sedated her beyond any hope of coherence. They shrugged. "Maybe I should ask how you got that shiner."

"You're so gentle..." she cooed. "I could tell by your... your eyes. I worried that when you had the evidence you needed against Papa, he might hurt you when you went for the arrest."

"Ernie did this?"

She didn't nod, but the intent stare from her uncovered eye confirmed everything left unsaid.

"He screamed that Tru's work was trite! Flowery! Sensationalized—!"

That was the last of her statement I heard. I was already running in the other direction, towards the conclusion of this case.

※※※

When I entered the large ballroom hosting the NATPN convention's main meeting, the convocation had just begun. Rod was unable to lead the call-and-response without plugging his television show at the end of the proceedings. He stood near the dais. Although, for his persistent smoking, the figure I took could have been a fog machine with a necktie wrapped around it.

Rod's assistant was equally useless in such a gathering. He stood by the entrance to the ballroom, taking in the proceedings coolly. I nearly wondered if he might have been Tru's murderer, but I avoided red herrings when I could. The salt is bad for my ulcer.

Therefore, it fell to the group's treasurer, Chick-Chick the Horse, to open the proceedings. She stood at center stage, reading from the pages of the Scrolls of E'tynah.

"To whom did this happen?" the horse asked the crowd.

"It happened to them," they replied.

Chick-Chick continued. "The story is done. The players will not speak."

"We will tell the tale."

Chick-Chick whinnied involuntarily, but kept her composure. "Who is that third person? The one who was never there?"

The crowd's enthusiasm vibrated the deep-pile carpet beneath my feet. "I am not. You are not! They *did*! WE ARE!"

NATPN collectively erupted in applause. My backup and I took the noise as an opportunity to approach our collar without spooking him. As we got closer Ernie appeared to be guzzling from something that looked like a water bottle, but smelled even from a distance like a mojito. The sooner I had him in a cell, the better.

"Ernie, you are under arrest for assault on Peg, and the murder of Tru. You have the right to remain silent." The unis slapped handcuffs on him. "Although, I don't think you're going to have any trouble with that."

I finished reading Miranda as they led the infamous Papa out of the building. Rod, his assistant, and the rest of the NATPN convention-goers looked on, stuck in the perfect crossbreed of horror and inevitability.

"You've done a good job," Rod's assistant told me as I tried to make my exit from this nightmare. Beyond the exit and outside the building, I could still see the flashing lights of the ambulance preparing to take Peg out of my life. I had to tell her the good news that I had put away her attacker and Tru's murderer. I also needed to see her just one more time.

Someone had left the ambulance rear doors wide open, and yet I could find no human activity around the vehicle. Upon closer inspection, neither paramedic had left the vehicle. Someone had snapped the first one's neck in a manner closely resembling Tru's demise. A syringe filled with blood and some the remains of other dosage dangled from the other's temple. I saw no sign of Peg, aside from the swath of gauze that only minutes before had been wrapped around her head. Beneath the bandage on the ground was a piece of folded paper. I untied the single strand of red ribbon sealing it. It read, in Peg's ornate script:

My Dearest Detective,

By the time you read this letter, I will be far away. Take comfort that there was no other way, my love. In due time, someone would uncover the evidence to clear Papa and implicate me in poor Tru's grisly end. I confess!

It never occurred to you that I was strong enough to snap Tru's neck, did it? How perfectly sexist of you. I may be a narrator of romance novels, but that hardly means I don't know how to kill a man with my bare hands.

Don't try to deny you never suspected me, my dear. Remember, I can read minds.

Au revoir,

Mrs. Munnerlyn-Upshaw-Marsh

"Peg"

Damned headhoppers. I tore the letter in half. I looked out into the woods beyond the hotel, but found no trace of her. Rod proved to be the only other soul in sight. He stood a few yards away, maddeningly smoking his cigarette and assessing the final moments of my embarrassment.

"Two souls, nearly in love. One, a clairvoyant murderess. The other, the detective tasked with bringing her to justice. It's a match made, not in heaven, but in—"

"Please don't say it again," I begged Rod.

"—the Twilight Zone!"

/II∫ER/
BY KERRY GS LIPP

On my 8th birthday I discovered that cats can scream. It's a terrible sound. About a minute after that, I learned that a metal baseball bat will silence a screaming cat with one swing. My dad taught me.

It probably sounds like my old man was an evil son of a bitch, but he wasn't. He did the best he could, at least I think he did, and all things considered, especially the way all this ended, I believe that he gave it everything he had.

The events that shaped him into the man he became were out of his control and I suppose he could've made different choices, but I think his heart was in the right place, or at least in his own mind, even if his mind had been poisoned since the day he got the news about the car crash that killed my mother, my two sisters and my brother.

It hurt us both. Hurt our home and the farm too.

It happened about a year ago and I was supposed to go with them to go school shopping, but dad broke my heart that morning when he told me that I couldn't go because he needed help with some chores around the farm to prepare for the coming cold months.

I hated Dad that day, and when the shock of what happened to my family hit me, I really wasn't sure what I felt after that. I kind of went numb.

But like I said, he tried his best and we struggled to recover over the last year. He wouldn't give up the farm or on the farm. I helped, but the two of us could only do so much. Dad was too proud to ask for help or hire anyone else. We both sort of pretended not to notice things beginning to slip and then outright fall.

To celebrate my 8th birthday my dad drove me about 30 miles into the nearest town, Kleaton, and took me to play putt-putt golf and then to the baseball diamond to hit a few balls and then out for ice cream.

All in all, we were only gone for about four hours, but those four hours seemed to last forever. On that birthday, with no farm work and nothing but my favorite things, I savored every breath.

I remember staring down into my brownie sundae at the ice cream parlor. Eating slowly and enjoying each spoonful. With every bite, I watched the sundae shrink just a little bit more and I knew that I couldn't wait too long because the ice cream would melt, but if I ate too fast, I'd just be sprinting to the end of my birthday. Then we'd have to go back home, and back home was getting depressing. I think they call it the downward spiral.

I studied at the last few bites for a long time and I didn't burst into tears, but I sniffled my way into them. They ran down my face and dripped onto the tabletop. I couldn't look at my father. I didn't need to, he knew. He ruffled my hair with his fingers and I said, "I know, son. I know." And he sat there with me, patient, while I took half an hour finishing the last couple bites.

We left and got back in the truck. I felt a little better, but I also felt tired. We'd spent the day outside, active in the hot sun and topped it off with ice cream. Even though I was supposed to be growing up, I was still tuckered out. I nodded off before the truck backed out of the space and took the first turn toward home.

❈❈❈

"Shit," my father yelled and I snapped awake. My dad hit the brakes. A fraction of a second later a thump shook the truck. And then I heard the screaming. Loud and clear and horrible, through the open windows. I had no idea what could shriek like that, it almost sounded like a person.

Still groggy, I didn't know what exactly was happening, but slowly my 8-year-old brain put it together.

Shit.

Brakes

Thump.

Screaming.

We'd hit something. My father put the truck in park and opened the door. Just before he got out, he looked over at me and saw that I was awake.

"We hit something Davy," he said. "Just stay here. I'm going to have a look."

"What's that screaming?" I asked holding my stomach. It might've been the sundae, but I think it was the screaming.

"I'm not sure. But I'm going to find out. Stay here."

He got out of the truck and closed the door. The screaming got louder. Pierced my eardrums. I looked out the back window of the truck. I still couldn't see what we'd hit, just the upper half of my dad and him shaking his head. The bill of his Reds baseball cap visible as he shook it from side to side.

Between the howling animal and the sundae, my stomach upset itself and I opened the door and darted to the shoulder of the road and vomited. Even the sounds of my gagging throat upchucking couldn't drown out the cries of the wounded animal. I turned my head in between dry heaves and looked.

I never should've done that.

I'll never forget what I saw. The front tire of the truck squashed the back half of the cat. The poor critter laid there, back legs sprawled in inconceivable directions half-flattened into the road. Some of its guts and blood had flown straight out its ass and sprayed all across the pavement. It's front paws clawed at the air, its head jerked all over the place and its mouth screamed.

My dad heard me retching and left the cat and ran over to me. He put a hand on my back and even as he held me I watched the cat twisting in agony. I spat bile, wiped my face and asked, "Can't we help it dad?"

And suddenly, as often happens when you finish vomiting, I felt a lot better. I stood up.

"You okay champ?"

"Yeah. Let's go help him. He's gonna die if we don't. We gotta get him to the vet."

Screams shattered the silence. Paws batted the air. Guts glistened in the hot sun. I think it was an orange cat, but it might've been part white, it was hard to tell with the different sprays of blood and fluid that matted the kitty's fur.

"Davy," my dad sighed. He looked away and then looked back at me. "We can't help him son. He's beyond help. He's in what they call misery. You know that word?"

"I think so," I said.

"It means he's suffering beyond repair and there's really only one thing that we can do to help him."

"What's that?" I asked, but I think I already knew the answer.

"We can put him out of his misery."

I said nothing.

"You're growing up Davy," my father said. "And as sick as it is, you growing up on a farm, this is probably a good lesson. They call it a rite of passage. Follow me son."

"You mean..." I started.

Stopped.

"Are we gonna..." I trailed off. I knew the answer.

The cat's cries grew more desperate.

I followed my dad to the tailgate of the truck. The hinges creaked as he unlatched it. He unzipped the bag in the back of the truck and pulled out exactly what I knew he'd pull out. My baseball bat. Some dirt still dusted the black rubber grip from my hands when I'd swung it at my dad's slow fastballs a couple hours ago.

"Come on Davy," he said. He took on a tone as serious as I'd ever seen. Except when he told me the rest of our family died. I don't think I'll ever see that in anyone ever again. He put his hand on my shoulder.

"Sometimes, there's just nothing you can do, and you've got to put 'em out of their misery," my dad said. "Do you understand Davy?"

I knew he was right, and I felt immature and ashamed that I hadn't realized it in the first place.

"Yes sir," I said, but looked at the ground.

"It's a hard lesson son, but you're growing up. What's about to happen might seem terrible, and it is, but son, it's right, and it's really the only thing to do.

Leaving it here would be wrong. We are human. God put us at the top of the chain, and it's our responsibility to end this poor critter's suffering. You'll see this on the farm from time to time, and you'll have to take care of it."

"Yes sir."

"Okay then. The poor kitty's been like this too long. I'll take the first swing, and son, I'm sorry, but you need to take the second."

My father raised the bat, looked at me, and brought it down on the cat's face. The screaming stopped.

I could tell his blow killed the cat, no doubt about it, but he handed me the bat anyway. I guess knowing that he'd already taken its life was supposed to ease me into the lesson of putting something out of its misery. I hesitated, but he looked at me and I raised the bat over my head, closed my eyes and swung like I was trying to ring the bell at the fair. I felt the leftovers of the cat's skull give. The weird sensation of bones crumbling reverberated through the bat and channeled into my young hands, my young mind, my young body.

I thought I'd feel sick, but instead, the blow brought clarity. I understood. The cat would suffer no more and we gave that to the cat. It felt powerful. It felt right. It lay there limp, its insides oozing out both ends, and my dad told me to get back in the truck.

From the cab I watched my father take a dirty towel from the bed of the truck and wipe the blood off the bat and put it back in the bag. Then he picked the cat up by one of its limp paws and tossed it into the ditch. He got back in the truck and rode the rest of the way home in silence.

The happiness and horror that made up my birthday vacated when we went inside the house. Reality came back swinging its big fists. The smell hit first as soon as we opened the front door, as we entered, the sight quickly followed.

Usually the smell wasn't so bad, but we were nearing the dead of summer, that time in which anything even a little stinky goes straight to rancid. Dad said that the farm was the priority, that's what made the money and that we'd get to the house when we got a chance. We probably should've spent my birthday cleaning the stacks of dirty dishes and doing laundry and vacuuming and killing the cockroaches, but my dad took me out for ice cream instead.

However, like we always did, we ignored the mess.

Dusk started setting in and he ruffled my hair.

"Let's change our clothes and watch a movie or something," he said. "It's been a long day."

"Okay."

"Meet back here in 10 minutes, son."

"Got it dad."

That had become one of our things after the rest of our family died. A time frame and addressing each other and emphasizing our "titles."

We met back in front of the television and dad had a beer for him and Coke for me. I could smell a frozen pizza baking in the oven. Our television only got a couple channels, and none of them were showing movies so we watched the Reds game together. Way better than a movie, and it just started.

Before the bottom of the fifth, I couldn't keep my eyes open any longer and since I couldn't stay awake, I didn't notice that dad topped off all his beers with heavy pours of whiskey. Though had I seen it, I wouldn't have been surprised. I could smell it. He drank, heavy sometimes, and didn't hide from me, and it didn't really bother me.

I woke up, just a little as my dad laid me down in bed. I feigned sleep, watching him stand in the doorway taking long drinks of his whiskey beer and sobbing at the sight of our filthy, silent, hopeless house.

I tried to go back to sleep, but I couldn't. I didn't want to get up. My dad didn't get violent when he drank, not even close, if anything, he grew more passive and depressed, but sometimes it made me uncomfortable. Laying in bed, I watched the ceiling and listened to him walk from room to room, looking at the empty beds and untouched furniture. Those rooms were the cleanest in the house. We never entered them; we just looked inside and remembered the memories, like little shrines to the majority of our once family.

I don't know how long I laid there listening to him, time has a way of playing tricks on you in the dark, but finally I heard him head to his bedroom, shut the door and then I just heard silence. I thought about that cat earlier, and how we put it out of its misery and that made me think about my dad. I wondered if he was in misery too, just his torn up guts were on the inside. That thought made me shiver despite the summer heat. I threw off the covers and went downstairs. I couldn't sleep and I needed some fresh air.

Looking at the clock on my way out the front door I saw it said 11:30pm. Exactly thirty minutes left of my birthday. I smiled at the great memories me and dad made today and that made me think about misery again.

What was it exactly? Was my dad miserable, like that poor kitty? Was he miserable all the time? Or just sometimes? Or maybe not at all? It was hard to tell.

Dad sure didn't seem miserable earlier today, but even at 8 years old I knew that people could be good at hiding things. My dad always tried to hide his sobbing and depression, but tonight wasn't the first time I'd seen him get drunk and pace around the upstairs and pass out, probably crying himself to sleep. Sometimes he didn't even drink; he just paced, and then went to his room and softly shut the door behind him.

I didn't really know what to do with all that. I tried to push it out of my mind and went outside for some fresh air.

The inside of our house was filthy and getting worse because we spent most of our time trying to take care of the farm animals. Without any extra help we couldn't keep up, and my dad was too cheap, too proud or too heartbroken to get any help. I didn't know for sure, but I'd bet on the latter two. And even though he knew how behind we were on chores and cleaning up after the animals he let us both take a day off for my birthday. I sniffled at the thought of that and realized that no matter how anyone on the outside might view him, my dad was one hell of a guy and a better father.

I'd gone out for fresh air and got hit in the face with the stink of pig shit. I was used to it, but it still stank, even worse than normal tonight.

I went for a walk around the house, staring at the clear sky the almost full moon and the bright stars. Patches of air here and there were clean and I enjoyed them.

Over the chirp of the crickets and croak of the frogs I heard something else and once it registered I couldn't believe I hadn't noticed it before. I should've heard it in the house, but I didn't. I guess I was just tired, but all the sudden the screaming hit me as stronger than the stink.

The pigs.

The pigs were screaming.

Since we spent my birthday relaxing and hitting baseballs and playing miniature golf, we neglected the pigs. Time ticked closer to midnight, but I wasn't tired and I thought knew how to care for the pigs. I wanted to make it right. Each step I took closer to the pen, the thick stench increased, almost became tangible. I grew up here and I'm immune to most smells that quickly turn the stomachs of non-country folk, but this was worse. A mass of unfed pigs, covered in slop and their own shit cooking in a summer oven disguised as a barn. I think the word is amalgamation.

I opened the door and the contents of my stomach burbled and I couldn't keep them down. For the second time on my birthday I vomited. The sight when I entered the barn was awful and worse was the smell, but the screaming sounds the pigs made that entered my ears the split second I opened the door assaulted me worse than anything. I got sick, felt a little better and slowly regained my composure.

The farmhouse was a mess, but the pig barn took it to a different level.

The pigs screeched in their pens. They must've been starving. We didn't feed them before we went to celebrate my birthday and we were too tired when we got home. I walked through the thick, putrescent air and looked around. It was atrocious before today, and no matter how hard we worked, we couldn't quite get it under control.

There was pig shit everywhere. Thick and deep and disgusting. Worms and maggots sprouted from the heaping piles and as I walked through I felt worse seeing the hungry pigs eagerly devouring morsels from the piles of their own crap.

We should've fed them.

My guts clenched again and I vomited into a sty. A pig watching with beady black eyes immediately turned away from the shit he was devouring and made short work of my puke.

The pigs ate and screamed, showed no signs of stopping. I looked into some of their eyes. The pigs' eyes were ravenous, desperate.

There was nothing I or even we, if I woke dad up, could do to fix this. Not tonight. Not ever. It was on the other side of the breaking point.

Looking at the miserable pigs I realize that there was only one thing left to do. When a creature was miserable, you had to end its suffering.

I thought dad would be proud of me learning and applying the lesson he taught me earlier that day. I couldn't take the pig sounds for another second and I couldn't imagine living in such conditions.

Such...

Such misery.

I went to the truck and got the metal bat.

Like the miserable, half-splattered cat, I had to put the pigs out of their misery.

Sometimes their misery is on the inside, I thought as I watched them swallow mouthful after mouthful of their own shit.

I went pen by pen as they ate hungrily from their own piles, and I raised the bat high, drove it home, and caved their skulls in. I swung hard and connected solid and occasionally if I had to swing twice I did, but finally, and I have no idea how long it took, but finally, the screaming stopped and their misery ended. The bat held up okay, but there were pieces of pig head stuck to it and it was dented in a couple places. I didn't think I'd be able to use it to hit baseballs anymore. Maybe for my next birthday dad would buy me a new bat.

I'd put them all down except for the last pen. That pen housed a mother and five tiny piglets. The sow squawked and challenged more than any of the others in the barn but the piglets were still too underdeveloped to make a peep. I thought about it and in a sick way, it resembled my family. I hesitated for a moment, but the piglets looked miserable in the filthy straw, all ugly and quivering. I couldn't care for them all. But one, I knew could handle one.

My dad, even if he was miserable (and I still wasn't entirely sure about that) had done a pretty good job handling one. Me. I thought maybe I could too.

I killed the mother first. The piglets attempted to scatter and tried to hide, but they couldn't. In no particular order I bashed them all, except the last one. I saved the last one.

After wiping the sweat from my brow and catching my breath, I picked it up and stroked it, the shit coating it smearing on my shirt and fingers. I cooed to it. To her I realized. Told her that her misery was over and that I'd take good care of her. And I would. With all these pigs out of their misery, I could focus on one and give it a good life. Like my dad tried to do for me.

Slowly, I became aware of the thick quiet that settled in the barn. No more screaming pigs, just silence. Pigs lay dead and bleeding out. I felt tired. I decided I'd take the piglet outside, hose us both down, and then we'd go inside and fall asleep together. Keep each other company. Keep each other happy. She nuzzled against my hand.

And then I heard the shouts coming from the farmhouse toward the barn.

"Who the hell's causing all this ruckus out here? I got a shotgun you better get the hell out."

The only sound was my father's approaching footsteps.

Then.

"Davy. Davy. Davy. DAVY. Is that you? Are you out here? Where are you boy?"

He didn't sound angry, just sort of drunk, maybe a little disoriented but mostly concerned. I looked at all the dead pigs, and had a sudden thought. Yes, I'd put these pigs out of *their* misery, *but what had I just done to my father?*

He stepped into the doorway holding a shotgun just as I was about to hide. My dad wore shorts and sandals and a wife beater shirt. His disheveled hair springing from his head in a bunch of different directions. His hair reminded me of the cat's legs earlier that afternoon. Dad didn't see me right away because he was too distracted by all of the dead pigs.

He pumped the shotgun.

"Jesus wept. What in the blue hell happened out here?" he demanded stalking through the barn looking around, visage visibly sick.

I could tell he didn't think it was me. He must not have checked my bed before he came outside. He probably just heard the screaming and saw the lights on in the barn. I knew he wouldn't shoot me, not even drunk. Not even angry. Not even after what I'd just done. He wasn't that kind of father.

"Daddy?" It came out like a question and I stepped toward him holding the piglet. He finally registered my presence.

"Davy. Jesus Christ. What have you done?" He asked. But he wasn't angry, his face instead composed of pure despair.

"The pigs Daddy, the pigs were miserable. Like that cat. Look at all the shit in here and we forgot to feed them today. They were miserable and they wouldn't stop screaming. We couldn't keep up Daddy. We tried, but just look at how they had to live. Their screaming wouldn't stop. So I... I put them out of their misery. I did 'em a favor right Daddy?"

"Oh Davy," my father said but couldn't finish. Tears glistened in his eyes.

"I saved this one though," I said and held up the piglet. "His family died like ours and I'm going to take care of him like you take care of me so he never has to be miserable."

The shotgun slid from my fathers grasp and clattered to the floor. He fell to his knees, weeping.

After a silent thirty seconds I went to him. I hugged my father and helped him to his feet and the three of us, me, my dad and the piglet went to the house. We didn't speak. Dad just put his arm around me. I didn't understand, at least not then, why he was so sad. I thought I'd done the right thing, and maybe I did.

He put me and the piglet to bed, and exhausted, we both slept without stirring.

Until the shotgun blast woke us both. The piglet, which I named Misery in honor of what I saved her from, jerked and murmured, but I held onto her.

With true childhood naiveté I thought perhaps my father had gone back down to the barn and found a lone pig still squirming with life and used the shotgun to end its suffering.

But I was wrong. My father used the shotgun to end his own suffering. When I entered my father's bedroom I saw his bottle of whiskey on the night table and his brains on the ceiling.

I didn't feel sad, or sick, or angry. I just felt numb. I think it had a lot to do with all the death I'd been a part of that day and the deaths of everyone I'd loved up until that point. Except for my piglet. Misery was still alive and happy it seemed. I set her on the floor and she went and licked at some dots of my father's blood. Misery also ate a couple pieces of something that the gunshot had blown loose.

I went to the night table, to the closest phone to call the police and I saw a few lines scribbled on a yellow legal tablet between the bottle and the phone. There were fresh dots of wetness dripped across the paper. Tears.

It said:

Son,

I'm sorry for everything that's happened to you in the first 8 years of your life. I'm so sorry. But I can't do this anymore. You were right, son, the pigs were in misery and I was in denial. You'll learn about all of that someday. Maybe you'll even understand and forgive me. And even if you don't understand you can forgive me anyway. I hope so. Davy, sometimes the misery is on the inside and not just on the outside and sometimes people have no choice but to put themselves out of their own misery. I pray to God that you never have to know misery like that. I'm sorry son. Be a good boy.

Love,

Dad.

I still felt numb. Felt nothing. Just empty. But I picked up that phone on the night table and called the police and told them what happened. Then I hung up and waited.

I didn't know what would happen next, but hugged my piglet tight to my chest and prayed she'd always be there to keep me company.

A Day in the Life of a Lame Fame Addict

by Shaun Avery

10:01 a.m.

I stand in front of the Fame Salon, a bundle of hard-earned cash in my hand.
I take a deep breath and look up at it.
Then I step inside.

10:08 a.m.

There's a queue, so it's a short little while before I'm standing in front of the receptionist.

She's pretty, chatty, flirty, wearing a low-cut blouse, plenty of cleavage on display. I don't think she's currently showing any signs of Fame Treatment herself, but you can tell she's had a little work of the surgical kind done. But then, who hasn't?

"Well, hi," she greets me. "I'm Sue." I could probably have guessed this from the nametag pinned above one of her half-exposed breasts, but I let the point pass. "Your name, please?"

I tell her.

"Ah yes," she says, head bent slightly, looking through the notebook on the desk before her. "You're here for a . . . ten forty-five session?" She looks back up at me. "Here bright and early, I see." Her eyes meet mine, and she smiles. "I like that."

"Thanks." I mean, what else can you say to that?

"If you'd like to take a seat," she says, "a technician will be with you shortly."

"Thanks," I say again. "Sue."

Then I park myself in the waiting area and the countdown begins.

10:33 a.m.

The place is packed, so I'm starting to suspect that the technician will be late, not early like me. But no, twelve minutes before the procedure is scheduled to take place a well-tanned man in protective glasses steps out into the reception area and calls out my name.

I stand up, dusting down my trousers.

You always want to look your best in a place like this.

I follow him into the Faming room, admiring his tan from behind as I do so. It's the type of tan that tells you he knows how to look and act around those who are getting famous, and it makes me wonder if he samples the goods he sells here. I wonder, too, if he gets any kind of discount as an employee. How brilliant would that be?

"Take a seat, sir," he says, and motions towards the item in question. "My name is Tad, and I will be your personal technician today." From nowhere comes a clipboard, and he's ready to write on it with a pen that has appeared in an equally mysterious way. "And what procedure can I interest sir in today? There's the Super Deluxe Bundle, and then there's . . ."

I let him go on.

But I already know what I want.

He frowns when I tell him, losing his professional front for a second.

"Are you sure, sir?" he says. "The Super Deluxe Bundle is much more popular, and lasts a lot longer, and it's only a little bit more expensive . . ."

He doesn't know it, but I already know all of this stuff. See, I've been in these places a lot. Now that they're so popular, there's pretty much a Fame Salon on every street corner in the city now. And it's a pretty big city.

"If sir would like to look, here are a few pictures of people who have taken full advantage of the Super Deluxe Bundle . . ."

He waves a photo album in my face, full of "Before" and "After" shots. I see a couple of people I recognise.

"And there's really not much difference in the price at all," he reiterates.

"I know." I push the album away. "I know all of that." I smile up at him. "But I'd still like the Standard Package please."

"If sir wishes," he says, and puts the album away. I can see that the "sir" doesn't come so easily to his lips now.

"Follow me," he says, then leads me to the chair, plonked down in front of the giant steel vat. "Does sir know how to strap oneself in?"

Sir does.

Sir puts oneself into the seat and puts on the special sunglasses and places his arms out straight on the arms of the chair with the vein sides pointing upwards so the needles that are hooked up to the vat with rubber tubes can come down and pump my blood full of Fame Plus Four Thousand.

"Very good," Tad says, and there's about a millimetre of extra warmth and respect in his voice now – guy's obviously playing for his tip. "If sir would prepare for the flash."

I do so.

That's why we all have to wear the glasses, back here.

No one can really explain the flash.

It's just something that happens when the fame meets the blood.

"Needles preparing," he says, and there's the sound of running liquid as the fame enters the tubes. "Coming down in five . . . four . . . three . . ."

I breathe in deeply.

Prepare myself.

And then all that fame hits me.

Fills me.

And before I know it, the time is 11:15 and I'm strutting on out of there.

Time to have some famous fun.

11:35 a.m.

First off, I know I have to swing by The Pad.

It used to be a warehouse, but that was long ago. Now it's a place where people like me go to hang out together and relax. Today when I enter there's about five or six people sitting around the first floor, all in various stages of a Fame comedown.

(Along the way here there were about fifty people who stared at me as I walked past them, roughly thirty of them whispering to whoever they were with "isn't that" and "what's his name again," trying to remember who I was, wondering if they'd seen me on TV or in a film or something. Had I mentioned that yet? No? Well, consider it mentioned now).

"Peter," Trudy says, looking up at me, eyes squinting. "Hey."

Stan crawls over and sniffs me. Then looks up at me. "Lame Fame?" he says.

I nod.

See, I guess I'd better now explain just what they did to me back at the Salon.

There are two types of fame they do, that you can have pumped into you. The Super Deluxe Bundle is stuff they get from people who are actually talented – actors, singers, whatever – and it lasts a lot longer. Thus, it's more expensive to buy – though not much more expensive, as good old Tad so helpfully pointed out.

Then there's the Standard Package, which comes from things like supermodels and reality stars, and it lasts less than half as long. Thing is, though, people like me and Stan and Trudy and the rest of the guys kicking around The Pad today, we don't call it the Standard Package. We call it the Lame Fame. Because when it wears off, lame is what you feel.

Plus, you know, it's all we can afford.

And even then only when we save up enough for it from doing odd jobs.

As if hearing this thought, Anna stands up and starts pulling a coat over her thin frame.

"Got to go," she says. "Got a job."

"What you doing?" I ask.

"Testing dog food," she tells me.

Which may sound pretty unpleasant.

But we have to get our Lame Fame money somewhere.

12:15 p.m.

Speaking of which . . .

I see Curtis through the window of a clothes shop, dressing up a mannequin.

He gets all excited when he sees me, and runs out to speak to me.

"Peter," he says, breathless, though he's just walked a few inches. "Peter, wait there! You've got to hear this!"

Then he stops, and looks me over.

"You been injected?" he asks.

"Yep," I say, smiling. I do a little twirl for him. "Just a few hours ago." I stop spinning, look up at his eyes. "Like it?"

"Yeah," he says, grimacing slightly. "I'm hurting for some fame myself." He motions back towards the window of the shop, through which I see what I assume is his manager frowning, looking out at us, his arms crossed in front of him. "Got to keep this slave-driver happy first."

"Yeah," I say. "Good luck with that one."

Then I go to turn away.

But he grabs my arm.

"Wait," he says. "You've got to hear this."

Then he launches into a story, but it's one I've heard before.

"See," he says. "I was at this party . . ."

Which may sound like the start of a good story to you. But you don't know Curtis. See, he was always "just at this party." And there was always "just this famous guy there." This time, apparently, it was an actor.

"He's making this movie downtown," Curtis goes on. "But he's getting bored of all the usual places he goes to when he's not working. He asked me to show him some place new."

I nod, make the appropriate comments. Because it's not like Curtis is a bad person, you know? He just gets a little carried away sometimes.

"So I thought I'd bring him to The Pad," he says.

"That's great, Curtis," I say. I put a hand on his shoulder. "You totally should."

That's when his manager raps against the window, patience seemingly wearing thin.

"I'd better go," Curtis says, hangdog expression on his face. "See you later at The Pad?"

"Sure," I say.

"Great." He heads back inside. "I'll bring my new friend!"

Yep, I think. Of course you will.

1:25 p.m.

From Curtis I head straight to a café to grab a little lunch.

They let me have it for free, once they realise that I'm famous.

After that, I take a walk along the street.

Two tabloid journalists are busy raking through bins and I stroll past. When they see me, though, they shout out "hey! Hey!" and start reaching from the cameras that are wrapped around their necks.

I let them take a couple of pictures.

I know, of course, that by the time the photographs they're shooting are printed the procedure will have worn off and I won't be famous anymore.

But I'm not about to tell them that, am I?

2:15 p.m.

Oh God.

What's this thing that's going on here?

I'm passing another Fame Salon, and there's a bunch of people marching around outside the place, chanting and waving banners about.

One of them, a woman in what looks like her twenties, comes over and hands a leaflet to me. But I'm so busy looking down the front of her blouse that it's a few seconds before I realise what she's saying.

"Eh?" I say, having caught just a few words.

"We're protesting against what they're doing in there," she says, pointing back towards the Salon. "They're preying on vulnerable people, and . . ." She stops, looks me up and down. "Don't I know you from somewhere?"

"Only from your dreams, baby," I tell her, and wave through the window of the Salon at a guy I know called Vince.

"Ah," the woman says, nodding. "You're one of them."

And she goes to grab her leaflet back.

But I hang on to it.

My eyes on hers.

"What's your name?" I ask her.

"What do you care?" she wonders.

"Come on, I'd like to know," I say. "What's the harm in telling me? Look, my name is Peter. There – now it's your turn."

A faint smile pulls at her lips for a second. Pressing my advantage I say, "Come on, tell me, I'm harmless."

"You're the enemy," she says. But the smile returns, and then widens, and finally she adds, "I'm Claire."

"Great," I say. "Pleased to meet you, Claire." I brush her fingertips with mine as I hand back the leaflet. "Now, how long are you protesting for?"

3:30 p.m.

"I still can't believe I'm doing this," she says.

"What?" I reply. "Having food?"

The one-liners always come to me a bit quicker when I've had a dose of Lame Fame.

We're in another café, and we've had some more free food. Well, actually,

Claire has had some free food. My plate still sits before me on the table, barely touched.

She eyes my plate. "Not eating?"

"I ate just a couple of hours ago," I tell her. "I'm stuffed."

She frowns. "So why'd you say to come here?"

I look at her. "I like to make the most of my fame, babe."

Which immediately puts a front between us again, and as she crosses her arms in front of her I immediately regret my words.

But why not tackle the subject head-on, right?

"Look," I say, "what's your big problem with the Salons?"

"Like I said earlier," she replies, "they're preying on the vulnerable, and –"

"Yes," I say, cutting her off mid-flow. "You did say that earlier. But that's all just a speech." I lean in towards her, table cutting into my belly a little as I do so. "I want to know what you think."

She looks me over, seemingly thinking about it.

Then sighs and says:

"I just don't think they're very good for people, that's all."

Her eyes meet mine.

"And I can prove it to you."

"Oh yeah?" I say, keeping my gaze on her, refusing to back down. "How?"

She stands.

"Let's go," she says.

But I remain seated.

"Go where?" I ask.

"You'll see when we get there." She's fidgeting slightly as she speaks, clearly not the most patient of people. "Come on."

"One condition," I say.

Here comes her frown again. "What?"

"If I go somewhere with you," I tell her, "you have to promise to come somewhere with me."

"I'll think about it," she says.

"Good enough for me." I say, standing. "Lead the way."

4:45 p.m.

"Huh," I say.

I'm standing on this guy called Dave's shoulders, looking over a wall.

"So that's where they get the Fame from," I say. "I always wondered."

"You must have suspected." This comes from a guy called Justin, who's lucky enough to have Claire hoisted on his shoulders, the two of them beside Dave and me. "Why else would it be in liquid form?"

"Yeah," I say, "I heard stuff." I shrug. "But I always thought that famous guys just donated it or something."

"Shocking," Claire says, shaking her head. "Isn't it?"

"I hope they check them out first," I say. "You know, for viruses and stuff."

"Would it really stop you taking the stuff?" she asks.

I look down at the source of all the Fame that's currently coursing through my veins.

"Probably not," I say.

But I'm starting to wonder.

6:15 p.m.

A deal's a deal no matter who makes it, so a short while later I'm standing outside of Claire's place when she changes into some new clothes.

The chemistry's there between us, so had it just been me and her I'm confident I would be fucking her brains out right around now. But since Dave and Justin helped us out back at the Salon I felt it was the least I could do to invite them back to The Pad, too. So here all three of us stand, waiting.

"You know," I say, just to make conversation, "I thought it would be better guarded."

"Some of them are," Dave says. "That one was a pretty lousy place."

I'm inclined to agree. Whatever they spent the five hundred pound I paid them last time on, it certainly wasn't security or decorating.

"It's not really a secret, as such," Justin chips in. "It's just one of those things they keep out of the papers, because it's the same guys that run everything."

I cringe inwardly, sensing the start of another speech. And he does indeed open his mouth to continue it. But that's when we hear the voice say, "Guys."

We look up.

And all the breath vanishes from my body.

Claire has changed out of the militant protester stuff into a dress and heels.

"Wow," I say to her. "You look . . ."

But I can't complete the sentence.

I don't know the words to do so.

"Thanks," she says, seeming to grasp my meaning, and she suddenly looks shy and turns slightly away and tucks a stray lock of hair behind her ear.

I shake my head, completely bewildered by what I am feeling. But then I try to strive for some assertiveness as I say, "come on, guys. Follow me."

6:30 p.m.

We're on our way there, and Claire links an arm through mine.

I like the way it feels.

I like the way she looks.

So I want to see more of her.

All of her.

But, I wonder, what chance could we ever stand when she's so morally against what I do?

7:01 p.m.

We arrive at The Pad.

There's a party going on.

Ed and Holly have come straight in from a Lame Fame injection. Always one to show off, Ed is still wearing his Salon glasses.

"Why do you even have to wear those?" Claire whispers in my ear, tugging at my sleeve to get my attention.

"No one knows," I say. "It just happens."

"I heard it's souls escaping," Justin says, "from the vat."

"Christ," replies Dave to this. "Even I think that's stupid."

I'm starting to think I could like this Dave character.

That's why I start introducing him to some of The Pad's single female revellers. I leave him to some of them, then whisper to Claire, "hey, he's not gay, is he?"

"No." She seems shocked. "Why would you think that?"

"Just checking," I say, shrugging.

You never can tell, with some of them.

I'm worried that this comment might colour Claire's opinion of me, might make her think I'm some kind of bigot or something. But she takes my hand as we move further into The Pad, and I gradually start to let myself relax as the night goes on.

By 7:30 p.m. I've had a couple of quick drinks and I'm approaching Mellow Fever.

Then, by 8:15 p.m. a bunch of us are sat around sharing Fame-based stories.

"I had five free takeout meals in one day, this one time," Stan says. He's stopped crawling on his hands and knees now, though the vast array of empty bottles around him suggests that he'll be reverting to that state soon enough. "One from a bakery place, one from a fast food burger joint, one from a Chinese restaurant, one from another burger place, and then I finished it all off with a kebab." He grins at the memory. "All I had to do was give the chefs an autograph."

"Cool," Justin says. After snorting something off a table he's starting to relax a little. "Did you give them your own name?"

Stan looks at him as if he's mad. "Course I did!"

"Cool," Justin says again. "Then what happened?"

I look around the group, all sat around Stan on the cold, bare floor. Claire is sitting next to me, and Justin is three people along. So where the hell is Dave? I wonder.

"I got food poisoning and couldn't get out of bed for three days," Stan concludes. "But it was so worth it."

Everybody roars with laughter.

Claire reaches over and touches my leg, smiling up at me.

And I smile back at her.

But I'm starting to worry.

Wondering where this can go.

Because I'm certain that tomorrow she'll be back to protesting. And me, my Lame Fame injection wearing off, I'll be trying to find the next day-job so I can save up for another fix of what I need.

I mean, how else can this whole thing end?

8:35 p.m.

The storytelling circle comes to an end shortly after, when we realise no one can top Stan's story.

Claire gets talking to Ed and Holly, wanting to get a little backstage gossip about the Salon they've just visited.

I leave her to it, and go a-wandering through The Pad.

I find Dave up on the third floor of the place, coming out of a room that's used pretty much exclusively for one thing. As if to prove this point, he's wiping his lips with one hand and doing up his flies with the other.

"Oh, Peter," he says. "Um, hi."

"Hey." I look over his shoulder, see a naked female form within the room he's just vacated. "You get lucky there, sport?"

"Um, yeah," he says, and brushes past me, embarrassed.

"How was her breath?" I ask.

He looks back at me. "Fine. Why?"

I wink through the door at Anna. "Oh, no reason."

That's when Ed shouts up the stairs, "Guys, get down here quick. You won't believe this!"

9:15 p.m.

Well, you know, what can I say?

None of us had ever believed him about anything.

But he was actually telling the truth this time.

Curtis has been hanging with someone who's famous.

Really, no-surgery-necessary famous.

And he's bringing the guy back to The Pad.

We're all huddled around the doorway, waiting.

Beside me, Claire squeezes my hand, and I can tell that she's excited, too.

But for how long?

I try to bite down on the doubt I feel, look instead to the door.

Which suddenly swings open.

A gasp rips through The Pad.

"Oh guys," Curtis singsong says, standing in the doorway, lapping up the attention. "Does anyone like movies?"

And from behind him steps a film star.

The gasp, this time, is even louder.

We're all amazed.

Even my three protester friends.

Friends?

I brush the thought away.

My eyes go to the film star.

And now I'm suddenly not so impressed.

It's not that he's old, in his fifties – I don't have a problem with age. It's not even that his clothes are crumpled and filthy, as if he's been sleeping in them for days. No, my problem's with the bloodshot eyes, the red and bulbous drinker's nose.

And as if confirming my thoughts, he steps into The Pad and looks around at us and his first words are, "where's the booze?"

11:02 p.m.

Well, with an opening gambit like that I suppose the ending was a foregone conclusion.

The star is passed out on the floor.

Curtis and Ed stand over him.

"I've never seen a man drink that much," the latter says, finally removing his safety glasses.

"I should have stopped him," Curtis says, running a hand through his hair, looking worried.

I come to stand behind them.

"You could have tried," I say, placing a comforting hand on Curtis's shoulder. "I don't think it would have done much good."

"But what am I going to do?" Curtis says. "He's due on-set tomorrow!"

I look over at Claire, sitting on a tatty couch, head turned away from me, talking to Dave.

Now that the party's coming to an end, I really have to think about where this "me and her" thing can go – if anywhere.

And suddenly I have an idea.

"I'll take care of him," I say, pointing towards the film star.

Then walk towards Claire.

"Just let me take care of something here first . . ."

"Hey."

She looks up at me.

"Can we talk?" I say, and nod towards an empty room.

We walk into it, shutting the door behind us.

I look at her.

I can tell that she's been having the same doubts as me.

How could it work? I'd been asking myself all night. Could my actions ever square up with her beliefs?

I had been uncertain.

Until now.

"I want to see you again," I say. "After tonight."

"I'd like that, too," she says. "But . . ."

And in that "but" lies all of the obstacles, the problems, that stand in the way of our desires becoming a reality.

But I think I've found another way.

"You're right," I say.

A sad look passes across her face.

I guess she thinks I'm agreeing with her last statement.

But she's wrong.

"I mean about the Lame Fame injections," I tell her. "Ever since what I saw today . . ."

My mind goes back to what I'd seen, peering over that wall. Malnourished has-beens being pushed with cattle prods into the back of the Salon, leering managers telling them, "next time read the contract, dummy!" Then the tubes being forced into their blood, drawing out their blood and pumping it all into the giant vat. Lastly, the used-up, drained-out bodies of the famous who had nothing left to give. Being tossed into a giant skip, just empty sacks of skin.

"I can't be part of that anymore," I say.

Claire strokes my face.

"That's nice," she says. "But you're just saying that."

"No," I say. I place my hand over hers. "I'm not."

"I can't ask you to give up something you enjoy so much," she says.

Of course, that had been exactly what she was doing when we'd first met. But chanting a slogan and waving a banner at a stranger is different than having a heart-to-heart with someone you've just spent a whole day with. And a pretty intense day, at that.

"You're not asking," I say to her. "I'm telling." I look her in the eye. "Besides," I add. "I think I've found something I like even more."

She comes into my arms then.

And we kiss.

11:57 p.m.

He opens one eye.

I'm standing there in front of him, one hand behind my back.

"Hey," he says. "Where am I?"

"My place," I say. "Like it?"

He doesn't take the chance to look around, though.

He's too busy looking at his wrists and ankles.

No doubt wondering why they're bound to a chair.

"See, here's the thing," I say. "I borrowed Curtis's car to drive you back to the hotel where you're staying. But halfway there, you woke up in some kind of panic attack, and you opened the passenger-side door and you leapt out." I pull my hand out from behind my back, showing him the knife. "I tried to run after you," I go on, "but it was dark, and there were a lot of back alleys, and I just couldn't find you." I smile. "At least, that's what I'll tell everyone back at The Pad. And anyone else who asks."

"What?" he says. "Why?"

"Your blood," I tell the film star. "Your famous blood."

And I advance on him.

See, if I'm not going to frequent the Fame Salons anymore, I'll have to get my fix somewhere else. And I'm not sure if it'll work, without the vats and the goggles and the pushy bastard technicians like Tad. But there's only one way to find out. Right?

I thrust and I slice and I find my thoughts, as I do so, are of Claire. She's promised to wait for me back at The Pad, and I can't wait to get back to her. Which means that this first blood-drinking session will have to be a short one, but I can live with that. With tubes and tourniquets and a little bit of planning, I'm sure I can keep Mr Film Star here alive for quite a while yet.

Of course, I'll probably have a problem when Claire wants to see my flat. But, you know, I'm a pretty resourceful guy.

I'm sure I'll have thought of something before then.

$\text{S} \text{Y} \text{/IIPHO} \text{N} \text{Y} \text{ OF } \text{S} \text{CRE} \text{A} \text{/IIS}$
BY KURT NEWTON

I. Adagio

The Goodwin Opera House sat in disrepair. The stately structure, once the architectural jewel of Southeastern Connecticut, was now a study in peeling paint, sagging support columns, and general neglect.

But that was about to change.

Francis Gregory Bellman III, the new owner, planned to introduce new blood, new life, into the aging edifice, one melodious scream at a time.

Francis (who preferred to be called Gregory, for obvious reasons) had acquired his wealth by living quietly and investing wisely. Up until two days ago, he lived with his overbearing mother, Mrs. Isadore Bellman, a woman who never met a discouraging word she didn't like, particularly when it came to Gregory's favorite pastime: music. In fact, it was Mrs. Bellman's excessive mockery of Gregory's musical compositions that led to her "accidental" fall down the basement staircase. Ironically, it was his mother's death throe shrieks and caterwauls as she lay dying that gave Gregory the inspiration for a composition on a much grander scale, a composition that would premier tonight before a very special audience.

Gregory stood center stage and bristled with excitement. "Savant!"

Gregory's voice boomed across the empty theater. Beyond the rows of red velour seats, in one of the side entryways, a shambling figure emerged.

"Savant—I need your help. Down in the orchestra pit—pronto!"

The orchestra pit—a semi-circular, below-stage-level, area—was empty but for six wooden chairs. In each of the six chairs sat a naked senior citizen—wrists, ankles, and waist leather-strapped. Three women, three men. The three women were once members of Mrs. Bellman's weekly bridge game; the three men, their dutiful husbands, who came looking for them when they didn't return home. With their heads hooded, it was difficult to tell man from woman. Aging flesh tended to separate from muscle, sagging and collecting in places that often confused gender.

One of the husbands—a still-muscular, white haired gentleman by the name of Charles Lumley—had managed to shake the hood from his head and free the gag from his mouth. "Why you fucking little punk! Wait till I get my hands on you!" The man shook and strained against the straps, but the chair remained bolted to the floor.

Gregory tsked. "Mr. Lumley... *such* vulgarities. Please, not in my opera house."

"Thank God your mother isn't here to see what you've become."

"Oh, she's here. Now sit back and relax, Mr. Lumlum. The performance isn't for another two hours. Savant!" Gregory clapped his hands together.

Savant grabbed the gag cloth and stuffed it back into Mr. Lumley's mouth. Savant's thick fingers worked to retie the gag, grunting with the effort.

"Tightly this time... or you'll be joining them. Understand?"

Savant nodded. He patted the old man on the head, replaced the hood, and cinched it tightly around his neck. The cinch loop was then reattached to the hook on the back of the chair.

The other five seniors had yet to wake up from their drug-induced state. Gregory gazed at the sextet. Stripped of their clothes, stripped of their dignity, the sight of them tickled Gregory's sense of impropriety. There was no better equalizer than nudity, and no better way to teach humility than through humiliation. His mother had taught him that. The smaller she could make him feel, the larger the lesson. *But, oh, how the student will school the teacher*, he thought, wringing his hands.

Savant stood idly by, waiting for his next command.

"Well? Don't just stand there. There's work waiting in the wings. Quite literally!"

Savant climbed out of the pit and dragged his clubbed foot backstage. Gregory watched him go. It was hard to believe that two weeks prior the poor man was wandering the city streets at night in search of food, the clothing rotting off his hunched back. Gregory had offered him a job and a ride to the opera house where new clothes, clean bedding, and a fresh meal waited. Though Savant could barely speak an intelligible sentence, he could follow instructions to the letter and was very good with his hands.

Francis Gregory Bellman the Third! Come here this instant!

Gregory tilted his head in the direction of the voice: the manager's office. He gritted his teeth and rolled his eyes, but stood his ground. He was the one calling the shots now. No one could tell him what to do if he didn't want to.

FRANCIS! DON'T MAKE ME WAIT!

Gregory flinched. "Coming!" he said aloud.

"Crayee ittle unk," mumbled Mr. Lumley beneath his hood.

Gregory kicked the man in the knee with the toe of his black leather shoe. Mr. Lumley howled in pain.

"Save it you old turd!"

Gregory hurried away up the aisle toward the lobby.

Twenty years ago the theater's manager's office was the opera house's opulent nerve center with its pinewood paneling, recessed bookshelves, plush carpeting, and large mahogany desk. The desk was now gone, sold at auction years back. The bookshelves hosted nothing but cobwebs and an abandoned coffee mug. The paneling wore a thick mold-like fuzz that gave the room a damp refrigerator-after-it's-been-unplugged-for-a-year odor. Advertising placards leaned against the wall. Spare light fixtures and cardboard boxes filled with old pamphlets sat on the matted carpet. In the center of the room stood a large green hand-truck. Strapped to the hand-truck, using half a dozen bungee cords, was Mrs. Isadora Bellman, Gregory's deceased mother. From the neck down her five-foot six-inch body was turned inward toward the handrail. From the neck up she faced the door.

There you are. Are you too busy now to come when I call you?

Gregory stood near the doorway, unable to bring himself closer. "I don't have to listen to you anymore," he said.

High-pitched laughter filled the air. Mrs. Bellman's chin rattled on her shoulder as drool dripped from the corner of her mouth onto the back of her red floral dress. Her cackle suddenly ceased. Her eyes, which haven't shut since he carried her lifeless body up from the basement floor, glared at him.

You will listen as long as I want you to hear me!

"Yes, ma'am…"

That's better. Now, Francis, be a dear and get me off of this contraption.

Gregory covered his ears. He wanted to snap her neck back to its original position to silence her, like he did when she pleaded for his help at the bottom of the basement stairs. Suddenly all the times he had pleaded for her not to call him Francis, the times she mocked his piano playing, the times when he wanted her to stop, just stop the constant carping, niggling, nitpicking, brow beating… all the times she ignored him as if he wasn't there, as if he were a cut-out like one of those placards leaning against the office wall—all of it came back in one blinding white explosion of rage (like it had two days ago when he had finally got the nerve to tell her of his purchase of the opera house and his grand plans to renovate it to showcase his music, and she just laughed and laughed and told him what a fool he was) and he screamed.

"I DON'T HEAR YOU I DON'T HEAR YOU I DON'T HEAR YOU!"

He screamed so loud his throat hurt. Tears squeezed from his eyes.

He quickly about-faced and left the room, slamming the door behind. He stormed into the main theater, down the aisle, back to the orchestra pit.

"Time for a rehearsal, Mr. Lumley," he said calmly, picking up a hammer resting on the lip of the stage. He brought the hammer down on the big toe of Lumley's right foot, splitting the nail down the middle.

Lumley howled again, only this time his body shook as a shockwave of pain rode through his system.

"A little pitchy. Let's try again."

Gregory brought the hammer down on Lumley's other big toe.

This time not only did the nail split, but the curved white tip of the toe split as well, gaping open like a squashed tomato, revealing the pinkish white bone inside.

Lumley released a series of whoops and screeches, as if he were stepping on hot coals. Blood poured from the wound onto the hardwood flooring.

"Fabulous. I knew you had it in you."

Gregory tossed the bloodied hammer aside, his energy spent. Time for another latte, he decided.

"Savant! I'm going to the coffee shop, can I get you anything?"

A grunt came from the shadows of the stage-right wings. "Jell-ee dough-nut?"

"Won't that go straight to your hump?" Gregory laughed. "I'll be right back. Keep working."

Gregory checked the time on his cell phone as he headed for the exit. Less than two hours till show time.

🕱🕱🕱

Savant watched the madman leave. He retreated into the shadows, back into the light of the prop room where he had been working nearly non-stop for the last forty-eight hours. Like the manager's office, most of what originally occupied the prop room had long since been sold or thrown out or stolen by curiosity seekers over the years. What little remained had been pushed into the farthest corners, creating an area large enough to setup a makeshift workshop. A jigsaw, table saw, and a miniature all-in-one mill-drill-lathe for metal-working, lined the back wall. A workbench and several saw horses ran adjacent. Islands of sawdust dotted the floor. The job Savant had been hired for—to replace cracked moldings and warped floorboards, to paint and stain where needed, and to perform general systems maintenance—came to a halt when the madman showed up two nights ago drenched in sweat and ranting about creating the ultimate composition, a "symphony of screams" as he put it. The madman came with sketches and diagrams of specially-designed chairs and other devices. He called them his "vox machina," but they looked more like props found in the dungeon displays of wax museums. Five of the designs were now complete; the final apparatus, still in progress. It was the largest of the set—a hospital traction bed-looking device with a center balance that rotated 360 degrees. It had been the most difficult to construct.

But "difficult" was the norm for Savant. His whole life had been difficult. The world was not designed for a hunchbacked mentally-challenged cripple. But he had managed. Although there were times when he thought God had abandoned him, he had to thank God for bringing the madman into his life.

As he measured and cut a two-by-four, he tried not to think about what the madman was doing, who the people in the orchestra pit were, and those who were chained to the tables in the dressing room. He kept to what he knew: wood and saw, glue, screws, and nails.

He climbed a step stool, leaned over the device, and attached the crossbar. Pleased with the fit, he screwed it into place.

He then thought about his jelly donut and how good it was going to taste.

🕱🕱🕱

From the small luxury box overlooking the left portion of the stage, Dr. Henry

Wadlow watched the proceedings below. He had been watching since Gregory first toured the opera house two weeks earlier with the real estate agent. In fact, he had been watching for the better part of the last one hundred and ten years. He could do nothing but watch, bound to the opera house the way a corpse if bound to a coffin. In life, Dr. Henry Wadlow had never received a proper burial. In life, the good doctor had disappeared shortly before construction of the Goodwin Opera House began. In life, Dr. Henry Wadlow was not the poster boy for moral behavior. Among his many conquests, he had seduced Charles Goodwin's lovely young wife, Celia, and Goodwin had repaid the favor by having him killed. Three thugs broke nearly every bone in his body before driving him out to the construction site and burying him beneath where the foundation was to be poured the next day. Goodwin himself had watched the burial. Wadlow knew this because he was still alive at the time.

One hundred and ten years of laughter and music and excitement and *life* trampling in and out of his final resting place like a revolving door, his only peace coming during the last twenty years—a slow, quiet decay—when the spirit of the building appeared ready to join him.

But, now, life had returned, he thought, as he watched this man who went by the name of Gregory exit the orchestra pit, the whimpers of the old man left in his wake swirling like a horde of insects. *Life in the form of blood from the old man's toe.* The blood had seeped down through the cracks in the floorboards, into the crawl space below, onto the cement slab, where more cracks sucked the blood down into the earth; over the very same location where the good doctor's body had been buried.

Drip. Drip.

The change was subtle at first. The air appeared to thin, but it was his spirit growing heavier. With each drop of blood that reached his bones, Wadlow felt a slight touch on the invisible surface of his skin. The drops seemed to infuse his ethereal body with an electrical charge, the way acid reacts in a car battery. The more blood, the stronger the charge.

And there would soon be even more. He had peered inside Gregory's mind and saw rivers of blood, enough to bathe in.

The prospect of this excited him, as he moved from the luxury box to the orchestra pit. He stood over the whimpering man and watched the man's blood soak into the floor with a quiet fascination.

This time his watching would have its reward.

II. Andante Misterioso

When Gregory returned from the coffee shop, he made it as far as the lobby door when he heard a growling noise. He stopped abruptly, his half-empty latte gripped in one hand, a small paper bag containing Savant's jelly donut in the other. He turned slowly, unnerved by the sound. It came from inside the manager's office. The growls turned to grunts, then turned back into growls again.

Gregory placed the donut and coffee on the marble ticket counter. He straightened his suit jacket and smoothed his hair back. He was stalling; he knew it. He took a deep breath and at last entered the office. What he saw he found difficult to comprehend.

His dead mother had gnawed through the top two bungee cords and was now working on a third. The top half of her torso was almost free. Her head snapped up on her broken neck when he entered, strands of nylon and rubber embedded in her teeth.

You don't think you can hold me here forever, do you?

"Mother—please, just stop."

Gregory looked for something to reinforce the cords. He spotted a roll of clear packing tape on one of the boxes and grabbed it. As he worked to find the start of the roll, her voice continued to gnaw away at his conscience.

After all I've done for you? The best schools, the best food. Are you forgetting the time I paid that cute little Mexican maid to help you loose your virginity?

"I'm gay, mother! Something else you never understood. And she was Filipino. And a nice girl. She told me you threatened her with deportation if she didn't sleep with me!"

He looped the tape round the hand-truck rail at waist level and began wrapping his mother back up. He avoided leaning close to her face. He could smell her breath as she talked, a combination of menthol cigarettes and cheese crackers.

You're father would have been so disappointed.

Gregory quickly ripped off a piece of tape and pressed it over her mouth. "You don't get it do you? Dad was gay, too. Why do you think he put that bullet through his head? You must have known. You must have sensed something. But like everything else, you only saw what fit into your perfect vision of the world. He was miserable. He hated you. But he loved *me*. So don't you dare say he would be disappointed with who I am. He's probably applauding me right now for doing to you what he wanted to do every moment of every day he was with you!"

By the time Gregory had finished his rant he had taped his mother up so tightly her eyes actually bulged from their sockets.

"Anything more to say?" He stared at her, waiting, feeling a sense of control, at last.

But her eyes began to flicker, moving rapidly back and forth like REM sleep. A deep bass line groan began to rise up out of her body.

Gregory stepped back. The tape fell from his hand and rolled away. The tape over his mother's mouth ballooned outward as the groan grew in volume. Gregory had backed all the way to the door when the tape broke and a sound like nothing he had ever heard poured out. It was the sound of something long kept in the dark finally reaching the light of day. It actually sent a shock wave across Gregory's body and drenched him with a cold sweat.

Once again he exited the room, slamming the door behind him. He didn't quite know what to make of the noise that had exited his mother's body. But then she had been talking away right up till that point and she was most certainly dead, so nothing should surprise him.

He discarded the occurrence with a brief shake of his head, grabbed his latte and the donut bag, and headed for the stage. When he got there he immediately peeked behind the stage curtains. His eyes grew wide with joy.

"Beautiful! Absolutely beautiful!" He stood admiring Savant's work.

Savant rolled the final apparatus onto the stage and set it down gently, completing the semi-circle Gregory had envisioned.

"We make a great team, Savant. Here's your donut."

"Jell-ee dough-nut." Savant pulled the donut from the bag and ate it in two large bites. Strawberry jelly squirted out the side his mouth like a bloody abscess.

Gregory checked the time on his cell phone again.

"Thirty minutes till show time, Savant. Time to get our players into place." He clapped his hands excitedly.

Outside, the sun was setting. The evening had just begun.

❦❦❦

Dr. Wadlow had found an interesting avenue to reach into the living world. It appeared the old man's blood acted as a conduit. Blood, after all, was living cells on its way to becoming dead cells. This transitional process apparently allowed him access to other living cells on their way to becoming dead cells. The woman in the manager's office was technically dead, but her decomposing body was still living matter. In fact, after death, the decomposition of living matter was quite an active process, one that could be easily manipulated if the right circumstances were present.

Wadlow enjoyed the look on Gregory's face when a hundred and ten years of stifled rage had finally been released. Perhaps he wasn't doomed to an eternity of insufferable boredom, after all. Perhaps, if he could successfully rid this building of the living, once and for all, he could at last achieve a measure of peace.

He concentrated on making the corpse of Isadore Bellman move. It was difficult considering her body was lashed in place by several bungee cords and now wrapped several times over with packing tape. But as he felt along the extremities of this recently deceased cadaver, he realized Isadore had kept her fingernails in extraordinarily good health. Half-inch tips, uniformly shaped. Her manicurist, no doubt, deserved all the credit.

Wadlow used those nails to push through the tape, puncturing the thin mylar. He eventually freed an arm, stretching it out to the side and working it like a marionette's appendage.

He didn't know just what he had accomplished, but he knew it would eventually come in handy.

❦❦❦

By now the six people in the dressing room had reached consciousness and slowly realized the helpless situation they were in. Some tugged at their shackles, others merely wept. All were gagged and stripped of their clothing. Any questions that may have had as to their fate were quickly answered when Gregory and Savant entered the room.

"Good evening instruments," Gregory announced. "I see you're all awake. Good… good. You don't know what a special evening this is going to be. Shall I tell you? I think I shall. You six will be the first to perform in my new opera house!"

Gregory's words were greeted with silence. The six sat like POWs, their backs against the dressing table legs, blindfolds masking the fear in their eyes.

"Come now..." Gregory clapped his hands together as if to magically transfer his enthusiasm. "My needs were very specific. Your size and shape and the timber of your voice were all deciding factors. You are the Stradivarius, the Steinway of your respective category: strings, brass, woodwinds, and percussion. I'm sorry we can't rehearse, but your first performance will also be your last. Savant!"

Gregory pointed to the man nearest the door and Savant unlocked the chains looped between his bound wrists.

"Take him to the first apparatus."

Savant nodded as he dragged the squirming, mumbling man out of the dressing room.

The remaining five people began to struggle in earnest.

"Please, don't expend your energy. You're going to need every last drop." Gregory then sang, "La la la la la la la la laaaah," running up and down the musical scale before exiting the dressing room.

Flashes of their first meetings flitted through Gregory's mind. The liquor store owner reaching up to select a fine brandy. The cashier at the 7-Eleven providing a smile when she didn't have to. The businessman stopped at the ATM, cursing his card's rejection. The parking garage attendant singing to himself and probably having the best night of his life. The bank manager stopping at the supermarket before heading home to cook dinner. A stripper leaning over him, asking if he wanted a lap dance. Gregory had collected them all in less than twenty-four hours, his harmless-looking face masking his masochistic intent.

But Gregory quickly cast their day jobs aside, along with any connection to the real world, and now viewed them only in musical terms.

He joined Savant on stage, where they loaded the garage attendant into the first device, face down, prone. A harness around the young man's waste, connected to posts on either side, kept him suspended an inch off the sheet metal surface of the bottom plate. Another plate, also covered in sheet metal, held aloft by four corner posts, was then lowered until the garage attendant was sandwiched in between with only inches to move.

"Untie his wrists and ankles, Savant, but leave the blindfold and gag. We don't want to make the others unduly anxious."

Savant did as he was told.

"Now step back."

An electrical cord ran from a junction box mounted near the harness to a switch held in Gregory's hand.

"Let's see how well this works." Gregory turned the dial slowly.

The garage attendant did nothing at first. Then his arms and legs began to rattle between the plates, producing a thunderous timpani beat. The higher Gregory turned the dial, the louder and more violent the drumming became.

"Amazing, isn't it, Savant?"

Savant clapped his hands together.

"Bring out our next instrument!"

Savant retreated to the dressing room and came back with the stripper. She was loaded into an upright device that looked like a gigantic automatic potato peeler. She stood on a small rotating platform, her feet secured in footholds, her arms stretched overhead and secured with wrist straps. The pole at her back was something she might have felt comfortable against. But this device was anything but comfortable. Mounted just outside the rotating platform was a second pole (which was actually a long Archimedes screw) that also turned. A top-of-the-line, ultra-sharp vegetable peeler, attached to a spring-loaded armature, traveled up and down the screw as the platform spun.

Gregory viewed the stripper as the clarinet of this small ensemble. Her voice will rise and fall, like the peeler itself, thought Gregory. He decided not to give this instrument a test run, choosing to save it for the actual performance.

The businessman (trumpet), the cashier (flute), the bank manager (cymbals), and the liquor store owner (trombone) were loaded into their respective vox machina. The devices had their own names: the branding iron, the windmill, the acupuncture chair, and the mousetrap. Each was designed to either burn, cut, puncture, or bludgeon the assigned instrument into producing a distinct yet harmonious vocalization.

At least that was how Gregory had envisioned it. As he stood admiring the full scope of his accomplishment, he had a Dr. Phil moment. He wondered why his mother never saw in him what he saw in himself? Was she incapable of expressing love? Was she totally self-absorbed and thereby oblivious to his needs? Maybe she was simply a bad person, one whose genetic makeup was the equivalent to burnt toast. Whatever the reason, it wasn't good enough to justify her treatment of him, he decided. And though she was dead, she would not get off that easily. Not until she saw what he had accomplished.

※ ※ ※

With only ten minutes till show time, Gregory wheeled his dead mother out of the manager's office, dragged her and the hand truck she was attached to up the twenty steps leading to the balcony section, down a narrow hallway to the luxury box—the same luxury box Dr. Wadlow had adopted as his favorite haunt. Gregory noticed that the bungee cords were indeed intact and his mother had not gnawed through them like he'd witnessed. He realized then that the reason he was still hearing her voice was probably because a small part of his mind had kept her alive. She wasn't really speaking to him. It was an illusion of his overworked imagination.

But it was strange that she hadn't said a word the entire bumping, thumping trip. Gregory had expected to receive an earful, something along the lines of, "Be careful, you fool! I'm your mother! What do you think you're doing?" But there was nothing. Perhaps the whole gay thing may have put a damper on her commentary and she was just being stubborn.

It was also strange how the look in her eye was no longer one of incessant ridicule, but more opaque, more like the look from a dead person's eyes.

He rolled the hand truck right up to the front of the box. As he stood behind her eyeing the best possible view of the performance, her hand latched onto his arm, her fingernails digging in. So shocked by the contact—she could mess with his mind but she wasn't supposed to be able to touch him—he felt his bladder release. Hot urine ran down his leg and stained his slacks.

He jumped back, disengaging her claws from his skin. Blood welled up from the tiny half-moons she left.

"You bitch!"

He was about to strike her when a sound like cracking ice greeted his ears. Her head slowly turned to face him. Her mouth moved behind the busted packing tape.

"Get out!"

It wasn't her voice. It was a good imitation, though. Good enough to send Gregory back tracking and nearly stumbling out of the luxury box. Her laughter chased him all the way down the stairs to the lobby, where he entered the men's room to clean up. Lucky for him he was going to change into his conductor's suit anyway.

III. Allegro Vivace Mosso

When Gregory returned to the stage he was dressed in an impeccable Armani tuxedo. He held a rosewood baton in one hand. Savant had already set up his podium. On the slant surface of the podium, where sheet music would normally sit, there were dials and switches instead. From the base of the podium electrical cords ran like tendrils to each of the devices.

The time was now.

Gregory instructed Savant to prepare the strings.

The strings were the six senior citizens sitting in the orchestra pit. The three women already had their devices strapped to them, hidden from view by their wrinkled folds: a masturbatory device called the Butterfly. It was pink, feminine, and battery operated. Ignoring their mumbled curses, Savant's thick fingers fumbled with each woman's private areas to turn their respective Butterflies on.

For the men, the chairs they sat in had holes cut out of the bottom, like an outhouse seat. Savant had rigged a four-inch conical-shaped vibrator to each of the cutouts. After slathering petroleum jelly onto the tips of the vibrators, he pushed the cutouts back into place beneath the chairs. The men struggled at first, clenching their ass cheeks together, but Savant's strength was deceptive for his size, and he succeeded in shoving them home. A couple of thumb screw brackets held each cutout in place.

With the vibrators plugged in, the senior's hoods and gags were removed. Savant then retreated to the stage wings to lower the lights to near darkness as the first notes from the string section began to fill the auditorium.

It was odd and dissonant at first, but the curses and futile calls for help quickly dissolved into a heaving, bellowing soundcape. With the sounds leveled to an eerily sensual backdrop, Gregory raised his baton. Overhead spots illuminated the six devices on stage with bright cones of light. Gregory slowly turned the dial on the garage attendant. A soft rumble emanated. The rumble grew louder, building toward the first crescendo of the evening. Gregory pushed the button connected to the acupuncture chair, initiating one of the randomly activated needles to plunge into the shoulder of the bank manager. Her scream topped the drum roll like a cymbal clash. Gregory thumbed the garage attendant back down to a low thunder roll while activating the branding iron and the windmill. A rhythmic sequence of shouts, screams, and gasps alternated as the businessman trumpeted the searing of his burning flesh and the cashier rotated end over end, her naked body whipped by a curtain of thin leather strips knotted with miniature x-acto blades. Her breathy exclamations were quick counterpoint to the businessman's extended screams.

Gregory was elated with the result. He glanced toward the luxury box.

His mother stared from the hand-truck, a spotlight circling her like a target. In Gregory's mind she was astonished and amazed by his sheer brilliance.

Gregory continued to turn knobs and flick switches. The devices started and stopped, revved up and slowed down. The mousetrap pummeled the liquor store owner with hammer-like mechanisms producing a baritone howl. Blood dribbled down the armrests and legs of the acupuncture chair. Blood splattered the stage in front of the windmill, creating a scarlet stripe. At last, the potato peeler whirled into action. The stripper shrieked as her skin itself was stripped, a wet thread unraveling onto the platform at her feet.

Gregory regaled, waving his baton and working the podium's control board with a Franz Liszt-type abandon. He glanced once again at the luxury box, to enjoy the look on his mother's face—the approval, the pride, and, yes, the love. But to his alarm his mother was now missing. Only the hand-truck stood in her place.

Gregory glanced around, his baton-work slowing, his maniacal manipulation of the vox machina waning. In turn, his musical composition lost its momentum. His eyes tried to pierce the darkness of the auditorium. At last he saw a figure along the center aisle approaching in jerky, unnatural movements. His mother, unbound, shambled toward him.

But how could this be? thought Gregory.

And then he reached the realization: there was only one person who could orchestrate such a ruse. Only one person adept in the arts of mechanics and craftsmanship.

"SAVANT!"

Gregory stormed from the podium, stopping to grab the hammer along the way. The vox machina continued unaided. The thump and rattle of involuntary spasms. The wailing caterwaul of punctured flesh. The mournful ululations of death's impending release.

"*SAVANT!*"

Meanwhile, the string section had achieved its orgiastic climax and had settled into a groveling vibrato.

Savant appeared from out of the wings, his hands held in a supplicatory gesture. "Not me," he uttered, "it is not me. There are ghosts here. Ghosts in the walls."

But Gregory was beyond incensed. He was beyond listening to poor excuses from someone so inferior. Savant had ruined his first performance. And, for that, Savant would not live to see a second.

Gregory struck Savant over the head twice with the hammer, breaking through the shorter man's upraised hands to connect with his skull. Gregory then grabbed the dazed hunchback by his shirt and dragged him over to the windmill. He tossed Savant just as the metal foot of the windmill was on the upswing. The foot caught Savant just below the Adam's apple and sank into his neck, lifting him up off the ground. But the weight of Savant's body was too much for the two-inch piece of crushed vertebrae, flesh, and spinal cord that held his head in place. Savant's body fell back while the head continued on, catapulted into the curtains that provided a pleasing backdrop for the stage. Blood, thick and plentiful, gushed from Savant's neck stem, creating a circular pool over the red stripe already there.

Gregory turned to face the audience—his audience of one.

His mother still walked toward him. She had skirted the orchestra pit and had reached the stage stairs. Her head had been roughly repositioned. Packing tape still clung to her dress. The compound break of her shinbone still pushed through the skin, poking in and out as she walked. She held out her hand. In its palm was something metallic. Gregory recognized it as his cell phone, apparently snatched from his pocket earlier when he'd wheeled her up into the luxury box.

"I've called the police, Francis. They've heard the screams. They're on their way."

And then she laughed. And then the laughter deepened from an elderly woman's cackle to a man's hearty baritone.

Gregory cowered as she continued to walk toward him. He sank to his knees in Savant's blood, holding his hands in prayer. He then curled into a fetal position, shielding his face from his mother's unblinking gaze.

"You've been a very bad boy, Francis... a very... bad... boy."

Gregory felt his mind slip, fluttering away like an escaped songbird. The songbird flew high up into the rafters of the opera house, as the symphony continued on without him.

IV. Adagio Tranquillo

One year later

Fuck me, said Dr. Wadlow, watching the men outside the lobby doors lift the placard that would become a permanent fixture outside the front entrance. The placard read:

The Goodwin Opera House

Constructed in 1897

Donated by the State of Connecticut

to the Historic Preservation Society

Wadlow thought for sure they were going to tear the place down. After the murders of eight people, and the psychological destruction of six others, by the brilliant yet insane son of one of the victims, Francis Gregory Bellman III, such a sordid history didn't appear conducive to historic preservation. But then one hundred and eleven years ago Wadlow never thought he'd get caught banging his business partner's wife.

Wadlow spirited himself back through the lobby and into the auditorium. He hovered over the spot where his bones still resided. *It looks like we're going to be here for a while longer*, he told them. He continued on into the prop room where Savant's earthbound spirit labored in his imaginary workshop. Wadlow pulled up alongside him and draped an arm over his hump and shoulder.

Hey, Savant, how's the napkin holder coming along?

Savant turned to him. *Good. Very good.*

Savant, I think you and I need to talk.

Savant stopped what he was doing and turned to listen to the good doctor.

Because your death was particularly violent, I guess that means we're stuck with each other as long as this building still stands.

Savant nodded. Wadlow didn't know if Savant understood or not. Just because one has become an earthbound spirit doesn't mean one has become any smarter.

There are going to be more and more people walking through here now, interrupting our afternoon siestas and our nightly reposes. A regular stream of the loud and the insufferable. So, here's what I suggest. I suggest we try to make it as uncomfortable for them as possible, okay? I can do that thing I do in the mirror, and you can bang and clang your tools all you want. I'm talking scare the bejesus out of them. And if we have to hurt one or two, that's okay. They have their own homes. They don't have to come here. If we make them all go away, the powers that be will have no choice but to tear us down. And then you and I can go home. For good. What do you say?

Jell-ee dough-nut?

I'll see what I can do.

He clapped Savant on the hump and took off to his luxury box to think. And to make plans.

It might take a while, Wadlow thought, but he was used to waiting. One hundred and eleven years and counting.

He grinned a sinister grin.

Hell, the next few years might even be fun.

Host

BY ADDISON CLIFT

It all started when Gina got a letter from her credit card company informing her that her data had been compromised. Once she got her new card the tiny charges began, billed to something called "bxp41.com." Gina hadn't been able to pay the minimum in months, so she'd been avoiding her statements. But for whatever reason she'd opened the latest and nearly gasped when she saw them, dozens of them, maybe a hundred, crowding out everything else like an invasive species. Most were between two and seven cents.

Frantically, she tore open the older bills. They'd first appeared in May, just two or three of them. Then more in June and more in July until by August, they represented about half the items. Now, in the October statement, they had multiplied their way onto a second page.

She looked online. The bxp41 website was complete gibberish—just weird sequences of letters and numbers. Not only that, but "bxp41" was referenced on other sites, equally garbled.

She felt funny about calling the credit card company, since lately they'd been calling *her* about the size of her debt, but she didn't see any other way. So after being on hold for a while, she was finally put through to someone in India who said, "Hmm, that is strange." He told her he would reverse the charges and block that merchant, although reversing what amounted to a few dollars didn't exactly make a dent in her $30,000 balance.

But a few days later she looked online, and there was a four cent charge from "xw9u6.com."

She logged onto a web forum and asked if anyone had had any issues with "bxp41" or "xw9u6." Later, when she went back to check for replies, the forum was effectively gone, the whole website just random sequences of letters and numbers.

☠☠☠

"Mommy?" Tyler asked.

"Yes, sweetie?" Something had been preoccupying him lately. Tracy at the daycare place had noticed it, too.

"What are those things that float in the water?"

"Well," Gina said, "What do they look like?"

"Like, squishy. You can see inside them. I saw them on TV."

"Oh, jellyfish," Gina said. "You mean jellyfish."

"There was one in my room last night."

Gina smiled. "There weren't any jellyfish in here, silly. I think you were imagining that."

"But I saw it."

"Sweetie, jellyfish can't live outside of the ocean."

"But what if they can?"

"Even if they could, we're almost a thousand miles from the nearest ocean. How are they going to get here, on the bus?"

Tyler giggled.

"Go to sleep, munchkin," Gina said, tucking his Toy Story blanket up under his chin.

But later, after she'd made Tyler's lunch, she went into her room and the stench hit her all at once. It was awful, corrupt, like animal rot, yet somehow sickly sweet. She noticed it was strongest right around her bed. Had something crawled into the frame and died?

Wrapping a towel over her face, she threw off the sheets and pulled up the mattress. She dragged the box springs off the frame, standing everything against the walls of her small bedroom. There was nothing there. She was in the process of pulling the dresser away from the wall when she let the towel fall off and sniffed the air.

It was gone. The stench was gone.

She slept on the couch anyway.

⟡⟡⟡

The next morning she woke up with a pounding headache. She figured it was from sleeping in a weird place. She also seemed to recall strange sounds during the night, but the memory quickly receded, probably a dream.

She and Tyler marched through their morning routine—zipper, shoelaces, hair, breakfast, teeth, coat, hat. Four stops to his daycare, then another three to Colfax Avenue, where she changed buses to get to her job. All morning the customers were even more dickish than usual, proclaiming that everything they sold was overpriced and wanting to know why they never had more lines open.

Around ten o'clock she started to get a pinched feeling up and down her spine. She waved Tim over and said her back was hurting and could he bag for a while. About ten minutes later, in the middle of ringing up someone's mass purchase of cat food, her lower back exploded in pain. She stumbled on her feet and spun around, thinking she was being attacked from behind. She reached back with her hand, expecting it to come away bloody.

"What's got into you?" said the unshaven man buying all the cat food.

Hunched over, Gina left her post, lurched through the staff locker room and into the restroom. It felt like someone was shooting her with a pair of staple guns, from the base of her spine all the way up to her neck. She pulled up her shirt and looked at her back, but nothing seemed out of the ordinary. She sat down on the toilet, her eyes watering.

"Gina?" It was Lynn, knocking on the door. "Gina, you all right?"

"Fine," Gina said, her voice cracking. "I think I just had a cramp is all."

After a few minutes the pain subsided. Howie let her go home early, but his tone spoke volumes: *It's always something with you.*

She got on the bus to pick up Tyler at daycare. The midday sun was far too bright for her eyes. She fished through her purse for her sunglasses but found them broken, so she had to cup her hand over her brow the whole way home.

❄❄❄

She made Tyler a peanut butter sandwich and put him in front of the TV.

"Mommy's not feeling too well, so I'm gonna go lay down awhile. You just be good and watch cartoons, okay?"

Once she was off her feet, Gina fell asleep quickly. She dreamed she was floating in a lightless void, but she wasn't alone. There was something else there, floating with her. It looked more or less like a prawn, except that its torso was glowing from within with a yellow-orange light, and it had tentacles that waved around in the ether like Medusa's snakes. She could see no mouth, but still it was speaking to her: speaking long sequences of letters and numbers, seemingly at random.

Tyler was screaming—she was back awake—*Tyler was screaming!*—she was out of bed and running toward the sound. She found him in the kitchen, his legs up on a chair, pointing toward the sink.

"Tyler, what is it?"

"There's a bug! A big big bug!"

Gina slumped against the door jamb, the rush of relief hitting her like a stiff drink. She looked to where Tyler was pointing.

"Well, why'd you leave the cabinet door open?"

"I didn't. The bug opened it."

She looked curiously at her son. He gazed up at her, wide-eyed, not a lying bone in his body. She crouched down to look under the sink. There was nothing there, but that stench again —putrid yet sweet—hit her so squarely she almost fell back on her ass. Her mind reeled. *What is this? What has come into my life?*

"Come on, Tyler," she said, standing. "Let's go to the playground."

❄❄❄

"I'm sorry, everyone," Howie was saying. It was just before the store opened; it was still dark out and people were huddled over coffee cups in the staff room. "Word just came down from corporate. We're to have no more full-time floor staff. Everyone is to be kept under thirty hours."

That roused the natives. "What the fuck, Howie?" Lynn spat. "How are we supposed to live on that?"

"What are they gonna do to make up the difference?" Aisha asked. "Hire more people?"

Howie nodded. Everybody groaned. Lynn called him a fat sack of loser and said his chin ought to be dusted for the CEO's ball prints.

Gina rubbed her brow. She had a headache again, a bad one, and as the day went on she noticed that the periphery of her vision was starting to darken and blur. By the end of her shift she could barely see anything that wasn't directly in front of her. But she didn't mention this to Howie as she didn't want to give him any reason to schedule her even less.

Once she was off the clock, she did some shopping for herself and for Tyler's birthday party. She hated having to use her Quest card at the store, but she knew she wasn't the only employee who had one.

Carrying her groceries to the bus stop, she saw a flyer stapled to a telephone pole. It was crudely made and said, in large black lettering, DO YOU FEEL LIKE YOUR BEING CONTROLLED BY DISTENT FORCES?

❧❧❧

Tyler and his friends had inhaled the cupcakes and were piling on top of each other in the living room, making a human pyramid. Gina watched with a mix of happiness that her son was having fun and wariness that someone would inevitably barf.

Her phone rang. She went into the bathroom to answer it, closing the door most of the way.

The voice on the line said, "Is this Regina Cascio?"

"Yes."

"I'm calling from PK16B Collections Services. We have recently purchased a debt in the amount of—"

"I'm sorry, did you say you're a collection agency?"

"Yes, PK16B Collections Services. We've recently purchased a debt in the amount of thirty-one thousand, two-hundred and eighty-nine dollars and ten cents. This is just a courtesy call to inform you that—"

"What was your name again?"

"PK16B Collections—"

"Why are you called that? Why don't you get a normal name like, um..."

Gina trailed off. Something was happening.

"Ma'am?"

In the mirror, the room fell away. Inky darkness sluiced down from some adjacent void. Her skin was gone; she was just a human shape outlined in tiny points of light, but her heart, glowing yellow-orange from within, was beating with profound vigor.

The voice on the phone continued, droning robotically: "*IKL02. 22NV669.7. 3.09U. 4. 54. BXP41. 999...07R. 48U. AA7.P8. 5554443.J6. 9...*"

Coordinates. They were some kind of coordinates.

Eyes opened in the darkness. Innumerous, insectoid. Each one accompanied by a silent scream, each scream ripping a new hole in her being until she felt the very life force rushing out of her like air from a balloon...

"Ma'am?"

Bathroom floor. No clue how she got there. *Tyler*. She rolled onto to her side and swung the door open; Tyler and his friends were chasing each other around the couch, squealing with delight. Breathing heavily, she lay her cheek against the cold tiles. She should have felt relieved, but something else was crowding the feeling out, some dread certainty descending like a slow guillotine.

"Ma'am, are you there?"

She'd been having a conversation with someone. Her phone was still in her hand—a strange, alien protuberance. Rote muscle memory guided it to her ear.

"Confused," she said, "I've been confused. My brain... weird things. We can't stop them. There's nothing we can do. I have to go, I think I have to go."

She let the phone drop to the floor and lay there, watching the mold spots chase each other around on the ceiling.

❀❀❀❀

Without going into the more baroque details, Gina gave Dr. Ramirez the rundown: headaches, nausea, tunnel vision, the weird smells, the hallucinations. He told her he was referring her to a neurologist.

"Do you think I have a brain tumor?" she asked, hearing the fear in her own voice.

"It's probably just stress," he said with a pinched smile. "But we do have to rule out any organic causes."

❀❀❀❀

The next day after dropping Tyler off at daycare, she walked up and down Colfax Avenue looking for a second job. Partly because it had now become necessary, and partly to distract herself from the feeling that she was schizo at best and terminal at worst.

Nothing looked promising. A fast-food place was hiring, but when she told the manager she already had a job, she said that wouldn't work since they needed you to be on call. A drugstore supervisor, a bird-faced woman with ugly saucer eyes, stood in front of the fake mistletoe of a holiday display and talked about their need for seasonal help—until her speech melted away, transmitting alphanumeric coordinates in its place. Tiny orange crustaceans poured out of every orifice in her head. Gina screamed and ran out of the store. Outside, the bright sun and traffic noise chiseled at her brittle senses. YOU'RE AN URBAN BOHEMIAN, proclaimed a billboard across the street, showing a green-eyed waif dressed like a Comanche. A man walking a Chihuahua nearby had a prawn for a head. Gina doubled over and vomited on the sidewalk. Great, stringy torrents of it cascaded out of her, wave after wave of yellowish-white discharge. The ground seemed to rise and fall, rise and fall with each tortured heave. When at last the well ran dry, she leaned on a parking meter for support and pulled herself up. That's when she saw another one of those flyers taped to a street lamp: DO YOU FEEL LIKE YOUR BEING CONTROLLED BY DISTENT FORCES?

The contact info was printed on tear-off tabs. She tore one off.

᠅᠅᠅

A few nights later she left Tyler with a neighbor and found her way to the basement rec room of an apartment building in Capitol Hill. Outside, more handmade signs directed her THIS WAY→ and MEETING↓. In the room below, all eyes were already on her as she descended the concrete steps. About a dozen people sat in folding chairs. A woman stood before them. She wore a surgical mask and had a pronounced tremor. None of these people looked well.

"Welcome," said the woman in the mask.

"Oh, she's got a good one," said a pale, pudgy man, regarding Gina with scientific interest. "Do you see it, Monica?"

"Oh, yeah," said Monica, sitting to his right. Her shoulders were hunched and her face appeared half-paralyzed.

"Look how well-defined the tail is," said the pudgy man.

Gina froze. *This is a mistake*, she thought. She didn't want to be here. These people were crazy and diseased and she didn't want to associate with them in any way.

"You can come sit down," said Monica.

Monica was smiling, or at least half her face was. To walk out now would be unbearably rude. But to stay? Seriously? Gina swallowed hard and forced herself to take a step closer.

"What were you talking about?" she asked. "Just now. The tail, or something."

"Your parasite," said the pudgy man.

Gina's hands reflexively went to her face.

"You probably can't see it yet," said Monica. "I'd say you're just Level One or Two. Mike and I here are Level Five. Once your parasite digs deeper into you, you can see them on other people, too."

Gina sat down, by herself, a few rows behind everyone else. She didn't even put her purse down, just left it draped over her shoulder. The woman in the surgical mask, whose name was Brenda, welcomed her and gave her the rundown, her eyes burning intensely even as her voice croaked and faltered. "These things, they first came like in the mid-90's, around the time of the internet. That's how they spread, the internet. First they showed up in Japan and Asia and now they're everywhere. All over the world. All we know about them is that they came from really really far away. From beyond the stars, that's what Lenny Caldera told me before he died. He figured out how to talk to his parasite. But we still don't know why they're here, or what they want from us. We do think there's a lot more of them coming."

As Brenda spoke, an older man, several seats away, cried out and his hands went to his head. He began shaking violently. Gina got halfway out of her chair, assuming everyone would spring into action. But no one else even stirred. After a moment the man stopped convulsing and slumped forward, a rope of glistening drool hanging from his mouth. Gina looked around, horrified.

Monica leaned back in her direction. "He's Level Eight," she said.

※※※

"Your scan is completely normal," the neurologist said, tapping on his milky light board. "No swelling, no glial neoplasm, no sign of aneurysm or meningitis. If I were a zombie, I'd consider this a prime cut." He laughed until he saw that she wasn't. "Your brain appears healthy."

"Then what's wrong with me?" Gina asked. Her relief wasn't as overwhelming as it might have been.

"Well," he said, awkwardly rubbing his neck, "At this point, that's beyond my ability to say. But I'd recommend maybe visiting with an allergist or if that doesn't work out, a, um...psychiatrist."

※※※

"Mommy," Tyler said on the bus home from daycare. "Last night the jellyfish told me you can stop going to those fucking doctors, because they'll never find what's wrong with you. It said they don't know where to look."

※※※

"Cappy is dead," Brenda announced. It took Gina a minute to realize that Cappy was the old man who'd had a seizure at the last meeting. "The official cause of death was stroke, but we all know what really did it."

"Them!" someone shouted, and soon they were all chanting it, an invocation cast in solidarity: "Them. Them. Them. Them. Them."

※※※

"I work in IT," Gordon said. "Nothing really interesting. I'm a support specialist for business clients. They call, I help them fix their problems. It's contract work. Never know which day's gonna be my last." He smiled and took a swig of beer.

Gordon was a black guy Gina met at the meetings. He was the only one besides her that seemed at least halfway normal. They were at a pub on Larimer Street, trying not to talk about Cappy. Or what it meant for them.

"I'm from Kansas City, originally," Gina said.

"Did you come here for the mountains?"

"I don't really like them."

Gordon almost dropped his beer. "You don't like mountains?"

"They terrify me," she said. "All they make me think about is breaking down up there, getting lost and snowbound, starving to death. I can feel them pressing down on me, even here."

"So I guess rock climbing is out," he said.

❧❧❧

Later, after a back massage, he went down on her, and she let herself get completely lost in it. It had been ages since anyone had done that. Certainly it wasn't anything Tyler's father used to do.

When they made love afterward he came right away, but she didn't mind. He awkwardly kissed her on the cheek and said he had to get up early. Once he was asleep, she crept quietly to the bathroom. She felt for the switch, shut the door all the way, and turned on the light.

There it was. In the mirror. It was wrapped around her head, thrusting, like it was fucking her in the throat. Glistening, alien, insectoid. Carnivalesque yellow and orange lights pulsed around its torso. A strange sort of gargle escaped from her and she ran back into the bedroom, waking Gordon.

"I saw it!" she yelled, looking back like it might be pursuing her. "I saw it, it's on my face!"

Gordon slowly reached over and turned on the lamp, clearly not sharing her sense of urgency. "Eventually you'll see them all the time," he said.

"Do you see it on me? Right now?"

He nodded. "It's blurry, but I can make it out. Mine, on the other hand, I try not to even look in the mirror anymore. That's why the beard. But I always know it's there. Feeding."

"What do they want from us?"

Gordon propped himself up on his elbows. "I don't know," he said, "But I guess now would be a good time to admit I had an ulterior motive in asking you here. Not just because I wanted to sleep with you. I want you to do me a favor."

"What."

"I don't want to end up like Cappy. I'm Level Six, so I may not have much time left before things start to get really bad on me."

"What are you asking?"

"I have a spot picked out in the mountains near Estes Park. The kind of place I wouldn't mind spending eternity. I'm going to get a gun. I'll go up ahead and dig the hole. I'm going to lie down in the hole and blow my head off. All I need you to do is cover me over with dirt."

His words hung in the air, untouchable. She couldn't even imagine how to respond. Just weeks ago, her biggest problem was credit card debt. She lay back on her pillow, looking at the rough brush strokes on the off-white ceiling, made lunar in the soft lamplight.

"What happens when you get to Level Ten?" she asked, just to puncture the silence.

"At Level Ten," he said, "You and the parasite become one."

Later, Gina couldn't sleep. She kept thinking of Tyler. Who would take care of him when she couldn't do it?

When Gordon awoke the next morning, she was gone.

❧ ❧ ❧

But at next week's meeting, it was Gordon who wasn't there. Gina wondered if he didn't want to see her after the way she'd left. As she took the bus to his apartment, she found herself hoping that was the case. Because that was the way life used to be. Things were so wonderfully complicated then. Men and women (like herself and Tyler's daddy) would push each other away over slights and misunderstandings, never really allowing themselves to be happy. Then this *thing* came along and made everything so grimly simple. She hoped Gordon was still well enough to make himself miserable on his own.

But one look at him told her otherwise. He came to the door in boxers and an old UC Davis t-shirt, hunched over and wincing in pain every few seconds. He was sweaty and he smelled terrible, like that stench Gina had encountered in her apartment. He said the thing had been "moving."

"What do you mean, moving?"

"It's a little hard to describe. You'll know it when it happens." He said he hadn't been to work all week, so he'd probably lost the job, not that it really mattered anymore. He said he thought the end was near for him, then he broke down and cried like she'd never seen a grown man cry.

❧ ❧ ❧

Mrs. Castellanos down the hall swore that watching Tyler was a pleasure, but Gina knew she'd been asking it of her way too often of late. "If I were your age, I'd have lots of boyfriends, too," she said, grinning. Gina hadn't told her anything about any meetings.

She thanked her neighbor effusively Thursday morning when she picked up her son. Since she was off that day, they went to the park. A light snow was starting to fall. Tyler ran and tumbled, tumbled and laughed. They fed the ducks, then she took him to McDonald's and bought him a Happy Meal.

The night before, Gordon had been doubled over in such pain she'd had the phone in her hand, ready to call an ambulance. He begged her not to. ("They know me there. They think I'm faking.") Buried under hospital debt and unable to obtain a simple prescription for a painkiller, he sweated and twitched all night, until she helped him drink himself into a stupor and he finally slept. The next morning she said she had to get her son, but promised she'd be back soon.

But the day was invigorating and Tyler was having a ball. Her head felt clear and she was in no pain. It went on like that into the next week. She felt a renewed energy. *Does this ever get better on its own?* she wondered. She avoided the next meeting. She was doing fine. She'd turned a corner. She didn't see Gordon. She made plans for a quick trip to Kansas City so she and Tyler could spend Christmas with her mom. For the first time since she couldn't remember when, she felt happy.

But one day on the bus home from daycare, it was as if some great clawed hand swooped down and tore away half the world. The bus and everything in it occupied the left side of her field of vision, while the right revealed an unfathomable void. And she heard a screaming, the howling of some astral wind—the terrifying sound of the cosmos itself.

"Mommy, what's wrong with your eye?" Tyler asked, genuinely concerned.

"Nothing, sweetie," she croaked. Her mouth tasted of broken glass.

She banged on Mrs. Castellanos' door and asked could she please take him, she was very sick. The pain had gotten so bad she could barely make it the rest of the way down the hall. She locked her door, even the chain. White hot daggers stabbed at her midsection. She looked down and actually saw it, pulsing nauseatingly on her belly. Was it moving?

The void that crowded out her vision had become the bottomless universe. Galaxies expanded and collided across her view. Millions of these things, maybe billions of them, flew through space, heading toward Earth. All the while, a never-ending sequence of cryptic coordinates thrummed in her brain: *490.A JM656 EE3...9000 D DH F.TY.69...*

With the tiny pinhole that remained of her actual sight, she crawled into the kitchen and pulled the biggest knife down from the rack. She ripped her shirt off. She could see it there, feeding on her torso. She attacked the places it had attached itself to her, peeling her flesh away with the blade. The pain this caused was negligible, since the pain this *thing* gave her was so much worse. She flayed at her skin, cutting into her arms and legs and sides, first avoiding her vagina, then, when she became convinced the creature was entering her there, slashing away at her labia. The blood cascaded out of her, pooling on the linoleum.

But the pain only got more intense, the visions more apocalyptic. The thing only seemed to dig itself deeper.

"Who are you?!?" she screamed. "What do you want from me?"

But of course, it didn't answer.

THE BREAKUP
BY FRANKLIN CHARLES MURDOCK

You best believe you're a dead man when I can spare the thought, Alejandro Padilla told himself as he cowered inside the worn acrylic of his old bathtub. Even that thought had been risky, the threat diverting his attention from...

His right shoulder slid free of its socket with a slick growl.

"No, no, keep it together," he said, hoping the others in the house hadn't heard him. He knew they were there — Iliana and her new screw, the asshole *palero* who'd put this curse on his head. Alejandro prodded his thoughts back to images of tendons and sinew, joints and bones, all intact and faithful. By the grace of instinct, his left hand had clamped on to the loose arm, pinning it against his ribcage before it completely detached.

"*Coño!*" Alejandro hissed, trying to fight off the panic growing in his belly. He could feel blood shying away from his face and nausea washing over him. He wanted to puke, but was afraid his stomach would lurch out of his trembling mouth like in a bad episode of the Twilight Zone.

He rolled to his side and onto his knees, meaning to stand before a sudden squelching stopped him. Again he fought the urge to vomit, focusing instead on thoughts of *whole* and *junto* and *one*. Despite his vigilance, Alejandro's right arm tumbled free from his left hand, landing with a meaty thud between his legs. There was no pain at the socket, no blood or torn muscle, only a slight burning sensation and the realization he was now ten pounds lighter.

Alejandro looked down at his severed arm, a cold sweat building on his messy hairline, and shook his head.

"*Hijo de puta!*" he screamed through gritted teeth. In the silence after the outburst, Alejandro scrambled to return to those images of togetherness and unity. He held his breath for a moment, hoping he hadn't distracted himself long enough to lose another piece of his body.

Ana, if I ever find you, he thought, knowing he was tempting fate. He felt his left ankle twitch as if on cue and bit his tongue to force back a scream. *Oneness. Complete. Junto.*

They'd both grown up in Camaguey, Cuba, though they hadn't known each other until college. They'd met during a party at a mutual friend's house one night, later hitting it off rather hard and fast in the guest bedroom while house music shook the walls and their heads swam with cheap rum. The next morning they'd called their respective partners with admissions of guilt, both of them naked and hungover. After those loose ends were tied up, they'd went another round, their raging headaches be damned. Two years down the line, they would be starting a new life in Miami, putting their business degrees to good use in the real estate market.

And now his hatred of Iliana was threatening to kill him thanks to the strange man she'd been sneaking around with for, what, months? Years?

Alejandro stood, almost collapsing again when he tried to catch himself with an arm that was no longer there. He regained his balance, averting his eyes from the severed limb, though he could swear it was still attached by the way he felt muscles flex beyond the stump of his right shoulder. He ran his remaining hand through the sweaty splay of his hair, though he was tempted to bring his fingers to the empty socket. A rising sense of disgust killed that thought and he turned to face the locked door of the bathroom instead.

Alejandro shifted his body forward to take a weary step onto the tile beyond the bathtub, hoping his left ankle was still working. He tested it with some weight and, besides a loud pop that reminded him of his arm smacking the tub, Alejandro was certain he could still walk.

"How did I even make it here?" he asked himself around thoughts of an imaginary thread sowing itself into joints and muscle to reinforce his focus. "I should be nothing now."

It's because you only ever think about yourself anyway, a voice cut through his thoughts. At that, his remaining index and middle fingers fell from his body with a knock he'd thought had come from the other side of the door. Alejandro growled, not just at his newest loss, but also because the voice in his head had belonged to Iliana. It was a complaint she'd had about him ever since their first year in Miami. That was when they'd stopped being happy and when she'd most likely gone searching for happiness elsewhere.

"Come on, Ale," he told himself beneath a long, hot breath. He could feel hatred rising inside him again, rage born that very morning when Iliana brought her new man back to the house to explain she was moving on. She'd said it'd been a tough decision.

Alejandro hadn't caught the man's name — hadn't cared really — because he was too angered by the confirmation of what had been going on behind his back. The man, who Alejandro had addressed as *Moreno* for their brief argument because of his dark skin, was tall and well-muscled. He also appeared to be a few decades older than Iliana.

Mercifully, that conversation was a blur now, though Alejandro remembered vividly how *El Moreno* had sneered at his insults before placing his large hands on Alejandro's chest and muttering something about *nganga* and *muerto* and *cuerpo*.

"*Vete, chico*," the man had concluded, "before the dead come to claim you piece by piece."

That's when the feeling of losing himself came and the fear that, if he didn't hold himself together with his frantic thoughts, he would fall apart.

He pushed away these memories from an hour ago, focusing on keeping himself intact as he stumbled to the bathroom door. Fueled by hatred for his lost love (and rage for *El Moreno*), Alejandro unlocked the door and forced himself out into the bedroom where they'd laughed and loved for so long. Perhaps too long.

If I'm going to die like this, cabron, he thought as his left ankle finally gave out, *I'm going to make sure you go down with me.*

Alejandro collapsed to his knees with a hard thud, but stopped himself from toppling when his remaining hand caught the edge of the swinging door. *Junto.* He growled again before his eyes were drawn upward to rustling from beyond the queen-size bed. *Whole.* He readied himself for the bastard who'd done this to him, who'd stolen his sweet Ana and, slowly, his life.

"Ale," he heard through his thoughts. "Alejandro?"

He tried to ignore Iliana's voice, knowing it would only bring death.

"Ale, *mi amor*," the voice continued from the far side of the bed. "Is that you?"

"Shut up," he replied. With that, he felt his left ankle finally detach behind him. *Together.*

Iliana pulled herself up the side of the bed, her face a stain of tears and smeared mascara. "*Lo siento*, Ale. Please forgive me."

"How dare you come back here," he said. "After what you and that asshole did to me."

"I know, *mi amor*," she said, her lip trembling. Alejandro narrowed his eyes on his wife and recoiled, having finally noticed why she looked so different — her nose was gone, replaced by the flat sprawl of her nasal cavity.

"What the hell?" he said in a voice that sounded distant and unclear. Then something hit near his knees and he knew before looking that he'd lost his ears.

"Ale, after what he did to you," she replied, her sobs cutting into her words, "I realized I was wrong. I don't want to lose you."

"So he dumped you and you came crawling back?" A tuft of his black hair dropped past his narrowed eyes.

"No, Ale," Iliana replied, "I told him I couldn't leave you and he pu-

There was a thud from beyond the bed and Iliana winced.

"He put the same curse on me."

Alejandro was silent for a moment as he tried to keep anger and confusion at bay. He steered his thoughts back to the invisible thread, hoping his imagination was strong enough to keep him alive.

"*Te amo*, Alejandro," Iliana said. "I just wanted to tell you that before I let myself go."

"What do you mean?" Alejandro replied. "Let yourself go?"

Iliana licked her lips and nodded. "Andres told me that one of us would be spared if the other…"

"Andres?" he replied. "Is that the asshole's name?"

"Ale, *escúchame*," Iliana said.

Another thump resonated through the floor, though Alejandro couldn't tell from where.

"I ruined our love," she continued, "and I want you to move on without me."

"Of course you do," he interjected. "You made that clear this morning."

"I mean you should…"

"The only thing I should do is stop listening to your bullshit!" He was screaming now, every other word muffled by dislodged molars and detached chunks of tongue.

"Alejandro, I only did what I did because I was unhappy."

"*Cállate, puta,*" he replied. "Get the hell out of here."

"I'm trying to…"

"Leave me alone."

"…make it better…"

"Go make it better with Andres."

Iliana was furious now, locks of her own long, black hair spilling onto the bed sheet where they'd made countless declarations of love over the years.

"*Vete, puta!*" Alejandro screamed, his face crimson with anger of his own. He tried to jab an accusatory finger at his wife, but there were no fingers left to point.

"You're such an asshole," Iliana replied.

"Get out!"

"*This* is why I left," she screamed back, hair flying from her balding scalp.

"Then you won't have any excuses when you walk out of here."

Alejandro felt his face sagging around an angry grin and quickly returned his thoughts to staying together. He was breathing in long draughts of air, his body trembling, but it'd felt good to scream at Iliana. He'd managed to say all the things he'd meant to that morning.

While her husband composed himself, Iliana hopped to the doorway on her one remaining foot. She was livid, her thoughts divided between self-preservation and revenge. She had returned to their home to apologize, to pay her due and sacrifice herself for the man she loved. But now there was only the anger that'd been simmering in the thoughts beneath thoughts since Alejandro had lost interest in her years ago.

At the threshold of the door Iliana turned back to her husband, her mind made up for the second time that day.

"Fine, Alejandro," she said with a grin. "*Ya me voy.*"

"Good."

"And you can say goodbye to *these*," Iliana said, pulling down her tank top to reveal the pert breasts that'd lured him into a certain guest bedroom so many years ago. Both her smile and his eyes widened in tandem. She relished that look of astonishment and what it ultimately meant.

Alejandro tried to avert his eyes and divert his thoughts, but he was an id-driven man with a weakness for beauty. He'd had his little affairs too, of course, but only because he'd been unhappy and restless. But now he understood how foolish they both had been.

As memories of those other girls flashed in his mind, his thoughts converged on the night years ago when he'd found real love. He thought of their drunkenness and the pounding music and those wonderful breasts rising and falling with his body. And he found himself missing Iliana as she once was.

Does she feel the same about who I used to be? he managed to think before Iliana blew him a kiss and turned away. He felt the imaginary thread slide free of his muscles and bones, his whole body overtaken with the slick growling of detaching limbs. And then, at last, he collapsed into a pile of body parts, his head rolling toward the woman he once loved.

But Iliana didn't look back because she knew her husband was already gone, had been gone since he'd taken that first girl to bed so long ago. So she, too, came to know temptation and distraction, though now her thoughts were clear, her own curse lifted upon the loss of her husband. And though she was missing a few parts (she mourned the loss of her beautiful hair the most), she was now ready for a fresh start.

Because now she could really let go.

About The Storytellers

Everyone knows that a gathering of crows is called a *murder*, but they're also called a *storytelling*. As writers, we aim to tell our stories, murdering those errors and fears that hold us back.

Please help us by reviewing this book. Whether you liked it or not, authors need your feedback and validation. It's like air.

⁂

To learn more about any of the authors or projects, visit http://www.amurderofstorytellers.com.

CPSIA information can be obtained
at www.ICGtesting.com
Printed in the USA
LVHW111354050921
697034LV00014B/182